São Tomé

Paul D. Cohn

BURNS-COLE PUBLISHERS

São Tomé —Paul D. Cohn
Copyright © 2005 by Paul D. Cohn

First Burns-Cole edition, April 2006

www.saotomethenovel.com

ISBN-13: 978-0-9645876-0-1
ISBN-10: 0-9645876-0-2

Cover design – Lynda M., Carson Welch

Cover photo – Lisa G. Shaffer

Burns-Cole Publishers
PO Box 5275(MSU)
Bozeman, MT 59717-5275
burnscolepub@aol.com

A *copy number* inscription inside the front cover is unique for this book.

PUBLISHED AND PRINTED IN THE UNITED STATES OF AMERICA

SÃO ✡ ✝omé

Foreword

The provenance of the Saulo Chronicle is nearly as intriguing as the life of its sometimes author, Marcel Saulo. The document was commissioned by Bishop Henrique Cão of São Tomé in 1497 and completed three years later. Shortly after its completion, Catholic reactionaries forced the bishop to flee Tomé Island. Cão returned to his native Congo where, in less than a year, he died of malaria.

Saulo's chronicle spans a period of five years, beginning in Lisbon with the kidnapping of Jewish children, and concluding with the arrival of a Portuguese military fleet to put down the Angolar rebellion on São Tomé. In 1485 the Portuguese Crown and Catholic Church began a program of kidnapping Jewish children, 'reeducating' the young conscripts as Catholics, and shipping them 4,000 miles to the West-African island to work the sugar plantations. At first the authorities stole youngsters mainly from refugee families fleeing persecution in Spain, but São Tomé had (and still does) one of the most virulent strains of malaria on earth, and the disease killed two-thirds of the conscripts within their first year. Saulo's chronicle begins in 1491 when the Portuguese demanded more conscripts from Jewish communities and began abducting resident children.

The chronicle remained in the São Tomé church rectory (under Bishop Cão's seal and apparently unread) for a hundred years until a Dutch fleet invaded the Portuguese island colony (18 October 1599), sacked the town, and in their Protestant zeal, burned the church. The parchment chronicle, along with shiploads of other spoils, briefly became the property of the Dutch captain, Pietier Van Der Vossen.

After the attack, the Dutch sailed west from Tomé for Brazil, hoping to repeat their deadly mischief in the Portuguese coastal settlements. Blown completely off course by an Atlantic hurricane, a few of the Dutch ships, including Van Der Vossen's, sought refuge in the Gulf of Paria between the Isle of Trinidad and the mainland. There they ran afoul of a Spanish naval squadron that quickly defeated them and recovered what remained of the São Tomé booty.

The Spanish captain, Carlos Márquez, recording that he thought the Saulo Chronicle dealt with the defenses of São Tomé, broke Bishop Cão's seal and read the document. After his reading, Márquez penned a damning letter and inserted it under the chronicle's lambskin wrapper. In part it read: "I find the biography of this vile Marrano, Marcel Saulo, an appalling slur upon all Christendom and our mission for The True Christ. I believe this slanderous blasphemy must be destroyed."

Fortunately the Márquez letter—written in Spanish—was likely misread or ignored by the Portuguese archivists. Faithful to the Spanish treaty with Portugal, the captain returned the seized goods to Lisbon in the summer of 1600.

In Lisbon, the Saulo Chronicle resided in the Archivo de Colônias for the next hundred-and-fifty years until it and thousands of other colonial documents found their way to the Archivo Nacional de Histórico Ultramarino after the earthquake that devastated the Portuguese capital in 1755. There it languished for another two-hundred years until the death of dictator Antonio Salazar in 1970 when many Portuguese national and colonial archives became available to research scholars.

The Saulo Chronicle came to my attention in 1998 via the Ph.D. thesis, *An Early History of the Portuguese Inquisition*, by Ervin Kolbertz of Brandeis University.

A few years later, while assisting me with the chronicle's

English translation, Dr. Kolbertz wrote: "In your efforts to preserve the authentic voices of the early 1500s—in particular Saulo's youthful vernacular—I suggest you adopt the language common to the Portuguese/English translations of the time." With this in mind, and using a thorough etymology, I made certain each word of the English translation (with a few unavoidable exceptions) was in common use before c.a. 1550.

—Paul D. Cohn, December 2005

Saulo

Chapter 1

The street before me surged with activity, horse wagons, vendors' carts, dogs, sheep, stray chickens and other animals, and throngs of people hurrying with their bundles. Everyone rushed to get ready for the Sabbath—not just any Sabbath, but the most important of all, our New Year 5252, first day of Tishri, and it would arrive at sundown. Because the sky was cloudy and the exact hour of sunset uncertain, we needed to be at synagogue with time to spare. The late afternoon breeze from the harbor carried the fragrant promise of rain; and everywhere women hastened to shake out and gather their laundry from balconies and overhangs. It had been a dry autumn in Lisbon (September 1491 by the Christian calendar) and though it had rained yesterday, more would be welcome.

Nearby a lamb bleated in pain as a cart ran into it. The woman of the house rushed out, cursed the driver, then dragged the struggling animal farther inside her doorway. I pulled the heavy gate of my father's brickyard shut behind me, closed the latch and tapped the wood stave into place. Across the street there he stood, the giant rabbi from Spanish Vigo talking with one of the Castilian refugees who petitioned our council last night. As if we did not feel enough foreboding these days, this hulking rabbi with his crazy manner and no pulpit seemed to sharpen our fear just by his presence. But with hardly a closer look, one could see it on the street: a mother's extra touch on her daughter's cheek, a father's arm around his son's waist jostling the boy in fun, yet the man's smile nowhere present in his eyes. Our entire community asked the same question, "Do you think they will come here?"

My father's answer was the most common: "It is only a matter of time."

I worked my way through the crowd toward home, nearing the intersection where the many streets of our Jewish warren ran together. As usual I had to go around the small lake that always formed there after a rain. On the opposite side an overloaded handwagon had dropped a wheel into the sewer channel and spilled some of its contents. A man and boy struggled to right the wagon and reload their goods, mostly thatch and rough lumber. To me they looked like refugees, and no one stopped to help—but I would, for that is my father's tradition.

"From where do you hail?" I asked, walking over to retrieve a piece of lumber from the water.

"Recently from Castile. Allariz," said the man without a hint of accent. "But like you, we are Portuguese. From Aveiro." I walked around to examine the wagon as the man dragged a soaked bale of thatch onto the dry cobblestones.

"I think we'll have to unload your wagon before we can pull it out," I said, and extended my hand. "I am Marcel Saulo." The man had a disordered beard and a fringe of dirty black hair protruding around his cap. He and his son appeared exhausted.

"We are the Saparows," he replied, not offering his first name. "This is my son, Germo."

The boy was small, perhaps two years younger than I, with sad and brooding eyes. I shook his limp hand, then began to gather more of their goods from the water. "I take it you're not refugees?"

"Not exactly," said Sr. Saparow, "but we fled Church persecution in Castile like all the Jews from there." He looked at me curiously. "Was it your father who spoke up

5

for the Castilians at the council meeting?"

"Yes," I answered, "for what little good it did."

The man put an arm around his son and drew him close. "The Crown authorities stopped us several times on our way here for questioning." He inclined his head toward his son. "The last time they did so I had to bribe the soldiers not to take him." The boy looked afraid and clung to his father. "For now it appears they're only taking refugee children. It's the *khateefat*—stealing of our precious children. The worst crime I can imagine."

Germo spoke for the first time, his voice hurried and fearful. "We saw wagonloads of little kids and lines of older ones on their way to Porto for shipment. The ones walking were strung together like slaves."

"Any idea where they're taking them?"

"Maybe Madeira," said the father. "No one knows for sure."

By now we had stacked the spilled goods to one side and made an effort to free the wagon. My legs were wet to my knees, but I didn't care. The wagon would not budge. Sr. Saparow climbed in and began passing things down to Germo and me. "What are you building?" I asked.

"A lean-to shed behind a friend's house. A place for us to stay when my wife gets here with our younger son."

"Where from?"

"Aveiro. My other son was too sick to travel." He nodded at a group of ragged-looking refugees who hurried by. "Every Jew wants to come to Lisbon. It's supposed to be safe here."

"For how long?" came a booming voice from behind us. We had been so occupied with the wagon that we'd failed to notice the rabbi from Vigo standing there. He strode over and considered the wagon, grabbing and shaking it at each point of his inspection, then looked at me and began to speak. As usual his manner was menacing and he stood too close. "Now consider this son of Saulo here. Only *his* father spoke out last night for the refugee delegation and pleaded that we intercede with the authorities. And the council shouted him down! Don't you think our brethren from Castile should get their children back?" He wagged his massive head and took a step closer. "That rabbi of yours, Saulo, and the council elders, what a sorry lot. Now if the council would grant *me* status—" He turned abruptly. With a violent heave he lifted the wagon and freed the jammed wheel. Senhor Saparow toppled backwards in the wagon-bed and sat down hard. The rabbi hauled the wagon up the slanted street to the dry cobblestones. "This is the most substantial Jewish community in all Portugal," he said furiously, "and they turn a deaf ear to God's Commandment."

Sr. Saparow got down from the wagon and offered his hand. "Thank you, sir. Who—?"

The Spanish rabbi put his immense hands in the air and backed away. "Tell them, Saulo, tell them. And tell your father he is the only man in this community I admire. The only one!" He stalked away into the crowd.

"What a strange fellow," said Sr. Saparow. "What's his story?"

We had started to load the spilled things back into the wagon when I realized how late it was. "I've got to leave," I said. "Will you be at synagogue tonight?"

"Of course."

"I will tell you about him after services. Then too, you can meet my family."

"Thanks for your help," they called after me. I hurried down the street.

• • •

"You're late," my mother said. "And why are your pants filthy?" My father, mother, and sister Leah sat at the table; they had already started dinner. I went into the next room and changed my clothes, telling them in a hurried voice what had happened.

I peeked around the corner to see my mother's smile. "You're a fine son for helping those people," she said. "Your lateness is forgiven."

I sat at the table, offered my Hebrew grace, and began to

7

eat. It was our traditional Sabbath meal, beet soup with onions, bread, and the last cucumbers from our brickyard garden, salty and flavored with nutmeg. We would eat the soup cold after sundown tomorrow, the end of our Sabbath fast.

Ah the Sabbaths. In ten days we would celebrate our Day of Atonement; and at services I would have to repeat the endless chant, *I have sinned, I have transgressed, I have done perversely,* then plead for forgiveness. As a child I remember sitting with my mother and Leah in our synagogue balcony, wondering at the meaning of these words. Growing older I began to search for my sins, but could not come up with anything that seemed to qualify—maybe a small lie occasionally or forgetting my prayers. Now that I am old enough to sit with the men on the main floor, imagining sins has become a way to occupy my mind when the service drags on. Now I can think of some that would qualify; a few even make my cheeks redden. Hopefully what Leah and I do at our father's brickyard does not qualify, although certainly to a Christian eye it would be a—

"Look at him," Leah said, "he's blushing again." I gave her an insolent smile.

"Finish up," said Father, glancing out the window. "We mustn't be late."

· · ·

The interior of our synagogue was a place for peaceful joy—darkly burnished wood, soft candlelight, and the last colors of day fading through the amber window above the Holy Ark. When Sr. Zelador, our shammes—the only non-Jew allowed inside our house of worship, and retained to do Sabbath chores since Jews are forbidden any toil on the Sabbath—blew the shofar and announced that services would start, everyone took their seats on the polished benches, the women and children upstairs, we men below on the main floor. Next Sr. Zelador dropped the heavy timber in place across our entrance door. The purposeful thud of this timber seemed to gave us all a feeling of safety, that we could forget—at least for an hour or two—the concerns of the day.

Our rabbi ascended the pulpit and began the service. He welcomed us, then bade the congregation stand and join in the responsive chant thanking God for our New Year. As the cantor called out our devotion and we answered him, I noticed a light flicker through the window above the ark. Others noticed it too. There sounded a thump at the synagogue door, not a loud thump—perhaps someone late for services—but enough to disturb our congregation. Some of us glanced about. We looked at one another, prayer voices fading.

Then our beautiful window shattered, showering the rabbi with glass. At the same moment there came a fierce crash at the entrance, splintered wood caving inward, a mounted knight atop our ruined door, his lance menacing the congregation, the horse defiling our house of worship. The king's soldiers stormed inside, the red Christian cross emblazoned on their gray tunics. The rabbi from Vigo rose like Goliath, raised a bench over his head and smashed it down on the helmet of a soldier. He swung the bench again, knocking two more of the intruders to the ground. Men around him threw themselves at the soldiers. Though a crossbow bolt protruded from his back, the giant rabbi rushed forward, seized the knight from his horse and slammed him to the floor. But quickly the soldiers overpowered our fighters and killed them all. We stood there stunned and shaking as more troops lined our walls, threatening us with crossbows, lances, and axes. The women and children trapped in the balcony continued screaming until the soldiers threatened them into silence. I looked up to see my terrified mother and sister. Near them stood an ashen Germo staring down. His father was among the dead.

Our rabbi lay lifeless on the pulpit steps, and at least ten Jews were dead or dying on the blood-soaked floor. The soldiers removed the horse and their wounded men, then the knight's body and the three soldiers killed with him.

They forbade us to tend our wounded. Through the broken door I saw more soldiers with torches outside in the street. I felt my father's arm around my shoulders. His face streamed with tears. I could not help but wonder if God had brought this vengeance upon us—His demanded atonement for neglecting our Castile brethren. Our trial was at hand.

Here now was the price of our cowardice, the calamity come home. We heard drumbeats, and a ghastly procession began. A tall priest marched inside accompanied by several others, all wearing white robes and devil masks. The tall one mounted the pulpit and, with animal indifference, stepped over our rabbi. This was the most terrible thing I had ever seen, and the priest spoke the most terrible words I had ever heard. "By Righteous Decree of His Most Catholic Majesty, King João II, all Jews, male and female, seventeen and younger, shall be removed from their district of residence and transported to the Holy See of Africa. These Jews shall receive the Beneficence of Conversion and Redemption in The Catholic Faith of Our Lord Christ Jesus. This decree shall apply to the districts of Estremadura, Porto, Aveiro, and Setubal." The congregation seemed to sob in unison.

At the devil priest's direction, soldiers went through the main-floor crowd, shoving all the boys into a space by the pulpit. My father gave me a strong hug, his face still wet with tears. "Be true to your namesake," he whispered. "There you will find courage." He looked up to my mother and Leah in despair. The soldiers grabbed my father and drove him and the other men from the synagogue into the street where the night rain poured down. The men spilled outside, black coats and hats in disarray.

Outcries came from the children and women in the balcony above as the soldiers harried them down the narrow stairway. At the confined exit of the stairs they seized all the children, including the infants, and forced the women into the street. They gave the infants to the older girls, thrusting a boy not a year old into my sister's hands.

"He's still on the breast," his mother pleaded. A soldier clubbed her to the floor. With the girls and children crowded together and all the women now outside, the soldiers pushed my sister and the others into a space against one wall.

The priest spoke again, this time to the girls, and appeared to be shaking his evil fist at my sister. "These are your Jew children, your responsibility. If any of them die, so will you."

I will never forget the look of terror on Leah's face.

Outside, the soldiers had driven the adults into the alley across from the synagogue. Next they prodded us over our shattered entrance and into the rainy street where the torches sputtered in the downpour. I had to step over the body of poor Sr. Zelador, one of the first to die defending our house of worship. Once we were assembled, they paraded us through the twisted streets, our families crying after, held back by angry swords. When we entered the Christian section, enraged mobs crowded in on us. At first they shouted only curses, but then a boy my age threw a paving stone. Soon we were dodging stones from every direction. A woman stepped from a doorway—her features savage in the orange torchlight—and threw a bucket of slops in my face. More slops showered down from balconies. As the crush of people came together they barred our progress, began to chant, "Assassinos de Cristo," and drag some of our children away. The soldiers feared for their lives and gained passage by offering up five of us. The mob took twice that many. Crushed of spirit, battered and stinking, we finally arrived at the harborfront.

My sister and all the girls with infants had been kept apart from us, but for a moment their group paused nearby. The little boy struggled screaming in Leah's arms. Clenched in his small fist were my sister's gold necklace and amber amulet, the sacred kamea passed down from our grandmother. "Marcel, my brother," she called, her face dirty and streaked with rain. "Pledge to me, Marcel. Pledge to me!" She looked down, seeing the child had broken the

11

fragile chain and pulled it from her neck.

"Pledge what?" I shouted.

"No matter what happens, I will find you. You must promise to find me too!" Leah worked the little boy's hand free and threw the necklace my way. As I reached for it, soldiers crowded between us, shouting, pushing my sister and the others away. One of the men stepped on the kamea and crushed the precious carving. Like tears of despair, the rain fell in sheets.

"I promise!" I shouted above the din. "Leah, I promise!" I fumbled in the sodden street until I found the broken chain, then shoved it into my pocket. Like the condemned led to the gallows, they marched us all into warehouses, the girls and children disappearing into one building, we boys into another. None of us could sleep that night, locked and alone in our filthy prisons of cold wood and stone.

Next morning our parents and other Jews brought clothing and provisions for our journey. Flaunting his disdain for our Holy Day, the priest had demanded this Sabbath violation from the pulpit last night. Soldiers kept everyone at a distance while they herded us into the harbor plaza. Our parents screamed our names and thrust their bundles at the authorities, pointing frantically. My father and mother stood in the very front of the anguished crowd, waving and shouting, peering between the lines of troops. Throughout all this I looked for my sister, but could not find her. Some of the girls and children were there, but many were missing.

The day had broken clear and hot; and to my left in the center of the plaza stood a large fountain. Vapors rose from its water spray and the pool beneath. I immediately recognized the ornamental masonry from my father's brickyard around the fountain's circumference. In spite of the terror within me, I had to smile, knowing what Leah and I had hidden there—the Hebrew letters yod-heh, heh, and sheen (symbols for our Jewish God, Yahweh) carved into the brick scrollwork. Even more amusing, we had carved the Hebrew mezuzah numerals from Deuteronomy into bricks destined for churches, crosses, and other Catholic structures. Though fear pounded in my chest, I worked my way through the confused crowd and over to the fountain where I drank and splashed water on my face. There were our symbols, evident to anyone who knew where to look. How my sister and I had laughed at our deviltry, yet knowing fully the penalty if the Christians found out. At dinner my father would say to my mother, "Elcia, I cannot imagine how two children could find brick-making so amusing," and Leah and I would giggle like possessed idiots.

Despite the prohibitions against Jews working the guild crafts, including the Mason's Guild, our brickworks had made a fine business for my family. Because our yard was the only one in Lisbon that produced ornamental bricks suitable for construction, we were partly exempt from guild restrictions and allowed to sell our special masonry to the Christian community. Since Leah and I were skilled at drawing, we often worked with our father—sometimes even with the Christian masons—to design brick decorations, carve the molds, and prepare construction drawings. Considering this now, my heart fell. Had our clever mischief turned against us? Why had God permitted this misery around me that now spread everywhere? Was Yahweh punishing Leah and me for misusing the venerated symbols?

The tall priest in the devil mask appeared and mounted a scaffold. The soldiers silenced the crowd, our noise reduced to flapping pigeons, gulls' plaintive calls, sundered families weeping. The priest paused before reading again his proclamation from the night before, appearing to savor the words, the mask this time covering only the upper part of his face, his smile the purest evil. Then he began, his speech like sand grinding into our eyes, confirming our dread in the light of day. The priest's words brought forth a collective mourn, the sorrow of two-hundred voices. "Order! Order!" he shouted. "Gather the provisions and restore order!"

I heard a familiar voice and turned to see my father

13

running, shouting, holding two bundles in his arms. Three guards chased after him while another aimed his crossbow. "Marcel, my son!" my father cried. I raced in his direction, feeling that if I were there, they would not kill him. We collided just as the soldiers seized and threw him to the ground. I covered his body with mine.

"Please," I begged, "he's my father. These provisions are for me."

"Two bundles?" a brutish soldier asked. "You don't need two."

"One is for my sister," I said, finding and showing him her name on the cloth.

"Where is Leah?" my father implored as they dragged him away. "Where is Leah?"

"I don't know," I shouted. "But I will find her."

"You'll find Hades," growled the soldier, taking both bundles and thrusting me back toward the other boys.

The priests and soldiers searched our pitiful provisions. Letters, mezuzahs, prayer books, worship vestments, all things family or religious ended their existence in a burning pyre. I could not help crying. With the exchange finished, the soldiers pushed the crowd back, forcing them to turn away. I saw my mother shouting things I could not understand. And my father, what would happen to him?

It seemed everyone received a bundle except Germo. The soldiers had recovered him in the early hours of the morning, returning the boy from a place where the mob had imprisoned some children. His face was cut and bruised. "Stay with me," I told him. "I will care for you." My words seemed so hollow, for how could I care for myself, much less another? I wondered what would become of the children the soldiers had not recovered.

Back in the warehouse a priest spoke to us. "You are going by ship to São Tomé." We boys looked at one another—none had ever heard of this place. "There will be prison convicts aboard. If you do not behave and love Christ, we will throw you to them. As of this day you are no longer Jews. By mercy of our Almighty Father you will

14

embrace The One True Faith and someday be baptized Catholic."

This could not be. I will always be a Jew. Last year I recited Torah to our congregation, and I go to Talmud school. I am now considered a man.

Chapter 2

The next day they loaded us onto the ship, a two-masted caravel. The boys had the center, a narrow space on the main deck with a place below to sleep. No surface on this strange deck was level. It had a bowl shape from the rear highdeck along its entire length to the bow, a saucer with ropes sprouting everywhere—more ropes than I'd ever seen. Tall slatted fences were erected on either side of us, the convicts chained in the bow, the girls and little children crowded behind in an enclosure like ours. I looked through a narrow opening for my sister, but did not see her. I saw a girl I knew, and asked, "Have you seen Leah?" A nun pushed her away and beckoned a priest who seized me with an iron grip and hauled me by my hair to the convict fence. I had never been so roughly treated.

"Useful hair," he said. "We won't cut if off until we get to Tomé." I thought of Samson. "Who wants this spawn of Satan for dinner?" he asked the convicts. The wretched pile of men leered at me like hungry dogs. Some of the convicts were dark of complexion, a few black as slaves. Moors, I assumed, Moslems imprisoned for their beliefs as were many Jews. "One more outrage," the priest told me, releasing his grip, "and over you go." I went back and sat with Germo.

The sailors threw lines to slaves on the shore. They pulled us along the bank of the Tejo backwater until we saw the ocean. I stood at the rail, watching the shore pass by. A fitful wind from the hillside scattered yellow leaves of

16

locust trees across the estuary, and they stirred like flecks of soiled gold in the ship's wake. With my family torn from me, I felt as helpless as these tiny leaves, caught in a wake of circumstance so desolate that only the depths without sunlight might provide solace. Never had my cup been so empty.

"Remember your father's words," I finally told myself. "'Be true to your namesake—there you will find courage.'" Among us there is the legend of the Just Man, the Saddiq, who endures all sorrows and protects others. I am called Marcel after my great-grandfather. He came to Portugal many years ago from France. People say Marcel saved a hundred Jews during uprisings against us, that he was the Saddiq. I vowed to God, "I resolve to be such a man."

As we moved along the shore I hoped to glimpse my house, but we had turned the corner at Almada with only the smoke of Lisbon visible above the hills. Many citizens from town stood along the pullway, including a few Jews who called to us. I did not see my parents. Had the soldiers released my father, or had they arrested my mother too? It seemed impossible I might never know their fate. As for seeing them, I had no hope.

When we approached the harbor mouth, small boats with oarsmen took the lines and towed us to sea. The captain gave the order, "Raise the sails." They swelled out and caught the wind. Thus began our voyage.

• • •

The captain, Alvaro de Caminha, an angry looking man with a short-cropped beard and waxed mustache on his stony face, stood near the rudder pole shouting orders to the sailors. His voice sounded full of malice. "Captain de Caminha is the colonizer of São Tomé," a fat priest in a brown robe told us. "He is the island's benefactor."

"Where is this place?" I asked.

"If you sorry Jews were true citizens of Portugal, you would know of our great conquests. São Tomé is our island colony on the African equator. There we grow sugarcane for the kingdom." He pointed to me. "You're going to be a farmer."

"How far is this island?"

"One-thousand-three-hundred leagues. Two months at sea."

Upon hearing this many of the boys began to rock back and forth and tear at their hair. I did not feel so afraid because I had a secret, one I could not be sure of, but something I hoped would sustain me through this journey. The secret was a letter I'd discovered while searching my bundle for a shirt to give Germo. My parents had hidden it in the yoke, and I felt it crinkle inside the cloth. I could not read this letter until I found a safe place away from the priests.

People crowded every inch of the ship, and left little space to move about. "How are we to survive," Germo asked, "with everyone packed together like this?"

"We'll make do," I said, but the truth was elsewhere. Earlier I heard two priests talking—when one asked a question much like Germo's. "After a month or so," his companion replied, "it will be less cramped. The captain told me half these convicts and Jews will perish."

On the second day at sea the nuns found a girl with a small prayer book. The priests tied her to the foremast, and her cries in the night kept us from sleep. Our sleeping area consisted of rough planks in the ship's hold just below the mast where she was tied. In the morning the fat priest baptized the girl and gave her a Christian name, wielding his cross like a club. "I commend your soul to the loving arms of our Merciful Savior," he shouted, and threw the little girl into the sea. This death made us gasp—one of many we would see in days to come.

"These are the cruelest of men," I said to Germo.

"My father told me it is because they take women, but do not take wives." He began to cry for his dead father. I put my arm around his shoulders.

One side of our enclosure lay exposed to the sea, and most of the boys feared going near this open scupper—few had ever been close to water of this size. But that's where the privy sat, and since many boys refused to use it, our area was soon contaminated with feces and piss. The priests called us filthy Jew pigs and forced us to clean the deck. They slapped and punched any boy found relieving himself outside the privy. After a while I began to sit along this open section and watch the ocean. Large fish the sailors called porpoises swam ahead of the ship, leaping gracefully in the bow wave. Occasionally they drifted beneath my feet and twisted in the green water to show their perpetual smiles. I did not know fish could smile. I envied their freedom and made a covenant with these playful porpoises, to let the priests' words wash by me as a ship moves through the sea—I, a ship's prow passing safely through murderous waters. Though I knew they would force me to learn this Catholic religion, possibly I could use it to my favor.

I wondered about the several boys who made up the ship's complement. There were three about my age and one a little older. I kept trying to catch their attention, hoping I might make a friend or two; but they so obviously avoided us, I assumed they'd been warned off by de Caminha or the priests. The three nearest my age had quite responsible stations, one was the captain's scribe, and the other two traded off as stargazer and compass squire.

One day a sailor speared a porpoise with a barbed lance from the ship's bow while others stood—crossbows poised—over the convicts. They hauled the porpoise aboard with hooked poles, the fish smiling even in death. Roasted in the fire pit, the meat smelled delicious, but they did not give us any; we had to be satisfied with our daily biscuit, raisins, a lemon, sometimes a few dates or rotten olives. They never allowed us enough water. As for beer of any sort, there was none.

I got sunburned as did many others. In Lisbon we spent little time in the sun or even outdoors except on our way to synagogue, school, or in commerce. Even then we worked in the shadow of buildings. Most Jewish parents kept their children safely inside to study. At least on this ship we could get away from the sun in the sleeping hold, but the convicts in rusted chains on the forward deck were completely at the whim of the elements. One afternoon a terrible storm blew in and we were ordered below. They closed the hatch and the hold became pitch black—no one had thought to light the lamps. The ship heaved and shuddered in the storm, seawater everywhere. Our sleeping place was next to the animal stable which reeked like a privy basin. Goats, cows, and a horse skidded together and kicked in the dark. We were very frightened. As animals and boys jumbled together, many got hurt. Everyone became seasick.

Mid-morning next day they opened the hatch. Although the storm had passed, the rough seas remained a sickening gray. Those of us who were able, clambered on deck, dying of thirst; we lined up for water. A gang of sailors went through the heap of convicts, chopping the dead from the chains with axes. As they rolled each body overboard, a priest recited a prayer. One convict threw a severed foot at the priest and hit him in the back. A sailor moved to strike the offender with his axe, but the priest whose name was Norte—the youngest of the four on this ship—stopped him.

Almost all the boys had cuts and bruises, one a fractured hand, another a broken leg. Through the fence, the girls and little children sat in miserable disarray, soaked, bloody and bruised, bemoaning their fate as the nuns worked among them. The sailors butchered the injured cow, winched the quarters up to be cooked, then put us to work bailing the stinking bilge. We handed bucket after bucket of filth up the ladder. They doctored the animals first, and tended later to us. The boy with the broken leg died the next day. The priests spent a long time with this boy and two children from the girls' enclosure who had also died, wrapping their bodies and blessing them with Christian names. After a ceremony in Latin, they dropped our dead comrades over the side. I wore my shirt with the letter inside so as not to lose it, though I feared it might be too soaked to read. They roasted the cow in the fire pit, and for the next few days we ate beef. We were so hungry for meat—it tasted even better than our lamb at Passover.

What would my family's Passover be like this year with Leah and I taken away? It had always been a joyous time, but the next—if at all—would be a heartache.

How we looked forward to the Passover celebration, the special food, the prayers, the Exodus story at synagogue, then the traditional question-and-answer parables at our family dinner, each person taking turn with their favorite part. From my earliest memories Mother would let me set a place at the table for the Prophet Elijah. And then when I was old enough—since we lived on the second floor—to open the window to welcome him. "Just ajar," my mother would say. "He mustn't think we're so presumptuous as to expect his visit." It seems when I was very young (or so they told me), that I thought Elijah's place was intended for Great-Grandfather Marcel, and I would sit in his chair, pretending to be the old man waiting for his dinner.

"Look at him," my sister Leah would say. "He thinks he's the Saddiq."

My mother would smile, hold Leah from behind, rest her chin on my sister's head and say, "Perhaps he will be a Saddiq someday," and then my father would add, "That is why we named him Marcel."

How could I live up to my family's hopes and find the bravery of a Just Man, to endure this cruel exodus without another Passover?

• • •

We came upon land, a Spanish port in the Canary Islands named Las Palmas. Captain de Caminha shouted Castilian at the soldiers who arrived in boats to inspect us. They rowed twice around the ship, all the while our captain declaring his peaceful intentions. After boarding and a short negotiation—de Caminha reminded them he'd provisioned here six month's before—several from the crew went ashore with the Castilians, then returned in large boats filled with supplies. The transfer of goods took two days during which the priests accelerated our conversion to the

Catholic faith. We had to sit very straight on the splintery deck. Sailors stood around popping whips. We knew these whips. A few days earlier, the sailors tied one of the crew to the rail below the rudder pole, stripped him naked and lashed him until he fainted.

The priests began by banning Hebrew. "Jews speak an evil language. You will speak Portuguese and nothing else except the Latin of our prayers." I thought them stupid in the way they addressed us, and wondered if they knew we were literate, quite above Portugal's general population. Did they know our tradition of religious scholarship? That every boy here was conversant with Hebrew Scripture, scripture identical to the Old Testament of their Catholic Bible? I squeezed shut my eyes. I must survive this insanity.

Marcel came to me, my Saddiq, in his black coat and beard, hatless, with mirth of eye quite unexpected, looking as much like God as any man. He said, "Marcel, my beloved grandson, take heart."

"How?" I asked.

"Don't you see? The Castilians have their hideous inquisitions, but these Portuguese give you perilous adventure. We will endure this travail and make—"

Shrieking— A sailor struck a boy's ear with the butt of his whip. A priest came forward and grabbed the child. "Punishment for the non-attentive," he proclaimed, and threw the boy over the convict fence. He landed on the deck with a dreadful thud and lay there dazed. I touched the comforting letter within my shirt's fabric. The priest's glare sought me out. "Who else wishes to visit our vessel's particular hell?"

We stared stupefied as a convict like a spider stalking crawled toward the boy. When he reached the end of his chains, he motioned to the others fastened with him. By his beckon they moved in ragged unison, enabling this terrible fellow to reach the child. The convict held him by a leg and began to talk. "You have nothing to fear from us. The priests are not men of God, they are craven animals who

22

enslave children." Despite these words, the child wailed in terror. "We have better food," the man went on. "If you stay and help us, we will feed you. We'll give these tyrants a lesson in kindness."

Contact with this foul-smelling convict was a fearsome experience for the boy. Except for Jews engaged in commerce outside our community, most of us had never been near a gentile. The boy sat up and rubbed his backside, though the man still held his ankle. The child began to bolt in fear. With the fence at the ship's edge closed, he could not flee back to our space. "Get me the water skin," said the man, "my friends and I are thirsty." Every eye fixed upon him. At this moment the priests forbade us to watch, demanding we turn our attention to them. I forced myself to ignore the boy's struggle.

After the lesson I approached the priest named Norte, one I had observed to be better educated and not given the brutality of his brothers. His name pleased me; Norte being the direction from whence we came. "Father Norte, may we write letters home? Leave them for the next ship going—"

"Letters?" he asked. "You are able to write?"

"We Novos Christãos are quite literate."

"No doubt the language of Lucifer," he said.

"No, no," I replied, "Portuguese, a little Castilian."

"We shall see," said Norte, and went forward to where the priests slept. He returned quickly with quill and ink, and handed me a sheet of rough paper, saying, "Let us witness this letter writing."

As if scribing my Torah lessons, I wrote carefully and deliberately.

Honored Father and Mother,

Life on this vessel of Our Lord Jesus is both challenge and adventure. I cannot tell you how hopeful...

The priests gathered round, commenting as duplicity scrolled from my pen. I paused and appeared to think, listening to their prattle. One said to another, "This one attempted the sign of the cross when you threw that brat to the convicts." I thought kindly of the letter in my shirt.

By now many of the boys had clustered about. "You say *all* of these Jews can read and write?" asked Norte. "Even the girls?"

"All," I said, and gestured to the children. "Every one."

He addressed another priest. "Why did we not know this?" They conferred together. "You may write letters in future days," he told us. "Thus we can assess your ability to learn." I felt sure every child listening knew the meaning of that—likely the priests would find our literacy a disadvantage; possibly they might find it daunting.

That night, a large and arrogant youth who behind his back we called Golem, appropriated the bundle of the boy thrown to the convicts. "Don't take that," I told him. "It's not yours."

"None of your business," he said. "I can sell these clothes to the girls." By the candlelight he began to sort through the bundle. "That kid will be dead by morning."

Golem was the son of the rabbi from Spanish Vigo. After fleeing a purge there three years earlier, the family settled in our community. The father hoped to teach in our synagogue, but our congregation did not welcome him, and the man reverted to his leathersmith trade, occasionally delivering sermons on the street in front of the synagogue and stalking our warren in his crazy manner. Golem, because of his size, foreign manner of speaking and family dishonor, found himself shunned by the other boys. Certainly not stupid, he could argue Talmud as ably as any.

"They murdered his father with mine," Germo reminded everyone. "The rabbi killed two or three soldiers and that knight before they ran him through." Under us the ship heaved and groaned, carried south by a tumult of wind that howled through the rigging. Las Palmas lay ten leagues behind.

"To take the boy's property dishonors your father's memory," I said to Golem who was much too big for any of us to fight. "Your father's bravery gives us all courage." I wondered how much bravery the Saddiq must have. Must he fight with bare hands against armed oppressors?

24

"The kid's as good as dead," Golem said with lessened conviction.

Though my hands shook, I stacked the boy's belongings on the bundle cloth and pulled it toward me. "In the morning if he's dead, you may sell these. But last I saw he dwelt with the living."

He bunched his fists. "I don't like you, Saulo."

"I am sorry about your father," I replied. Golem retreated to the shadows.

By now the priest assigned to us that night sat snoring in the corner. I chanced a peek at my letter. The paper was stained, the writing faded, but to my relief, legible. Seeing my father's familiar Hebrew script made my eyes brim with tears.

My father wrote of his love for Leah and me, his and Mother's sorrow at our criminal separation, and of our religious traditions: *Survive my son of bravery, keep our heritage alive in your heart. Despite distance, persecution, or passage of time, your resolve must never falter.* What followed filled me with dread: *I fear the seizing of Lisbon's children is only the first treachery by this accursed monarch, João. Everyone hoped the tyrant would not strike here, but soon he may steal our goods and expel us from Portugal.*

This I have never revealed: Grandfather Marcel's gravestone has a deep recess cut into its underside. There, packed safely behind a dirt stopple, I will leave notice of our whereabouts. Even if expelled, I can maintain a record. A trusted friend in Christian Lisbon will do this for me. With this knowledge and God's help, you, Leah, our family, will be reunited.

We are told letters are not permitted, but no matter, I will write. I and your mother hold... there the writing faded. I read the cherished words again, wondering if the authorities had released my father. Would this be the last I would ever hear from him? And what was the name of this gentile friend—a person of trust my father had never mentioned? I retrieved my sister's gold chain from its hiding place and folded it within my father's letter. I returned the precious

25

package to my shirt yoke, hiding it close to my heart.

Next morning an astonishing sight greeted us. The boy from yesterday, wrapped in ragged blankets, played jackstraws with a convict as several of his companions looked on. Golem appeared beside me and dropped the boy's bundle over the fence. "You might need this," he called. When the kid glanced over, the convict withdrew a straw. "He moved it," another convict growled. The boy whirled with reproach. The man raised a grimy hand and replaced the straw.

Fr. Norte arrived. "It seems hell hath a visage unforeseen," he said, opened the gate and withdrew the boy who protested he'd not finished the game. Norte treated him gently at first, but when another priest appeared, he dragged the boy roughly and said, "I see pointless games command your attention and piety does not. We will devise a more effective punishment." With this the boy scurried into our midst, cringing as he remembered the rough deeds from the day before. The convicts glared and muttered.

During our morning meal I saw Golem talking through the fence to one of the girls. As restrictions against this exchange had slackened, I'd earlier taken the opportunity to ask about my sister. "I last saw her at the warehouse," a girl told me. "All girls with infants too sick or young to travel stayed in Lisbon." I prayed this meant Leah was again with my parents.

While we assembled for morning doctrine, Golem showed me a list of names written in charcoal on a square of cloth—names of our dead who dwelt in the eternal sea. "Tonight we will offer kaddish for each of these," he said, and hid the list within his clothing. "The girls will offer also." Thus he became our rabbi, fulfilling the treasured role denied his father.

That night when the priests were gone, Golem brought out a tallith he'd made from an old shirt—fashioned with a knife, fringes ragged and dyed black with ink. Wrapping it across many shoulders we whispered kaddishim for our dead. Afterwards he said, "I hear the name that everyone calls me, a name that could otherwise offend. My family and I saw things in Castile to freeze one's blood. *Our* situation perils us in like manner. Until we are free of these accursed priests, they shall know me as Golem."

As he folded the tallith and hid it away, I said, "If they find that, they will kill you."

His eyes misted, likely thinking of his father. "Not before I kill some of them." Then he began to cry, something I thought I would never see. Golem noticed my look—well, all of our looks—and angrily wiped the tears with the back of his hand. "Never thought you'd see your rabbi cry, gentlemen?" He turned to me, but so the others could hear. "Rabbi, Saulo? Do you know how dear my father held that title? Do you know how much he wanted the community to call him that?" No one answered; we us just looked down. "Don't worry, gentlemen. Oh, it was the same in Vigo. My father usually spoke out when he should have kept silent. Always an outcast, the Jewish community there considered him a mad man. And his size made him so visible. Everyone feared him, yet the Christians teased and threw rocks, and often the soldiers taunted him. He couldn't fight the whole country; and any outburst against a Spaniard—"Golem's eyes glistened in the candlelight. "Well, even if justified it meant the rack or death.

"Enough, enough," he said, and turned away.

• • •

One evening after Vespers, Fr. Norte came to sit with me. We stared across the ocean into the setting sun. Norte was awkward of carriage, tall and gaunt with a hawk-nosed face, the youngest of the priests. Below us an occasional porpoise ran silently in the bow wave, its back flashing golden. "The sea can be quite beautiful," he said. "I never tire of—"

"Each day takes me farther from my home."

He turned silent, then removed a book from his vestments and began to read, his lips moving with the words. Finally he said, "It is God's will, Saulo, that we are here."

"What book do you read?"

27

"I read only one book, the Holy Scriptures. This is Genesis."

"Genesis?"

"Yes. Where we go may be nearly as unspoiled as Eden. I myself have never been to São Tomé. I read Genesis for guidance."

"May I see it?"

He responded slowly, then cast an eye to the sea, afraid I might share his treasure with the porpoises. "You do not know Latin."

Norte showed me the worn opening leaf revealing beautiful lettering, words straight, uniformly scribed and well rounded. "In The Beginning God created the ...," I read.

"No. I do not believe it."

"I have the Pentateuch in memory. We call it The Torah. By eighteen, most of our men can quote Old Testament word for word."

As the evening fire fell over the edge of sea, a forktail bird flew out of the sun. Following it eastward, I saw land for the first time in many days, a low thrust of hills lit yellow against the sky.

"Africa!" cried the stargazer from the high deck. "Africa!"

A world away, I thought, and pictured my family at our last dinner together. My loneliness overwhelmed me.

Chapter 3

Two days later we entered a bay south of Cabo Branco and anchored off Arguin Island. A cluster of grass huts stood near its shore. The inhabitants looked especially poor. The sailors told us they were fisherman and called them "heathen Moors." When the scrawny blacks spotted our ship, they fled with their children and old people to a far shore, scrambled into their canoes and paddled away. The sailors laughed at the sight. One said, "We killed a bunch of those devils our last time here."

We unloaded all but the large animals onto the island. Some of the children, fearful that this was São Tomé and not believing the priests' explanations, screamed in protest. The next morning the captain ordered we older boys and some convicts back to the caravel. The ship sailed a few leagues to a place on the mainland where a ramp made of stones and logs sat at the bay's edge. The boat glided between two poles jutting from the water and nosed into the ramp. Using the net webbing, we clambered overboard. Golem, Germo, and I waded on shore, setting foot for the first time in Africa.

The ramp had been built for ship repair by earlier generations of Portuguese seafarers. As we prepared to pull the caravel onto it, a large group of savages—ones different from those on Arguin— emerged from behind a sand hill. They approached us cautiously, then removed their stalked headdresses and prostrated themselves facedown at the captain's feet. He acknowledged and motioned them to stand. With great ceremony the natives produced gifts of ostrich eggs, crocodile skins, and vests and caps of feathered knitwork. De Caminha must have expected them; he gave their chieftain two knives and a bag of religious coins. They watched us fasten the ropes and pulleys, then helped haul the caravel from the water. The captain ordered Golem and Germo to scrape the ship's hull and work with the cleaning crew. He considered me for a moment. "Go with the sailors. They will teach you to hunt seals."

Here I saw an opportunity to get to know some of these men, and had hoped that a boy or two my age from the crew would go with us; but de Caminha held these younger ones back with the hull-cleaners. As far as the sailors on the hunt were concerned, I was surplus baggage.

In two boats we rowed down the coast to a rocky island named Heron. We saw seals on the island that did not seem afraid, moving only after we came within a few feet of them, the animals large, brown, and much bigger than the gray ones in Lisbon harbor. We beached our boat behind a low hill and crept to look down at a noisy group on the shore below. As we waited for the other boat to round the corner, a sailor near me pointed farther down the beach. "There's what we want, those elephant-looking ones. They'll make two casks of oil each."

They didn't look much like elephants, but were certainly the largest seals I'd ever seen—many times the size of the ones below us. The other boat came into view and rowed to where the big animals rested. The men got out and killed several of these giants before we made it down the hill. The remaining animals milled frantically, bellowing in protest, struggling to regain the water. These immense creatures died a slow death, even when lanced through the heart. They bled into the wet sand, pleading to the end. One rolled over an iron lance and bent its shaft like a green twig.

Though some of the animals still clung desperately to life, we carved large sections of skin and blubber from them, stacking the pieces in the boat. Sailors brought the other boat around and we loaded both to the gunwales.

Canoes with the same savages from this morning came round the island. They helped with the butchering, started a fire in the beach wood and began to smoke the meat, curing it with seawater. The blacks also butchered the heads, extracting the dog teeth for ivory. The dripping fat sputtered in the fire and filled the air with its uncommon smell. We ate the cooked meat which tasted much like the cow we'd eaten two weeks before. Stuffed with food, we stacked slabs of red flesh on top of the blubber and labored slowly back to the caravel. Once there, we spent the night on the beach. The captain, sailors, and convicts dined on seal meat, roasted seaweed, and shelled worms cleaned from the caravel's hull. "Try one," a convict said, drawing the worm's raw body from its shell and swallowing it whole.

Golem shook his head. "No thanks."

"Go on," a sailor said mockingly, "they're a delicacy."

Golem, talking Hebrew, turned to face me and the other boys. "I've never heard of these, but shelled creatures are abominations, excluded in Leviticus." That was agreeable with me.

De Caminha glared across the firelight. "The devil language. What did you say?"

I hoisted a piece of seal meat. "A prayer of thanks, honored captain. For the seal meat, for the souls of us all."

"Not for the worms?"

Meat in hand, I crossed myself. "To the worms."

The air turned cold and we slept close to the fires. In the night more fires appeared down the beach—the savages had returned. At daylight they helped us float the caravel. Towing the two ladened boats from the day before, we reached Arguin late that morning. We spent the next days rendering oil into casks, smoking seal meat and feasting. Everyone got involved, including the nuns and little children. Dogs from the village begged about. For sport, the sailors shot several with their crossbows. They also killed two goats who wandered in from the sand hills, adding their meat to the smoke fires. On the third day, as we loaded the caravel, a canoe of villagers paddled by. The sailors goaded them by setting their huts afire.

This troubled me, and I asked Golem, "Why do they hate the fisherman but not the ones on the beach?"

He gave me a weary look. "The beach savages play for the captain, wear crosses and grovel. You saw them. That's what we'll have to do." He stared at the flaming village. "When we were tarring the ship, Saulo, I thought I might run away, follow those blacks across the sand hills into the Wilderness. Like the Biblical Jews with God's magic to guide them."

"We need to stay together."

He clapped me on the shoulder. "That, my friend, is why I'm still here."

We sailed into the dusk, a fair breeze at our heels, the fires of Arguin our guide to deep water. Free of land, the compass squire took readings by his lamp and counted down the hourglass.

As our journey continued south, the polestar each night fell closer to the north edge of earth. From the dark the stargazer sang the headings, his chant rising to the fading North Star, to Africa, to the unknown sea:

> *Regiment of the North, guide our way*
> *Stella Polaris, The Savior's gift*
> *Sentinel of the night*
> *Coax forth God's Cross from the southern sea.*

• • •

In the week following, our ship rounded Cape Verde and our heading turned from south to east, sailing always within sight of land. Throughout the journey the sun had set starboard; now it set to the ship's stern. A priest told me, "We sail along the earth's equator." I did not know what to expect, but longed to set foot on land again, any land—after weeks at sea with only Arguin to break the ocean's sameness, I would welcome even unknown São Tomé.

One day we spotted a two-masted caravel much like our own. At sight of this Portuguese voyager returning home from Africa, Captain de Caminha and his crew cheered with great excitement. Our vessels hove-to a short way apart; their captain and two others crossed over in a small boat. De Caminha greeted the men with great salutations and clasping of hands. One, an immensely fat, serious-looking man, wore a gold jacket and a cumbersome white hat made from winding cloth. His skin had the color of vino tinto, a complexion I'd never seen.

Immediately after the greetings, this strange man expressed an interest in examining us. In the company of de Caminha, he spent brief moments with the girls and small children, then entered our enclosure. For some reason the captain pointed at me. The visitor came close. "Remove your breeches," he ordered. This demand left me aghast. Because of his thick pronunciation, I feigned misunderstanding and turned away.

De Caminha grabbed my shoulder and spun me around. "Do as he says!"

As the captain moved to strike me, Fr. Norte came between us and said, "Saulo, he merely wants to see your privates. His culture practices circumcision, and we told him that Jewish males are thus disfigured. He wants to see for himself."

I tightened the knot at my waist. "No." My heart pounded, every eye settled on me. The boys exchanged glances and laughter. De Caminha beckoned a sailor who strode forward with his whip. "Lower your breeches or I will beat you and every Jew on this ship within an inch of his life." The boys turned silent.

I closed my eyes tight, my legs began to tremble; I wanted to run. In this terrible instant Great-Grandfather Marcel appeared, smiling as ever. "Teach them," he said.

"How?"

He inclined his head. "By your compliance, you save your fellows. Their derision turns to respect." With these words I undid my waistcord and exposed myself. My face flamed with humiliation.

I jumped back and drew up my breeches when the evil

visitor reached to touch me. He spoke to the captain in his thick Portuguese, displaying yellow teeth. "One should respect these Jews. They come from a culture possibly more venerable than your own." The captain glared, reached to his waistband and pulled a dagger from its sheath. Everyone gasped. The visitor turned his back to the threat, put an arm over my shoulder and walked me along the fence. "Your captain will endure my insults because he needs me for his enterprise. Besides, my brother is the overseer of his plantations on São Tomé." As I tried to wriggle free, the man tightened his grip. "I was on my way to visit your country when we encountered this vessel. De Caminha plans a call in Porto Novo to purchase slaves. That city, young man, is my place of business—I am a famous broker of slaves." He eyed me. "And you are called?"

"Saulo. Marcel Saulo."

He offered his hand. "I am Nasic. I have seven wives, many concubines, and live in a palace by the ocean. Would you like to see it when we stop in Porto Novo? Have you ever had an African woman? I will give you the gift of one."

Again I tried to escape his grasp. "No."

"Very well then. Although I have heard of your people, young Saulo, you are the first I've met. But I am sure to meet more. According to the captain, that King João of yours intends to populate Tomé with young Jews. Or should I say those who survive conversion? What have they told you of the island?" I shrugged. We turned to walk back along the fence. "It is a dreadful place which I refuse to visit. Tomé has a pitiless fever that afflicts everyone— slave, master, and soon your people. You will do well to remain with me in Porto Novo. I can arrange it with de Caminha, an extra slave or two." When I offered nothing in response, he left and returned to the captain on the high deck. The two parleyed, looking my way.

I went to sit with Germo and Golem, the former staring fearfully, Golem laughing. "That man is a slave trader," I told them. "He will sail back with us to a place called Novo where de Caminha plans to buy slaves." Golem's laughter grew louder. *"What?"* I demanded.

"You, Saulo. I have never seen anyone get into trouble like you. First you're friends with that gargoyle, Norte. Then you drop your britches so everybody sees your tsaat-sooa. Next the captain draws his dagger. Now you're adopted by a tent head." Germo and the others rolled with laughter.

"Silence!" De Caminha shouted from the high deck and thrust a fist at us.

Nasic remained while his boat went to the other ship. On its deck, tethered and roasting in the sun, lay slaves—a tortured pile of anguish. Soon the little boat returned with Nasic's baggage and his personal slave. The black, taller than any man I'd ever seen, wore a white robe and head wrapping. He also wore a heavy chain around his neck with a short piece like a braid to the middle of his back. Clearly visible on the man's forehead was a brand shaped like a horseshoe, a depressed scar. I touched my own forehead and winced at the thought.

As we watched Nasic's boat unload, Germo said, "Marcel, ask Farther Norte to send our letters home." His request stabbed my heart, knowing what tragedy his family suffered. I sought out the priest and he agreed to do so. As they completed unloading Nasic's goods, Norte waved our letters wrapped in hide leather and announced they were heading home. Our two camps, boys and girls, cheered.

With the transfer complete and sails raised, we tacked east. Nasic, standing near the rudder pole, saluted me. Ignoring his wave, I stood at the rail as we neared the other ship and pondered the miserable lives of slaves, their desperate eyes. I imagined each forehead with the loathsome horseshoe, wondering if they would brand us in like manner. Something thrown from the home-bound vessel splashed in the water. When we neared, my spirits sank into the sea. "Our letters," I whispered, and glanced at my two friends. Sorrow in their eyes told me they had seen it too.

Three days later we dropped anchor at Porto Novo. Before Nasic went on shore he again suggested this port as my new home. I told him I'd decide before we left. I wondered which prison, Colony Tomé or Porto Novo, could I more easily escape? In my view from the ship, Porto Novo appeared a hateful place, some low grass huts, a long wooden building, and a slave enclosure of stacked logs topped with woven thornbushes. Fires blazed day and night around the enclosure. Guards marched endless vigils on its circumference. Though I could see nearly a league along the shore in either direction, Nasic's castle was nowhere in sight.

Around noon the second day, boats loaded with slaves began to arrive. All of us watched with growing apprehension. Would this to be our fate as well? Was there no limit to the cruelty of this voyage? On the shore, guards with prods and whips herded a dozen Africans at a time from the enclosure. Nasic and the captain sorted through them, segregating the few of de Caminha's choosing. The guards then drove the others back to their prison. Those selected for our ship and not yet branded immediately received the burning horseshoe on their forehead. Though nearly a hundred yards from shore, we clearly heard their howls and pleadings, and smelled the execrable odor of cautery. Once on board, many of the new arrivals continued their lamentations.

The slaves occupied the forward deck with the convicts. In preparation, the sailors erected another fence, dividing the space in half and crowding the convicts to port. With their chains re-fitted and much shortened, they protested loudly. As the slaves arrived, sailors goaded them off the boats and up the rope webbing, first detaching the gang chain so that one slip would not drown them all. The slaves were very fearful. Even those not freshly branded shook and begged as they ascended the web.

I watched two slaves fall from the net, one into the boat, the other into the sea. The man who fell into the boat hurt his back and remained in the bottom of the craft. The one who fell into the sea sank from sight, dragged under by his leg iron. He surfaced and struggled to climb into the boat. He did so with help from the sailors, but not before the most terrifying fish came after him, a demon three times the size of a porpoise with an immense gray head, long slash of mouth, rows of jagged teeth, and eyes like dull pewter. The monster lunged through the water at the thrashing man, twice missing him.

"Hakifi! Hakifi!" the Africans screamed as the fish continued to prowl around the boat, a terrible shadow in the water. The boatmen shouted and poked the creature with their oars, but failed to drive it off.

As the last slaves worked their way up the web, the sailors pulled the injured man to his feet from the bottom of the boat. Nasic stood looking down from our ship's rail, encouraging the slave in his native tongue to climb. But the unfortunate African, even with assistance, could not stand. After the man's vain attempt at the web, Nasic made a dismissive gesture. The sailors removed the black's leg iron and threw him overboard. He must have expected this fate; with dignity he chanted quietly—perhaps a death chant— moving his arms in a circle to stay afloat. The giant fish took him silently from behind, dragging him under in an instant.

Of all the death we had seen, this was the most horrible, made more-so by Nasic and de Caminha who watched with indifference. As the final swirl of bloody water closed over the man, the slave broker removed a book from his purse, made a notation, and showed it to de Caminha.

Females made up the last boatload, and included girls much younger than Leah. Except for scant adornments, they wore no clothing. I had never seen a woman without clothes before. As they came on board I felt ashamed, but watched anyway. They chained the females on the fore deck closest to the rail, separating them a short distance from the males. These young girls and women were most pitiful, many just branded—their blistered horseshoes the same shape as the iron crooks sunk into the deck to anchor slaves.

I did not need Great-Grandfather Marcel to help me choose São Tomé over Porto Novo—in this there was no choosing: Stay with my comrades. At the first opportunity I told Nasic. I did so in a courteous way, believing that if angered he might force me, with de Caminha's blessing, to stay in Porto Novo. I had become fearful of the captain since the day he threatened to beat me. "I am disappointed," said Nasic, but he accepted my decision. Though I did not understand his friendly treatment, I realized I might someday benefit from knowing this evil man.

That evening they gave us bananas, the first fresh fruit we'd tasted in weeks, and we savored every bite. Along with other supplies, bunches of the fruit had been brought on board in the afternoon. We lay the night at anchor while a strong breeze blew from the north, salting the heavens with constellations I had never seen before. The slaves just over the fence lamented in their strange and haunted tongue. In the night, as waves washed against the ship and slaves whispered sorrows, I saw three convicts escape over the side. Their chains had been fastened in error that afternoon.

At dawn the sailors discovered the missing and frantically searched the ship. "How could they risk the hakifi?" I asked Golem. "They prefer that peril to São Tomé?"

"They know what we must learn," he said.

De Caminha grew furious at the escape. He directed the sailors responsible stripped naked and whipped without mercy. With the captain's lash and moans of beatings ringing in our ears, we set sail. The wind bore us away from Porto Novo, slaves silent and wide-eyed, convicts cursing those fled, beaten sailors in a bloody pool of seawater thrown on them for their wounds, and we Jews fearful at what awaited. Only the priests, captain, and nuns seemed to understand the purpose of this unhappy voyage. Just five days to the south, Tomé waited.

On the third day the wind failed and left us in a lifeless

calm. At the time no one considered it a problem—we had been so burdened before, usually for less than a day. But as the second noon crept by, everyone became restless—in Porto Novo we had stocked food and water for only a week. The sailors began to talk of the dullens, a windless condition that could last a month.

In the midst of this the slaves fell ill, then the convicts. The illness went unnoticed for two days, since no one except Nasic, who'd stayed in Porto Novo, spoke the slave language; and everyone considered the Africans complaining by nature. The convicts also remained silent, knowing the likely fate of any found ill. Soon almost the entire company had the ruinous malady, some much worse than others.

Upon consideration, my affliction was mild, certainly so when compared to those who died. I had a terrifying headache, burned with fever, and could not rise for three days. In my fever-madness I prayed to see Great-Grandfather Marcel—if I were to die, he would guide me. Marcel did not come; instead the devil priest appeared and cursed all Jewry. I became Samson. The devil fled before my sword.

My illness did not produce the purple skin spots that afflicted many who came to their end on this death ship. When I had nearly recovered, a priest came to me and said, "You will assist the barber and bleed sick Jews." While this method for treating the ill was contrary to our custom, I complied because we had nothing else available. It seemed nearly all our number were sick, some far beyond help. The boy who survived the night with the convicts was among the first to die. This child, so courageous in life, lay dead next to a boy in fever-madness and covered with skin spots. As we worked over the living and gave comfort to those we might save, I whispered kaddishim for the dead. By now we had been in the calm for seven days, the hard sun upon us. They doled food and water in short allowance. As I further recovered from my illness, hunger and thirst overcame me.

During this time—despite warnings of deadly punishment—most of us ate from the animal grain crib and secretly provided this coarse sustenance to the girls. The sailors petitioned de Caminha to butcher the goats, but he forbade it, saying these animals were brood stock for Tomé. We the living dropped our dead overboard with only the slightest ceremony. Hakifi circled and fought over the spoils, worrying the bodies in mindless frenzy. Except for those demons, this ocean seemed void of life.

I'd not seen Fr. Norte and asked another priest about him. "You will see him in due time," he said. "He is not ill."

On the afternoon of the eighth day a drenching storm appeared. Heavy rain fell and we stayed the night on deck to wash the sick and collect the blessed rainwater for ourselves and the animals below. Sometime in the night another blessing appeared—dozens of flying fish stranded themselves on our deck. These beautiful winged creatures, called little angels by the sailors, were common during our journey and often littered the deck after a storm. We always gathered them for cooking. On this daybreak the slaves shouted and whistled as we collected the fish, showing with pride they could eat the fish raw. Several of us tried. First we stripped the skin with our teeth as the Africans did, then gnawed meat off the bones. Certainly eating uncooked fish, though I could not cite the exact stricture, violated our dietary laws for the thousandth time on this infernal voyage. But their bluish flesh tasted better than anything I ever remembered. In early morning with clear skies, our sails gathered a fresh breeze and carried us on.

With the wrathful illness laying waste the ship's persons, I took stock. Of the original twenty slaves, eleven lived. Following the Porto Novo escape, seven convicts remained on board. Of these, only one had died. The ship's compliment, originally sixteen, now totaled twelve. Of the four priests, one had died. Two of the four nuns had perished, with another so ill on deck that no one expected her to live. Upon leaving Lisbon, we stolen Jews numbered thirty-four, fourteen boys, thirteen girls, seven children. Five died before we reached Porto Novo; after the illness only nine boys, ten girls, and three children lived. I said many prayers to God in silence, asking over and over, Why are innocents punished like this? I could not reason it out, so I thought to ask Norte. Perhaps his God had an explanation.

I remembered our intense sorrow at the first deaths among us. Now, surrounded by dead and dying, we'd become sadly accustomed. Poor Germo was still too ill to rise; his skin eruptions and fever would not yield. The barber bled him daily, but it seemed of no help. Golem and the few others who had not taken ill helped with great zeal. During the illness the fence stayed open between the girls and us and no one moved to close it. Neither de Caminha nor the ship's officers had the illness. I continued to worry about Fr. Norte—I had not seen him for over a week.

The second midday after the cleansing storm, we saw the first hint of São Tomé, a column of smoke that rose from the sea. The two priests walked among us. "There lies our destination," said one. "Norte thought it The Garden, but in truth it burns with the fire of Hades." At end-of-day the wind quit. Tomé had risen from the edge of ocean to reveal a long, low-shrouded mountain, smoke rising several times the mountain's height. Indeed it could be hell—how does an island burn?

With no wind, de Caminha raised a smudge fire in the cooking pit in hopes someone on the island would notice and send boats to tow us. By night they set pitch torches in the rigging. The sailors prepared the two small boats for towing. If our sails found no wind by sunrise, we would start the tow. Here the ocean's current flowed against us, and pulled us away from Tomé. The distant island became a frightful vision; orange fires burned from beneath its smoke and serpent tongues of lightning struck along the mountain backbone.

Next morning Fr. Norte, his wrists locked in chains, sat inside our enclosure, resting his back against the fence.

Scratched on his cheek was a bloody M for Marrano, or pig, a term used for Jews of failed Catholic conversion. I brought a cloth and water to cleanse him. "It seems inquisition reaches even to Africa," he said. He stared blankly as I dabbed his face.

"You?" I asked. "How could this be?"

"The priests, the nuns, the captain, they all accuse me. They say my friendship with Jews brought the sickness. I must confess or be put to the stake."

"Can you stay in São Tomé?" This priest was my only hope among these Catholics.

"No Saulo, I am corrupt, forbidden to leave the ship. They will return me to Portugal for trial."

Two boats were now in the water in an effort to tow. Though the sailors strained at the oars for hours, the island appeared no closer. In the afternoon de Caminha came to us, pointing. "Time to save your rotten skins and ours too. You boys can relieve the rowers." While I had never rowed a boat, it seemed an agreeable task, made all the more interesting when we found ourselves teamed with slaves and convicts also pressed into service.

A sailor who acted as both coxswain and slave master directed us to our seats, four rowers along either side, each with his own oar. At first I enjoyed this new chore. An hour later rowing became torment; my shoulders and arms ached as never before. They gave us leathers to protect our hands, but mine were soon blistered and bleeding. I drenched my handcovers in seawater, though it did not help. The convicts and slaves were much better rowers— few of us boys had ever done labor of this sort. Even work in my father's brickyard had not prepared me for this. How could I ever be a farmer in some alien land?

More than a mere maker of bricks, I had hoped to be a mason, perhaps someday a builder. In Lisbon, Leah and I admired the buildings, the churches and universities. Foolishly I imagined myself in service to the João Court, their designer of great Portuguese churches and public buildings—the first Jew of that position. The Court of

Castile had master builders who were Jews, some even
with the title of Architect. We'd heard they were forced to
convert. What insults did they suffer? Worse than on this
damnable ship? And you, Saulo, now you are the servant of
torment, your hopes in ashes, your only task to survive
until the Catholics allow rest for your bloody hands and
aching shoulders.

After what seemed forever, we returned to the ship.
With my hands aflame, my body in agony, I could barely
climb the web. Fr. Norte, his chains removed, attended to
my hands, smearing them with lard. Another breach of
Law, but otherwise comforting. In the night we talked
while others of the crew labored in the small boats. Across
the sea, the island glowed its hellish hue, the mountain
crowned with lightning. "That does not look like Eden to
me," I said to Norte.

"Nor to me, Saulo. And the fires are not of Hades, simply
fields burned after harvest, customary in the agriculture of
sugar. Though I do not doubt the lightning's intent—I
believe it is God's displeasure at what we do."

We took care of Germo who was little improved, and
Golem and another who had grown ill while rowing. I went
below to sleep, not knowing what to do with my throbbing
hands. Around midnight a change in the ship's creak woke
me. The calm had broken. The ship began to move.

Just past first light we dropped anchor in a shimmering
cove, our destination before us. In the near distance I saw a
brown-sand beach edged with palms. A rough track led
inland where I could see a church and buildings of russet
stone. Behind the town rose thick clouds of smoke, a
curtain that hid the long mountain. The jungle seemed to
dominate everything in view. Following a prayer of thank-
fulness on the high deck, Captain de Caminha, the officers
and priests went on shore. A group of men, which included
waiting priests, greeted them. On the beach another
ceremony and the staking of a cross.

They first unloaded the animals. Men ferried a long
ramp out to the ship and we put it into the hold. We prod-

ded the goats, horse, and the two remaining cows up to the deck. Sailors had removed a section of rail at mid-ship and they bullied the protesting animals overboard. The men in boats waited, took ropes and swam the beasts to shore. I had no idea farm animals could swim, but each did. These creatures had been our companions on this long voyage, and we looked after them with well-wishes, wondering as to our own fate. Supplies and personal goods went next, along with the large sail which needed mending.

As they prepared to unload the slaves and convicts, de Caminha returned to oversee— and to deliver his ominous message. "I will allow only those healthy to go on shore. The rest will stay shipbound to either recover or die." Anger swelled in my chest. Earlier with great care they had moved the sick nun to shore. I wanted to speak to this unfairness, but feared de Caminha.

Golem, who had weakened during the night, wheezed, "If I could only swim I'd—"

The captain's words broke in. "We will anchor a half-league off shore to keep those tainted from befouling our colony." He turned to Norte. "*You,* traitorous priest, you will vicar this floating spittle house. I will reclaim my vessel in a fortnight when I must prepare for voyage. Those who are recovered will join my colony. For the others who remain ill, God in his wisdom has chosen to maintain their affliction. They will be disposed into the sea."

At de Caminha's direction the sailors sorted through the convicts, chained the sick together, and prepared the others to depart. Many of their sick struggled to stand and pleaded to go on shore. To stay, they knew, meant death. The slaves understood and began their own protest, helping the ill among them rise. A second gang of sailors moved quickly to quell the disturbance and separate the sick.

After transport of the convicts and slaves, we Jews suffered the fateful sorting. The sailors went through the girls and children first, leaving the sad few who still had the sickness. They helped or carried those not sick down the rope web into the waiting boats. The ones left looked on hopelessly as their comrades were rowed to shore. The boats returned with supplies of food, water, and wood for fuel. We boys helped unload, pulling baskets of goods up to the deck and putting them in place. The supplies seemed meager for our number, but did include bread, black sugar syrup, dried fish, and a basket of oblong fruit I'd not seen before.

"I will see that everyone is well cared for," said Norte.

I did not feel assured—I had spoken these same words to Germo so many weeks before. Now it was time to say good-bye to Germo and Golem, to the two sick girls and a small boy who remained ill. Golem stood shaking at the rail. Germo, his fever-eyes filled with tears, could only signal farewell, a frail smile from where he lay.

Marcel came to me. "The bad luck of this," he said and made a cup of his hands, first offering it to São Tomé, then to Germo—a confounding gesture. "Your cup overflows with opportunity."

"What opportunity?" I asked. He vanished with my words.

Since the wind blew directly landward, two large boats with rowers stood off-bow for towing. My companions lined at the rail, ready to depart. The barber went among them, cut close their hair and clipped their sidelocks. As the newly shorn climbed down the web to the boats, I became terrified at leaving. I summoned my courage and approached the captain. "Captain de Caminha, sir?"

He was giving instructions to the few crewmen who would set the ship for its fortnight's stay. He turned to glare. "This upstart boy again. What do you want?"

"I wish to stay with Father Norte. To care for the sick."

"I should have left you to Nasic. He would have taught you manners."

Gesturing to the remaining Jews and the souls chained on the fore deck, I said, "You have toiled these many weeks to bring us here. The more who live, the more will benefit your colony."

He glared at Norte. "You put him up to this."

45

"No captain, but an extra hand would be most helpful."

De Caminha eyed me and pointed to the barber. "You are a slick-tongued Jew who mocks civility and corrupts our priests. Take your place with the others and—"

He looked to the island. With a shift of wind, dense billows of smoke carried the smell of burning fields, the ship's rigging rattled, a twilight settled. The captain studied the remaining sail tied to the yardspar, then me. "It seems providence has brought a favorable breeze," he said. "I will honor your petition, though I distrust it." He directed the sailors to mount the small sail and sent a man forward to wave off the rowers. "When you return," he told the crew, "bring both rowboats. I want no pestilence on our shores."

We sailed a ways from the island, passing through smoke to open water and clear skies. The crew dropped anchor, reefed the sail, and abandoned us in their little boats—their scornful laughter drifting back on the wind. Fr. Norte and I watched them depart, the long mountain before us, resplendent green above the smoky gloom of São Tomé.

Norte looked pleased. "Well done, Marcel. It appears you may keep your hair a while longer." He turned to the sick. "Come, Saulo, God calls us to His task."

Chapter 4

During the evening of our first day, Germo's illness reached a dreadful intensity. I cradled him through the night while his body burned with fever. Minutes after sunrise and without waking, his breathing ceased. This was the saddest moment of my life. Germo, perhaps the last of his family, his history lost to eternity. Norte tried to comfort me, but I could not accept it.

"It is because of you accursed Catholics my friend is dead. And all of us lost in this foreign sea."

"He is with God, Saulo." Norte made the sign of the cross.

"Whose God? Not mine. Without proper burial and eaten by hakifi? And *your* God? Your God is the reason he is dead!" My words shocked me, but I was so sad, so angry.

He looked from me to Golem who had recovered enough to help with sick chores. "I understand your sadness. If you will not tell the others, you may bury Germo in accordance with your custom."

"And if another Jew dies?"

"Do as you wish, Saulo. My supposed treachery is well known."

And so we prepared our poor friend for sea burial, first wrapping his body in a cobbled sackcloth of dirty rags. Golem offered kaddish; Norte prayed quietly behind us. Golem removed his precious tallith—tearing the fringes for burial—and gently tied it over Germo's head and under his chin. The sun's heat and swarms of flies from the stable forced us to abandon our friend to the water sooner than intended. Discarded slave shackles attached to his ankle bore him to the deep, hopefully away from the hakifi.

• • •

I saw that Norte had changed clothes from his robes to that of a sailor's—brown oil pants, a blue shirt and short leather boots. "I believe we should remove the leg irons from both slaves and convicts," he said. "One man is well enough to help us, and the others will do better if they can shelter from the sun."

"What's to keep them from slitting our throats?"

Without a word he produced a key and we began to remove shackles. We first unlocked the two African females and moved them to the girls' enclosure, one so ill we carried her there on a litter, covering her face to keep flies off the festering brand on her forehead. The other was a girl about my age. We settled them with the two remaining Jewish girls, first washing, then clothing them in our unhappy surplus of women's garments. We moved the Jewish boy, Hiem, from the girls' enclosure to ours. We next unlocked the remaining male slave, and lastly the two convicts. One convict, a Moor, went with us; the other, a mixed-blood, refused our help after we freed him. The Moor spoke a little of the slave language, and thus enabled us to talk with the Africans. I noticed I had picked up a little of the language too, a tongue called Guinea.

"We will make a hospital," said Norte. He directed us to unlash the small sail. We did so, tying its yardspar to the high deck with the loose end pulled across to the forward mast where we lashed it in place. This gave us a large area of shade between the high deck and mast. "Put everyone under the canopy," Norte told us. We moved all except the resisting mixed-blood.

Norte considered our handiwork. "These innocents must not go to God without the Sacrament of Baptism." He then prayed over each and sprinkled drops of water on their brows. When finished, he turned to Golem and me. "As I allow your Jewish prayers, you must allow mine. We will pray for their souls, their return to health, and our souls." Golem and I joined in while the mixed-blood glared hatefully at us from where he sat.

Over the next days our wards improved except for the slave woman. The male African, the first to get better, immediately began to help with the black women. Besides aiding them with food and water, and keeping the flies away, he applied seawater and lard to their sores and made an ointment from tar to kill the fly worms in the brand wound on the one woman's forehead. Despite his efforts, she continued to linger between life and death.

The Moor, whose health had returned, often sat with the black slave and mixed-blood on the bowsprit, the three of them dangling their feet over the water. The slave taught them native songs which they chanted while gazing at the island. Golem found a supply of lime, and we spread it in the holds and elsewhere to kill the flies. We also cleaned the holds of animal and human waste and removed spilled slops from the deck. The ship became more habitable.

In the evening Norte produced a cask of spirits, and we set about drinking. I had never before tasted spirits and, though the liquor burned my throat, after a few drinks I found it quite to my liking.

Norte raised his cup to Golem and me. "It seems some of the devil-lore about Jewry may be in error," he said.

"You mean you're not poisoned by our touch?" Golem asked.

Norte took a drink and offered me the cup. "Nor do you have tails or cloven feet."

Golem reached over and pulled at my mop of hair. "But Saulo still has his horns." He took the cup from me and drank. "And do you believe we drink the blood of infants?"

The priest opened his hands in resignation. "You do not drink blood or have horns anymore than I."

"No more than say, a Jew named Christ?"

"Enough!" shouted Norte, swaying to his feet. "I have been forced to confront many things on this voyage. These insights will cost me both cloth and life." He staggered to the rail where we heard him vomit, then shout against the night, "I cannot imagine a hell worse than the trial I face in Lisbon!"

Golem stared through the lantern's light. "It is good to see these Catholics feed upon themselves."

"This man is different," I said, reminding him of my father's letter and the unknown gentile friend back home. "Not all of them hate us."

In the dark Norte gasped and cried out. We took the lantern and rushed to the sound. The mixed-blood, his eyes wild, held Norte with a knife to his throat. "Kill me and be done with it!" Norte cried, and began to pray in Latin.

Angrily the mixed-blood began to shout the same prayer over Norte's voice. Then he began to wheeze. "I once trained in the priesthood until the Church grew tired of its black experiment."

Golem rose to his full height. "You cannot kill us all. Saulo and I will die for this priest. And where will you go?"

"They threw me in prison because of my color. Before I was a free man, now I am a slave."

"Killing Norte won't change that."

Norte reached up, put his hand over the convict's, and pressed the knife to his own throat. "I am sorry for this injustice, brother," he said in a strangle.

The mixed-blood appeared so weak from his illness that he could barely stand. "Brother?" he repeated. Golem reached over and pulled the man's hand from Norte's throat. The mixed-blood stumbled away.

Next morning, the three of us bleary from drink, worked the sick chores. Norte brought food to the mixed-blood, letting him know he held no malice from the night before. Breakfast was a dreadful concoction, a soup of long-neck sea worms which the male African harvested from the ship's hull. He'd found them while drawing seawater. As we'd heard once before, Norte declared the worms a delicacy.

"Are we the Jews of Egypt or the Wilderness?" I asked Golem.

He shielded his eyes from the ocean's glare. "Why?"

"Pick one."

"Egypt," he answered, as if he'd read my thoughts.

50

"God did not forbid abominations until Moses and the ancients had left Egypt. We are still in Egypt, not yet the Wilderness."

He took a bowl of worm broth and began drinking. "It is not the same, but I'm hungry."

While we ate, Norte touched the old plague scars on his face. His voice shrank as he talked. "Becoming a priest seemed God's destiny for me. The pox killed my mother, my father, my whole family. I was about seven and we lived in Évora. After the plague, nuns from the abbey went through the village and collected orphans. They found me cold and shivering in the doorway of my house, my family dead inside. The Church became my family, the Abbey de Monsaraz and the priesthood my community."

"The Jews of Évora suffer at the hands of that abbot," commented Golem.

"Christ's Gospel teaches tolerance, even kindness to non-believers. But for non-believers to suffer in hell—" He rubbed his eyes to clear his thoughts. "The Church teaches that the most lasting kindness is to convert them so their souls will be welcome in heaven."

"At what cost?" I asked.

"The Jew suffers no more than any commoner," he answered. "The Four Horseman ride amongst us all. As for heaven, I am more convinced of its beneficence than I am of sitting here."

"But what you said last night? If you go to the stake?"

"Last night I said my *trial* would be hell. But I expect whatever outcome to be blessed. If acquitted, my service to the Church continues. If condemned, the fires will cleanse my sins. Heaven will welcome me."

Golem and I looked at each other, not knowing what to make of such reasoning. We turned to the mixed-blood.

"I will not say if I differ," he grumbled. "I prefer slave to heretic."

"You may speak your mind," Norte told him.

"Opinions are my peril, priest, I will not risk it." He stood, walked to the rail and at once shouted, "I see a sail!"

51

We rushed to join him. In minutes the sail became two, two caravels beating northwest, bound for São Tomé.

We knew when they spotted us, as both came about, dropped their tack and heeled to the breeze, sun dazzling their flanks. If not for the blood-red crosses on their sails and their trade in human despair, these ships made a glorious sight. They arrived swiftly, lowered their large sails, trimmed the small, and paused close starboard in an opal sea. Norte and one captain conversed in shouts, the latter shaking his head when he heard our circumstance. I pictured Germo's eyes watching us from the deep.

Oh the sad endowment of their decks, one fully covered with slaves and convicts, the other with brethren Jews— children and young adults, Leah nowhere in sight. "Welcome to New Egypt!" I shouted in Hebrew.

Norte's face blanched; he stared at me. "Oh Saulo, that cannot be undone. I hope no one understood."

A priest from the ship yelled, "What did that cursed Jew say?"

"Nothing," replied Norte, "a greeting of some sort." He turned and cuffed me so hard I fell headfirst into the rail. "I am sorry," he said after me.

"Lash him," the priest shouted.

"Be assured, father, I will," called Norte, then quietly to me, "Stay down, Saulo, he must not see you."

As the ships prepared to leave, Norte whispered, "Your careless words threaten every child on that vessel. How do you know they won't beat a translation from them?" He hauled me to my feet and summoned the convicts. "Tie him to the mast. Make a show of it." From the corner of my eye I saw Jews on the receding ship watch grimly while two priests and a nun looked on in satisfaction. I felt great shame for my mistake.

With the caravels fully gone, Norte untied me and examined my bruised face. I said, "I am sorry, Father Norte."

"I too, Saulo. Let us hope my apparent beating appeased them."

"Apparent?" I put a hand to my cheek.

"Perhaps some spirits tonight will provide wisdom and heal your pride."

That night the mixed-blood sat with our drinking club and spoke freely, but refused to imbibe. The Moor and male slave sat a short way off, listening to our discourse. The Jewish boy, Hiem, slept at our feet, health nearly regained. Of our three remaining wards, the African girl had recovered, the Jewish girl less so, the African woman unchanged, though she still clung to life.

"My mother was a Moor," the mixed-blood told us, "the mistress of Vicar Duarte de Vincente. After my birth the vicar banished her but kept me. At age seven I entered the Abbey Vincente and began my studies." He struggled to his feet and began to pace, his steps angry and measured. "The vicar was greedy and sought too many benefices. Soon novices with wealthy sponsors filled the place. He threw me and the one other black into the street. My father, the vicar, refused my claim. For a while I worked as a free man in Lisbon. Then they declared men like me slaves and put us in chains."

He stopped pacing and settled next to Golem. "And then there are victims of indulgence. You Jews are victims of a *grand* indulgence." He looked at Norte. "Tell them priest."

"It will not change—"

"If *I* know, surely your telling it violates no secret."

Norte said, "In the shadow of death, King Afonso petitioned Pope Alexander for absolution. For two-thousand gold reis, His Holiness granted the request; but Afonso died before the final payment of five-hundred. When João II ascended, he offered satisfaction for the remaining debt: ten-thousand converted Jews."

"How do you like that?" the mixed-blood asked. "Ten-thousand souls for five-hundred pieces of gold."

"That Pope got a bargain," said Golem.

The mixed-blood, irritated at Golem's glib tone, said, "And you will know hell on São Tomé."

Norte raised his cup of spirits. "Tell us, brother, what

53

you know of it?"

The mixed-blood looked to the night sea. "I know but little, from a slave who once worked the syrup mills there. Fernão Gomes discovered Tomé about twenty years ago. No natives, the island a-run with animals, lush fruits, and an abundant sea. Gomes claimed the island for the kingdom and named it St. Thomas, that being the Saint's Day on which they found it. On their return to Portugal, most of the ship's company became ill with Tomé fever—the same that infects all who live there. Many died. Afonso granted title of the island to Gomes. By some means, a marriage possibly, the grant later passed to de Caminha. About ten years ago they discovered that sugar on Tomé grows far better than on Madeira. With slaves and convicts, the captain built the town and plantations. Now the commerce of sugar lines his pockets and those of João II. No matter that half the workers perish before a year passes."

"More like two-thirds," offered the Moor.

• • •

Next morning two boats appeared rowing toward us. We recognized de Caminha's pennon and several of his crew. The captain's presence likely meant we would return to the island. We rushed to get the remaining sick on their feet. For the African woman we had little hope, she was doomed, unable to rise. The Jewish girl, though her spots were fading, seemed less improved this morning. Golem, Fr. Norte and I washed her quickly, exchanged sick clothes for fresh, and set her upright. This girl, about age nine and named Sara, stood for a moment, took a few steps and fell. "Let me die," she pleaded. "Please let me die."

"Hide her," said Norte. And we did, putting Sara below deck in the stable.

The male slave and African girl began to lament over the slave woman. We helped move her forward to the old slave enclosure. Norte appeared from his quarters; he had changed into his vestments. We put on our best face as we lowered the web and welcomed the captain. An unfamiliar priest and stern-looking bailiff accompanied him. The latter carried a brace of chains, undoubtedly meant for Norte.

De Caminha examined our use of the small sail. "Who did this?"

Norte fingered his rosary. "I did, captain."

"I did not think you so ingenious, priest. Captain de Santarem from yesterday told me you wore sailor's clothes. He wondered if you were indeed a priest."

"I am still in Christ's service." On hearing this, the bailiff and priest looked with derision.

"We shall see," said de Caminha "At any rate my vessel returns to harbor. Soon after they left Porto Novo, our comrades were shadowed by pirates. But the brigands manned cumbersome galleys with poor sails, and our captains outran them. A Portuguese ship would be quite a prize to those devils." He surveyed the deck. "How many of these fools still have the sickness?"

Norte crossed himself and gestured forward. "Just the African woman."

De Caminha beckoned two sailors and pointed to the woman. "That one still lives. Finish her and throw her overboard. If any resist, kill them too."

Not a person to lie, Norte looked miserable. As I stepped forward to speak, Golem seized me by the arm. "Let's help mount the sail." In this deadly situation for Norte, I held my ground. If caught lying about the Jewish girl, the captain would kill him on the spot.

"Captain," I said, "I am accountable for one other. A Lisbon girl. Sara. Despite Fr. Norte's orders, I moved her below deck. I believe—"

"And?" asked the captain.

I addressed Norte. "With all respect, Father, I believe Sara is over the illness, just not—"

"Bring her!" commanded de Caminha.

While the captain directed the sailors to raise the sail, Golem and I retrieved Sara. "You are well," I told her, and brushed away the straw. "Just weak from the illness. You must appear healthy."

"I will try."

When we presented Sara to the captain, several sailors were waiting. "I believe these Jews need more than a beating," he raged. "Throw them in the water." Norte prostrated himself before the captain and pleaded for us.

"I don't know how to swim!" I screamed as a sailor lifted me over his head. Though I held on to his shirt, ripping it, I plunged into the ocean. My first thoughts were the hakifi. Sara splashed next to me. She grabbed my leg and pulled me under. I groped for a handhold on the ship's hull, feeling the mass of long-necked worms. At first they broke loose, but when I gripped a larger handful, they held. I drew up my leg and forced Sara's arms loose, pulling her to the surface. She sputtered and cried.

I put my free hand under her chin and said in Hebrew, "I can save us if you do not struggle. Hold on to these worms." She did so, but barely. Ahead I saw the rope web. "Grip my waist and I'll pull us." The effort was agonizing. The worm shells cut my hands. When I made it to the web, I hooked my arm through and guided Sara's in like manner. The African woman's body floated a few yards away. The wind freshened and the ship began to move in a circle. I could have climbed the web, but Sara needed my help and I would not leave her.

The rope web began to shake. Above me I heard the sailors laugh. "Get off you stupid Jews. Go to your God." They began to pull the web upward. I clung for a few seconds, but Sara could not. Letting go of the web, I seized a handful of worms on the hull and held her too. The boat began to move more quickly; the pull of the water made our task painfully difficult. My hand broke loose and I grabbed at more worms. Again I broke loose. I needed both hands, my one bloody and quickly tiring. Sara could not hold at all. The Saddiq should let go, die comforting this girl, join Germo in the deep.

As I adjusted to my new fate, something brushed my side. I thought hakifi, but it was Great-Grandfather Marcel. He handed me a rope that trailed in the water. The

56

ship's narrow turn had floated the line from the tethered rowboats within my reach.

I clamped the line under my arm. "Bless you, Grandfather." Getting a better grip on Sara, I held tight as the ship pulled us along, but soon tired. With my arm thrown over the rope, I slid down the belly and kept the line taut with the ship while the rowboats still drifted in the eye of the turn. *If I could just get inside one, or at least have it support us in the water!*

The moving ship suddenly took up the slack between me and the rowboats. The line snapped tight and jerked me into the air. I lost my hold on Sara. Below me she struggled in the water, rolling against the hull. "Grab the boat line," I shouted, but she made no attempt and quickly washed past the ship. Marcel appeared next to her, cradling Sara's body before they vanished beneath the water.

"Survive," I heard, and glimpsed Golem above me. Someone seized him from behind and he disappeared.

Sliding along the line, I grasped the first rowboat. As time passed, Fr. Norte and Hiem called from the ship's stern. "Climb in," they shouted. Too weak to do so, no longer fearing even the hakifi, I held on, hoping my travel to the island or to my death would come swiftly.

I did not believe I could last another minute when I saw the sail lower and the anchor splash. Sailors pulled the rowboats to the rope web and climbed down. Too weary to beg for my life, or perhaps unwilling to do so, I waited in the water. They heaved me into the bottom of a rowboat and stepped over me like a corpse. A sailor poked me with his foot. "The captain told us to leave you; but since you're tough for a skinny Jew, perhaps we should not."

"And brave," another muttered.

De Caminha looked down from the rail. "Why is that one still alive?"

"Honored captain," a sailor replied, "a boy this strong will do a fair day's work."

"I should have killed him myself," the captain snorted. "We will see if he's more than disobedience and talk."

Chapter 5

A dozen bodies were scattered on the beach. A snarl of
dogs, pigs, vultures and fish eagles fought over the remains. Led like cattle with ropes around our necks, Golem,
Hiem, and I trudged through the town. Despite my ordeal,
I fared better than Golem. De Caminha in his rage had
lashed my friend, then strung him to the longspar by his
hands. Both shoulders were out of their sockets, his pain
intense. Hiem and I supported Golem as we labored along.
The slaves and convicts followed in chains. At places along
the route, lifeless eyes watched our progress, the heads of
men both black and white stared down from iron poleaxes.

Golem looked at them and said, "I now live for the
purpose of killing de Caminha. By my hand he will join
those dead."

"Where is Norte?" I asked.

Hiem answered. "On the ship. Chained."

"Doomed," added Golem.

We stopped at the church where a priest and barber
waited—the former blessing us, the latter cutting our hair
and sidelocks while he cursed under his breath about dirty
Marranos. "Do not worry," said Golem, trying to make light
of his pain. "It'll grow out. You even show a little chin hair,
Saulo."

They put us in a walled yard behind the church. Three
dead Jews lay in the mud next to the gate. Inside, a few
boys sat against the wall, sick and suffering, without spirit,
the rest gone to labor in the fields or sugar works. Over a
low dividing wall rested a number of girls, some also sick,

several very pregnant or with infants.

"We've been here since spring," a pretty girl named Miriam from Algarve Province told me. She had dark eyes and her hair was covered in a dirty kerchief. "They took every kid they could find. My father was a chartmaker in the king's fleet and we had a life of privilege. But when it came our time, no one was immune."

"We heard rumors," I said. "Our elders denied them."

"And now this." She nodded at the infant in her arms. "The sailors, the priests, even our brethren make us whores."

"What do you eat? Everyone looks starved."

"We eat little. If you're ill and cannot work, you get what others sneak back. They give us food only in the fields or at the mills." She gestured to a building beyond the wall. "There are women next door who work for the priests. They take pity and sometimes bring food."

"What about the Catholic training?"

"A farce," replied Miriam. "We are plantation slaves, nothing more. Only a few times have the priests lectured us on religion."

I pointed to the street. "The gate is open. There are no guards?"

"Where would you go? Town or the jungle? In town without a pass, soldiers from the garrison will beat you or worse. We are locked inside at night."

"How does one get a pass?"

"You look too young. Some of the older boys have them. They have taken common wives and live as peasants outside the enclosure." She looked at her baby and shrugged. "Because of him, I can never be a wife. He needs to be circumcised, but there is no one here to do it."

It began to rain, and since the girls had little shelter, we went back to our side and crowded into a shed that extended from the wall. When the rest of the Jews returned that evening, I saw almost a hundred boys and nearly as many girls, an astonishing number. From their clothing they produced a variety of things. Snakes, lizards, a little dried fish and meat, and various fruits. A kid from the ship greeted me. "We eat everything. Dogs, cats, rats, sparrows, pig flesh, and this." He handed me a string of dried meat.

"What is it?"

"Something we get from the blacks. An abomination, and you don't want to know. We're fortunate to have it. Get used to it."

The rain started again. Some of the boys built fires inside the shed and cooked the reptiles, sharing the food with those too sick to work that day. A few of these sick were beyond help and would not last the night. Since Golem could not use his arms, Hiem and I fed him. He was nearly mad with the pain. A boy came up to us. "I have some medical knowledge. You must restore your friend's arms or he will never use them."

"Do you know how to do it?"

"Yes. It is very painful."

We held Golem to the ground while the boy pulled his arms and moved them back into place. Though Golem's face contorted in agony, he made not a sound.

The yard, surrounded on all sides by a twelve-foot mud wall, was topped with a tangle of savage thornbushes. Though locked in at night—and the wall seemingly impassable—the boys had found a way out by raising a section of bushes from the top of the wall to create a hole large enough to crawl through.

Next morning, Hiem and I assembled outside the gate with the others. An overseer summoned us and said, "Jews earn six copper reis for six days work. If you miss a day, your week's pay is forfeit." They divided us into several groups. My group walked a quarter league to the sugarmill where I spent the day carting bricks from an old ruin for use in a new part of the mill. Once they started construction, perhaps I could benefit from what I'd learned in my father's brickworks.

Almost everyone fell ill with Tomé fever. It came and went, a few died. For days, many remained unable to rise, then it would lift quickly. "You will have it soon," everyone told me. "It's only a matter of time."

• • •

Now it was early Tevet (January by the Christian calendar). It rained every afternoon and often into the night. During the heaviest of rains we took shelter in the shed. The area beneath the roof could not cover everyone, so we drew straws for the privilege. I spent many wet nights propped against the wall with only an immense jungle leaf for shelter. Finally along the east wall—the driest place—we built larger lean-tos made from sticks and leaves.

The girls' yard sat next to the rectory and an assembly hall. The building remained closed to them and they had no shelter. At night we helped them build lean-tos, begging rope and other things useful from the black women who labored for the priests. While working on the girls' side, I often asked new arrivals about Leah, but learned nothing. Golem seemed compelled to tell everyone about Sara and my attempts to save her. Not one girl from our ship remembered Sara, and few boys remembered Germo. And no one believed I saved myself from the water even when Hiem and Golem told the story.

"Will all our deeds and friends be lost to history?" I asked Golem.

He looked at me stupidly. "Since when, Saulo, are Jewish martyrs remembered anywhere except in the Bible? I know of hundreds of families in Vigo destroyed without a trace, Jews, Christians, Moors." Golem swept his hand across the yard like Moses. "You expect too much from these children."

"But—"

"Tell me," he asked angrily, "do you know the names of the boys who died last night? Do you remember the names of your family dead, your brothers and sisters who have passed on?"

"Not all. Of course I remember Leah—she's two years older than I—and I know of my two predecessors named Marcel."

Golem laughed, then stopped as he raised his arms to stretch. In the past two months his shoulders had started to mend. "You are the *third* Marcel in your generation?"

"Yes, my mother had seven children. Only my sister and I survive. You've heard of my great-grandfather Marcel, the Saddiq. My father is determined to have the family name live on."

"My father's twice married," said Golem, "yet *I* am the only living child of— I think, nine. Now he is dead and can seed no more." He made a grim smile. "So, Saulo, you are a continent away. With your family believing you Catholic or dead, will your father name his next son Marcel?"

"You'd like that, wouldn't you?" I pondered the idea. "The world could always use another me."

He slapped me on the back. "Third Marcel, you'll have to do."

• • •

We often heard the girls cry out in the night. Looking over the wall, we saw men with torches taking some away. Most of these girls returned in a day or two, ruined; a few never returned. In Portugal, a Christian caught fornicating with a Jew could be put to death, although the crime was rarely enforced. Usually it was an accusation added to particulars for those condemned, or a confession extracted in torture and used as an excuse for execution. Here in São Tomé, the men considered it sport.

"The rape of these girls is wrong," Golem said.

"Yes, but what can we do?"

He clenched a fist and ground the knuckles into his palm. "We can stop the Jewish boys; I'm not so sure about the outsiders." Lately Golem had adopted a sinister demeanor and usually sought work in the fields with the mixed-blood and blacks from our ship, speaking in their manner and using face paint. This morning, an hour before dawn while I held a fragment of brass mirror and a candle, he blackened his eyebrows with oiled charcoal and extended the line along his temples to his hair. He paused, studying his work. "My outcast father seems to speak to me at times, Saulo. To fight on God's side with courage and cunning as Ahab did against the Assyrians. If needs be to die a hero as my father did."

I turned the mirror to myself, surprised to see the almost-man who stared back at me, my eyes dark and brooding, more determined even than Golem's. And my face was dark, too, much darker than my usual olive complexion. "The priests will think you're a demon," I said and handed him the mirror. "They will burn you like Norte."

Golem again studied his reflection. "They may not have sent Norte to Lisbon as we were led to believe. I think he's imprisoned at de Caminha's."

"Tell me."

"I found a prison last night while I snuck around the captain's residence. In the nearby jungle there are cages. One of the prisoners might be Fr. Norte. This night I will bring something to occupy the guards while I get a closer look."

"I'm going with you."

The day seemed to last forever. By nightfall I could hardly wait to set out. Sometime near midnight when the rain stopped we crept over the wall and ran behind the rectory. If we found Norte he was most likely starving, so we carried food and water for him. Near the rectory a black man waited in shadows cast by a clouded moon.

"You say come out when rain stop," he whispered. "You pay now."

Golem gave him some coins. "Half now, half later."

The man scowled and showed us a skin. "Bring holy wine from priest church."

"Good."

"Take slave path."

As he turned, Golem caught his arm. "How do you know where we're going?"

"You not only spy on this place. Eyes watch everything."

"Whose eyes?" I asked.

"Not until we know you better," he said to me and gave Golem a poke. "Maybe know this big outlaw fellow."

Golem grew taller in the moonlight, and his face took on the look of defiance. "Enough talk." He pushed the black forward.

Light from torches appeared through the trees as we approached the cages. We counted seven; each held one or more prisoners. Golem pointed. "If it's Norte, he's there."

"Money now," our companion said.

Golem gave him more coins. "Extra for dice."

The man gripped the money tightly. "You good fellow." He walked leisurely toward the two guards and bounced the wine skin on his head, making drinking sounds. They talked and drank, soon noisy, drunk and gambling.

"Norte," Golem whispered when we neared the suspected cage. The man looked up with hollow eyes. Though nearly a skeleton, it was him.

"You have come! The Virgin answered my prayers! Did you bring water, my sons? Did you bring food?"

"Yes, both." I handed him the skin and food through the bars.

He drank, then began to eat the fruit. "Bless you, Saulo. Bless you Golem. I prayed for this." Tears ran down his cheeks. "I will eat slowly. I know fasting."

I looked past Norte's cage to the next. The two men inside were dead. In another cage, a man sat in a stupor on the body of his companion. In the moonlight it appeared he had eaten one of the dead man's legs. I touched Golem's arm. "What now? We can't leave him."

Golem examined the cage's heavy brass lock. "Eat and drink, Father. We will come again soon."

Once away, Golem said, "We reached him just in time. Another day and he'd be gone. The mixed-blood told me they give them only one stalk of sugarcane a week. For water they depend on what rain they catch."

"How will we free him?"

Golem thought for a moment. "Freeing the priest is not the problem. It's where to hide him. We must draw suspicion elsewhere."

"If they suspect at all, they will torture and kill us."

"I will think of something."

"We will think of something."

"If they have our trust, Saulo, there are blacks who might help."

"Why would they?"

"In a way they see us as hostages, not free, yet not slaves—possible allies." The moon hid behind clouds and we stopped to get our bearings. When it reappeared, we moved on. "A fugitive slave named Tjange lives on the mountain," Golem continued. "He has enough people that the Portuguese fear to pursue him. Having Norte, a be-trayer priest in their camp, would be a stroke of luck for them."

A few days later Golem and I caught the fever. It lasted only a few days. We felt fortunate—many people told us if the first sickness was mild, the infection would not kill you when it returned. We lost four days work and two weeks wages—our illness had spanned the Sabbath. During this time Golem taught me to cheat at dice, tricks he'd learned from the slaves. In a few days we had won two-hundred copper reis and five silvers from the boys in the yard. "We should stay here and gamble," I said. "It's better than working."

He looked at me darkly. "We have enough money for Norte. Time to act."

While we were sick, Golem and I had paid Norte's guards to give him food and water. As we prepared for our first day back to work, Golem said quietly, "I will make arrangements today with the mixed-blood. Tonight we tell Norte our plan." Since I labored at the sugar works and he in the fields, we did not meet again until that evening. He told me his news with great excitement. "The mixed-blood escaped the convict camp. He is with Tjange."

"So will they help us?"

"Of course. Now the mixed-blood will fight with them against the Portuguese."

In the night we waited for the rain to stop, then hurried to see Norte. Though improved in health, he recoiled when he heard our plan. "I refuse to go with this Tjange. You must not free me."

"The Portuguese will let you die."

"*I am* Portuguese. I will stand trial in Lisbon."

"They starve you." I pointed to the cages. "Most of these men are dead. And they bring new ones to die every—"

"Starving on this island is also my trial, Saulo. Now I must live. By God's hand you arranged sustenance."

"Money arranged sustenance, we cheat at dice."

"*Please*, Father," Golem said, "let us free you."

He considered for a short time as he drank the wine we had brought. "Young men, I will pray on this. Return in a few days."

"These Christians are insane," I said on our way back. Golem agreed.

When we returned to the yard we saw two boys dragging a girl over the wall. Golem reproached them. "We do not defile our women. They are ours to protect." Up to this time no one had challenged his edict, but these two chose to assault him. At the first blow, Golem flew into a rage and beat the two until they pleaded for mercy. He forced them to lie in the mud and ask the girl's forgiveness. For the rest of the night we kept her with us, returning her through the gate in the morning.

• • •

Everything had changed with Norte when we next met him. "Saulo, Golem, I have prayed over this. With a certain requisite, I consent to this rescue."

"Requisite?"

"It must be known that I am an unwilling captive and wish to return in service to the Church. If I request it, Tjange must free me."

"I can ask them," said Golem.

Norte continued. "I do not plan to live out my days as a fugitive in the jungle. Perhaps my detractors, the priests and governor, will take heart and embrace my return. I hope for absolution."

"You have nothing to absolve."

He made the sign of the cross. "God has his reasons."

A few mornings later we counted out the money and put it into two monkey stomachs. Golem hefted both pouches. "Half today, half tomorrow."

"Why not just bribe the guards?" I had this absurd image of Norte and Tjange disappearing arm-in-arm into the jungle.

He eyed me. "You, friend Saulo, are an idiot. Does this place look like Lisbon? Where would the guards go with their new wealth? The rescue must appear forcible or they will lose their heads." He smiled broadly. "De Caminha returned yesterday from his voyage to Africa, just in time to suffer the loss of his heretic priest."

That night we met the same man who had gone with us the first time, and whom we had relied upon to deliver the bribes. Nearing the cages—too late—I knew something was wrong. Soldiers swarmed from the jungle and threw us to the ground. Norte's cage sat empty. De Caminha rode from the trees on his white stallion, the same horse which had traveled with us to the island. The animal's apricot eyes blazed in the torchlight. Next came more soldiers leading five blacks, arms trussed, roped together, legs hobbled. Behind them they dragged two bodies, a black man and the mixed-blood.

The soldiers forced us to stand and face de Caminha. "Sons of Judas, here is Tjange and his henchmen."

From the ground the mixed-blood gasped our names and cried, "The priest Norte has betrayed you, betrayed us all!"

As a soldier moved to silence him, de Caminha raised his hand. "Spare him for the moment. It is my pleasure is to see all these criminals burned at the stake."

The soldiers removed the bodies from the cages, and heaped them to one side in the grass, cutting the throat of one man discovered still alive. Next they shoved us inside and did not bother to unbind our hands. De Caminha posted guards and left. I could not see Golem; they'd put him in a cage a distance away. To no avail I asked to be untied.

In the morning, thirsty, hungry, and aching, I watched soldiers bring more prisoners, Hiem, two other male Jews, and several blacks. They put a black and Hiem in the cage with me. The black, a man I did not know, ignored us. Hiem shook with fear. "They claim I conspired with you, Marcel." He began to weep.

"Unfasten my hands, Hiem. In some manner we will find comfort."

He worked at the knots, his voice failing with every word. "They say Fr. Norte betrayed you. That he is now cleansed of his ties to us Jews."

"He must tell me himself. Otherwise I do not believe it." I pulled at my arms and rubbed my wrists. Could this true about Norte? Why had his cage been empty?

Hiem continued his lament. "They will torture and burn us. Even worse, twelve more Jews, six girls included, are to be burned as an example. Everyone blames you and Golem. And do you know who the inquisitor is?"

I shook my head.

"They say it's Norte."

Chapter 6

We lived in the cells without food or water for several days, then our inquisition started. Soldiers and priests led Golem, me, and the others to the rectory and put us below ground in solitary cells. Golem said only one thing on the way. "They did this to Jews in Castile. Confess, that is your only hope for survival." They silenced him with a blow to the gut. I settled among the rats and, like everywhere else on São Tomé, the ants. Scattered in one corner were the bones of a human arm. The only light came from a distant candle down the hall. I found it curious that the Portuguese had built these cells. Did the priests use them for cloister and meditation, or were they always intended for prisoners?

The next morning (I could only assume it was morning) they brought me a cup of water and a piece of salt fish as hard as wood. I softened the fish in the water, the latter now too salty to drink. In a short time my mouth burned; I called for more water.

Two priests, their faces covered with black hoods, came to my cell, unlocked my chains and led me to torture. They strapped me to a post, leaving one hand free. The free hand they tied to a little table that reached in front of me about chest high. I could not look down because of a thick chain wrapped under my chin and hooked to the post above my head. "Where is Fr. Norte?" I cried. "I must know—"

"Silence Jew! Norte will see you when he is ready. Then he will hear your confession." One put a tiny cup to my lips. Water, blessed water. "To oil your tongue." The other priest held a large black nut in front of my eyes. "This is a seed

69

from the stone tree. We learned its use from the Africans."
The nut's long end had a finger-sized hole in it. "While we
do not have the modern devices of home, God has shown us
primitive means that also work."

I felt them do something to my free hand, to my little
finger. They had fit the nut to it and twisted. Unbelievable
pain! My finger splintered like a dry twig. I screamed, my
voice fading into insensibility.

They splashed water on my face With my mouth so
terribly dry, I licked eagerly for the few drops within reach.
"What do you want from me?"

"Jews are the Dominion of Heresy. We want naught from
you but your confession and death." The priest's eyes
flickered inside the hood. Did I know this man? I could not
be sure.

While I slumped without senses, they had switched
hands. Now my right lay on the table with the nut attached. I felt cracking, searing pain. Vomit rising, I tried to
do so in the priest's face, but the man had expected this. He
stepped back and avoided the stream that spewed from my
mouth. "You are ruining my hands. I will be unable to sign
your confession!"

"Sign *my* confession."

"My confession! I will be unable to sign it."

"By the time we are through, you will sign even if you
have no arms, eyes, or nose."

They dragged me to my cell and put me back in chains.
In the next days, as I faded in and out of agonized stupor,
many screams came to me, some mine, some others—
Golem, Hiem, the Africans. Other Jews? I did not know.
Why had Marcel not come? Why had I not called for him?

Sometime in those days Marcel did come. "You believe
yourself forsaken, that is why you did not call."

I showed him my hands. "I am forsaken."

"I am here, therefore you are not forsaken."

"How can I endure this?"

He took me in his arms and showed me his hands,
fingers twisted like mine, but healed. "My hands will

become yours. Together we will endure this."

• • •

The torture went on. I learned to drink water and eat little. I saw no one except the inquisitors. They broke my next two fingers, then started on my feet. Over and over I offered to confess, but they ignored me. I screamed "Kill me!" and they laughed. "The stake is the only place where you will die. There you will receive Christ's mercy."

How long it went on, I do not know. I became without sense, the pain of torture flowing through me like a stream of brimstone. From the second day, I could not walk; later I could not rise. They dragged me to torture and dragged me back. At some point I signed a confession with my broken hand and pledged my soul to Christ. If Fr. Norte took my confession, I did not know it.

After I recited my confession many times, the torture stopped. A priest came to pray with me each day, bringing a little food, wine, and water. Sometimes Marcel appeared with him, saying nothing, oblivious when I questioned him. The priests thought me mad, talking to someone they could not see. I watched their hands—which ones were my tormentors? A physician attended my wounds, telling me I must be healthy to die at the stake. "Others are not so lucky," he told me.

One day Nasic came to the cell in the company of Great-Grandfather Marcel, the latter smiling strangely. In the hallway slaves waited with a litter.

"Nasic, how can you be here?"

"I am Nasic's brother, the plantation overseer."

"He told me about you." I vaguely remembered seeing this man before at the sugar works.

"My brother suggested you were a bright young man, and I believe it."

"People burned at the stake are very bright."

"Perhaps." The man's Portuguese was much better than Nasic's. "My name is Nawar." He smiled like Nasic, show-ing yellow teeth. "Our father had an affection for the N." A slave brought a chair. Nawar sat and looked down at me.

Though I could not know it at the time, this man was offering me the blessing of friendship. "You worked at the mill before your arrest?" I nodded. "And you made bricks?"

"Yes."

"Did you make the short wall? Some pattern for a new construction?"

This could be a dangerous question. "I cannot remember."

"The mason declares you did. You used bricks with holes in them. This pattern of yours appears quite useful."

"Useful?"

"You must explain this construction. Since you cannot walk, we will carry you."

They carried me on the litter to a spot behind the sugar boiling house where the men made bricks, the air heavy with the smell of sugar and parched clay. Off to one side sat the little wall I had built. The chief mason came over, looked down at me and crossed himself. "He is the one."

Nawar tapped my wall with his walking stick. "How did you come up with this? Explain its use."

I blessed my father's brickyard and the mason skills I had learned there, then felt dread—I could not remember where in the Jew yard I had hidden the remnants of his letter and Leah's gold chain. At the same moment our gentile benefactor's name came to me: old man Diaz, a sometimes gravedigger who carted and sold our bricks in the Christian community.

They moved my litter next to the wall. "My father owns a brickyard in Lisbon," I said. "Jewish businesses are not allowed to compete with Christians, so they limited us to making decorated bricks not available elsewhere. But we also made plain construction bricks for the Jewish community." I motioned to some on the ground; Nawar's slave handed me one. "My sister Leah carved the molds." Her image came to my mind and I stopped talking, remembering how she protected me from bullies when I was little. Will I die and never see her again? I focused again on Nawar. "One day she made some bricks like these with holes in the center. We put wood shafts through the holes as bolsters. A wall, when mortared and built in this manner is sturdier than usual construction."

"Your *sister* invented this?"

"Yes, Leah. My father and I thought it a fine idea." I brushed the little wall with my hand. My monument to nothing, I thought, but it will outlive me.

• • •

Although I received better treatment after Nawar's visit, the torment around me continued. Men and women and children dragged down the hall, broken bones and screams. My cell had no door, just a narrow slit for an entrance. Chained to the far wall, I had a limited view of the hallway outside the cell. A few times I thought I saw Golem or Hiem in the dim light. I did see children taken by, some of the victims so tiny that the inquisitors pulled their bodies as a child might drag a doll.

I had often heard the Portuguese were a merciful race, a people who tolerated minorities—never a Jew's experience in Lisbon, and certainly not here. A priest came daily to prepare me for execution. On one of these visits I asked him, "If you're going to kill us, why do you continue the torture?"

"Our Savior demands Pure Truth from sinners. They must confess all sins to procure God's Absolution."

The belief struck me as absurd. "I am sure we sinners have confessed to your satisfaction."

The priest looked indifferently—torture was a province of his faith. "Not to *our* satisfaction, only to God's. Their confession must be sincere and inclusive. Otherwise you and your fellow sinners will not be welcome in Heaven."

Such cruelty. How could I make this fool understand? "They will curse heaven if the path is painful."

"You know nothing of this. Execution at the stake releases pain, purifies body and soul. It is clearly set down in our *Modae et Applicare*." He went on for a while, calling death by burning virtuous, then asked me to pray with him. I refused. Why should I pray with these people who planned to kill me? He prayed anyway.

I wondered if I did not pray, would they again torture me? "Was *my* confession sufficient?" I asked. "Why am I no longer tortured?"

"We maintain your health for God's purpose. Besides that, I cannot say."

At hearing this I did not know what to feel, left alone while my friends and others suffered. In the end, death would unite us all. The priest went out and abandoned me to misery. Preposterous that they claimed interest in my health—their torture had made me a cripple. My hands were of little use, neither were my feet. Because of my hands, I could not use a crutch; I could only hobble with help. Would they carry me to the stake? They must surely carry the others. These cowardly inquisitors—nameless behind their hoods and masks. More people dragged past my cell, screams. I prayed to God for my deliverance, deliverance for us all.

Days went by. I asked the priests for the date of execution. All claimed ignorance. Finally they announced it a week hence, on the Christian Sabbath. I asked to see Fr. Norte, Golem, and Hiem, asked the names of the other Jews, asked if the mixed-blood still lived. They refused answers, saying, "You must heed only your Salvation."

Nawar came to see me two days before "Burning Sabbath" as I had begun to call it. His slave carried a chair. He brought news both welcome and terrible. "After Sunday, they will set you free. All others in the conspiracy will die."

"Why should they perish and not me? I choose to die with the others."

"You are now my property, Saulo, so you will live. De Caminha wished mightily for your death, but I paid his price."

"What do you want? Look at my hands and feet. I cannot work."

"You will help with construction. Your masonry skills have value." I tried to sit up and could not. Though I scrabbled at the wall for support, I fell back. Nawar summoned his slave; the man brought the chair and helped me sit. "You can thank me for your better treatment," said Nawar, "and for your freedom."

I did not feel grateful. "Spend your money for the others. If they die, I can never be free. I will die with them."

He rose to leave. "I have struck a bargain for you life. You will witness the burnings and return to the Jew yard."

With all my strength I screamed. "You cannot ransom me with the blood of my fellows! I will starve. I will never work for you."

Nawar addressed his slave. "It seems I have acquired an idiot. Put this stubborn Jew back on the floor. Now I may have to pay extra to keep the priests from killing him."

He moved to leave. "Wait! I wish to see Norte."

Nawar turned with an air of futility. "Unfortunately you will indeed see Fr. Norte. He is to die in good company with you." He left without explaining.

Later a priest came into the cell and I asked about Norte.

"Norte has confessed to instigation. He will burn like the others."

"Your tortures produce false confessions. He never—"

"One more day and your blasphemy will be silenced."

Despite my many insults, these priests had always stayed to pray with me. This man left in silence.

All morning of Burning Sabbath I begged to see Marcel, but he did not come. Around midday a church bell rang, the first I'd heard since arriving on Tomé—something special to mark the occasion. A short time later priests, soldiers, and slaves went through the cells and took prisoners out, some silent, some crying softly, others who screamed in helpless sorrow. I listened for Golem and Hiem, but did not hear their voices. No one spoke to me. I prayed for my friends and myself. How I needed Marcel! Of all I had endured, this was the most cruel.

The hall grew quiet. Had they had forgotten me? A priest appeared. "You are the last." He came in with two soldiers. They unlocked my chains, dressed me in the white cloth of penitence, and pulled me along the hall and up the stairs. The priest walked ahead, praying. The sunlight blinded me. Oh, the sky so blue, the clouds milk white, the heat wonderful on my skin.

They had set the burning place in the town square, full of people come to watch, the stakes in a triangle—a total of ten—four in the last row, then three, tapering to one in the front a slight distance from the others. The condemned stood—some in pairs—bound to every stake but the first. I saw Golem and cried out to him. His chin rested upon his chest and he could not respond. I called to Norte who answered wordlessly. I did not see Hiem or the mixed-blood. There were fewer Jews than I expected, the missing likely dead from torture. A few on the staked cried aloud and pleaded for mercy. They lifted me up, onto a pile of wood and sugarcane refuse, and chained me to the front stake, facing the others.

The people in the square taunted and threw rocks. The Jews among them cursed Golem and me. The pain of my hands and feet destroyed my spirit. Even without Marcel, I felt ready to die. Earlier they had dragged me though puddles in the street—it must have rained that morning. Now I felt the wood wet beneath my feet. Before I could hope they might postpone the burning, carts of dry sugarcane refuse arrived. De Caminha directed the men as they piled it around each stake. Although they had nearly a cartfull left over, they put none around me. Would I die in the agony of a green fire?

Nawar appeared in front of my face. "Courage, Saulo. This torment will not last forever."

"Put dry wood under me. I wish to die with the others." He did not answer. I felt someone behind me place a strap across my forehead, pinning it painfully to the stake. Two priests took Nawar's place. They pierced my eyelids, sewed open my eyes, and attached the threads through my forehead. As I screamed in rage and pain, blood clouded my vision. There was a time during my torture that I thought I could never hurt worse, but now I did. My pain was beyond

76

imagination.

De Caminha came close. "So you may never conspire against my authority, witness all that happens here."

I strained to shut my eyes, to tear the lids from the threads, but could not. They threw water in my face. I knew the others would die and I would live—live with each death on my soul.

The crowd silenced as a priest read the warrants of execution. Finally Golem, face terribly disfigured, looked my way, though I could not tell if he saw me. Norte mouthed a prayer. Through the orange haze of blood I searched the stakes for faces I knew and called their names aloud. "Norte, Golem, Lael, Tjange, Simon, Galvão, Dorthea, Bernard, Anyce, Ruth, Laura," and those not there, "Hiem, "Mixed-blood" whose proper name I never knew, "Sara," and "Germo." *I must remember them all!*

The orange haze became fire. The crowd cursed and denounced us. Water again splashed my face. The figures before me pleaded, cried and screamed. Their voices rose with the fire's crackle, faces aswirl in flame. A few stayed silent, but all leapt as the blaze consumed them. Someone pitched a burning stick at my feet. The crowd approved. I cried blood and died with my friends.

Chapter 7

I was on my back somewhere, facing into a warm rain. A few drops at first, then a heavy stream. Someone stood over me pissing in my face, burning my eyes. The threads were gone; at least I was alive. I rolled over and put my face in the dirt. "Stop!" The piss continued. I heard derision and laughter, and recognized the boys of the yard. A sharp kick to my ribs, curses. "Golem's not here to protect you, Saulo. He is burned to a crisp." More kicks.

I awoke later that night, hurting everywhere, my eyes clotted and infected, hands as sore as ever, my feet even worse, likely burned. I stank of urine and vomit. "Marcel," I cried, "Marcel."

Footsteps came near. "He calls to himself. What does he want now?"

"Please don't kick me anymore."

"A dozen of us died because of you and Golem. All for that rotten priest. Our treatment has worsened since your rebellion. You are despised, an outcast, the overseer's indenture."

"I'm sorry. I tried to be a friend." They walked off, deaf to my words. I lay in the dirt in agony.

In the morning after almost everyone left, I crawled to the cistern, drank, and washed my face. I saw my feet were indeed burned—toes broken, swollen and blistered, dead flesh oozing. The soles, which I could not see, hurt worst of all. I tried to rest in the shade by the shed, but the flies and mosquitoes drove me mad. The few boys remaining in the yard ignored me.

Sometime later Nawar came by, angry when he saw me.

"I told these damn Jews to take care of you. I left bedding, clean clothes and food. Where is it? I sent the physician. Did he see you?"

"No, I am an outcast here."

"So I see. You look terrible. I will take you to the hospital when they have room. Right now it overflows with the fever, but you are my property and I expect it to be protected." He walked around to the girls' yard. His slave stayed, concern in his eyes. Nawar came back with two girls, explaining that he would pay them for my care. He and the slave carried me next door and placed me on a grass pad. I became a ward in the common nursery the girls ran for the infants.

They cleaned and washed me, tended my wounds, changed my clothes, and helped me to the privy. One said, "You and Golem came to our aid when others preyed upon us." She told me about their weapons, mostly clubs and a few spears. "In the last month we have driven off every intruder. No stranger comes in now without asking."

"Do you believe our rebellion put everyone in peril?"

"Yes." She looked around to make sure no one overheard. "But Norte was a good priest. He deserved your help. Most of these Catholics are a vengeful bunch. In one way or another, we all run foul of them."

"Still, at least twelve dead and—"

"Oh it's sad, but the fever kills that many each month." She continued to tend my feet, carefully washing them, the attention so welcome.

"Can you do anything for my eyes?"

She brought her face close to mine. "I don't know what to do. I think the doctor is coming today."

I glanced around the yard. "How is the young woman Miriam, the one from Algarve with the little son?"

"She is at work in the fields," the girl said. "I expect she'll be back with the others."

Later in the day the physician did arrive, the same man who treated me in prison. He wore a Portuguese hat of soft wool felt. Beads of sweat sprouted along his brow. He looked at me and shook his head. "I came to see you last afternoon. Some boys barred my way, told me you had died. They were preparing you for burial."

"A secret Hebrew ritual."

"Since you still live, we will continue." He motioned to his assistant, a black woman with large, soft hands and piercing eyes. She held up my feet and hands for examination. The doctor summoned two of the girls and explained the treatment as he went. At last the doctor tended to my eyes, washing them with a warm solution. He showed the girls something in a vial. "This is a powder of pearls and sulfur. You must wash his eyes three times each day and apply this sparingly." He made a puddle in his hand of water and powder and dribbled it into my eyes. If it helped, I felt nothing.

I held up my hands, fingers useless, twisted and swollen. "Can you do anything about these? And my feet?"

"I plan to. The burns on your feet must first heal. I can do little for your toes now except extend the fractures. That will help the healing. I will do the same for your fingers. Since they are not burned, I will splint them. In time you will heal. Tomorrow I will bring my instruments. Prepare yourself, it will be painful."

Near nightfall the girls crowded back from work. Miriam came to see me, her baby slung in a length of kanga cloth. The little boy stared at me without blinking, his head a mass of black curls. Miriam responded with the same cringe I'd seen from everyone. I made a weak gesture at the throng of girls and children. "I see many new people. I was too feeble last night to notice the boys. Are they equally crowded?"

"Yes, new boats arrive weekly. There is another off-anchor with many sick on board." She knelt to get a better look at me, then shook her head. "You seemed so full of promise when you arrived, helping the ill on your ship. Now your witless enterprise has brought you to this." Her baby began to pull at her braid. I thought of my sister and the little boy thrust into her arms by the soldiers, of the mother's anguish and Leah's. Oh, my sister, if not Tomé, where are you?

I ignored Miriam's reproof and squinted at her little boy. "Your youngster looks well, what do you call him?"

"Joseph."

"A name of patience and fortitude."

She held him to her face, smiling, though her eyes remained sad. "'Youngster,' if he lives that long. So many die in their first years. One should not get too attached to babies." Her smile turned to scowl. "And then we have boys like you and Golem who risk everything for nothing."

"If you disapprove, why do you visit?"

She thought for a time; the baby began to fret and squirm. "Perhaps I made a mistake." She got to her feet and walked away.

The physician returned the next morning. Besides his assistant, he brought two men to hold me. They moved me to a bench where he examined my eyes. "It seems the Jewess nursery takes good care of you. How do you feel?"

"The same except my eyes; they are better. It helps to be clean."

"Nawar must believe you have promise. The pearl and sulfur powder is quite expensive." He laid out his instruments and described the course of treatment. The black woman held my left hand while the two men pinned me to the bench. "This is going to hurt." With his hands and clamps, he re-fractured my fingers, fixing splints as he completed each extension. It reminded me of when we restored Golem's shoulders. In tribute to my dear friend, no matter how much it hurt, I did not cry out; but my chest shuddered and thrashed. The doctor commented when he moved on to my feet, "You are strong not to complain."

"Torture prepares one. You should try it."

"I have seen too much torture." Behind the doctor stood my long-absent great-grandfather, his hands raised, clasped together triumphantly.

I spoke with a strangled voice. "Grandfather, why have I not seen you?"

The doctor looked up. "What?"

"Nothing, my mind wanders."

Marcel moved closer. "My beloved child, I have been nearby, watching. You have endured this ordeal without me. My heart swells with pride."

"How am I to be the Saddiq, the Just Man? My people despise me." Marcel did not answer; my question turned him to vapor. The doctor ignored my words and continued his work.

The next days were arduous, yet hopeful. I felt my health improve. The doctor brought crutches which I used cautiously, and a book of Chaucer. I read the stories eagerly, my eyes better each day. I felt encouraged, trying to move my splinted fingers, praying my hands would regain their strength.

Miriam's turn at the nursery came. I tried to talk with her and, though Joseph grinned at my prattle, she ignored me, only mumbling an occasional assent. "My circumstance is impossible," I told her. "I am indentured to Nawar, but have vowed not to work for anyone in league with these Christians. With my friends sacrificed, I—"

"Nawar rescues you and you complain?" Miriam frowned, looked down and crushed a line of ants into the dirt with her sandaled foot. "He has given you a position of sorts, while the rest of us..." She began to trample ants with both feet, then slung the baby in his kanga over her back. "Starve, Saulo, that's your choice. You are more fool than I imagined." She walked off, her work left unfinished.

• • •

In the week following, the doctor took me to the hospital. "You will convalesce here. The Jew yard is unsafe for an outcast who can't defend himself." By now I could use my hands a little and get around on crutches. Since my right thumb and forefinger had not been broken, my writing hand worked. I found a journal among the discarded possessions of a dead man and began to keep a record, bringing up to date my experiences so far.

Nawar showed up at the hospital the same day. He

found me sitting in the shade drawing pea fowl as they stalked the black and green lizards that scurried everywhere. He studied my work. "Can you design hearths for my new boiling pots? I wish to use those bricks of yours."

My life as an indenture had begun. I considered my situation: the Saddiq as serf. "Yes," I answered grimly, "I need details."

The mason and Nawar's slave arrived the next morning. The slave helped me to the harbor where the copper boiling pots, recently shipped from Portugal, were stacked on the beach. On our way through town, my opinion of the hearth project began to change. Indenture or not, here was my first commission as a builder. The little wall I had constructed had saved my life and given me a beginning. Could a simple boiling hearth provide me with real opportunity? Along the way, the mason and I discussed the project. Then, when I asked, he explained Nawar's arrangement with de Caminha. "Though Nawar is in the captain's employ," he said, "he owns shares in the sugar and saw mills. He is also a freeholder of sugar land."

"Freeholder? How is that possible for a Moslem?"

The mason shrugged. "I'm from Madeira. The religious stricture on my island and here is very different from the mainland. Away from Portugal, the Church yields to commerce."

"Do you own shares?"

"Yes, a small share in the sugarmill and my own plot of land." He nodded to the slave. "I also have a quarter of him for my use. He works my garden; we raise yams and maize. He gets a portion of that, and sugar and other goods from Nawar."

"I hear some married Jews will get shares."

"If the governor believes them true Novos." The man crossed himself. "It does help to be a Catholic."

At the beach, the mason told the slave to get some men from a nearby unloading crew so we could measure the pots. They hefted the heavy pots and separated them, moving each a little distance from its neighbor.

"There is a rumor," the mason said, "because of the sickness and runaway slaves, de Caminha may offer slaves freeholding after a period. My wife is from the Niger. Through our marriage she is free."

Marriage, I thought. If I were back home, in a year or so I would be expected to have a wife chosen for me. With no one to arrange it, who would do that here? Then I remembered the pain of the blacks on our ship. "Is your wife branded?"

"Yes, but not our children. They are also free." With a look of displeasure he touched his forehead. "Branding is an affront which I believe should be abolished."

"Some of the Jews take African women."

"That is the policy—produce offspring, replace those who die."

We measured the pots, their rivets evenly spaced, the seams clean and finely soldered. I admired their quality. "Who made these? Excellent workmanship."

"The Aviz shipwrights in Lagos. They supply much of our metalware."

When we finished, the slave gestured to the unloading ship. "Very fine Congo goods sirs." The mason bought fresh onions and dried fish. He lent me a few reis, and I bought a pound each of pistachios and dates.

Near sunset we set off for the hospital, passing groups of people just returned to town from the fields and mills—new Portuguese families with young Jewish wards in their households. Since my arrival five months before, the town had almost doubled in size, the most recent citizens crowded into roughboard hovels and canvas tents. We also passed more substantial construction, two sugar warehouses, a public garden next to the hateful burning square, and a common bath.

We stopped at the bathhouse where I examined the stones. "These come from a Lisbon quarry."

The mason again crossed himself. "Indeed so. Intended for the church at Porto Alegre."

"Why not use local bricks for the bath?"

"Politics." His eyes narrowed. "The Church disputes Governor de Caminha's sovereignty over the island. He counters by using consecrated stones for the public bath."

While I found this humorous, I kept it to myself. Back at the hospital I handed my food purchase to the slave. "Take these to Miriam in the Jew yard." I described her and Joseph. He nodded and trundled off. The Saddiq as slave master.

Next morning we went to the boiling house. I studied the old hearths, made rough drawings, and saw ways to improve the current design with a simpler draft and means of support. The mason remained helpful and I concluded, though he was Christian, his origins on Madeira made him more tolerant than others. We discussed construction changes. "If we use my bricks for fire enclosures, the bolsters must be iron rather than wood." I saw this as an opportunity to contact my father through Diaz. "I know a merchant of construction materials in Lisbon."

"No, no. We will get the rods from Lagos. Nawar and I have shares with the Aviz shipworks, as does de Caminha."

Ah commerce. No matter, even dealings with Lagos held promise that I might get a letter to my father. I had to think he was safe, released from the authorities and back with my mother.

In the early evening Miriam and the baby, escorted by a slave carrying a torch, showed up at the hospital. She thanked me for the food and handed me a package of flatcakes tied with string. Delicious, and like all foods of Tomé, sweetened with black syrup.

"These aren't much," she said. "Yamcakes with your pistachios and dates." The baby gnawed on a piece and played with her braid. "Better if I had the sort of things we cooked with back home, wheat flour and spices, and olive oil." Her face grew sad. "In Algarve we had a pantry full of spices and the most beautiful kitchen."

"When we first met, you told me your life was privileged there."

"It was, but I did not consider it unusual. Because of my

85

father's profession, we were part of a mixed community, Jews *and* gentiles. I *played* with Christian children, and we entertained my father's associates and their families in our home."

"To my knowledge, nothing like that ever happened in Lisbon. Were you invited to their homes?"

"Of course; they were our friends. Mother said they even took on some of our customs."

"For instance?"

"The Christians began including their children at their dinner tables. And they would bring them to our home for parties. Oh we had the best parties." She adjusted Joseph in her lap and looked away. The baby dropped his flatcake. Miriam broke off another piece and gave it to him. "I baked these at the home where I'm visiting."

"Whose home?"

"The foreman's at the Crown plantation."

I tilted my head at the slave. "Is he theirs?" Suddenly I felt very angry.

"Yes, from the sugar farm. He's one of three slaves who belong to the foreman's family. The family's from Almodovar in Beja—"

"I know where it is," I snapped.

"Why are you angry?"

"I've heard they will abolish the Jew yard. That we have to live with Portuguese families or the damned priests."

"That's true, Saulo. With everyone jammed together there, the fever breeds. All of a sudden they've begun to treat us better; we have more food and freedom. Some believe your rebellion has changed things." I knew the truth of this, but did not wish to hear it. We had paid too high a price. Miriam shook her head and continued. "You're always angry, Saulo. Why?"

"You—" I hunched my shoulders. "I am sorry; it's just that all of us have become like them." She remained silent. "Are you going to live with the foreman's family?" I asked.

"They have invited me. I will stay there a few days to see."

"Will you convert? You will, won't you? You have to."

"We all have to."

"I am angry about that too." I took another bite of cake. "These are very good."

Miriam bounced the baby on her lap. "Today Joseph said your name."

"No, how could he? He has never heard my name. He said 'mamma' and it sounded like—"

"He's heard it!" She spit out the words. "Marcel Saulo. He heard it!" She began a bitter weeping. "Do you know what happened to the girls on our ship? What happened to me?"

"If you wish to tell me, do so. On our ship both nuns and priests treated the girls cruelly, but never compromised them."

Her body racked with sobs. She could barely speak. "We had no nuns on our ship. I don't know who my little boy's father is."

"I'm sorry."

Miriam beckoned the slave. Without saying more, the two of them left. Oh how I missed Golem. He would know what to do, how to comfort a ruined girl with a child, a charming child at that. Had Joseph really said my name?

Chapter 8

Over the next days with Miriam on my mind more often than the project, I drafted plans for the boiling hearths and made visits to the mill and beach. On one trip to the oceanfront I bought a jewel of pink coral from a Guinea trader—its color the same as the Lisboa marble from my father's brickyard—hopefully someday a gift for Miriam. And the feelings that possessed me: What was it about this girl? It seemed my soul transformed inside me whenever I saw her, a welling up.

As for my hearth design, the mason approved it with only a few changes. At week's end he examined my latest drawings. "Excellent, Saulo. Where did you learn to draw?"

"If one learns to scribe Hebrew, drawing is easy." I saw no reaction from him other than approval. This man appeared truly tolerant. I imagined Norte smiling his approval also.

The mason brought Overseer Nawar to look at my plans and tally the lengths of iron rod we needed. They talked eagerly about the new hearths. "We will procure the iron and start as soon as possible," said Nawar. "The order to Aviz will go out with the next ship." He scribbled on the margin of my drawing, mumbling as he went, "With favorable winds, four weeks to Lagos, a month to make the rods, five weeks back." He looked at us. "Make bricks and remove the old hearths while our supplies are in transit. Three months, and we can start construction." What he said next gave me great concern. "We'll present this design to Governor de Caminha. I want the two of you to explain it."

"I cannot meet with him," I stammered. "I cannot! He murdered my friends."

"He will demand your presence."

The mason stepped in. "If Saulo won't do it, I will present the design myself." Without resolving this, we finished our work. In my mind I began to compose the letter I would write to my father.

The following day I wrote the letter, stressed my masonry work, did not mention indenture, and left out my travail. I addressed it to Diaz and gave it to Nawar, asking him to send it to Lagos for forwarding. I felt encouraged when he accepted it without question. I also sent a note to Miriam and asked her to visit. By now I was doing well with crutches, even able to walk a little without them.

For three days it rained. Miriam arrived the first evening without rain, bringing a skin of beer and a bowl of crushed chickpeas spiced with garlic and salt. "Compliments of my mistress."

"You've moved to the foreman's?"

"Yes." The slave stood nearby holding a torch. Miriam nodded to my lantern and addressed the black. "Put out the torch and sit over there."

"Where is Joseph?"

"My mistress cares for him."

"'Mistress?' You sound like a foolish Christian." I ignored her pointed stare. Miriam as gentry. "Last time I faced a difficult choice, you answered with scorn. Regardless, I now seek your advice." I told her my dilemma with de Caminha. While she considered, I added, "Your father worked for the Court. Did he face this sort of thing?"

"The Court did much of which my father disapproved, so he complained. Yet because of his position he had no choice but to make his maps."

"He complained about the mistreatment of Jews?"

"Yes, a formal complaint to the king's chartmaker."

"And then they stole you from your family. Think of the conflict your father now faces?"

"Think of the conflict *I* face. We are thirteen-hundred leagues from home, the fever kills many more than do the Christians, and we must survive."

"You did not answer my question."

She shrugged and continued. "I have my son to consider." Then she whispered, "I also hate the Catholics, but they dominate us like a force of nature, like the fever."

"Often, Miriam, you show true wisdom. I have given this much thought. We should marry. I am asking you."

She looked at me and laughed, astonished. "You are just a boy—not fully grown and likely a cripple. I have no dowry. After what happened to me, do you really think I want a husband? There is nothing I want from you or any man."

"Once you said, 'I can never be a wife.' I will provide for you, give Joseph my name. A strong son, *he* will be your dowry. And together we will have more sons."

Miriam studied the candle flame; the yellow light illuminated her smile. "What do you know of having sons, Marcel? Have you ever been with a woman?"

"No, but—"

"How old are you?"

"Sixteen," I lied. "My birthday was last month while they tortured me."

Her smile faded. "I am sorry, but I do not need a husband. My situation with the foreman's family is quite good."

"I will not always be a cripple, and I will take a wife. God wills that all men must marry."

She gave me a sharp look. "Marcel, God wills that women not be raped." She stood to go. "And God wills that we should not be kidnapped. Everything that happens here violates God's will."

"Regardless, Miriam, will you consider my proposal?"

She lifted my lantern and carried it to the slave. The man removed the glass and lit his torch with its flame. As she returned, Miriam appeared thoughtful. "Thank you, Marcel. I will think about it." She turned to leave.

I picked up the beer skin. "Wait."

"Keep it. I will come back in a day or two with my answer."

Miriam did not return in a day, nor the day after, nor the week after. My thoughts of marriage turned to other girls. Many girls in the Jew yard would consider a mason in the overseer's employ a good catch—virgins without a child to care for. Yet none appealed to me like Miriam.

• • •

I prepared drawings of the brick molds and details of the hearths. Each morning Nawar's slave met and helped me to the mill where I watched over brick production. We tore down a hearth and I laid out the foundation for a new one. The mason put me in charge of this work while he stayed busy elsewhere.

One day, too tired to go back to the hospital, I took a nap in the shade, covering myself with a mesh to keep the pests away. After only minutes the mason called my name; I woke with a start. The governor and Nawar, the latter with my finished drawings rolled under his arm, stood looking down at me with indifference.

The mason helped me stand. Too dazed to think clearly, I drank water from a skin and splashed some on my face. De Caminha spoke. "Explain these square hearths. How does a square enclosure accommodate a round vessel?"

Did the mason intend this as a trap? He did not need me to answer these simple questions. Nevertheless, like a tamed parrot, I responded. "It is easier to build a square hearth, and this design will operate better." The slaves had moved the boiling pots to the site and we circled them as I talked. "These new ones are quite sturdy, so we can brace the rims at four points on the hearth walls and place supports underneath. The hearth's open corners are the chimneys." I hobbled around the foundation trench and showed him the location of the fuel doors. "With the open corners it will be much easier to remove ash and empty the pots." At one corner I drew a circle in the dirt. "To clean the pots, a worker can stand here. Easier than cleaning from the rim."

They asked more questions. As we talked, I realized my fear and rage had softened. Is this what happened to Miriam's father? If so, it did not work long for me. My rage at the governor quickly returned. I seethed while our discussion continued.

When they departed, leaving me alone with my crew of brick-makers and diggers—slaves and convicts assigned to me by Nawar—I went back to the hearth foundation and found the circle I had drawn in the dirt. "Please God," I prayed, "do not deny me this mischief." Around the circle's margin I scratched The mezuzahs Numerals from Deuteronomy. I vowed tomorrow to hide a mezuzah in the boiling house, hide them everywhere. That night I began to inscribe the Torah from memory, concealing the pages within my folder of drawings, vowing that when I had sons, together we would copy my Torah onto a sacred scroll.

• • •

Later that week, just as the slave arrived for our morning trip to the boiling house, citizens began to run past the hospital with children and possessions, crying, "Guinea pirates! Flee!"

A boy I knew and his wife ran by. I shouted to them. The wife, heavy with child, gasped for breath as they hurried over.

"What's going on?" I asked.

"On the beach! Slave hunters. They'll pillage the town."

"Where are the Jews from the yard? I don't see any."

"The garrison took refuge in the yard. They are holding the Jews with them."

"Why?"

"Too many pirates. De Caminha's at the beach offering terms."

"But *why* are they holding the Jews?"

The couple looked back fearfully. "Don't know, Saulo. Maybe to ransom the colony." They ran off.

I turned to the slave. "We're going to the beach."

"No master sir. Guineas make me galley slave."

"Then take me there, and leave if you want." We started out. People streamed by. We passed the Jew yard where soldiers stood guard outside the gate. They looked more frightened than the townspeople. I could not allow my brother Jews to be used for tribute.

At the beach I beheld a strange scene of ghastly death, military council, and nature untroubled. Just off the beach was a caravel overtaken by the pirates. The Portuguese crew stood at the rail, stripped naked, two of them hung by their feet over the side, disemboweled, their entrails dipping in the water. Hakifi splashed in the sea and pulled at the guts, dragging the corpses to and fro. Between the caravel and shore, a pelican flock worked a shoal of anchovies; the water flashed brown and silver-blue with feeding birds and scurrying fish. Two enemy galleys sat beached in the shallows a few feet from shore; a hundred of their crew stood at arms.

Governor de Caminha in full armor, flanked by two hastily equipped squires, sat astride the white stallion facing the horde, his lance at the ready in his left hand, battle sword laid across his saddle. His horse, wearing a gleaming breastplate and red-ornamented side mail, pranced and snorted in anticipation. I had never seen such a display of courage. This man whom I hated, at this moment my protector—the man Golem swore to kill—held the entire enemy company at bay. Before him stood their chieftain surrounded by fierce-looking warriors. At their feet in a gory jumble were several of their dead. I could not help thinking of a hundred years past when Crusaders slaughtered thousands in the Holy Land.

As I moved closer I saw de Caminha's sword dripping blood, the side of his horse bloody also. Nawar, who spoke the Guinea language, stood beside the governor interpreting. As they spoke, de Caminha nudged the horse forward to stand on the dead; the animal trampled the corpses with a slow, rhythmic motion of his hooves. My companion next to me grunted approval. He had not fled, and we both stood in awe of the spectacle.

In terror of the mounted knight and horse, the chieftain backed away and consulted his warriors. Nawar followed him, talking quietly, then returned to the governor's side. In a minute the Guinea chieftain left his warriors, walked up the beach, and bade de Caminha follow. After a sufficient pause, the governor and Nawar complied. The three of them parleyed. When they parted, the chieftain returned to his men and de Caminha sent a runner to town.

After a long wait, soldiers appeared. They led a goat and carried three squealing pigs trussed on poles. The Guinea pirates fell upon the animals, butchered them and started cook fires. I turned to Nawar. "I thought Moslems did not eat pig flesh."

The overseer's face was full of malice. "De Caminha knows they're starving. He shames them subtly—without the goat they would be fully disgraced. Pay attention, Saulo. Next morning we will crush them."

I watched the savages as they swarmed about the fires. The chieftain, who appeared in low-spirits, stood a short distance from his men. Did he know what fate awaited? A cohort brought him a shank of goat, the meat still bloody. He chewed on it as he walked toward us, glaring at me and talking at length with Nawar. I understood most of it, but pretended I did not, and wondered at what I'd just heard. Nawar burst out laughing. He turned to me and said, "The scoundrel asked what happened to you and why I make company with a cripple. I told him you're a little daft and often hurt yourself."

"And what made you laugh?"

"Oh, well... uh, so you wouldn't be a bother, he offered me the favor of killing you."

I looked at him intently. "That's not all."

"You understood?"

"I understood enough. You told him I am your adopted son, and though an idiot, your wife had grown fond of me."

Nawar became flustered. Before he could answer, de Caminha walked over followed by a squire leading his horse and two seconds carrying his armor and helmet. He nodded to Nawar and the chieftain, then to me. "You will come with us, Saulo. See how we honor visitors to our humble colony." Nawar translated for the chieftain who called three of his lieutenants to join us.

The governor mounted his horse. We marched in odd procession up the beach and into town. I took up the rear, helped by the slave who mumbled curses about feeding dead men fresh meat. I asked him how he knew. "Just know, master sir. Just know."

At sundown, de Caminha held a banquet in the public square for the pirate chieftain and his commanders. He treated them with dignity, presenting the leader with a silver-appointed saddle and the promise of a charger to go with it. In exchange for a five-year treaty of peace, he offered them safe harbor at Porto Alegre and supplies of sugar, black syrup, and yams.

During the celebration I encountered the Crown foreman. "How is Miriam?" I asked.

My question seemed to distract him. He considered it briefly. "She's fine," he said, and walked off. His manner left me puzzled and concerned.

As the evening progressed, strong beer, wine, and spirits flowed. The Guineas, apparently unaccustomed to drink, quickly became intoxicated. We could have overwhelmed them at any time, but the governor kept his surprise for the next day.

As I found out later, when the alarm first sounded that morning, de Caminha sent runners the nine leagues through the jungle to the new colony at Porto Alegre where two caravels were moored. More runners stationed themselves at points along the island shore, lighting beacon fires so the caravels could navigate at night. The two ship captains, both Burgundian Knights, marched up-island with the Alegre garrison ready for battle.

• • •

Next morning Nawar woke me before dawn. "A spectacle awaits us, Saulo; one we must not miss." At first light we walked through the town square. The bodies of five pirates with their throats cut lay grotesquely in the street. We neared the beach and the clash of battle. In the harbor the enemy galleys had just erupted in flames, their escape blocked by the caravels from Alegre. On the blazing galleys a force of Portuguese sailors dumped their dead adversaries overboard. Our caravel captured the day before had been freed. Over its side hung pirates, replacing our dead from yesterday. Pelicans, oblivious to the chaos around them, bobbed in the water.

The water's edge surged with men from the São Tomé and Alegre garrisons. De Caminha and the two other knights roamed the beach at will. These newcomers were poorly mounted compared to the governor. One rode a stallion without armor and the other an unadorned mule, likely the only mounts available. They galloped across the wet sand, their squires running afoot to catch up.

Swords flashed in the new sunlight, hacking left and right. A pirate lance took the knight's charger straightaway and tumbled the man over the horse's head. The knight on the mule rode to help, repelling the enemy with blows from his sword. Within seconds the mule-rider went down, his animal mortally wounded and bellowing, a spear protruding from its side. De Caminha, the squires, and more of our soldiers came to the rescue, forming an impenetrable thornbush of steel. In moments the enemy found itself surrounded by our fighters. They gave up weapons and surrendered. Now only small knots of the enemy remained for killing or capture.

Bloody and flushed with victory, the governor directed the captives stripped and tied together by their necks. He drove them up the beach where their chieftain and the pirate commanders had been held before sunrise. With the assistance of his squires, de Caminha dismounted, removed his armor, and put on his dress of governorship. Soldiers brought stout poles and forced the captives to dig holes in the sand. Soon, nine stakes stood where the beach and jungle met, the enemy chief and his lieutenants naked and lashed to them. Marking the chieftain's chest with a sword cut, the governor addressed the crowd; his booming voice drowned out the Guineas' frantic caterwauls for mercy. "With the help of our Almighty Savior, we today have won a stunning victory over the infidel." He paused and placed the point of his sword under the chieftain's chin. "We will make their last days on earth most unpleasant—as unpleasant as they would ours had not God been with us."

A priest sprinkled Holy Water on the staked men, his hands fluttering in prayer. He then blessed the forty-or-so other captives. Scavenger animals began to stalk the dead on the beach. Priests and soldiers walked among the bodies and assisted our wounded. They also removed the Portuguese dead to a place safe from the animals and killed any pirates left alive.

As he had done before—and always confusing to me—de Caminha sought me out. "Saulo, do you share our joy today in victory for Crown and Christ?"

I met his eye. "Joy that I did not suffer the alternate fate."

The governor looked fearsome, sweating fringes of blood where his squire had missed cleaning him. His smile tightened. "Nawar has foolishly requested your presence in his home. The overseer is a Moslem, and my permission for non-Christian households is required. Against my better judgment I continue to grant favors in your behalf, and you continue to—"

A cheer from one of the caravels interrupted him. He motioned me to follow and strode into the water. I limped behind. The knight who had ridden the mule joined us. He shouted to a barge as it pulled away from the caravel. The barge rowers took notice and cheered back. De Caminha clasped the knight and introduced me. The man, his face in a suspicious pinch, did not extend his hand. The governor drew him closer. "Captain Álvares, greet our most productive Novo. He tends the sick, shows mastery of the mason's craft and even withstands torture."

He did not acknowledge, saying, "I must tend to my cannon."

De Caminha accepted his excuse and turned to me. "I am about to demonstrate a formidable new weapon, a maritime cannon sufficiently portable for land use. I know little of its operation, but Álvares and his sailors do. Perhaps your knowledge of machines can be put to further use."

It was nearly noon, and the sun bore directly down, the Guineas feeling the worst of it, crying for water. The soldiers gave them seawater and explained they would soon have no need for drink. The cannon barge nosed into shore. The sailors extended a plank and rolled the cannon onto the sand where it promptly sank below its wheels. It took three hours—with the aid of many planks and two mules from town—to free and roll it up the beach into place.

The passage of time worked havoc on the captives, a considerable number of them fainted, dragging down the others tethered to them. With the cannon in place, the governor ordered a halt and had canopies erected. He served lavish food and drink to the victors and encouraged long oratories. The vanquished acknowledged their fate and hurled insults at the revelers. With the afternoon grievously hot and great quantities of wine and beer consumed, the celebration turned riot. Our people attacked the Guineas and killed several before the governor stopped them.

The soldiers herded the mass of prisoners a few yards away from the staked men and leveled the cannon loaded with small beach rocks at the pleading mob. With an incredible roar, louder than a nearby thunderclap, and to the lunatic delight of the crowd, the hailshot turned the prisoners into a writhing pottage of gore. Shot gone astray killed two of the staked men and wounded others. The governor and the knights went through the mess, examined the cannon's effects and dispatched those not yet dead.

Tired of carnage, de Caminha directed the Alegre contingent to retire. He gave beer to the Guinea chieftain and the men staked with him, then doused them with seawater and black syrup, leaving their fate to the sun, the flies, and the ants... always the ants.

• • •

A few days after the battle I moved into the Nawar home. His wife, a Congo woman named Yasemina, greeted me pleasantly. Nawar pointed out his offspring—children of all ages and hues, many old enough to work the yam plots and cane fields. "Some of these, Saulo, are from my mainland wives, and some belong to Nasic." He gestured to Yasemina. "The Christians allow me only one resident woman at a time. Is it true Jewish Law allows only one wife?"

"One God, one wife."

"Some confusion of Scripture no doubt?"

"If I could find just one, I would be happy."

Unlike the wood or canvas houses of the Portuguese, Nawar's was of African design—a large floor with a thatched roof and open sides, the structure elevated on three-foot stilts from the ground. He explained this feature had great advantage, as it kept ants, rats, and other crawlers from coming inside. "What you smell is a mix of tar and tree sap. The children smear it on the pilings and steps. It stops our little friends."

Whether from conformance to his position or indifference, his family kept only one Moslem tradition, that of washing one's feet and wearing special sandals when inside the house. A shallow rock cistern by the entrance served the purpose. He smiled his peculiar grin and said, "One might justify this custom as Christian cleanliness."

During the next weeks my physical health improved, but as I adjusted to the domestic surroundings, my longing for a mate burdened me more than ever. Letters arrived from Portugal, including some from Jewish families, though none for me. As everyone talked about events back home, my yearnings grew. With no word from Miriam, I decided to pay her a visit. I asked Nawar's slave to deliver a message. Had I caught a master's indifference? I'd known the man for two months, yet had never called him by name. He brightened when I did

"Kiman," I said, "please take this to Miriam at the foreman's house." He looked at me strangely—for what reason I did not ask. He started to speak, then put the paper in his belt and said he would go that afternoon. When he returned in the evening, Kiman remained silent and avoided me. I sought him out. "What's wrong?"

Obviously he carried ill news and did not want to displease me. He stumbled with his words, then said, "Foreman not let you see Miriam."

"Why?"

He refused to answer, shifting his weight from one foot to the other.

"Did you give her the note?"

"He take paper, say, 'No visit.'"

"This morning— You knew all this?"

He looked at me blankly. "Yes, master." He began to palm a hand across his brow.

My heart sank. "Tell me, is she all right?"

"Miriam all right... Foreman know she like you. Use her... he use her."

"How do you know?"

"Slave there tell me. Say foreman wife very angry. Everyone fight."

"We're going to see her. Early, before dawn. Will you take me?"

"No master, it—"

"Don't call me master, call me Marcel."

He nodded uncertainly. "Farm long way. You bent feet."

"We will go even if you have to carry me."

That night I barely slept as worries surged through my mind. The nighttime heat and flies assaulted me without mercy. The next day, less than a league into our journey, my feet failed and Kiman hoisted me onto his back, trotting unhindered along the trail to the foreman's. Nearing the house—in the gloom just before dawn—we passed a small cemetery with two freshly dug graves. Once at the house, we saw only a female slave tending to many small children, Joseph not among them. The girl greeted us. Fearful for those whose graves we saw, I asked about Miriam and Joseph.

She ignored me and jabbered to Kiman in Guinea. She kept repeating, "This is a sad place. Sad place." The graves were of a male slave and a child who had died of the fever. Miriam and Joseph, she told us, worked the cane a short distance away. She knew who I was and looked at me with scorn. In Portuguese she said, "Foreman be angry you here. Go back." She glanced at the children clustered around us. "Children talk talk. Tell foreman." Kiman took her aside. They whispered together.

When they turned back to me—knowing Kiman would understand my meaning—I told him, "We will return to Nawar's."

"Yes master." He lifted me onto his back. Once away from the house, he turned on a trail through the jungle that took us to the fields. We entered a forest clearing thick with sugarcane. Everywhere the cane rustled and swayed as workers removed sucking pests from the stalks. The thickets were lush-green this time of year, about six feet high, and tightly packed. We saw slaves, free men and convicts working side-by-side as they drew the canes through their hands, stripping off the green, inch-long pests to eat or crush underfoot.

I spotted Joseph first, toddling near Miriam who worked with her back to us. She turned when we approached and threw herself at our feet. "Oh Saulo! Saulo!" She looked frightful; bruised and scratched, her hair cut short and ragged. "I am ruined! Twice ruined." Joseph silent and brooding looked worse—welts on his face and arms.

Kiman put a finger to his lips. "Shh! Hear us."

I pulled her to her feet. "We'll take you back to Nawar's."

Miriam hissed, "Marcel, I can't. The foreman will kill me." Joseph began to cry.

"He will kill you if you stay. Let's go. It's over."

Still weeping, she nodded and wrapped Joseph in his kanga and put him over her back. We walked through the cane thickets until we reached the jungle, then moved quickly along the trail to town. My feet began to fail, and I'd soon need Kiman's help. As we crossed the path to the foreman's, I asked her, "Do you want anything from the house?" She hesitated. I had never seen her so unhappy. *"Anything?"* I demanded.

She stared at me. "He rapes and beats me, drags me by the hair. I cut it short so he could not." She reached over her shoulder to touch Joseph. "His wife and children hit us like animals. I cannot go there."

"They won't know until later. The slave girl has the children away."

Miriam turned and walked ahead of us toward the house. Once there, she hurried inside, returning with a small bundle. The foreman and three of his workers came out of the trees on the other side. "What is that bitch stealing now?" he snarled. Miriam crouched behind Kiman. In the short time standing there, my feet had stiffened. I hobbled toward the four men and faced them by the house. The foreman shook his fist at Miriam. "What could she want from a crippled Marrano?"

"We are going to Nawar's," I said. "If you follow—"

"Follow? I will kill you here. There'll be nothing left to follow." He moved closer, his face knotted in anger.

Miriam appeared at my side. "Marcel, it's all right. I will stay." She walked toward the house.

I plucked a rust-red ant from my arm and placed it in my palm, then spoke in a voice I had never heard. "You know I have the ear of Governor de Caminha. Harm us and you will die at the stake. Eaten alive." I flicked the ant at him.

He took a step backward, uncertainty crossed his face. At the edge of my vision I saw Miriam stop. I motioned to Kiman. "Take her back to Nawar's," but she returned next to me. Joseph began to fret. I caught Miriam by the shoulders and turned her. "Go!" I stood my ground and held the four men in my gaze, waiting until Miriam and Kiman neared the trail before I limped painfully to join them.

• • •

At first Miriam did not take to life in the Nawar household. Despite her ill treatment at the foreman's, she had adjusted to their patterns. Yasemina, ever solicitous, soon won her over. Joseph remained quiet and fearful, always insisting for a place near his mother. One day Miriam said, "All the boys in this house are circumcised. Joseph must be too."

"Yasemina told me Nawar knows how. Since the Christians forbid circumcision, he does it himself."

And so with Nawar's help, we held a little brith for Joseph, recalling what ceremony we could. Joseph, of course, fought like a demon and hated it. In the midst of his screams, Miriam became upset. "We never should have done this," she cried out. "He's too old." In this supposed celebration (at least for the adults) I thought of my torture. I had never considered circumcision in this light before, and realized it too might be torture. Afterward, poor Joseph became more fearful of everyone, including his mother.

About a week after Miriam joined us, the foreman showed up, standing in the yard with one of his slaves. He had a rolled-up petition in his hand. Nawar looked outside, then turned to me. "Saulo, I knew this might happen. Come with me." We both walked out to confront the men. The foreman kept his stare on the house, I assumed looking for Miriam.

I spoke first. "She is not here."

He pursed his lips and offered the petition to Nawar. Nawar dusted his hands in refusal and said, "I know what's in it. There is no use—"

"Your upstart indenture took my Jew girl. I've lost a field worker and need her replaced."

Nawar grew angry. "I know you already appealed this to the governor. He told you the girl is a resident here now, and that I would provide another worker. For going behind my back I could have you removed from your position and flogged." Next he told him an untruth, but I liked it. "Saulo recommended a public beating for your treatment of the

Jewess. Only my intervention prevented it. Mistreatment of anyone, Jews or freedmen, is prohibited, and you know it." The foreman began to scrape his foot in the dirt. Nawar continued. "Tomorrow I will send two of my larger boys to work in the canefields. When the work is caught up, send one back. If there is ill-treatment of anyone, they will report it to me." The man left without a word.

As we paused to wash our feet, Nawar responded to my questioning look. *"Politics,* Saulo. Out of courtesy to Alvaro de Caminha—even though Miriam had already taken refuge in this house—I requested her presence here. The governor is supposed to approve households for all non-Catholics. He said 'yes', but also warned me."

"Of what?"

"He warned that the priests complain about our non-Christian house. He told me to appear as Catholic as possible." We walked up the steps and put on our sandals.

"Does that mean going to church?"

"Perhaps. He will inform me. He holds what you did at the foreman's residence in great esteem. De Caminha suggested I punish the man. I talked him out of it."

"Why? He should be punished."

"I agree, but a public lashing might draw more attention to this household. And despite the foreman's rotten conduct, he is skilled in agriculture."

• • •

Miriam often referred to herself, Joseph, and me as "us." I seized on this, obsessed with the idea of family, also with thoughts of laying with her. I asked her to marry. Again she disappointed me. "It's not possible, Marcel. After the way I've been used, I trust no man."

"We live in the same house. I obviously care for Joseph and will willingly give him my name." I found her refusal baffling, and her opinion about the rescue equally so.

"You did a stupid thing, Saulo. The foreman might have killed you."

"I stood ready to die, but here I am. For you to leave there, Miriam, it took courage. For that I admire—"

"Ahgh! You do not understand, Saulo. You just—"

"I understand! There is more courage in this world than anyone knows."

"Where did you come up with *that?*"

"My friend Golem said it, and he is the hero of this tragic place. I honor him." She put her hands on her hips and glared. I returned her look. "I believe I've acted bravely on your behalf, Miriam. Now you insult me! Who else will marry you?" I stalked off, regretting my words.

She burst into tears. "You just don't understand!"

• • •

A few days later Kiman and I returned from work at midday. Miriam was in the front yard retching. Nawar's wife held Joseph a few feet away. When I ran over, Yasemina looked at me angrily. "Why you here? Sun not down."

I knelt beside Miriam. "What's wrong?"

She appeared unable to talk. I looked up. "She take potion," said Yasemina.

"What potion?" Yasemina shook her head. "Damn you, what potion?"

In a choked voice, Miriam said, "I carry the foreman's child. I took a remedy."

"Remedy?"

"To lose the baby."

"Yasemina, do something. She's dying."

"Most not die." She turned and carried the screaming Joseph back to the house.

Miriam did not die, nor did she lose the baby. When she recovered I asked why she had taken the potion.

"Because of what you said, that no one would marry me."

"I will marry you. I will give the new baby my name. Our name. Promise you will never take that again."

"You're more fool than I thought, but I promise." She gave a weak smile and patted her belly. "After this baby, I will consider marriage."

105

Chapter 9

Miriam's pregnancy seemed to last forever, and I busied myself with rebuilding the boiling hearths. They worked without a flaw, which pleased Nawar and de Caminha. We had a surplus of iron rods, so I devised a way to bend them in a uniform arc to use in a masonry kiln with a curved interior. The design proved superior to the square kilns in use—their uniform heat provided better quality bricks. After he inspected my work, the governor asked me to use my rods for arched ceilings and curved walls in a new chapel near his home. The Saddiq as church-builder.

Finally Miriam gave birth to a boy she named Lael. By then I had convinced myself this was my child. "Lael Saulo," I called him privately. On the eighth day we celebrated his brith. I found myself squeamish, taking Joseph outside when Lael began squalling. Our surgeon, Nawar, made light of my concern. "These babies don't feel a thing. Some of my boys slept right through it."

"The last one didn't."

"Likely I am losing my touch. At any rate, congratulations." He handed me a letter. "This came enclosed in a parcel for me yesterday."

With hands trembling, I broke the seal and opened it. My father's Hebrew script jumped out at me, the first I had seen in over a year. I touched the place above my heart, remembering how I had once hidden his letter there. "How did you get this past the censors?"

"I have many friends in Lagos. When you sent your

letter by way of our esteemed shipworks..." He brought forth another letter. "It seems Miriam's father, the chart-maker, often visits our facilities. He has also penned a letter." Miriam gave a little cry when he handed her the letter.

"Thank you," I said and embraced him. "This never could have happened without you." He left us to our reading.

As I read my letter, savoring every word, so pleased that my parents were safe, Miriam feigned despair. "Grievous news, Saulo." She sat against the wall, nursing Lael, and gave me that wan smile I'd grown to cherish. "I wrote my father five months ago and he has replied. He knows nothing of Joseph or"—stroking the new baby—"this one; but he has given me permission to marry. Unfortunately there are conditions."

"What?"

"That my husband be both a Jew and taller than I."

"I am taller."

"Only because I am sitting down."

"Not so. I—"

"Marcel! you stupid boy. If you still want to marry me, I consent."

• • •

Most common-married Jews cohabited until the priests tracked them down to impose baptism and a sanctioned wedding. Sometimes neighbors turned them in, but more often house-to-house searches by priests exposed the Jewish malefactors. Miriam and I agreed, regardless of Church interference, that we would discreetly live as Jews—candle blessings on the Sabbath and an occasional fast. Only our home with Nawar made this possible.

A few weeks before Miriam and I married, São Tomé's first vicar, Gaspar Vilhegs from Coimbra, visited the island. Vilhegs was a nonresident whose primary duty rested with his congregation in Portugal. The vicar became a permanent resident when the fever killed him only a few days after his arrival. From his deathbed he ordered the local Church to keep exact records of all Novos to ensure compliance with their new faith. The priests began to enforce this edict, so I feared they would soon visit our household. I told Miriam my concern and plan for action. "I'll bribe a slave at the rectory to destroy the ledgers."

"I forbid it, Marcel. I will not be a widow."

"But I owe it to the Jews who have held out. To my father. His letter—"

"You have responsibility first to your family!" She handed me Lael and took Joseph in her lap.

"My great-grandfather Marcel was a Saddiq and I—"

"Oh don't tell me! Don't tell me, Marcel, you believe in that Just-Man obsession? They are fools with no regard for their own lives."

"But there are also Just Women. Deborah for instance. And Miriam—*Rebellion*—your namesake."

"I am not that Miriam! I am Miriam from Algarve. I live on a wretched island where everyone dies. I am Miriam over a thousand leagues from my home. I have two bastard sons and I am fated to marry a fool."

I expected her, as she often did, to burst into tears, but she stared at me calmly, her anger cold and fixed. I said, *"Do not* call our sons bastards, they will have my name."

"Only if you live, Marcel. Only if you live."

Outside, the night settled upon us bringing flying blood-suckers and oppressive heat. Yasemina had built a smudge fire, and she and the children stood within the smoke and smeared camphor on themselves to repel the mosquitoes. Nawar joined us. He'd heard the commotion in the house and gave me a stern look. "You Jews need to be harsher with your women."

"It is not my nature."

"And Miriam knows it. No female would ever talk to me that way."

Yasemina, her eyes lowered, began to rub camphor on Nawar. I unfolded my father's letter, reading it again by the firelight.

I and your mother are joyous to hear from you and know

you are prospering. We pray this letter finds you well. We hear such terrible things about São Tomé. How proud we are that you succeed in the mason's trade so far from home. You must always work hard and do well.

We have no word from your sister, but understand from escaped brethren that she is held in a convent near Coimbra. The Catholics send many of our stolen children there before shipping them to Tomé. Rumors have it that they will send more of our little ones to Madeira, or further south like you.

You are a smart boy to guess our friend in Lisbon. I believe now you may write directly to me, but in the most benign Portuguese. Most all the children are gone now; a few remain hidden by parents or neighbors. Some we sent to live with gentiles. The priests and soldiers go through the neighborhoods searching and torturing Jewish suspects. No young ones go to school, and rumors of expulsion abound. We hear of riots against us in Castile, and inquisitions in Aragon.

My son, we live in a time when life is fleeting. After all we have lost, you and Leah must survive. Only God knows why we have been swept into this terrible time of history, but so much of an enduring life is will. God gave Grandfather Marcel that will, perhaps He gives it to us also.

So sad about Germo Saparow. I will add his name to the kaddishim. I sent word to Sr. Saparow's wife, but we never heard back. We hear that a deadly fever stalks your island. Is it like the plague that kills so many here? We pray for your health and that of Leah's...

I thought of the letter I would write my father in reply: about marriage to Miriam of Algarve, but nothing of our sons; about boiling hearths and brick kilns, but not the governor's chapel; about the death of Golem and Hiem and Sara, but no details. And what would I invent for Nawar's household? I could not risk telling my father about the concealed mezuzahs or my bricks with disguised Hebrew symbols. I longed to discuss this with someone—certainly not Miriam—but the Saddiq would surely tell his father everything and never lie. I hungered to see Great-Grandfather Marcel, too-long absent.

In harmony with tradition—announcing our marriage two weeks beforehand—Miriam and I told the Nawar family. Yasemina and Nawar cheered, raised urns of beer in our honor, and announced a feast for our wedding day. The children ran about squealing with delight. I offered Miriam the jewel of pink coral fitted to Leah's gold chain, recited my declaration, and repeated it in Portuguese for all to understand: "Behold! You are consecrated unto me according to the laws of Moses and Israel." Miriam accepted the necklace and my declaration, and offered me a tallith of her own making—white silk with alternate black fringes. I received her gift with great pleasure and presented our marriage contract. We signed and offered it to Yasemina and Nawar. "Your witness honors us," I told them. Yasemina called Kiman from the slave camp. He welcomed the news with excitement, adding his mark to our contract.

"When we lived in Alexandria," said Nawar, "Nasic and I attended many Jewish ceremonies. We will give you a real Hebrew wedding."

This news astounded me. "I thought you hailed from the Indies? When I first met your brother, he—"

"We did, though we spent years in Alexandria before crossing Africa. Egypt is where I converted to Islam."

"But when I first met Nasic, he said he'd never seen a Jew."

"Ah, my brother. One never knows the truth with him."

We set a Sunday for our wedding day—fittingly on the Christian Sabbath. Miriam and I began our fast at sundown the evening before. In accordance with our status as Novos Christãos, we went that morning to church. Upon our return we joyously erected a four-post wedding canopy in the Nawar home, and arranged it so we faced northeast to Jerusalem.

Thus began our marriage. Miriam and I stood in the yard as Joseph poured a pitcher of water down the steps and over our feet. Delivered unto Israel—through the sea out of Egypt—we ascended barefoot, my disfigured feet carrying me into the house. At the threshold, surrounded by the children, Kiman and others, Yasemina placed an Indies veil of luminous blue over Miriam's shoulders, around her head, and over her eyes. Arm-to-arm we arranged ourselves under the canopy, our bodies joined at the waist by my new tallith. Nawar raised a clay goblet filled with spiced claret he'd procured for the occasion. With raised cup he recited three of The Seven Blessings: "To the Wine. To God the Creator of the Universe. To God the Creator of Man." Yasemina recited the Blessing To God the Creator of Woman. Miriam and I recited the Couples' Blessings To the Nation of Zion and our Fertility, and To the Rejoicing of our Lives Together. I recited the final Blessing To All Jewry, and my Torah verses from Genesis 2. We drank from the goblet and together crushed it underfoot. They left us sitting under the canopy to break our fast with a honey and pistachio marzipan of Yasemina's making.

Yasemina, her daughters, and the slave women had prepared a sumptuous feast of goat with coriander, yams, fruit, strong beer and the special wine. The celebration and dancing lasted well into the night. Ever-thoughtful Nawar had set off a corner of the house to give us privacy, but Joseph insisted on sleeping with us and Miriam complained it was too soon after Lael's birth. So, much to my displeasure, the consummation of our marriage was put off.

I slept little that first night—four of us on the pallet— and rose before dawn to start the cook fire. Carrying a mug of heated yerba buena, I walked the short distance from the house into a clearing where I watched the rising sun illuminate the green mountain. In the blush of first light, two fish eagles left the highest reach and began their spiral descent into the lowlands. The pair searched the treetops, hoping to catch a gray monkey or other tree-dweller. The gray monkeys were also human prey, trapped for miniver and meat. One eagle dove into the foliage and emerged seconds later with an animal clutched in its claws. With its heavy burden, the bird struggled aslant the treetops, unable to regain level flight. As it came nearer, part of its catch came loose and fell into the trees. I marked the spot where the thing fell and hurried to it. On the ground was a baby monkey. He appeared lifeless; though by the time I got him to the house, he began to move. Yasemina took the monkey and cooed as she dripped yerba buena into its mouth. "Lucky, lucky. Maybe live, Saulo. Guinea say little monkey good luck."

"If he lives, we'll call him Mazal."

"What that mean?"

"My word for luck." I looked closer at the gray infant, his fur silken and clean, the hair thin in places where I could see pink skin. He had a solid gray coat, except from the outer crease of each eye three black stripes ran down his cheeks. Mazal looked at us with an adoring face.

"Need milk," Yasemina said and handed me our new arrival. She went outside to find the goat.

Miriam appeared with Lael in her arms. Joseph, who chewed on a goat shank abandoned by the dogs, trailed behind her. My new wife looked at the monkey. "What is that?"

"Like Moses, an orphan."

"Oh?" She reached to touch it. The animal's eyes brightened and he scrambled along her arm to nestle by Lael. Miriam smiled. "Next he'll want me to nurse him."

"He'll make a fine pet. Yasemina said 'A little monkey is good luck.'"

Joseph dropped the bone when he saw Mazal, reached up and cried, "Mama," the first real word we had ever heard from him. Miriam smiled and bent down to give him a better look. He put his hand on the animal. "Mama," he cried again. Mazal hissed like a cat, whirled, and sank his teeth into Joseph's hand. The boy reeled in pain, clutching his hand as blood ran between his fingers, a face etched with hurt, eyes shut tight, struggling to hold back tears. Catlike again, the monkey returned in repose by Lael. I seized the animal and threw him into the yard, then bent down to comfort Joseph. To my shock, Joseph slapped me in the face and toddled outside. Miriam, who seemed indifferent to all of this, put Lael under her shift to nurse.

With the taste of Joseph's blood in my mouth I glared at my new wife. "That pig of a monkey just bit our son! How can you ignore him?"

Jarred into action, Miriam finally said, "Get Joseph, Marcel. I will console him."

I walked outside, astonished by her momentary indifference. My son stood in the yard and poked Mazal with a stick. The monkey scooted pitifully as he tried to flee, appearing to have an injured back and broken leg. How had he survived the fall from the eagle, yet fell hurt from my casting him into the yard? Had Joseph struck him with the stick? Yasemina walked over, leading the goat. "What happen?" When I explained, she covered Joseph's stick-hand with her own and raised it to strike the monkey. "You kill bad monkey." Joseph screamed and wrenched away. Yasemina handed me the goat rope and knelt by Joseph. Miriam joined us, Joseph continued to scream. "I fix hand," said Yasemina. "Bad monkey bite." She took him into the house.

I pointed to the monkey. "What are we going to do with Mazal?"

"Mazal?" said Miriam laughing. "Mazal *Ra!*"

I cautiously picked up the trembling animal. He rested quietly in my hands, seeming to show more pain than even poor Joseph. Yasemina, after she ministered to the boy, splinted the monkey's leg and put him in a crib. She covered the opening with gauze to keep him inside. Mazal's confinement lasted only a minute. He struggled and snarled, finally tearing a hole in the gauze cloth and making his escape. He limped across the room, labored up a chair to perch on the railing, and hissed at anyone who came near. Joseph, cudgel in hand, watched from a distance.

Over the next days—at Yasemina's urging—Joseph and

Mazal overcame their mutual fear. The boy began to feed the monkey, giving him sugar cane to chew and dribbling goat milk from a hollow twig into his hungry mouth. During the feedings Joseph showed Mazal the bite marks on his hand and patiently scolded him. The animal responded by tilting his head curiously. Miriam found Joseph's chatter particularly pleasing. "The pet's good for him," she said. "I though he would never start to talk."

Mazal attached himself to Joseph, and Joseph to Mazal. The boy carried him everywhere, gossiping to his ward like a rabbi's wife. He also started to talk more to us. Several times I took Joseph and the monkey with me to a mill project or my construction at de Caminha's. After six weeks we removed Mazal's splint and he scampered about as if never hurt. Joseph looked happier than I'd ever seen him. Miriam, in a rare state of mind, said one day, "You do very well with children, Marcel."

"Oh how well I would do with a son of our own."

She smiled and looked down. "We shall see."

• • •

About this time—the start of our dry spell and not the usual season for the illness—fever swept through the settlement. It seemed the entire population fell sick and many died. Our household was spared only briefly. Soon everyone had it except me, Lael, and Nawar. As we cared for our sick, he asked, "Have you ever had the fever, Saulo?"

"Only once."

"And you?"

He shook his head. "Never."

"Is it strange that some people seem protected from the illness?"

He gave comfort to his nephew, a son of Nasic's who hovered near death. "If it is God's will, I see no pattern to it. This boy is a hard worker and never trouble. Oh what a sad letter I must send my brother."

In the end, five of our household died, Yasemina's daughter from a former Congo husband, Nawar's two daughters from a mainland wife, Nasic's son, and a Portuguese convict. These deaths left us in a bewildered anguish with nothing to do but bury our dead in the town cemetery. We settled them among the fresh graves, graves so numerous the priests were hard-pressed to give everyone a Catholic burial. We conducted discreet Moslem ceremonies, though with an occasional nod to the priests who circulated through the misery around us. As we returned, walking through the town, Nawar in his grief remarked, "I notice few of the slaves get the fever, and even fewer die. Why are they more durable than us? How is that God's work?"

"Because we oppress the blacks, God inflicts us. Evil deeds bear evil fruit."

"So now Saulo quotes the Qur'an?"

• • •

Miriam and I grew closer during her illness. She allowed me, without complaint, to care for her and Joseph. Shortly after her fever left, we consummated our marriage. I had great zeal for our coupling and found myself eager at any time to be with her. One day, with an unusual light in her eyes, she expressed surprise at my ardor. "You have a little madness, Saulo. At this rate you will soon have your son." The Saddiq as lover.

In celebration of the fever's lifting, and to cheer people after so many losses, the priests organized a festival following Sunday Mass. Part of the festivity, they announced, would be a native dance by the freed blacks and slaves called a Shamba. As we headed to the public square, Nawar said, "I wager these Catholics have never seen a Shamba. If they had, they never would have sanctioned it. It's not like anything you have ever seen."

Indeed it was not. Late in the afternoon, with everyone full of food and strong drink, the black men appeared with white face-paint and headcoverings of long, yellow grass. These nearly naked men danced lewdly to drums, pipes, and beaten sticks. Soon the women joined them, wiggling their behinds as they enticed the men to select partners. The priests, who as a group had drunk more than anyone, revived from their stupor to protest. The townspeople reacted to the Churchly censure and irresistible rhythms by joining the dance. Miriam and I found ourselves in the middle of it, carrying the children, with Mazal on one shoulder or another, all of us wriggling with the throng. After a while the music trailed off and the dance ceased. Many of the revelers drifted away to private activity.

• • •

During the following weeks life was good for our family, and improved for the Nawars as their grief waned. Miriam and I found moments together while Yasemina watched the children. Both my sons were strong and healthy, with Joseph less sad as he laughed and played with the other children, the whole crowd of them sharing games with Mazal. Miriam seemed happy, days spent caring for the children, helping Yasemina, or going with me to my projects. A year ago Nawar had forgiven my indenture; now he and de Caminha paid me a wage. In the time since, I had saved a considerable sum, almost three-hundred silver reis. I kept them safe in de Caminha's treasury. The Portuguese Crown continued to open new sugarmills, along with land for yam and cane cultivation. Shares in these ventures were available for purchase at a small cost, with future payments to the Crown from operating profits. I began to imagine a home of our own, a garden, and a plot of land for sugar cane.

Though no one knew it on the Sunday it happened, the Shamba insult to the priests worsened the conflict between the Church and the island's governance. A month or so after the Shamba, with the governor absent from the colony, the dispute took an ugly turn. One day, while I worked on de Caminha's chapel, Nawar came to warn me. With the roof finally completed, he stood and watched as my workers and I set a scaffold inside to plaster the ceiling. At the governor's request, the chapel had a domed interior and a box steeple fashioned after the cathedral at Santarém. At one end of the building, above where the altar would stand, I had built a round opening in the wall for a stained-glass window. The glass, currently on its way from Portugal with the governor, would be the first of its kind on the island. Again, de Caminha had defied the Church by acquiring sacred property for his personal use. Nawar looked up at me and shielded his eyes from the circle of light. Though he commented favorably on my work, he looked glum. "There is much bad news. A damned Aragon zealot named Tomás Martínez arrived on our island yesterday."

"Martínez? What's a Spanish priest doing here?"

"This one claims Portugal and Spain will purge the infidels and reconcile. He sailed part of the way in convoy with de Caminha."

I climbed down from my ladder and sent my workers outside. "Where is de Caminha?"

"A month delayed on Island Arguin. A repair of some sort. Listen, Marcel, this pious Martínez is the worst kind. People say he eats nothing, sleeps on a bed of stones, wears thorns and haircloth, and fills his shoes with pebbles. They say—"

"Yasemina knows the witchman Igbo. He'll give Martínez the fever."

Nawar glanced outside at the workers, relieved that none were listening. "This is no joke, Saulo. After you left this morning a priest and soldiers came to the house. The priest drove a stake into the ground and read a proclamation. The settlement priests convinced Martínez the Shamba was witchery, that we infidels and blacks conspire to kill Christians with the fever. That we killed Vilhegs."

Miriam appeared at the door with the children and Mazal. "I have brought you noon supper, Saulo." Despite her calm manner, she appeared as troubled as Nawar.

Nawar nodded to me and addressed Miriam. "Your husband thinks that priest this morning was a joke. Tell him."

"I will, friend Nawar. Yasemina wants you back home."

He frowned a hasty good-bye and took his leave. I looked at Miriam. "I've never heard you call him 'friend' before."

She put a hand to her face. "Oh, Saulo, I have betrayed them. I think—"

I motioned her to stop. "Not yet." My three workers peered through the door and waited for instructions. "Eat your supper and come back in an hour," I told them. Happy for the unusual respite, they faded from view. Joseph remained outside with his monkey-pet, and Lael slept soundly in his kanga at Miriam's breast. I cleaned the dust from my hands and gathered my family in the shade of the chapel. We sat down to our supper—cold yams flavored with ginger, dried fish, and black-syrup beer. She'd brought food enough for several days. "Whom have you betrayed?" I asked.

"Nawar and his family. That evil priest frightened me so. They're coming back for all of us. With this food, we can hide in the jungle."

"We need to stand up for Nawar. He's done so much for us."

"But we are helpless against the Church."

"Take the children," I told her. "Go back and help Yasemina."

She threw herself against me and sobbed like the Miriam of old. "Oh, Saulo, this morning before that priest came I wanted to surprise you today. Now our lives are in danger."

"Something like this can always happen. We will face it. And what is your surprise?"

"I will tell you tonight. I can't now." She left, and I called my men back to work.

Halfway home that evening I came across Miriam, the children, and Kiman on the trail. The slave led an ass on which Joseph rode. Miriam rushed forward when she saw me. "They've taken the Nawar family!" she cried, her face pale. "Kiman found me and saved our lives."

"We go fugitive camp in jungle," said Kiman, his voice flat and resolute.

Dread rose in my chest. I recalled my torture, and my feet began to throb. I took Joseph down from the ass, forcing myself to sound calm. "How do you fare, Joseph?"

"Mazal gone," he replied, and buried his face in my shoulder.

I looked back along the trail. "We must do something for Nawar."

Miriam shook her head. "Kiman said they tied everyone to trees and waited for our return. When we did not come, they took the family away." She handed me a notice. "They tacked this to the doorway. A warrant. You are named." The thing listed names and accusations. The list against me included children not baptized, un-sanctioned union, conspiracy to afflict Christians, unlawful Jewry, violation of Guild Law... On it went.

In rage and frustration I yelled at Kiman. "Why didn't you come get me? Why didn't you help them?" Joseph squirmed down from my arms and ran to Miriam. Kiman looked puzzled, as if he couldn't understand me.

Miriam gave me a strange look. "Marcel, you're yelling in Hebrew."

"I cannot bear to think of Nawar being tortured, and Yasemina and the children!" My feet began to ache. My senses had left me.

Kiman spoke. "No yell Ma'am Saulo. She carry son."

I looked at Lael in Miriam's arms. "Kiman, I know that."

"Marcel," Miriam said—she patted her belly—"I carry a new son. Our son."

I wept—wept harder than I could ever remember. I sat on a log at the edge of the trail and put my head in my hands.

Chapter 10

We found the fugitive camp a miserable place, unsuitable for agriculture or humans, yet here we were. It sat on the south flank of the green mountain, more than a league inland from Porto Alegre. Here was a region of São Tomé that we had only heard about, an area of thick, wet jungle that covered two-thirds of the island, a place of permanent twilight. It rained constantly from a dark cloud that hovered over the mountain—much more rain than at the Tomé settlement. Oh how I wished to be back at our home with the Nawar family. This camp was a terrible place for Miriam to carry our child, but given the circumstance, our only refuge. We were determined to make do.

Looking south toward the bay and Alegre, one could see sunlight and clear skies beyond our mantle of gloom. We yearned to dry ourselves in the sun, to feel its warmth. Leech-filled mud puddles covered the ground. The fugitives had built paths of raised logs so one could walk without sinking into the mire. We had plenty of food, though not much to our liking, mostly meat from jungle animals, gruel starch from a boiled root of some sort, and stew made from leaves, leeches, grubs, and other unsavory forest dwellers. Miriam refused to eat the stew, calling it "abomination stew."

"When we were starving on the caravel," I told her, "Golem and I conjured absolution when we ate abominations."

Miriam looked with repugnance. "Only Catholics get

absolution and you're not starving now." I made the sign of the cross over Joseph and Lael's bowls. Miriam placed a hand on her belly, her look undiminished. "Our new son will never eat such things."

The camp's population consisted mostly of escaped slaves—black Africans along with a few from Portugal—and some white and mixed-blood convicts, about thirty souls in all. Everyone dressed in the African style, loincloths and little else, the women bare-breasted. At first they watched us with suspicion and, if it had not been for Kiman, they might have run us off or perhaps worse. There were few women, and most seemed to share favors with any man. The men eyed Miriam with lust, causing her to stay close to me and Kiman.

A crowded common hut with a thatch roof sat at the camp's center. There we prepared meals and slept. The Rio de Sul ran nearby, so we had plenty of water for drinking, bathing and laundry. The fugitives caught fish and other creatures in the de Sul by walking downwater, herding their catch into nets strung across the stream. For the first week all of us were sick, vomiting and diarrhea, Miriam so ill that she began to bleed, frightened she might lose the baby. She did not tell me until she had recovered. Everyone thought a demon in the food caused the illness. Demon or not, we felt better by week's end and kept our meals down.

On the second day a white convict approached and said, "Jew, do you remember me? Two years ago on the ship from Lisbon?" I remembered him vaguely. "You've grown up," he said. "A wife and sons, taller, hair on your chin." He asked about some comrades, and described each man in detail.

"Unfortunately, all dead," I told him. "Two executed, the mixed-blood and another. The rest dead from fever."

"I heard of the executions just after I fled here. The spirit of Tjange still roams this mountain."

Much of the first week Joseph cried for his lost Mazal. The little monkey had grown rapidly at Nawar's and could climb the highest tree, coming down only when Joseph called. A camp woman took pity on the child and gave him a monkey doll made of sticks and dry grass. He carried the doll everywhere, pretending it was his real pet, feeding the doll, then scolding it for running off. Kiman offered to return to Nawar's and find Mazal, but I forbade it. Before we fled, the monkey had started weaning himself, eating leaves along with his usual goat milk and sugar cane. "Mazal's all right" I told Joseph. "He's in the trees by Kiman's house, chewing leaves and waiting for us."

"No!" Joseph yelled, and stomped off through the mud with his straw doll.

Some commerce existed between the fugitive camp and Alegre thanks to slaves from the town who traded goods for the boiled root-starch. Many Africans preferred the root paste to both ground maize and yam. Near the end of the first week a slave woman named Anyz from Alegre told us that Jewish families had taken refuge there. Miriam and I made plans to go to Alegre, perhaps to hear news of Nawar and find a place to stay, a step towards our return home. "Anything would be better than this mud pit," I said. I gave the woman two copper reis and asked her to return with answers to our questions about our safety. She did not come back. We feared she had been arrested and might disclose our whereabouts.

A few days later a strange-acting Jew I did not know arrived with a slave from Alegre. The Jew appeared troubled beyond words and had paid the man to bring him. The slave handed me two reis. "From Anyz," he said. "She not come. This man Shemal tell answer to questions."

I addressed Shemal. "Tell me what's wrong. Why are you so upset?" He gasped and blubbered, unable to talk. He had a peculiar manner as he opened and closed his left hand, then held it to the side of his face. "What happened to him?" I asked the slave.

"Soldiers take Jews to Tomé. Take man wife and daughters. March back in chains." With this, Shemal began to moan, then threw himself in the mud and rolled from side to side.

I could not stand to see him thus. "Kiman," I said, "take Shemal to the river and wash him. Keep him there until he can talk. Give him whatever he needs." He and the Alegre slave lifted the crazed man from the mud and helped him away. Many in the camp had looked on, amused to see a white man so afflicted. Miriam and I walked to the stream and watched Kiman tend to Shemal. "Our only hope is de Caminha's return," I told her. "He will not let this insanity continue."

"You said he's a month at sea."

I nodded my head but did not reply, just watched Kiman bathe the man and set him on the bank. In a while they came back, Kiman leading Shemal by the hand like a drunken goat. They had tied the Jew's long hair in a knot at the back of his head. I stared at the left side of his face, his ear thickly disfigured and cheek scarred. The rain began, curtains of it rushing through the trees. I walked Shemal into the common hut and gave him a cup of yerba. The others there made room for us. Miriam seated herself nearby, eager to hear the man's story. "We grieve for your family," she told him.

He answered in halting Portuguese, his accent Castilian.

"Speak Hebrew," I suggested.

"My family is from Burgos in Aragon," he said blankly. "Inquisition is there. They arrested the Jews and kept us in an old Roman circus, a filthy place used for cattle slaughter. We had no food or water; they tortured us, mistreated everyone, taking a few at time for conversion." He painfully touched the side of his face, now realizing it was exposed. He untied his hair and pulled it forward to conceal the scars.

"Your family was with you on the mainland? Your wife and daughters?"

He began to shake and clutch his hand again. "Yes, my family. Portugal. The Christians persecute everyone now, Jews and Moslems."

"How did you end up in Portugal?"

"At Burgos there was an uprising. The townspeople

stormed the circus and intended to burn every Jew. Just a few of us escaped to the countryside. We fled to Castile but the Inquisition there is even worse, thousands of displaced Jews, all attempting to flee. We heard we could find safety in Portugal. For a price."

"My father wrote from Lisbon," I said. "He thought it might come to this."

Shemal's words poured out. "We crossed the border at Vilar Formoso, tormented the whole way by Castilian soldiers and townsfolk, robbed, beaten, spit upon, charged fortunes for the most vile food. They even charged us to drink from their wells. Perhaps two-thousand Jews were held at the border in Portugal, and more came every day. A city of desperation. Those who could pay the entrance tax received a pass and were allowed to go on. Families like us, who could not—" He broke down, weeping.

I reached to console him, unable to keep my eyes from the scars visible beneath his hair. In a short time, he started again. "My family had plenty of money in Burgos, but the journey to Vilar Formoso reduced us to beggars. I was once considered a rich man, we were merchants of glass, the finest of pieces, valued by Jew and gentile alike. I also imported colored panes for stained-glass windows. They were used in synagogues and churches. I told people that, but it made no difference. At the border the Portuguese gave us two choices: Go back to Castile and convert or be killed, or travel under guard to Lisbon and ship to São Tomé."

"How old are your daughters?"

His face clouded further and he could barely speak. "So young, three and five. We had a son too, barely a year. We lost him in Castile."

Miriam and I looked at one another, not knowing what to say to this tragic fellow. Finally I said, "How long have you been on the island?"

He hung his head. "Just three days. When we arrived in the Tomé harbor, our ship captain discovered the inquisition there, so we came around the island to Porto Alegre.

They put us on shore and told us we'd be safe; but as soon as the ship left, the priests and soldiers showed up and took everyone back to the settlement. I escaped. I had to!" He lifted his hair and showed me the scars. "I abandoned my family to that monstrosity Martínez. I had no choice. We had heard rumors of him in Burgos. Now he follows us here. *The Inquisition has followed us here!*" He began to blubber again, and pulled at his hair. "You see my face? Do you know what did this?"

"No." Although I did.

"In Burgos the priests took you for questioning—" His eyes turned wild as he struggled to contain his torment. "If you did not convert or they did not believe you, the inquisitors dropped melted lead into your ear. If, on the second night— Well, we escaped. At least I have one ear that works. Don't you see? Yesterday I had to run away. I could not let them catch me again."

"We understand, Shemal," Miriam said. "Do you know what's happening in the settlement?"

"The priests hold the non-believers in a place called the Jew yard. They must convert or suffer the consequences. All commerce, farming, everything has stopped."

"How many Jews on your ship?"

"Nine. Two families. Mine and another. All survived. An easy voyage from what we've heard."

"So few Jews. Were there others?"

"Yes, many. Fifty or more. Degradados. And a second boatload behind us. Many prostitute women for breeding. We heard they want to replenish all who have died here."

"Degradados?"

"Criminals, thieves, prostitutes. Mostly from Lisbon prisons or pulled off the streets and held for exile. Their choice is shipment here or prison there. They become freedmen once they set foot on this stinking island."

Shemal talked through the evening and into the night as he recounted his sorrows across Aragon, Castile, Portugal, and all the oceans to São Tomé. I could hardly listen to his stories of mistreatment—my feet ached with every word;

though I had the curious thought that despite the situation, it seemed good to talk Hebrew in a safe place with another Jew. Sometime during his story he reached for Joseph and held him on his lap as he talked. My son fell fast asleep there, clutching his tattered monkey doll, a comfort to everyone.

Camp life did not set well with Shemal. He adjusted poorly, complaining and wringing his hands constantly. I assured him that we would do something to rescue his family, for we too had family in peril; but I had not the faintest idea what to do. A few days later two soldiers showed up, one black, one white. They carried a truce flag and told us they hailed from a ship anchored off Alegre. The men of the camp, prepared to repel any attack, took the two into the common hut and threatened to kill them. I put myself between the soldiers and the mob. "Two men can do no harm to us. Let us hear them."

The black soldier did most of the talking. Obviously they had planned this visit carefully. "We stand ready to reclaim the settlement from the Aragon priest, but we are insufficient in number and need your help." The white soldier went around the hut and gave a copper reis to each man. "These coins are specially marked. If you march with us, the coppers can be exchanged for two silvers. After the battle, each of you will be declared freedmen." The men of the camp examined the coins, discussing the proposition in many tongues.

Shemal stepped forward and took one. "Count me in." The fugitives began to chant in agreement. The soldiers smiled and asked each man to come up and pledge his mark in a registry.

The camp headman, a fiery African named Owo, protested. "This trick! Take us slaves again." He walked along the line to challenge each man. Three stepped out and stood with him at the back of the hut. Owo took their coins and dropped them scornfully on the open registry.

"What do you think?" I asked Kiman who had not joined the throng. It occurred to me that he might stay in the fugitive camp.

"Not know, Master Saulo. Maybe trap, maybe no. Maybe die in fight."

"Have you thought of staying here?"

"This bad place. Nawar better. I number one slave at Nawar. Buy freedom someday." He went to the front of the line, took a coin, and returned to my side. He held it up. "Buy Kiman freedom."

Realizing that defeating Martínez was my only hope to regain our home, I walked over and picked up a reis. "When we get back," I told Kiman, pocketing my coin, "my two silvers are yours."

A day later, in company with soldiers of the Alegre ship, we marched from the camp. Connecting to the trail along the east side of the island, our little troop set out for the Tomé settlement. Miriam, our children, and several of the camp women, along with their children, decided to go with us. We were armed with light pikes. The soldiers carried poleaxes and crossbows. The ship, the soldiers told us, would sail up island and blockade the bay at the settlement. I felt confident—this was the second time I'd traveled this trail without my feet hurting. After an unpleasant night in the jungle, we arrived at the settlement midmorning. I found myself excited for battle but fearful. I knew nothing of warfare and hoped the soldiers would show us. I suspected that Shemal, who boasted loudly about his fighting skills, knew even less than I.

At the edge of Tomé, soldiers from the settlement garrison blocked our way. They waved a white flag and lowered their weapons. "There will be no battle," the sergeant told us and crossed himself. "The priest Martínez is in chains."

"How is this possible?" I asked.

"Yesterday Martínez ordered three of our priests held for heresy, including the garrison chaplain. Our soldiers rose up, arrested this dangerous Spaniard and freed his captives from the Jew yard. We no longer need your help."

Though we welcomed this news, I grew suspicious. "How did you know we were coming?"

He hesitated. "The caravel from Alegre. The captain told us this morning."

The soldier who led our troop—the same black who had signed us up two days before—turned to his men. "Collect their weapons." His soldiers brandished crossbows and poleaxes and quickly took the pikes from the fugitives. A few backed away, unwilling to comply. More soldiers appeared and disarmed them, wounding two, killing one. The fugitives howled in protest. I grabbed Shemal by the arm and pulled him to where the women and children stood. Kiman, threatened by the soldiers until they recognized him, joined us. The fugitives, overwhelmed and surrounded, shook their fists and cursed.

From somewhere behind the raised poleaxes, the fat and boisterous personage of Nasic appeared. He gestured to the soldiers and pointed our way, flashing his yellow-toothed smile when he saw me. "Get those slave women and ninnies out of there. Put them with the others." In shock I watched the soldiers pull these poor blacks from our group and push them in with the fugitives. Nasic's slave—the same giant I had seen two years earlier—came forth with a bench covered in embroidered cloth. He placed it at his master's feet and helped him stand on it. The slave merchant addressed his captives. "You are my property and I reclaim you. Your leader Owo is dead. I have those who remained with him at the camp in chains." He seemed to take particular delight in his next words. "Your women and children are also my property." The fugitives lamented their terrible fate. Nasic let the commotion fade before he continued. "You white convicts may step outside. By order of Governor de Caminha, you are now free men." These few whites passed through the soldiers to freedom. They stood next to Nasic and grinned back at the captives.

"What about us?" the black and mixed-blood convicts shouted. The soldiers crossed lances and kept them within.

"I will decide later," said Nasic from his pompous station. "Your servitude will be measured against your deeds." Then to the soldiers, "Take them away."

With the help of his slave, he got down from his bench and came to where Miriam and I stood. She moved closer to me as he approached. "Ah, Saulo, my brother told me you'd matured to a fine young man." As he had done once before, Nasic put his arm around my shoulder and tried to walk with me.

I shoved him with my elbow. "Get away. This is treachery."

He eyed Miriam and the children. "I rescue your family and you cry treachery?" He raised an eyebrow. "Ungrateful Saulo curses the agent of your governor?"

"Are Nawar and Yasemina all right? That's all I—"

"My brother and his family are quite safe."

"How are you de Caminha's agent?" I could not stomach this man's arrogance.

"What little you know of these matters, Saulo." Always the fox, he looked at Shemal. "And you must be the Jew from Aragon Burgos?" Shemal nodded. "Well, if you will walk with Saulo and me, I will explain our situation."

"Is my family safe?"

"The Family Shemal? All safe of course. I saw to it myself."

Nasic amazed me. He seemed to know everything, and I realized his Portuguese was vastly improved since I'd first met him. As his slave walked a short distance behind us, we set out. "You Jews could learn a lesson from the Portuguese," Nasic said. "They have a genius for turning adversity into advantage. Take this—"

"We Jews taught them," offered Shemal. He'd taken a quick liking to this slaver.

Nasic put his arm over Shemal's shoulder. "You see, Saulo, your comrade admires my intelligence. It is only you who misjudge me." I kept silent. "You ask how I am agent for de Caminha? The governor did not stay in Arguin, but sailed just a day behind the Spanish monk. He found me in Porto Novo, gave me his ship and captain, and the delightful task of freeing this miserable settlement. Paying... let us see." He counted on his fingers. "Perhaps twenty male slaves, some females and children. Mmmm... five-thousand silver reis."

"The governor should do his own villainy."

He smiled and jostled Shemal. "Another sensitive matter. Since the Crown sent Martínez and his little inquisition to São Tomé, de Caminha could hardly oppose him, much less be the man's executioner. The governor knew the monk's presence here would quickly disorder commerce, so he sent me.

"So none of the sergeant's words were true?"

"My brilliant fabrication."

Wondering where this man's humanity lay, I said, "I grieve with you and your family at the fever's taking your son."

For the briefest moment his smile faded. "Thank you, Saulo. He was a lovely boy. I will visit his grave tomorrow. With death so commonplace—" He lowered his head. "If I believed in Allah as my brother does, perhaps my son could be in Paradise."

"What will you do with the slaves? Your trickery will make them surly and useless in Tomé."

"The Portuguese intend to build a new slave port a hundred leagues west of Novo at Elmina. I plan to move my business there. These Guineas I've captured will be my first shipment. A fine lot."

"And Martínez?" A discomforting thought—I relished his execution.

Nasic brightened at my question. "Ah, I forgot to count that priest and his henchmen. I've five of them on board the caravel. They will bring me good trade with the Bakongo king who supplies my slaves. To a bush king, a healthy white man is worth two blacks." His grin expanded. "They do things with them."

We turned and walked back toward Miriam who waited impatiently with the children. Shemal ducked from under Nasic's arm and took his leave, heading to town to find his family. "Take Kiman," I told him, "he'll help you find them." As we neared Miriam, a three-wheeled cart drawn by two slaves pulled up.

"Excellent," said Nasic. "My chariot." His white-turbaned servant helped the slave trader up to his seat and settled next to him. Nasic reached down and gestured to Joseph. "Let the little boy ride with me to my brother's house." Miriam started to hand him up when she saw my pained expression. I gave a subtle shake of my head, and she pulled him back. Joseph began to yowl. Nasic threw his hands in the air and complained to the heavens. "Saulo sees evil in everything I do. He is as insolent as a Turk."

I considered the situation and said to Miriam, "Let Joseph ride in the lap of the slave, you behind them on that step." I reached for Lael to carry him. "I will see you at Nawar's." When they were in place, I lifted my pike from the ground and handed it to her. "If the slave-trader touches the boy, knock his head."

Nasic glared down at me. "You insult me beyond words, threaten my person with a woman?"

"Enjoy the ride," I called as he set off for Nawar's. "She's more the Turk than I." With the slaves in trot, they wheeled past me. Joseph, eyes full of wonder, looking everywhere.

The scene at Nawar's was one of unbridled pleasure. The entire family and slaves—Nasic in the middle of the revelry—stood in the yard drinking beer and celebrating. On the steps sat Joseph while Mazal scampered about. "You see," I said in greetings to my son, "your pet did well while we were gone."

"Mazal good good," he replied.

After an embrace with Nawar and Yasemina I went to the hiding place to look for my Torah. There I found it, undisturbed beneath our pallet of straw. I read the last words I had written—Numbers 11, God's Commands to Moses in the Wilderness, the same passage I'd quoted to Golem so long ago. Miriam peered from behind me. I turned the page facedown. "You're not supposed to know about this."

"Marcel, you stupid boy, I have read your words every

131

day for almost a year. I am proud you're writing our sacred text. More than halfway finished."

"I thought—"

She stopped my words, pressing her fingers to my lips. "I am frightened by the fire I see in you, frightened the Church will see it too. This business about the Saddiq is dangerous, but now we will have our son. I want him raised a Jew. Secretly if we have to."

I held her to me. "Our child could be a daughter."

What Miriam said next so lifted my heart, her eyes alive with anticipation. "Just as the Tsoanyahs do back home, Yasemina has looked into my face. She knows our child will be a boy."

• • •

In a few days Nasic left with his cargo of fugitives and priests. De Caminha arrived later that week and summoned Nawar and me to his home. A squire met us at the door, ushering the overseer and me through the cool, tiled hall into the parlor. The governor stood in greeting, inquiring as to our health and that of our families, then took us to a nearby room where the stained glass window rested against the wall. He crossed himself, tolerant of the fact that we did not. "It is beautiful, no?" He smoothed his mustache as I knelt to examine it.

"Beautiful," I repeated.

"You have done a fine job with my chapel, Saulo. I am greatly indebted to you."

"The debt is mine."

"And you, overseer— It appears our commerce has survived the Spanish invasion."

Nawar smiled and bowed. "Thank you, sir, it has. And also good to see my brother."

"Ah yes, Nasic has been a great service to our colony."

We returned to the parlor where we seated ourselves at a polished table. A slave dressed in white served Madeiran wine in zinc goblets. The governor slid land titles across to us, his manicured fingers resting there as he talked. "I am giving each of you fifty acres of Crown land. You, Nawar, for your continued service to our island's commerce—fifty acres adjacent to your current holdings. And for you, Saulo, your initial holding, three leagues south of town. The Rio Vascão runs quite full there, a good place for a sugarmill and perhaps a sawmill."

I had dreamed of owning my own farm, and here the Crown was *handing* it to me. Yet something told me to be cautious. "Thank you, sir," I said. "This seems extraordinary. I am already well paid for my work."

He raised a hand. "No, no. Nasic told me you personally delivered the fugitives to him. This is your reward."

Reward? So here lay the trap—to be rewarded for delivering those unsuspecting souls to Nasic? "Not so," I protested, "Nasic exaggerates. We were all prepared to fight, but I did nothing specific." Though I dearly wanted this gift of land, I slid the deed back. "I cannot accept this."

Nawar moved uncomfortably in his chair. He mumbled something, then swallowed it. De Caminha glared at me. "You will accept it, Saulo. That is final."

Though his words vexed me, I took the deed and rested my hands on it. The Saddiq, the compromised slave monger.

Nawar broached another subject, one which concerned me also. "If I may ask your Excellency," he said, "what is your policy in regard to the degradados? At best they remain a contrary lot, at worst a danger to everyone. Many just started work on the plantations; only a few are satisfactory."

The governor nodded. "Using them to replenish our fever losses was my idea; of course with Crown approval. I am fully aware that these low citizens are a devil's bargain. Perhaps as back home they should be supervised with vereadores." He signaled for more wine. "The demand for Tomé sugar grows faster than our production. We need more workers. We'll soon import hundreds of Africans and must balance these with sufficient whites." He focused on me. "And it seems our Jews are not well suited for menial labor. They have a strong inclination for, uhm... shall we say, running things. Don't you agree, Saulo?"

Upon hearing this I felt both pride and anger; and humiliation at being forced to live here. "Sir, it is a mixed blessing."

De Caminha smiled. "Ah, Saulo, I can always count on you to—" He paused to drink as he considered his words, then raised his goblet. "With plentiful sugar, there is a new mainland industry, spirits and strong beer. Evidently when beer is brewed with sugar, the result is nearly as strong as wine. Just think, gentlemen, our little island in league with the drunkards of Europe. But more about the degradados. With Crown permission I will set an expanded policy, one I hope will give our new citizens some passion for work. As you know, upon arriving here we make them freedmen, though unable to own land. With my new policy, after three years' service, I will allow them to own land. Further, after the three years their banishment from Portugal will be lifted and they can return home if they wish, free of course. But once invested here, my hope is—"

I shot to my feet and crushed the deed in my hand. "And what of us Jews? When can *we* return?"

Nawar also jumped to his feet and held me by the shoulders. "He did not mean the insult, sir. He is—"

"He is as arrogant as when first I met him," muttered the governor, sucking at the corners of his mustache. "Though now he is an established member of our island community." He pointed to my shaking fist and the crumpled deed. "Tear it up if you wish, Saulo. Regardless, I have placed a copy in the settlement registry. The landholding is yours, like it or not."

"But why are we Jews—?"

"'We Jews' has no meaning here. Officially you are Novos Christãos, *not allowed* to return to Portugal. At any rate, although I do not agree with the Crown in this matter, your brethren will soon be banished from the homeland." While he stood and drained the last of his wine, his eyes stayed on me. I tried to shake his gaze, but could not. "Our meeting is over, but consider this on your return home. By my protection neither of you practices Christianity. If I so choose, that could change." He left the room and summoned a squire to show us out.

Nawar and I walked in silence from the governor's house and along the forest road. Finally I said, "If my words brought you threat, I am sorry."

"All life is a threat, Marcel. This is nothing. Think of that priest Martínez as a Bakongo slave. As fervently as he loved his Christian God, how abandoned he must now feel."

We reached the main road and continued home, passing a group of slaves returning from the fields. A few glared at me and hissed curses in Guinea. I smiled, shook my head, and answered in tongue, "You are wrong, I betrayed no one." To Nawar I said, "I will ask Kiman to say a good word for me."

"Right now he is more disliked than you. They believe he's become a planter like us." We bought some fruit from a woman peddler and ate as we walked. "It is a strange thing," Nawar went on, "almost any slave on the island could have run to the fugitive camp, yet few did. Everyone knew the inhospitality of the place. But now that it's gone, all the blacks and convicts seem to miss it. A puzzle indeed."

"It does not puzzle me. If you wished, you could leave here; I cannot. Even if freed, I would likely stay, but the possibility of freedom would give me comfort."

As we neared home, Nawar said, "With your new landholding, I guess you'll move one day. The money you've saved— Well you will need it to buy slaves."

"I've wanted land for quite some time, but I never thought it would come so cheaply." I shrugged. "Trifles really, just my dishonor and lost integrity. As for slaves, the notion of owning them is very disagreeable to me."

Nawar put a hand on my arm and stopped walking. "There is something I need to say and this is as good a time as any. You have a way about you, a manner that inflames people."

"*Inflames?*"

135

"A poor choice of words, perhaps. You are persuasive and steadfast, but in a way that is aggravating. If you could only hold it in check."

"You mean with de Caminha today? More than once the man has tried to kill me!"

"But no longer, Marcel, don't you see? Except for my brother, there is no man alive who could talk to him the way you did and live to tell it. You misuse your gift. And why are you so angry?"

"Oh I have stewed about this ever since I got here. How my father encouraged me to study, to become a mason, and someday an architect. Now I build Christian churches on an infested island and fear to tell him what I build." I thought sadly of my sister, how bitterly she cried when my father told her she could marry a mason, but never be one herself. "You know," I said to Nawar, "my sister was a talented mason—an artist really—and my father forbid her to seek the trade. But I promised Leah that I would employ her if I ever got the chance. Now she's lost and I'm a world away. Wouldn't that be enough to make *you* angry?"

By now we had reached home and Nawar ignored my question. We walked across the yard, eager to tell the women our news.

In the morning, when I asked Kiman about the slave community, he replied, "Yes, Saulo, they believe we betray fugitives for money."

I remembered my pledge and put four silver reis in his hand. "My two and your two. You see, we indeed did it for the money."

His face shadowed as he tried to hand them back. "Why you give?"

"They never paid us for Martínez. Keep the money for your freedom. Now the Africans can have a real reason to hate you."

Next morning I asked Kiman to go with me to survey the new property. Miriam prepared a noon supper, and all of us set out, taking the children. As usual, Joseph and Mazal ran ahead. We settled the family by the river and spread

136

out my crumpled deed, finding the marked corner of the property from the plat traced on the document. Kiman and I paced the remaining corners and set stakes. An established canefield sat to the north and it looked in fine shape. I knew the planter's reputation, a Catholic Portuguese named Nuño Horté, a brutal man, infamous for cruelty to his slaves. Kiman said, "Maybe get plant start from Horté. Know woman who work there. Good tops for seed plants."

"Why would you want me to do business with him? He beat a slave to death last year."

"Best cane plants in Tomé, Master Saulo."

While I had never talked to this neighbor, I had grown curious about his violent nature. Also at this time I realized I truly admired Kiman and thought it fine if this strong-willed African worked for me. "I doubt Horté will sell me anything," I said. "He doesn't like Novos."

"Why that?"

"Many of the Christians do not trust us. Just like the slaves, they know we live here against our will."

The afternoon rain started early and drenched us to the skin. We returned to the family, wading across the river at a shallow place, the smooth rocks slippery with mermaid hair. My family had moved, sitting huddled in the trees near an elevation of black rock. They were dry, having covered themselves with a single jungle leaf as big as a tabletop. Lightning and thunder crashed all around.

Ignoring the rain that dripped through the leaves, I recited our discoveries to Miriam. She and the children peered at me from under their green cover. "A watercourse above here drops swiftly through a narrow place. We could put a single wheel there for a crushing mill on one side and a sawmill on the other. There's plenty of high ground for a boiling house. I saw no clay for bricks, but we'll find some."

She pointed to the rock table behind her. "The children and I climbed up there. It's a good place for a house, high enough that it will never flood, and not so many crawling things. Let's build an African home like Nawar's."

"That should please the neighbors. Nuño Horté and his

clan own the farm over there." The rain stopped and a steamy sun appeared. Miriam handed out supper. Kiman took his food and went down by the river. Joseph followed him, pulling Mazal on his jungle leaf like a sled.

Miriam looked after them. "I wish that man was our slave. Would Nawar sell him? I know Kiman is number one there, but Nawar's got plenty of others."

"I've had the same thought. You know owning a farm of my own gives me pause."

"You don't want to be a slave owner?"

"I loathe the idea." In the distance I could see my son and the black man as they ate by the river.

Miriam looked down at Lael just curled into his nap. "The Just Man remembers our bondage in Egypt and cannot own slaves. You said de Caminha will permit some slaves to be freedmen, so make Kiman an indenture."

How proud I felt. "The wife of the Saddiq is wise."

"The wife knows her stubborn husband."

"I want to try some of the new crops, ginger, cotton, even pepper. The three of us can't run a farm this size, and there are fifty acres I'd like to buy south of here."

"Hire degradados or buy slaves. We don't have to get rich overnight. Indenture the slaves and give Kiman a tenant share to pay himself out." There were tears in her eyes and she looked away.

"Something else?" I asked.

"What you lack in wisdom, Marcel, you make up in kindness. And there is so little kindness in this world."

I took her hand. "You are the wife I have always prayed for." And now it was my turn to be sad. "My mother and father would be so proud."

I put a sleepy Lael on my shoulders and climbed with Miriam through the green foliage to the top of the rock table. Indeed she had discovered a fine place for our home—flat, fifty yards across, short grass, a few trees and bushes, a good view of the farmland and river. Near the east edge I put five black rocks together. "Genesis to Deuteronomy. Our home will go here."

Elmina – 300L

Lisbon – 1,300L

Ilhoa de Cabras

Slave Port

swamp

R. Negro

São Tomé Settlement

N

São Tomé
{1495}

Nuño Horté farm

R. Vascão

Saulo farm

R. da Névoa

Brazil – 1000L

Atlantic Ocean

R. d'Ouro

△ Pico São Tomé

East Road

West Road

Angolar camps

Pinda – 75L

□ Fugitive camp

R. de Sul

0   ½   1   2 Leagues

Porto Alegre

Chapter 11

In little more than a month we had completed our home on the table land, the location better than we first thought. Rainwater did not collect in muddy puddles as it did in the jungle, and frequent breezes kept the flying pests away. We deepened and lined two rocky basins where clean water could be collected, planning to augment the cisterns with riverwater during dry spells. In tribute to Nawar, we chiseled a small basin next to the house for footwashing.

Kiman turned out to be an able foreman for our African house-building. Nawar reluctantly agreed to sell him to me for two-hundred-fifty silvers, accepting thirty as initial payment and requiring one day a week labor from his ex-slave. Once I explained to Kiman that he was a tenant and would share in the farm profits, he became thoroughly devoted. I set him to clearing and planting, and instructed him to purchase what labor he needed. On the days Kiman worked for Nawar, I toiled with the field hands and experienced the brutal, dawn-to-dusk drudgery these blacks endured.

Nawar received a shipment from the mainland of ginger roots, cottonseed, and pepper vines, selling me enough to start small gardens of my own. The first year's yield would be mostly seeds and cuttings for larger plantings next year. We set up small areas for these crops in the fertile ground close to the river for irrigation. The first fifteen acres of sugarcane ground was cleared and ready to plant by early Sivan (June by the Christian calendar), but this was the start of the dry season, so we chose to keep clearing land

and build our stock of rooted cuttings to plant when the rains would start in about four months. Though I knew I could get cuttings from Nawar, I decided to ask the notorious Nuño Horté.

When I told Miriam, she looked irritated. "Horté's got a vicious reputation", she said. "He probably thinks we're blaspheming Novos. He won't sell you anything."

"I will test his manner. Make a dozen yamcakes to win over his wife. For the cuttings I'll offer him half last year's price. Everyone will have plenty of good plants this year, so other than mine, he'll have no income from green starts."

"A waste of money and food. Nawar's got a fine crop and he will *give* them to you." When I said nothing, she turned on her heels. "Suit yourself, Saulo, you always do."

I went to Horté's on Sunday afternoon. He emerged from his tent house when his slave-camp dogs announced my arrival. Several children followed and he shooed them back; they, along with his wife watched from the open door. Despite a limp from an old injury, he crossed the littered yard quickly to confront me. He was a short, stocky Portuguese with deep olive skin. Using both hands, he shaded his eyes from the sun. "What do you want?"

I offered him my bundle of yamcakes, and opened the leaf wrapper so he could see inside. "My wife made these for your family."

"Wait here," he told me, and carried them to the tent. His family came outside and began to eat the cakes greedily. Horté returned. "What do you want?"

"I see you have a fine canefield next to my new ground, lush and beautiful."

"You're not here to discuss my sugar cane."

"But I am. I would be honored if you sold me cuttings. No work for you. I'll have Kiman—"

"I did not see you in church today. I never see you there. This is The Lord's Day. I do no business on the Sabbath."

I made a respectful nod. "May I come tomorrow or—"

He stepped closer to me, a face of dark hatred. "You may not come at all. Everyone knows you and that heathen

141

Moor have put a Jew-spell on de Caminha. I have no business with you." He spat, turned abruptly and limped away.

• • •

Our rains started on the first Saturday of Tishri and reminded me of Lisbon—the knight crashing through our synagogue door, the soldiers taking us. What would life be like if I were still in Lisbon? Likely preparing to flee with my parents and sister, sailing to a new home in Turkey as things got worse in Portugal.

A letter from my father confirmed Shemal's warnings, unjust laws and riots against Jews. Of my sister he wrote, *We hear that many of our girls were forced to become nuns at the convent in Coimbra. We pray that Leah is well and has not suffered the tyranny of conversion. Though we have no word from her, another person (You can guess why I do not write the name) wrote that Leah is now at the Convent Silves.*

Since Miriam's family lived only four leagues from Silves, I quickly returned a letter to my father, letting him know that Miriam had asked her parents to inquire about Leah. I also wrote, *My lovely Miriam who enjoys good health expecting our first son just two months away now, says you and Mother would be welcome in her father's home.* I gave him the location in Lagos and told of conditions there. I went on, *If you have to flee Lisbon for Turkey, Porto Lagos is a good place from which to depart.* With inquisition everywhere, I knew my father would not count on life continuing well for even the Jews of Lagos.

I also penned a hopeful letter to my sister at Silves, told her all the news, but avoided any mention of Catholic tyranny and, because of the censors, only hinting at our pledge to find one another.

Once the ground was thoroughly soaked, we began to plant our canefields with cuttings from Nawar's. Through rain and clear weather I joyously worked with the slaves— our first sugar harvest would be just six months hence. My ginger and pepper plots flourished, the cotton less so. I decided to save the seed from the cotton and try a different location next year. In all, we had forty-five acres under cultivation. In the weeks before planting, I had prepared drawings for a crushing mill and boiling house where the Vascão fell through its narrow course. I also devised a plan to use the sugarmill wheel for a sawmill on the stream's other side. Kiman and I staked out the construction, dug foundations, and made ready to start building. How proud my parents would be when I wrote them of our accomplishments.

We had a happy home life. Our new son kicked in my wife's belly. I could feel him at night as Miriam rested against my back. The boys liked to feel the baby too. Year-old Lael babbled on about his baby brother, seeming to tell Joseph and Mazal little stories about 'new boy' in his odd mixture of child talk, Hebrew, Portuguese and Guinea.

My tenant camp consisted of canvas and wooden buildings on the flat below my house—two Guinea families and a house for Kiman who had recently taken a wife, a Christian free-black from the Congo city of Ambasse. I wondered if my tenant arrangement with Kiman and the opportunities of São Tomé had attracted the marriage broker to suggest this woman. If so, some of her family were bound to follow.

Kiman had sought my permission to travel to the African mainland and wed. I had no qualms concerning his marriage, even though—once back on Portuguese Tomé— his union to a free woman would make him a freeman and set aside his indenture. Just as it does for females, Crown law unbinds a male slave or indenture when he marries a free woman. Kiman's wife provided a substantial dowry, and I assumed she must come from a wealthy family. When he returned, Kiman again proved his honor by giving me a skin of silver reis. "Buy freedom," he said. "From wife dowry. Two-hundred-fifty."

I handed them back. "You're free. The debt is canceled."

"Most thank you Master Saulo. But one debt not. How much you still owe Nawar?"

"My concern, not yours."

"How much?"

"About one-ninety."

He set the skin on the table. "You take. Have plenty money. Build new house near slave camp. Kiman buy land someday."

"Will you work here until harvest?" At any time he was free to leave.

"Yes, yes. Good farm here. You fine master."

"Thank you, but I am not your master anymore." I opened the skin and dumped the coins in a bowl. I counted sixty, put them back in the pouch and handed it to him. "This is your wage so far. The rest I give to Nawar. All debts are canceled."

When choosing workers, I had exercised my influence with Nasic by insisting he provide me men with intact families. Although Portuguese degradados were available at a fixed wage, I preferred the harder-working, self-sufficient Africans—though the latter were more expensive and Nasic required full payment on delivery. When I acquired my first Negroes, I decided—in addition to setting them up as indentures—to add the further incentive of tenancy shares. This way they toiled even harder, understanding that work bought freedom, and at harvest time put a few reis in their pockets. The farm seemed to prosper under my labor scheme, but only time would tell. My first harvest was still nearly a half-year away.

Be they complaints from 'Old Christians,' as the Catholic-Portuguese lately called themselves, or Novos Christãos—everywhere I heard angry comments about my tenant plan, particularly from farm owners. As I oversaw construction on many of the new Crown-financed mill and boiling-house projects around the settlement and in Alegre, often a planter would say to me, "This scheme of yours fosters slave rebellion."

"But de Caminha already plans to free the original slaves after a period of service," I said.

"Also a dangerous notion," an ill-tempered farmer told

me. "If Novos such as you attended church as good Christians, you'd have heard Nuño Horté denounce your plan from the pulpit."

"Oh come now. You say he denounced the *governor* from the pulpit?"

Fear showed in the man's eyes. He made the sign of the cross. "Well... *after* Mass. He only inferred the governor when he denounced you."

I pointed to the slaves who toiled in his crushing mill and at his almost-completed boiling house. "Next time you fault the Crown, remember who gave you the money to do this." The Saddiq as King's proxy.

• • •

As always with the onset of the rainy season, Tomé fever swept through the colony. People thought the rain and bad air caused it. My use of African labor again proved wise, as fewer blacks caught the fever.

Many of the new emigrants died, including poor Shemal and his wife. Their tragedy had come full circle. We took in their daughters, Louisa about the age of Joseph, and Michal, two years older and able to help Miriam. These girls, having suffered much, began to thrive in our household. They doted on the boys and jabbered about the baby to come. It had been a long time since I'd seen Great-Grandfather Marcel, but I knew he would approve of our taking in Shemal's children. I yearned to tell him about my wife and our son in her womb, and to tell him that Miriam has a good opinion of her husband, the hoped-for Saddiq. Even though I could not see him, I felt certain he knew every moment of my life.

On a day when we had nearly completed our cane planting we heard the faint ring of the Angel bell in the settlement. It was only midmorning, the time much too early. The three degradados who worked with my planting crew knelt to their noon prayers. The bell continued its toll throughout the day, fading in and out with the wind. A runner came from town in the late afternoon, crying out so everyone could hear, "His Excellency, Governor de

Caminha, is gravely ill with the fever. All citizens must pray for him."

I offered a prayer for this man, prayed as hard as I could. If he died, many calamities might befall us. I said also kaddishim for those who had died by his hand, Golem and Norte, Tjange, Hiem, the Mixed-blood, even Germo and Sara— many others, their names gone from my memory, so much death among us. I next said a kaddish for de Caminha. If he were to die, the Christian God might forgive his ill-deeds, but surely Yahweh would demand His due.

Our prayers were of no avail, and de Caminha died at week's end. The day after the funeral his wife, mistress, horses, squires, and children sailed for Portugal, their home and my nearly completed chapel abandoned, the stained glass window claimed by the Church. Many months might pass before a new governor arrived. We finished our planting in a somber mood, anxious about our future.

The island's governance fell to the garrison constable, a Novo Christão in the Catholics' pocket. With de Caminha gone, the Church—with urging from fanatics like Nuño Horté—renewed its campaign against non-believers, citing the governor's death as God's punishment for his lax policies on religious adherence.

To counter the evil that might assail us, and since I had only three pages of my Torah left to finish, I worked through the day and night to complete the sacred text. As night settled the following evening, Nawar and Yasemina came to celebrate with us. They, along with Kiman and his wife, sat attentively as I read Genesis through 4:16—when God banished Cain to the land of Nod, and concluded my reading with Deuteronomy 34, the death of Moses in Moab. "Though Moses led the Israelites to the Promised Land," I explained, "God did not permit his entry."

"A fate reserved for Prophets to come," explained Nawar, who knew the writ as well as I.

Miriam spoke up. "This island is the fate reserved for us."

"The soldiers and priests have begun to round up people," said Nawar. "They could require our conversion at any time."

"Will you flee?" I asked.

Yasemina looked to her husband and shrugged. "Don't know, Saulo. Must decide soon."

Nawar stared into the gloom outside, the rain falling without pause. "You are lucky, Marcel, with your farm so far from town. The priests will come here last, on their way to Alegre." He gestured to Yasemina. "We cannot take another agony in the Jew yard. Let them plant their damned cross. We will convert." He stood up and poured the last of the wine into our cups, then grasped Kiman's hand. "Kiman," he said, "loyal servant and friend." Yasemina withdrew a scroll from within her garments and gave it to Nawar. He in turn handed it to his ex-slave. "This is a legal paper which I have prepared. It authorizes you to run my farm if anything happens." He looked to me next. "I assume this is all right with you?"

"Of course," I said. "But what about the plantations?"

"The devil take them. No one cared when they seized me the last time. Let the Crown farms run themselves."

• • •

As if God cried at the passing of our governor (I had such confused feelings about de Caminha), the rain fell relentlessly. The Vascão flooded my ginger plot and left many of the thick-rooted plants floating in the muddy water. Miriam and I labored with the workers to build a dike above the garden, directing the water into a ditch around the flooded field. In the late afternoon, as the sun peeked under the clouds for its last look at our rain-soaked earth, I saw Miriam begin to strike her hoe carelessly in the water. "What's wrong?" I called.

She looked at me, face pinched, her eyes red with tears. "Oh my husband, I have caught the fever."

Fear struck my heart. "Go to the house and bed yourself. I will fetch Yasemina." I sent a tenant woman to look after her. I sent another to Nawar's.

147

An hour later Yasemina's oldest daughter arrived. "Mama sick," she said. "Sent Igbo this." She unwrapped a smelly poultice and applied it to Miriam's forehead. The children stood around and watched, eating their dinner and making faces. "Mama say woman with baby inside not often fever-sick. Get well soon." The girl listened to Miriam's belly. "Baby fine." She moved the poultice to my wife's swollen belly.

Miriam told me she felt better. I did not believe her. Why was she sick at all? The children crowded onto the pallet, pushing all together to help her sit up. "I am not so ill," she said, and patted her belly. "Only a week or two, my husband." She nodded at the woman who had made our dinner. "Go eat, Saulo."

I did find my wife better in the morning, so I sent Yasemina's daughter home. I smiled at Miriam. "Stay and rest."

She sat up and said, "Do you know what day I think this is?"

"No."

"I believe today is the first year's date of our marriage. I will fix a special supper tonight. Think of it. A year ago we had just two sons. Today we have our two sons, almost another, and two daughters."

I kissed her on the forehead to show my affection, but also to see if the fever had left. It indeed seemed diminished, though her color remained ashen. "Rest," I repeated. "You can fix a special supper tomorrow or next week." Walking outside, I found Michal sitting in the shade with the children. This dutiful daughter of Shemal had proved a blessing to our family, and I often thanked God for his gift and that of her sister Louisa. "Help Miriam with anything she needs," I told Michal, and left to work in the muddy fields. The sun was shining for the first time in days. The weather steamed.

Sometime late morning I looked toward the house and saw Michal hurrying my way. She splashed through the muddy water, running, slipping, and crying, soaked through by the time she reached me.

"What's wrong?"

"Mama bad sick. You come home."

I picked up Michal and called a tenant woman to follow. My first touch of Miriam brought the fear again. I told the woman, "Go, bring someone from Nawar's."

My wife lay drenched in sweat. She burned with fever. I had the children get wet rags to put on her forehead and chest. Miriam forced a smile. "Oh my husband, this is not the anniversary I planned."

"Shhh," I whispered, "tomorrow." Michal brought the poultice from the day before and applied it in the same manner. The children and I sat with Miriam who drifted in and out of fever dreams.

The tenant woman, who seemed to take forever, ran into the house with a fearful look. "Nawar family gone! Only little children left. Guineas —"

"What happened to them?"

"Guineas say they go with priests."

Miriam wakened, heard the news and clutched my hand. "My husband," she moaned—her eyes shone with tears she would not cry—"our son is dead and I will soon follow."

I stared at her. "No, no! It's just the fever. You'll both be fine."

She placed my hand on her belly. "He stopped moving this morning, just after you left."

"I'll get the midwife from the village."

She tightened her grip. "No one can help. Stay here." She laughed in a pained, uncontrolled way and gestured to the foot of the pallet where the children stood. Mazal played with a feather, offering it, then scampering away when anyone grabbed for it. "Oh, Saulo!" Miriam gave me a haunted look. "I so wanted to give you a son. But now you are the father of God's joke, two bastards, two orphans and a monkey."

I shouted at the tenant woman who stood behind the children. "Go to the settlement. Hurry! Bring the midwife."

She just looked at me, shook her head, and backed away.

149

"No good, master." At the doorway she began to cry, put her hands to her face and hurried outside.

I ran out to the steps and screamed, "Go or I will beat you!" With no one to help me, I returned to Miriam's side. She sank further. I lay next to her on the pallet, the children cried softly and watched in dread, all of us sweating in the cruel heat.

Miriam died so quickly.

I had fallen into a stupor of failed prayers, into a fever dream of my own, wishing Marcel would come to help. At the end she said only, "Take care of our children, Marcel," finally whispering words I could barely understand, "love" and "Saddiq."

Then Miriam left me forever.

The pain screamed in my gut and doubled me in two. I cried beyond grief. Cursed Marcel who did not appear. Cursed God. I wanted to reach for the children, but could not. They wailed in chorus with the Africans who had gathered around us, screaming, stamping their feet, mourning in the same manner. We lamented all day, joined by other workers. Kiman came to sit with me. "Ma'am Saulo," he cried, and put a hand on my shoulder. Finally he and two others lifted Miriam's body onto a litter and carried her away, the children and black families trailing after.

I remember little of the funeral, just that I went to the evil-smelling cemetery where a priest took charge. The children were there, and Kiman and the rest of my blacks. Nawar and his family absent—and my not caring. Perhaps a few Novos showed up, people who knew us.

Afterward, I sent the children to sleep in the tenant camp. Someone brought me food I did not eat. I asked God why he had taken her. Who would bear my sons, sons of my seed, Jewish sons? I pleaded for Marcel to explain this thing. I cursed Gabriel, asking, "Is this The Time Of The End?" I cursed God.

Someone had brought my wife's coral necklace from the cemetery. I kept Leah's precious chain, but wrenched the jewel loose and threw it into the cooking pit. Two women came in with fresh straw to clean the pallet. I sent them away. I got onto the pallet where Miriam had died, and I wept, not caring where the death-spirit lingered. I lit our Sabbath candles and put them by my head. Within the straw my hand touched a torn page of Torah, one I had discarded after finding an error. I held it to the light.

Strangely I could read only a little of the text. I struggled with the words as they dissolved into senseless scribbles. I retrieved my Five Books and could not read them, could not read a word! I shook my fist at God. "You render me blind to my faith? I render myself blind to you!" I heard the Angel bell ringing. At night? Impossible. I put hands to my ears. Louder it rang.

I set the Torah page on fire and threw it on the straw, threw the candles after, then the Torah itself. I found Miriam's clothes and burned them. My workers came and I fought them off. The ceiling, though wet from afternoon rain, caught fire inside and burned with a mighty heat. The workers returned and dragged me outside. Crazed beyond understanding, I watched my house consumed. What remained of the soggy roof fell into the burning ruin. I threw myself onto the steaming pile and with my fists beat ashes into my eyes. "I will blind myself!" I screamed. "They should have blinded me at the stake. Torture's pain is bliss compared to what my heart feels now!"

In the days following I cared naught for myself nor the children, though they often came to see me. My heart held the bitterest thoughts. Who were these children? I thought of my parents and their dead offspring. Who were they? I could not be sure. Only the names Marcel and Leah survive—perhaps only Marcel. I thought of all the dead, the dead more numerous than the living. Maybe these Christians had a better plan, a destination for one's soul.

My workers cleared away the charred thatch and put canvas over part of the house. I lived there, midst the filthy ruin as rainwater poured across the floor. Some men came to see me, the constable, a priest I'd not seen before named

Bartolis and his child squire, and the plantation foreman. The foreman carried a petition for the return of Lael. "His rightful son," the constable read.

My grief had rendered me lunatic. "Take him," I said. We walked to the tenant camp where we found Lael. They left with the little boy. I could hear Lael screaming for the longest time. The priest and his squire remained, and I returned with them to my wrecked house.

Bartolis had the look of a woman, lips a-pout, clean of face, high forehead, blue eyes and thin eyebrows. Though I did not ask, he told me about the Nawars. "Now truly Novos Christãos. His family has embraced the True Faith." When I did not respond, he continued, dabbling his fingers together as he spoke. "You must do the same, Saulo. The terrible loss you have suffered will be reversed. The Saints will smile upon you."

I looked to my muddy garden plots where workers hunted through the muck, finding an occasional ginger bulb. Others re-strung pepper vines broken by the flood. My cotton plants no longer existed. "Is there a saint to repair this calamity?"

"Yes," answered Bartolis. "I will pray to St. Benedict, the patron saint of farmers. You must pray also."

"My prayers for my wife and the governor did no good."

"The saints respond only to those baptized. You must offer yourself to the font on Sunday. The congregation will witness your conversion."

"You pray to saints, not God?"

"Only the ordained may pray to Christ and The Father. The Church serves the Trinity, man serves the saints. In return the saints serve man." With these words his squire knelt, crossed himself, and began praying, fingers touching his rosary.

Chapter 12

The following Sunday, my hair cropped short, face shaved clean and sidelocks gone, I embraced the Christian God, or gods as it seemed. I wondered if Yahweh and Marcel witnessed my baptism, my fitting revenge— baptized on an island named for a Jew who had abandoned his faith. The priests told me their Father God, the Father of Christ, is the same as the Jewish God. I decided—with all the Latin and so on—this new religion might not be much different from my old. Regardless, since they believed their Father and Yahweh are the same, that still left me with a betraying deity.

Nowhere on my farm could I escape the spirit of Miriam. Inches from madness and unable to attend my destiny, I became a wanderer of the settlement, taking work in the fields and mills. Every Jew and Moslem who'd held out previously had now converted. Threatened with loss of property, children, earnings and freedom, all—some fervent, some indifferent—had become Catholics. The Old Christians boasted about these conversions. One told me, "When he arrives, the new governor will be pleased that all Tomé is Catholic."

"God's plan," I replied. The man paid me extra reis that day.

Following my conversion the constable assigned me to a vereador, a man named Felix da Tavora who insisted I address him by his surname. Use of vereadores (warders for degradados) was common in Portugal, but not so on the island until criminals took several plantation owners

153

hostage for ransom. The constable eventually tracked down the felons—five degradados—and hanged them, but the citizens remained apprehensive. Shortly before his death, Governor de Caminha ordered that all degradados be supervised by vereadores.

As the island's temporary governor, the constable began to assign vereadores—in my case da Tavora—to all distrusted Novos, and publicly cited Nawar and me as two of the most suspect. These vereadores exercised a terrible power over their wards; they could order beatings, fines, torture or jail for any transgression. Senhor da Tavora had a reputation of corruptness and often dealt severe punishment for the slightest offense. Faced with this threat, I carefully maintained my piety. But even with the hated da Tavora not witnessing a transgression, any person in exchange for a few reis might report something to him.

The public bath, reserved exclusively for planters after midday Mass on Wednesdays, became my refuge from da Tavora. If the vereador cared to spy on me, he had to do it from the street while I bathed inside. At first I disliked the bath, save for the asylum it provided. It is a tradition among Jews never to be seen without clothes, even in the privacy of home or by one's wife. But these Christian men seemed completely at ease, and I soon found myself less bothered by nakedness. On my fourth or fifth visit Nawar showed up. I had seen him previously in church where he expressed his true sadness at Miriam's passing, yet for some reason I still avoided him and had stayed away from his farm. I had also stayed away from my home. When I saw him at the bath, I found myself eager to talk. On this occasion a noisy group of black farmers had assembled in a corner of the pool. Nawar and I situated ourselves near them so as not to be overheard by the whites. He had grown noticeably in girth, and I was surprised to see how little hair he had on his body, and that he had been circumcised like me. "Were you circumcised in Alexandria?" I asked.

"Yes, by a mullah." I winced at the thought. He looked

me over. "You look healthy, Saulo. I see work has hardened you."

"Hardened against the fever I hope. These days everyone seems to have it. I pray Yasemina is well."

"She is well, as are the children."

"The bath enables me to escape da Tavora."

"I saw him idling outside."

"I thought he might go pester his other wards."

"You're his favorite," said Nawar with his usual jollity. In the past months I'd missed this man's manner.

"Da Tavora is dangerous. He's had people beaten, even jailed—and for nothing. What should I do?"

"Pay him to leave you alone. I bribe mine with strong drink. I keep him drunk." A woman who worked at the bath brought us soap and offered to cleanse us. I'd heard one could purchase favors from her and others. Since she could have been a spy, Nawar accepted the soap and waved her away. "Have you seen your farm?" he asked.

"No."

"Well you should. Kiman and his workers have done well. You have fine stands of cane."

As a group the blacks left the pool. I acknowledged them, greeting one I knew by name. He and his fellows mumbled curses. "No one is happy with their lot," I said to Nawar. "Two years ago they were slaves; now they're freedmen, have their own little farms, and they resent my worker policy. You'd think if I freed their kinsmen—"

"Sugar, slaves, and money, the combination corrupts everyone. Those blacks own many slaves. Your policy threatens their status."

I though of my farm and burnt house. My heart ached. "At the farm, what about my children?"

"They live in your house tended by one black girl or another. Your workers restored the thatch and cleaned the place."

"I cannot bear to go there. I miss Miriam so much."

"I know, but you're not the alone. After two years Yasemina still grieves for her daughter killed by the fever,

155

and I grieve for my two that died. Everyone loses family. You've a farm to run. How long will you remain a vagrant of sorrows?"

The ache stayed in my chest. "Is Lael all right? Have you seen him?"

"Lael's fine. I see him when I go by the foreman's. The wife cares for him nearly like her own; and the foreman knows I will break him to serfdom if any harm comes to the boy."

"I don't know how I could have let him take Lael. I must have been mad."

"No doubt, but if you want him back, the foreman can be persuaded for a few silvers. He owes two months' wages to the dice-players."

"Yes. Of course. That boy was more my child than any other. I should have never given him up." We rose from the bath and sat on wooden benches. Two women approached to dry us. They stared at our privates and made eyes. I felt my desire stir. "Leave us!" I growled, and took the towels, giving one to Nawar.

He laughed. "You need a wife. Or perhaps a consort."

"Jews do not take consorts."

"And fish do not swim. At any rate, you are now a Christian and can behave as they."

"Would you take one of those women?"

"No, I have three wives. Yasemina here and two in the Congo. And no woman is worth Yasemina's wrath."

"Wrath? Back a while you told me to follow your example, be harsh with women. So now?"

"Yasemina has found a place in my heart. For you, perhaps the pretty black girl who—"

I waved the thought away. "I cannot think of such things."

As we dressed he said, "You've seen they're bringing slaves here for shipment north? And some of the priests leave the Church to become slavers? Money will buy anything these days."

"I've heard the Church even pays the local priests in

slaves, six per year. So my worker policy threatens them also. That's why Bartolis chastises me. He expected me to change that too when I became a Christian."

Nawar gave his yellow-toothed grin. "You have an ally in me, Saulo. I have made three of my best workers tenants." He set his jaw and glanced at the planters dressing nearby. "To hell with them," he grumbled quietly.

In the same manner I said, "These Tomé Catholics seem so careless with their faith. In all Iberia there is inquisition. Yet here— Well, only we Novos are suspect; though many Christians are as indifferent as I'd like to be."

"This island is prosperous, so commerce overcomes faith. Bide your time, and soon you and I will be as unsuspect as any." He grunted as he bent down to tie his sandals. "Three weeks ago I returned from the Congo where I fetched more of my kin. Your fond admirer, Nasic, tells me that slaves are the future commerce—they ship hundreds north every month. He claims there will soon be thousands. The collusion with the slavers includes blacks in high office. There is this Bakongo who's visited Rome and Lisbon and calls himself Henrique, a Christian name. This supposed Congo King intends to make all his realm Catholic, even as he enslaves his own people. He has a son, Cão, a priest who studied with the Roman Curia and now lives in a Portuguese monastery. Imagine that, a Catholic priest in the family, and the father's minions sell entire villages to my brother?"

"I can imagine anything from these Catholics. We had a mixed-blood convict on our ship who once studied the priesthood. Because of his color they arrested him and shipped him here." I pulled my shirt over my head and tucked its ends beneath my waistcord, my thoughts yielding to the women who laughed with the other planters. "You say I need a wife. Who?"

"One of the girls who cares for the children is very pretty—quick of wit, with a bright smile. Take her, she'll make a fine wife."

• • •

In the next week, returning from a farm northwest of the settlement, I visited the slave port, a place of complete despair. The Africans were separated into two camps, those for shipment to Elmina and points north—to Lisbon and as far as Amsterdam I'd heard—and those destined to stay here. The sick, culled into a separate area, had been left to die. Slaves selected for shipment were branded on the forehead with the despised horseshoe. I felt Nasic's evil hand in all this. The slave children destined to stay on the island—ages five and older (big enough to work)—were kept separate from their families in another enclosure, cared for by older girls just as the Portuguese had done to us.

Two men, both ex-priests who called themselves captains, commanded the port. The condition of the slaves sickened me, but I chose to say nothing, for there was nothing I could do. Is this what Christianity wrings from men? No, wealthy Jews and Moslems kept slaves in Lisbon, and I imagined more would keep slaves if they could afford them. Commerce or war is the excuse, for slaves have been kept always.

A captain approached me. "Master Saulo, do you wish to buy slaves today?" He gestured to one enclosure. "Those are available. Would you like to inspect a woman, perhaps a prize man or two?"

"Another day. But tell me, where do these slaves come from?"

Since I was not buying, he showed a flicker of irritation. "Most from the Congo, some from Angola."

"I have heard of Angola, though I don't know where it is."

With his walking stick he traced the coast of Africa in the dirt. "Here we are in Tomé, northwest across the sea from the Congo. South from there, also on the mainland, is Angola, perhaps a hundred-and-fifty leagues. We call slaves from there Angolars."

"And where is Porto Elmina?"

"About here, west and north—three-hundred leagues

from us."

"So why do we have a slave port on our small island?"

This so-called captain brightened at my question, eager to show his knowledge. He poked the Congo with his stick. "Whether captured here or shipped north from Angola, our cargo is kept in barracoons at Porto Pinda—just seventy-five leagues' sail from the Congo to here. Two days with a favorable wind." He seemed to relish his next words. "At Porto Tomé we can sort them, keep the best for ourselves, and ship the others." He traced a line. "You can see we lie directly on route to Porto Elmina. Without a stop here, we would lose many blacks to the crowding sickness." He pointed again to the enclosure that housed the Tomé slaves. "Are you certain you don't wish to purchase slaves today?"

I ignored his question, happy I'd not been asked to help build the barracoons. I said, "These structures are particularly elaborate. Who paid for all this?"

"The Crown, of course. Just as they finance our farms and mills." He pointed with his walking stick. "Over there we're building other enclosures. We expect many more slaves soon."

I had heard enough. "Thank you, captain," I said, and headed back to the settlement.

The day had one minor triumph. Da Tavora had followed in the morning, hoping to catch me in some mischief. As I idled around the port, he grew restless. At my suggestion he agreed to ignore me for fifty copper reis per month, then left to spy on someone else—fifty coppers, an unreasonable sum, but worth it.

At Sunday Mass, Fr. Bartolis preached the sermon. I continued to puzzle over his womanly appearance and that of his young squire who served this day as acolyte. The boy appeared birdlike, so frail I wondered if he might be a girl, then considered if he were perhaps a Jew. I felt sad for one corrupted so young, and made up my mind to find out more about this child.

At the sermon's conclusion, Fr. Bartolis announced, "I

have received word from Lisbon that our new governor, Luis Doria, has embarked for our island and, God willing, will be here within the month. When Governor Doria arrives, he will bear a grand message: Because São Tomé is now all Catholic, King João has petitioned His Holiness Alexander VI to establish The Diocese of São Tomé. When granted, our far-reaching see will include the Kingdom of the Congo. The diocese will be a bright star in the constellation of The Holy Church."

While quiet hallelujahs greeted his announcement, to me the iniquity of slave commerce had fully revealed itself. Including the Congo in the diocese would give the Portuguese a monopoly in the slave-trade and secure income from Spain, the Dutch, France and England. Vast amounts of money would flow into the Crown treasury and thus to the Church. Porto Tomé had become the valve by which the Portuguese would control the entire slave enterprise. My cynicism grew. Crown and Church had made an odious compact.

After Mass I went with Nawar to his home. I felt great pleasure at seeing Yasemina. She hugged me and said, "I'm pregnant," and happily showed me the small bulge in her belly. With her smile and lively manner, I understood Nawar's fondness for her. She handed me two letters. "Man bring yesterday. Say not find you for a month."

The first was for Miriam, the second for me from my father. I looked at Nawar. "These come from Spanish Málaga, far from Lagos!" I shoved the letters at him. "Take these, I fear to—"

He grew angry. "Read them, Saulo. Be responsible."

I retreated from him and opened my father's letter, watching sadly as an infant son of Nawar's played on the floor with his older sister.

My Dear Son Marcel,

I pray this letter finds you and your wife Miriam well. I also pray that your first child is born and healthy, and a son as we all wish. Miriam's family, along with their many relatives who fled the Inquisition to Málaga with us, also send greetings.

I so wish we had good tidings.

I felt impossible pain. So much had changed, so much gone wrong.

About two months ago agents of the Inquisition arrested our trusted Christian friend in Lisbon. I fear they have killed him. All around us Jews, Moslems, and suspect Christians were taken into custody and tortured, their homes looted. Since we had a hopeful refuge in Lagos, I and your mother sold what we could and traveled there. The roads were clogged with many souls fleeing as we. Spain and Portugal are devoured by inquisitions.

Miriam's family welcomed us, but actions against Jews had already started, so all of us fled to Porto Málaga. The Castilians in this region permit Jews to pass, but for a price. At each district border they robbed us, so we have no money left for passage. I lay bricks, and Miriam's father draws maps and building plans to earn enough to leave this place. The women take in laundry and clean Christian homes. Life for Jews is misery, but at the moment Málaga is free from the Inquisition.

Before we left Lagos, an uncle of Miriam's sought Leah (at great risk to his person) at Convent Silves. They told him she was once there, but refused to disclose her current whereabouts. They claimed she is a nun who cares for children.

And so, when we have the money in hand, we will sail with a merchant to the Levant, Egypt or the Ottoman, for we hear Jews are welcomed there more than any place in Christendom. Sadly, we understand Jerusalem is forbidden to us. As with Jews always, our families are cast asunder.

If your child is a son, Marcel, you know the name I most prefer.

Oh the sadness, the cruelty of God, seeing the rest of his letter in Hebrew and, try as I might, I remained blind to it. How could I not read a language I'd known all my life? The punishment for burning my Torah? I so missed the comforting sounds of my father's tongue.

More sadness fell over me as I read Miriam's letter from her father— the same hopeful salutations for his dead daughter and our child, both gone forever, his letter much like my father's. Within the father's letter I found a contemptible missive from Miriam's mother. In part it read:

We have endured much with the Saulos, and I think them generous and kind, but I must add that they are coarse in manner and much too devout for our taste. The father, a common brick mason, raves about an ancestor Marcel, supposedly a Just Man. Every day, that's all we hear from him. I certainly hope your Marcel is "just" (good) to you, and that he is more cultured than his father and mother.

A while back, in a situation of much peril, your uncle Luis went to the convent at Silves to ask the abbess about the Saulo daughter. He found little; but regardless, Sr. Saulo showed no appreciation for his efforts.

I think they expect us to sail with them to the East Mediterranean, but that is not our plan. There is a colony of Jewish Catalans who fled to Majorca before us. Like Father, they work in the science of maps and navigation. Our plan is to go there with all the family. Compared to the Levant, Majorca is promising, a shorter less dangerous journey, and not as far from you. Without question, that is where we will go.

We were fortunate that everyone made the dreadful journey from Lagos to Málaga without injury or death. It felt like a breath of fresh air when we escaped the tyranny of Portugal, and it will be more relief when we depart Andalusia.

The mother's letter ended with a hopeful note for her lost daughter and grandchild. Saddened and piqued, I handed it to Nasic. "Read this."

After reading it, he laughed aloud. "Well, now you know about mothers-in-law."

"I know nothing about anything."

"What does your father's letter say?"

"The same, but no affront to Miriam's family."

"You must write them, Saulo. Let them know."

I wrung my hands. "The letters are three months old. They may be gone."

"What is wrong with you!" He came over and pulled me to my feet. "Look at me, look me in the eye. Do not let some new religion divert you from your legacy of Marcel. I've known about the Saddiq business for some time. Miriam told me. *Live up to it!* Write the letters."

Yasemina came between us. "You men are trouble," she said, and shooed the children away. "I fix supper. Eat and calm yourselves."

After eating, I gathered my courage and went to my farm. I climbed to the house from the east side, away from the tenant camp to avoid seeing anyone. Unfortunately, I encountered a girl there with the children. Although I told her my name, she screamed, covered her face and ran off. The house looked better than I could have imagined. The children stood in the entrance and looked at me, then filed down the steps, Michal, Louisa, and Joseph who hung behind. Mazal came last, scampering into Joseph's arms. I didn't know what to say. The children stared at me strangely. I had not seen them in over two months.

Kiman appeared and seemed to understand. "Take you cane fields, Master Saulo. Do fine. Bring children." He called down to the slave quarters. "Jubiabá!"

"Who is that?"

"Screaming girl you scare. Niece of wife. Care for children."

"Why does she have a Portuguese name?"

"Take name in school. Want go Lisbon someday. Very good speak."

Jubiabá arrived from the camp and stood next to Kiman. She was the most beautiful black girl I had ever seen. A second girl joined her, Jubiabá's younger sister it turned out. The older girl spoke. "I am sorry, Master Saulo that I ran away. You frightened me." Her Portuguese had a lovely African sound to it.

For some reason I felt quite flustered. "Nawar tells me

163

you do well with the children."

She made a curtsy, something I hadn't seen since Lisbon. "I will tidy the house while you go with Kiman. My sister, Suryiah, will care for the children."

Michal spoke up. "Father, we want to go to the fields with you and Kiman."

At her words my knees buckled. "All right," I said, barely able to speak, "all right." I turned and we walked down the hill the way I had come so we could look first at the gardens, Michal and Louisa right behind, chattering in Guinea, Castilian, and Portuguese. I waited until they caught up and patted them both on the head, looking back to Joseph who walked solemnly beside Jubiabá's sister. I stopped and knelt. "Come on Joseph, let's have a look at you." The sister pushed him forward. He ran to her back and hid his face there, his small hands clutched around her middle. Holding his hands to her waist, Suryiah dragged him forward and turned as she came near. As I reached for Joseph, Mazal who had stayed a few feet behind, ran at me and hissed, baring his teeth.

I had not cared for my family as Miriam wished. I put my hands to my face and sobbed. "I am sorry, children. So sorry." The girls patted me as if I was a hurt dog. Joseph stared for a moment, then walked over and slapped me on the side of the head. Everyone looked horrified. I laughed, wiping my tears on my sleeve. "Joseph, that is the second time you've done that, and this time I deserve it." For the briefest moment he let me hold him, then pushed free and picked up Mazal.

"You see," he told the monkey, "Papa been very bad, but you may not bite him."

I looked at Kiman. "Where did he learn to talk like that?"

"Children go school three days week. You not know?"

"I guess I did." Around the time Miriam died, the Crown opened a school in the settlement. Whether bound or free, all children had to attend. I'd paid little attention.

At the garden we inspected the plots. The ginger plants,

rescued from the flood, were doing best of all. Some even had flowers. At the edge of the forest many of the pepper vines looked healthy, a few had climbed their host trees higher than I could reach. They showed clusters of small flowers that would soon berry. Kiman had a new cotton crop started. "Nawar give seeds," he said. I wondered if Fr. Bartolis's prayer to St. Benedict had helped my plants flourish. As the evening approached, we examined a nearby cane field while the children hid among the stalks and laughed. Kiman tipped several canes to show me the green tops. "Good harvest soon. Very glad you home, Master."

We returned to the table rock where I could see my house illuminated inside with oil candles and a low fire. Jubiabá sat on the lower step, then stood as we approached. She wore a colorful shift and had red shells woven into her thick hair. She looked quite the lady of the house. For the second time that day the smell of good food whet my appetite—a delight after the poor fare at the labor camps. Kiman took a torch and led the children and his younger niece toward the slave camp. Jubiabá, eyes down, continued to stand by the entrance. As the voices of the others faded, she said, "Come in, Master Saulo. I have fixed your dinner."

It was the best dinner I'd ever tasted, pea fowl roasted with figs and coriander, honeyed onions with pistachios and red peppers, and a date pudding made with sour goat milk. Jubiabá served the pea fowl and onions, poured a cup of beer, and stood back. I looked up at her. "Have you eaten?"

"No. I eat after you."

"I will not eat until you sit at my table. Bring your dinner. In my home, that is what we do."

"With a wife, perhaps. Not with a Congo girl."

I crossed my arms and pointed my nose at the table. "Sit."

She brought a plate and sat across from me, her face lovely in the candlelight. I could not believe her beauty. When I took my first bite, she also began to eat. I looked at her. "Your Portuguese is polished. Where did you learn it?"

"My family is from Ambasse. I went to a church school there, one run by the nuns. I am Catholic."

I lifted my cup of beer. "Thank you for this dinner. It is excellent."

After the pudding we lay together. I then realized how much I missed the comfort of a woman. I must have fallen asleep, because the next thing I knew Jubiabá had rejoined me in bed. Outside the rain fell. The table had been cleaned and a single candle burned at its center. She placed herself beside me and I again became aroused. Though my thoughts of Miriam in this bed with me filled me with self-reproach, Jubiabá and I coupled eagerly; and she took much pleasure in it.

She rested next to me and purred like a cat. "I must ask my uncle's permission before we can marry." I gulped loudly and she looked at me with humor. "If you want, I will not ask until morning." I did not know what to think. For a second time the idea of a black wife had been suggested by Nawar that afternoon.

In the morning, the birds calling at first light, Jubiabá brought honeyed yerba buena and a warm cloth to wash. She looked down at me and removed her shift. Again we coupled. Afterward she tickled me. "My goodness, Saulo. Get up, you've a farm to look after."

Kiman appeared with a smiling face that morning, but did not ask about his niece. The first thing we did was to look over the drawings for my mill site on the Vascão. As we walked past the garden plots, Kiman said, "Jungle grow over mill ditch, but easy fix. I also find clay for brick."

Once at the site, we cleared the vines and trued the foundation trenches. "Where did you find the clay?" I asked. He pointed. "How far? That's Horté's property."

"I look all over farm, on acres south and free land. Find no other. Only clay on Horté."

"Is he using it?"

"Yes, but I steal. Make business with Horté slave."

"A bad idea. I can work out something better." I knew

Horté did not have a mill or boiling house, and no kiln to fire bricks. To make his clay useful to both of us, I needed a kiln. "He gets his cane ground at the Crown mill. He knows he'd make more money if he did it himself." I stopped and leaned on my shovel. "We can't do much without fire bricks, so I will have to buy those in town. After we build a kiln, perhaps I can entice Horté to share his clay for fired bricks."

As we walked back to the house, I saw the children and Jubiabá weaving baskets in the shade below the table rock. Kiman pointed. "Niece happy here with children. She like you."

"We just met."

"She know you, Saulo, I tell. She want Lael back."

"As do I."

When I remained silent, he said, "If you no marry, Jubiabá not stay. She work teach school. Live in settlement with nuns."

Kiman knew his niece. Within a few days Jubiabá began to shun my advances. By week's end she left for the settlement, replaced by her sister who dealt with me in silence. When I told Kiman I missed the girl, he shook his head. "Pretty niece want marry white planter. If you no, other will."

In the next month we finished the house repair. But more important and with dear Nawar's help, thirty silvers to the foreman, and much rejoicing at my farm, Lael rejoined our household. Jubiabá used the opportunity to visit her family and spend time with the children. In league with her sister, the two ignored me, and I continued to be flustered in Jubiabá's presence.

I purchased fire brick in the settlement and built a kiln at my mill site, then paid Nuño Horté a visit. Despite his prejudice and stupidity, he agreed to let me mine clay in exchange for fired bricks sufficient for his sugar works. Nawar was right again: on São Tomé, prejudice yields to commerce. When we concluded our spoken agreement, I extended my hand to Nuño. He refused and stepped closer, standing just inches from my face. "There is not one second, Saulo, that I believe you are a Christian. I do business with you only because it suits me. And also that I won't have to be around those Jew-Novos and free niggers at the government mill."

I stood my ground. "Nuño, you more than I, are the child of the True Savior. For your kindness I will supervise your mill construction to assure the best result." With a baffled expression, Horté crossed himself, backed away, and left without a word.

Chapter 13

In some of my fields the cane began to ripen. Kiman and I made plans for our first harvest. The island's new governor arrived with little notice and moved into de Caminha's residence. We first saw Luis Doria on a Sunday when he greeted his subjects from the pulpit. The church was jammed with two-hundred citizens overflowing into the square—so many that a crier had to relay the governor's message to those outside.

Doria was a tall man, perhaps thirty-five, with light complexion and brown hair. In contrast to his mannerly demeanor, he dealt sternly with officials who appeared slow to accept his rule. The constable and two lackeys were the first to feel his iron fist. The three, accused of taking bribes and not maintaining public records, were given the choice of the lash or deportation to a prison in the Congo. Since the latter amounted to a death sentence, they chose the lash.

I left at the end of services that Sunday to avoid the spectacle. Nawar found me in the square as I worked my way through the lunatic mob. "You're not going to stay for the festivities?" he asked.

"Public savagery is not to my taste."

"Nor mine," said Nawar, "but at least it's the constable and those other two."

We reached the edge of the crowd and moved up the

street. "The charges seem transparent," I said. "This island's rife with bribery, and the constable is no different from any other official. And records were never part of his duty."

The bloodcry of the crowd signaled the prisoners' appearance. We quickened our pace. Nawar looked at me curiously. "The charges are an artifice of power, Saulo. What do you know of Doria's intrigues?"

"Plainly not enough."

"Because the charges are clearly false, Doria can demonstrate his authority. The constable offended the governor by submitting a list of civil duties he wished to retain. He should have prostrated himself and pled his case, begged our new monarch to bestow what favors he might."

"How must we deal with this man?"

"I've already met with him. He holds court in the church rectory where he has an office."

"Not at de Caminha's?"

In the distance the mob cheered as the lash found its mark. "The public is no longer welcome at the official residence. It seems our governor has something to hide. Rumors have it it's a woman, a mistress, and that he does not have a wife. We will see what female shows up with him at church."

"How did you fare in your meeting?"

"Very well. As Crown Overseer, I am an asset. He treated me with dignity. The more money the plantations make, the more he pockets. It seems de Caminha kept extensive records, so he knows all about us." He raised an eyebrow. "The governor asked about you, Saulo."

"Uh!"

Nawar smiled. "As Crown mason, he—"

"He called me *that?*"

"And more. He's angry you've neglected your duties."

I shrugged, feeling indifferent. Nawar continued. "It will be interesting, my friend, to see if you can stay on his good side."

"I've been wanting to ask, after you said you knew Jews

in Alexandra, did you know Jews in the Indies?"

"Oh, yes, many. Mostly merchants. Some quite wealthy. In a class denied to my family."

"Denied?"

"My country has a caste system. We were Shudra, the workers, only one step above untouchable. No one can be in a profession that is outside his caste, and merchants, the Vaisya, were above us. When Nasic and I told our father we hoped to be merchants someday, he beat us and drove us from our home." Nawar gave a muffled laugh. "My father had no room for all his children. Anyway, a Jew who sold metalware hired my brother and me as apprentices and took us in. When my father found out, he hired a mob to drive us from the city."

"How strange. So you fled to Egypt?"

"Yes, and my brother and I embraced Islam. A lovely faith, Marcel, where God believes all men are equal."

When we reached the crossroads to our farms, I felt the wind. "The season is changing," I said. "Our drytime is upon us. Maybe an early harvest?"

"Indeed," answered Nawar. "May I visit? I've heard good things about your crops. I would like to see for myself."

"Of course. Lael will be happy to see you, as will all the children. I am still in your debt for returning him as well for as the seeds and starts. I'll have the girl make supper."

"She hasn't poisoned you yet?"

"A rotten thing to ask." I knew where this led.

"Did you bed her sister?"

I felt my face blush. "I could not help myself."

He smiled. "No man could resist a woman as pretty as Jubiabá. Why then do I see her in town?"

"You ask this to spite me. I'm sure Kiman's told you everything."

"Not everything. I speculate you haven't said anything to the girl—the worst sort of disappointment. Is it because of her color?"

"I don't know."

"Sure you do. Yasemina is black, and you don't object to

171

our union. And one of my mainland wives is black."

"That's your business. But don't you see? There are black Moslems and white, Moslems of all shades. People see Yasemina and consider you have married someone of your own religion. Jubiabá is so obviously not a Jew, everyone will know."

He wagged his head in annoyance. "No one cares but you, Marcel. We are all supposedly Catholic. Marry this beautiful Sheba and be done with your grief."

• • •

Governor Doria's summons arrived a few days later in the person of the constable—the man much chastened and servile. Though one of the most steadfast Novos, even the constable's sincere conversion and faithful service had not saved him from the official lash. Since I had also suffered official mistreatment before, I wondered if I would again.

The governor's clerk had set my audience with Doria after Wednesday Mass. I wore my best clothes, expecting to see him right after. He sat in a private pew near the altar and turned to look at me. Though I acknowledged each time he looked my way, he seemed not to notice. When I entered the rectory hall after the service, I found a number of suppliants waiting ahead of me. The nearest was the foreman who gave me a stare of hostility. I stood close and dared him to make a move. Under his breath he whispered, "Cuckold, how do you like caring for my bastard son?"

This was an immense insult, and if I had a weapon I would have killed him right there. But this rectory and the crowd made any action impossible. I held my ground, crossed myself, and said, "My son Lael? I pray for him every day, just as I pray for you." The clerk who guarded the door ahead hissed, "Silence!" The foreman cursed and turned away.

With the hallway stifling hot and my stomach growling, I walked past the others, gave my name to the clerk, and left to find food. I bought fresh figs and roast pig from a street woman—the ex-Saddiq sups on pig flesh. The figs were very juicy and, not realizing it, I dribbled them all over my shirt. Stained, drenched with sweat, and irritated, I returned to the rectory hall. The line had not moved, the foreman ahead of me, and I still last. After an hour with only one man admitted, I found a chair and went to sleep.

Someone called my name. I awoke, and without thinking, wiped my face on my shirt, staining it further with sweat and drool. "Marcel Saulo, the governor will see you now." I labored to my feet and passed the four men still waiting, receiving sour looks and ill-wishes.

The governor sniffed when he saw me. "Well Saulo, what have you been up to? You look a mess." The room was spare except for the massive chair in which he sat and a nearby table stacked with papers. At a small desk, a scribe sat recording. Doria motioned me to sit.

"Thank you for seeing me, governor."

"You were summoned, Saulo, because I wish to berate you. I see no record or invoice for your services. You have neglected your Christian duties as Crown mason."

"Since my wife died I have had the melancholy." Again I found myself surprised by his use of a title for me.

"No excuse. Work is the cure"—he smiled wryly—"and of course another woman. In a place where so many die, one should not grieve long." He looked at a paper. "Did you know the hearth at a new mill failed? The hot syrup killed a slave. Two others were scalded."

"I did not know."

"Well you should. It was a Crown-financed project and I hold you responsible."

"Sir, I—"

He raised a hand. "I am not finished. Governor de Caminha, bless his memory, left notes about you. Here he writes: *Saulo is a malcontent, yet he remains a skilled craftsman and productive member of our community.* Are you a malcontent?"

"Yes."

"He also states you are painfully honest." The scribe smiled to himself and bent to his task. "I believe the landowner at the mill where the hearth failed did not request your help because you are roundly disliked."

"No more than most Novos."

The governor stood up. *"Most Novos* back home get roasted at the stake! In our colonies, including here, converted Jews have privileges Marranos on the mainland never have. In contrast to our island's prosperity, back home we have plague and inquisition. Here the Crown gives you land and position. In Portugal your family—"

"My family fled Portugal to the Mediterranean." The conversation had become absurd. I felt as if my anger might overwhelm me.

Doria seized a whip and blustered around the table. I stood to confront him. If he struck me, I would defend myself. Surprised by my action, he stopped, but close enough that I could smell his perfume. "What do you think will happen to your family in the Mediterranean? Killed perhaps? Captured by the Barbarossa, the men sent to die on the galley bench, the women made whores for the sultan?" He slapped the whip on the table and returned to his chair.

"My family had to flee, sir. What choice did they have?"

He shook his head with displeasure. "You are truly as de Caminha described. Regardless, you remain a Crown subject. Count your blessings."

"I will fully resume my mason's duties."

That did not satisfy him. "Unfortunately this leads me to another subject—that of your tenant policy. It sows discord among landowners and slaves."

"In all respect, sir, I do not understand. It has been the policy to make freedmen of the original slaves. Why should it not apply to mine?"

"Again you take matters in your own hands. The policy is a Crown practice and does not apply to slaves privately owned. I command you to indenture no more slaves."

He dismissed the scribe with a flip of his hand and asked him to wait outside. When the door closed, Doria continued. "Between us two, we have sufficient free blacks on Sugar Island—that's what they call us in Lisbon, you know. But soon the commerce of slavery will far exceed that of sugar." He rose and began to pace. With the scribe gone, the man's manner changed. "I pray for your family, Saulo. By leaving Portugal, they saved their lives. The Spanish infection, as most back home call the Inquisition, has no bounds. Even the most authentic conversion does not guarantee safety. Many innocents are tortured and burned. It has little to do with religion and much to do with greed and envy."

As if he'd explained too much, Doria paused at the door, cracked it open, and motioned me to leave. Then he spun toward me, his face giddy and flushed, sweat in the corners of his mouth. He pushed the door shut with his foot. "I will tell you a story, Saulo, a story about the future of slave commerce. About ten years ago this lunatic Christopher Columbus— You've heard of him?" I shook my head no. "Well, he's a Genoese navigator who presented a scheme to King João about sailing west to the Orient. In those days I sat on the Maritime Commission, and though we thought the navigator's science faulty, we favored the voyage as a worthy gamble. But João said our African adventures were sufficient, and ruled against us." The governor put a hand to his face and looked at me between his fingers. *"I knew* this fellow would succeed. Christopher Columbus – *Christopher, The Bearer of Christ* – he carried The Patron's name!" He uncovered his face with a futile wave. "Well, he went to Isabella and Ferdinand and pled his case. Three years ago the Spanish funded the expedition. Columbus returned after he discovered a new land. Not the Indies or Cathay mind you, but some gigantic, wild place hinted at only in legend. Of course the Spanish claimed it, a land that should rightfully be ours.

"Still, Saulo, we will profit. The future of the slave trade is bright, and the demand for labor in these new lands will be immense. With our allies in the Congo, Guinea, and Angola, and our new diocese, we will control African commerce. Though we Portuguese will not own this western land, we will reap a fortune by supplying its labor."

175

Doria returned to the entrance. "Now I hope you understand the importance of a firm hand when you deal with blacks."

He opened the door and called for his scribe, then turned to me. "Again, I pray for your family. Understand that I care less for ceremony and more for hard work." As his man entered, the governor said, "Remember your pledge to me, Saulo." He crooked a finger at the next person in line.

I walked along the street, not believing my conversation with the governor. Was I truly better off in this damned colony? A Novo? Worse, a Marrano? This place lacked the sharp class distinctions of Portugal—a true benefit—and my lot was certainly better here than fleeing the Inquisition. Does history offer Jews only such choices?

As I turned onto my road, I came across Jubiabá, Suryiah, and the children returning from school. Jubiabá, who looked as beautiful as ever, left without a greeting. The sister offered her usual indifference. She carried Lael in a kanga, though he was far too big for it. "Why did you bring him? Next time leave him with a woman back home."

Suryiah handed me the boy. "He cries when I'm gone; he's no trouble."

I set him down in the road. "You can walk now." He ran ahead. Mazal, who had been riding on Joseph's shoulder, jumped down and scampered after.

She gave me a sullen look. "Jubiabá teaches the ninnies Portuguese, and I help." Something I already knew. "My sister must leave the school soon. The nuns will send her away."

Michal and Louisa began giggling, and Joseph ran after Lael. "Why?" A stupid question—Jubiabá was probably pregnant. I had a queasy feeling.

"My sister will tell you when she is ready."

I walked ahead and scooped up Lael. "Come on boys, we can walk faster than the girls."

About halfway to the farm a wind-driven cloud of smoke churned our way, the plume too large for anything but cane-burning. This made no sense—few fields had been harvested, and none were ready for clearing. Out of the smoke ran Kiman and all from my tenant camp, some of Horté's blacks, and other planters and slaves. Many of the men carried weapons—crossbows, pikes, poleaxes and swords. Kiman ran up, out of breath, drenched with sweat and scared. "Angolar raid. Kill Horté. Burn everything!" The other planters confirmed the mayhem. All the fields and houses had been set aflame. We faced a major rebellion.

We learned later that slaves from Angola had slipped their chains and seized their ship as it rounded Ilhoa de Cabras, a rocky island just east of the slave port. Unable to operate the vessel, and all the sailors dead or overboard, the slaves drifted with the burning ship until it grounded a quarter league off Tomé. Unable to put out the flames, the Africans took to the sea and swam for shore. About half of them drowned in the process. The guard and captains at the port elected to make a stand, but the rebels killed them all, thus no alarm reached the settlement. We faced a force of Angolars and escaped slaves, perhaps three-hundred crazed individuals.

As we hurried back to town, a knot of fifteen Angolars— soon all the rebels would be called thus—came at us from the jungle. They carried rough wooden spears and fire-brands. When they saw our number, they retreated toward town, shouting at our blacks, motioning them to join in. I don't know if our slaves understood the language, but none left us. In the days that followed, however, some local slaves joined the rebels, including most of Horté's.

Closer to town we could see buildings afire and people fleeing. Here and there soldiers from the garrison ran through the smoke chasing the rebels. A small company of defenders near the church were about to be overwhelmed. As we ran forward, someone handed me a poleax. With our weapons much superior to the Angolars', we routed the attackers quickly. My axe was slippery with blood. I had never killed a man before, but in a few seconds I had killed two or more.

Our men with crossbows retrieved their bolts from the dead and dying. They cut the throats of any left alive. I found Kiman, his breath coming in gasps, bloody sword in hand, a serious gash in one arm.

One of our men had been wounded in the groin. Some of our people bound up his wound and carted him to the hospital. The dead Angolars were a sorry lot—thin to the point of starvation, covered with sores and without shoes. Many had the marks of iron on their necks and ankles. One soldier said, "Go to the garrison. You'll be organized and given proper weapons." On the way there I bound Kiman's arm.

I suddenly thought of the children and whirled about. At a distance through the smoke I saw a nun with some children as they hurried away. I prayed the nuns had also found mine and would care for them. If not, Suryiah would know what to do. We rushed the short distance through the flaming town to the garrison. Over a hundred male citizens milled in the street there, about a third of them black. For the first time I worried that a large number of armed Africans among us might be a threat, but seeing the eagerness of our slaves and freedmen to defend the settlement, my concern left me. The bodies of dead Angolars revealed that the garrison had just repelled an attack.

The constable walked from the building and addressed the crowd. "The soldiers will pass among you and hand out weapons. Break into companies of twenty men. A soldier will be your captain. Select an alternate among yourselves."

"What about the fire?" someone shouted.

The governor, dressed in the same clothes from the afternoon, appeared next to the constable. Oh how we needed a knight of de Caminha's caliber. Doria had revealed himself as no such warrior, merely a Crown official. He cried out, "We can do nothing until the rebellion is crushed. Let the women fight the fires." It was strange to see him allied with the constable after last week's beating.

I admired the constable and felt pride for his Jewish beginnings. He'd rescued himself from humiliation at the governor's hands, though the lash wounds had to be still painful.

A soldier I knew approached me and nodded to my bloody poleax. "Saulo, you hold a seasoned weapon. You will be my alternate, I am your captain." He swept his arm at the men around me. "Count twenty and move over there. Choose a second in case you are disabled."

I did what the soldier asked, picking Kiman as my second. In a few minutes the constable called from the garrison door and motioned us inward. "Captains and alternates, to orders!" Inside we found scribes at work as they completed rough maps of the settlement and nearby farms. It seemed the constable's military skills were remarkable, and I wondered where he'd learned them. He designated us troop four, with eleven troops in all. The constable handed out the maps, mine with an area *4* circled on it. Next he and Doria went around and marked the maps to show the location of adjacent troops. Nawar stood nearby, also an alternate in his troop. "Good luck," we wished one another. Outside, the uproar in the town continued.

With the map drawings complete, the constable addressed us. "Each group will scour the settlement area within your circle and return here. If you cannot hold your own against the Angolars, retreat to a troop close to you and combine forces. I expect the slave port is now back in our hands. Take your captives there." He looked outside. "We have less than three hours of daylight. You must return here by nightfall for guard duty."

We filed outside and gathered our men to us. Father Bartolis offered a prayer to St. Adrian, "The saint of soldiers," he told us.

We set out through the burning town, passing dead Angolars and injured townspeople everywhere. We saw that the soldiers had driven the attackers away from the hospital and saved the structure. Our captain carried a crossbow and sword; Kiman and I along with a few others carried poleaxes; the remainder carried a variety of weapons, swords, pikes, maces, and crossbows. Our troop was to scour an area north of town, between the swamp and the slave port. Except for the fighters sent to the port, ours was the most distant from the settlement. Places even more distant, including my farm, would have to wait until morning. Ahead of us was a large plantation and two smaller farms.

At the first farm we found only smoke and ruins, the cane fields still smoldering. This area had to be one of the first attacked. The second farm revealed a scene of brutal carnage—mutilated bodies both black and white, the Novo farmer, his family and slaves slaughtered. The condition of the dead sickened me. I had heard of such savagery in Castile and Burgundy, but never considered it in Africa. The amount of damage done to our island in this short afternoon was frightening.

As we skirted the east side of the swamp, about a half-league from the main house of the large plantation, we encountered our first enemy, five Angolars who fled ahead of us. The captain thought if we followed it might be a trap, so we waited at the edge of a blackened field. As we discussed what to do next, a mob of Angolars charged screaming from the trees. Outnumbered, we ran directly away from them, stumbling across the field into the forest. We assembled in a small clearing, panicked that they had us surrounded.

Our captain and two others had been hit with bolts, the captain in the chest. He went down, slumping against me as he fell. This meant the Angolars had armed themselves with weapons seized from the plantation or the slave port.

The captain's death put me in charge. With evening approaching, none of us had any desire to take on the Angolars who blocked our retreat in the direction of the road and closest troop. The rebel force smelled blood, and I had to act quickly. Since no more crossbow bolts came our way, we assumed they did not know how to respring their weapons.

"Help the wounded," I ordered and knelt to close the captain's eyes.

Kiman gestured through the jungle in the only direction clear to us. "Island in swamp. Defend good."

"Can we wade it?"

He nodded.

I directed five men to lead. Supporting the wounded between us, we set out. Our fighters with crossbows guarded the retreat. As we neared the swamp we entered onto an open shore of sand and mud. Kiman pointed to the island about two-hundred yards out. We could hear the rebels as they gathered at the edge of the jungle. I set a third of my force to guard our escape.

Dragging our two wounded men into the water, we headed for the island. The water, chest deep in places, began to panic me—I had never learned to swim. But ahead I went. It was time for courage. As we neared the island, I called our rear guard to join us. When our men entered the water, the Angolars emerged from the jungle, but they feared our crossbows and did not charge.

Out of breath and grateful to be back on land, I helped my men out of the water and onto the island. The light began to fade. A long, hungry night loomed ahead. The rebels assembled on the open shore; the whole mob of them jeered and pointed. Just as we'd suspected, they were well armed. "Gwema! Gwema!" they shouted.

"What's that?" I asked Kiman.

"Crocodile. Angolar think we food soon."

The flesh-eaters were least on my mind, having been cleared from this swamp long before I'd arrived on Tomé. My men's enterprise pleased me. Without my directing them, they attended to chores and the wounded. Someone produced a flint-and-steel—a true stroke of luck. Flying bloodsuckers buzzed everywhere. A smudge fire would soon dispel them. A hunt of our tiny island for turtles, crabs, birds, eggs—anything edible—yielded nothing, and the water was too salty to drink. Soon we sat in a drift of smoke, wishing we had food, awaiting an uncertain dawn.

Daylight left quickly as it always did on Tomé, so different than the lingering dusks of Lisbon. On the shore we could see the enemy fires and to the west a partial moon floated in the clear sky. Hopefully the enemy's fear of crocodiles and our crossbows would keep them in place. I considered the moon; we would have complete darkness in a few hours. Perhaps this would allow us to escape, or even attack the Angolars.

I set five men at watch and told the others, including Kiman, to sleep. In two hours I woke Kiman. "Set a new watch. Wake me when the moon is down."

It seemed I had barely slept when I heard his voice. "Moon gone."

"How are the wounded?"

"Maybe die, maybe not. No more bleed."

I considered a plan. "Change the watch again. Have those sleeping lie in front of the fires. Move the wounded there also. Stoke the fires once, then let them die." Kiman sent a few men to gather wood. "How well do you know the jungle above the Angolar camp?"

"Know it."

"Well enough to get through in the dark? Get behind the rebels?"

Kiman smiled broadly and adjusted the wrap on his arm. "Easy, Saulo."

"If we go that way, how do you know the water isn't over our heads?"

Again the smile. "Maybe master learn swim someday. Kiman hold up."

We waited an hour, then woke the men and had them put mounds of sticks where they'd slept. I laid out my plan. "We will leave our wounded comrades and later retrieve them. We'll go ashore above the Angolars and stage a surprise—trap them between us and the swamp." The men thought it a good plan, although some who couldn't swim protested. "I cannot swim either," I said, "but we will alternate. A swimmer in the lead, followed by one who cannot. All of us holding to the waistcord of the man ahead." Fortunately we had an excess of swimmers.

I spoke to our wounded, assuring them we would return, then led everyone in a prayer to St. Adrian as Bartolis had done. In the pitch-black we crept to the rear of the island and entered the water, probing ahead with our pikes and poleaxes, Kiman in the lead, I next, the Angolar fires our marker as we cleared the island. A short distance out Kiman stopped, pulled me to him, and put one of my arms around his neck. Understanding the signal, swimmers along the chain prepared likewise. Kiman kicked quietly through the water while he pushed his poleax ahead. I reached down with mine to test the bottom and found none, yet felt no panic.

Kiman was a born leader. When he regained the bottom, he stood, moved ahead, and motioned to those behind so they could quickly find their footing. We lined up again and moved silently forward. We had to swim one more time before we reached the shore.

Once inside the forest, I counted my men. We'd left our island with nineteen; everyone had made it. An animal trail lead west, revealing itself by yellow leaves fallen in the path. We came to a freshwater channel and everyone drank. A man next to me shrieked in pain. Without a thought I shoved his head under and clamped my hand over his mouth, then pulled him back by the hair, the writhing snake attached to his cheek and around my arm. Kiman felt for the serpent and hurled it away. "Water mamba," he hissed. The man thrashed violently and tried to scream. Someone cracked his skull with a pike and he went limp, rendered senseless, a blessing. He would soon be dead, as the bite of this snake is always fatal. I whispered a prayer and we moved off.

When I estimated we had passed the rebel position, I sent three men through the forest to spot the their camp. They returned in a short while. The man I'd appointed leader, a friendly Novo planter, said, "We saw them. Straight from here will put us in position." He laid a hand on my shoulder. "Must hurry. There's light in the east."

In a few minutes we reached the edge of the forest—fifty yards across the grassy shore lay the sleeping enemy. The lingering smell of their food from the night before assaulted our hunger. Kiman crouched next to me and pointed to the brightening horizon. "Sun in eyes soon." I made a hurried plan and we snuck from the forest. At twenty-five yards an Angolar shouted the alarm. My crossbowmen knelt and shot, then let us pass as they reloaded. My column split and formed a semicircle around the enemy, cutting off their retreat except to the water. As the confused Angolars struggled to their feet, a flurry of bolts came our way. They had learned to respring the crossbows in the night, though had not perfected their aim. Fortunately the enemy cross-bows felled only one of my men. Initially they had outnum-bered us two-to-one, but our crossbowmen quickly im-proved our odds. My men shouted "Gwema!" and pointed their weapons, causing a brief panic among the Angolars.

Still outnumbered, our only hope was an immediate charge, and this we did, the clash quick, brutal, and defi-nite.

Guarded by my men, a dozen Angolars cowered face-down on the ground. Nearly twice that many were dead around us. My men went among these dead and dispatched any who appeared still living. Two enemy bodies floated in the water. I counted my troop's number. I had thirteen healthy, two dead, three wounded. "Let's kill the rebels!" one of my men shouted. Others hooted approval.

"No," I commanded, "enough killing for today. We will take them to the port." I pointed to the piles of stolen food and supplies, setting four of my men to prepare food while the others guarded the prisoners and tended our wounded. Kiman found a coil of rope and began to truss the prostrate Angolars in the customary slave chain—single file, neck-to-neck, hands behind their backs.

I sent men to retrieve our wounded from the island. They returned with only one alive, the other dead, the latter a skilled carpenter who had worked with me on de

Caminha's chapel—the structure likely burned to ruin like everything else. The death of this carpenter, one of the best-liked men on the island, brought forth new shouts to kill the captives. I again ordered, "No," and put myself between the prisoners and the shouting men. One man pushed me. I brought the shaft of my poleax down on his shoulder. He crumpled to the ground. I glared at the others in challenge—all of us armed, a dangerous situation. "I will kill the next one." I prodded the man at my feet. "Tie him with the prisoners." Kiman and another man did as I ordered.

With the insurrection suppressed and some food in our bellies, we set out for the slave port, leaving a guard for our wounded. One of my fighters found a bloody square of cloth, attached it to his pike, and strode ahead with his banner. A discussion of our battles ensued. What my men said gave me pause. At no time had I hesitated to take action, and viewed success as the only outcome. I said, "The violence I have seen instructs me." I pointed back to Kiman who marched with the captives. "He's seen it as well. De Caminha's campaign against the pirates was a complete victory. And a year-and-a-half ago we saw Nasic trap the Alegre fugitives and sell them for a fortune."

"We should sell ours for the rebuilding," someone said. "We'll need the money."

I felt sure of the Angolar's fate: hanging. Their only possibility for survival was to work in the settlement, then be sold off-island after rebuilding.

Ahead, beyond a grove of low trees, was the slave port. Beyond the trees the masts of two slave caravels tipped at anchor in the harbor. These ships sealed the fate of the rebels. With sufficient replacements at hand, the Angolars would be executed. We trailed from the grove, emerging along a black sand beach. Bodies of drowned Angolars bobbed in the harbor and lolled grotesquely at the water's edge. Scattered throughout the dead were women and children—up to this point an element of their lives I'd not considered. Small red-eyed birds with vicious beaks pecked at the remains, and large-clawed crabs swarmed over the bodies clicking their pincers. Our captives began to yowl. Ahead we saw a rough gallows set inland from the slave enclosure, some with two or three bodies hanging from a single rope, a pile of dead off to one side. Surrounded by garrison soldiers, a sorry group of rebels waited their turn. At seeing the gallows, our prisoners threw themselves to the ground and refused to move. The man who'd pushed me was the only one left standing. "Release him," I ordered.

He said, "You have my gratitude, Captain Saulo. I regret my behavior."

I ignored him and sent the flag-carrier ahead to ask the garrison soldiers for help. The Angolars pleaded in a tongue that sounded much like Guinea. Despite my ruined harvest and my zeal for defending our island—and despite their savagery—I pitied the Angolars. We had killed men fighting for their lives, souls ripped from their families who floated dead and bloated a few yards away, souls who sought vengeance in this foreign place.

An officer came running forward with three men. "Saulo, where is your captain?" He eyed our captives.

"Killed last evening. He fought valiantly." I pointed to our prisoners. "Take these Angolars, Lieutenant. We must attend our wounded."

His soldiers prodded the captives to their feet. "Good work, Saulo. This a fine catch. The most of any troop. How many did you kill?"

"More than enough." I told him where to find the bodies and looted goods.

"Do you need help?"

"No. We have five of our dead to collect, including the captain. We will leave them there for you."

He saluted and ordered his soldiers forward with our luckless prisoners. I turned my men and headed back. I wanted to get away from this port and back to town as quickly as possible, to get away from the dreadful scene unfolding behind us.

Two of our wounded needed stretchers; the other two

could hobble. I sent men into the jungle to retrieve our dead. The rest of us readied the wounded for travel. We fashioned litters using clothing from the dead and pikes for poles. Before we left, I again led the men in prayer, thanking St. Adrian for our victory. I commended the souls of our departed to Christ—a prayer allowed only to priests. Though I received astounded looks from some of my men, I smiled grimly and began our march.

The journey back to town was long and solemn. In town, the hospital and garrison appeared to be the only buildings left standing. At the hospital we found chaos, bodies strewn about the courtyard, the building itself overflowing with the injured. A woman in childbirth, tended only by her frantic husband, screamed the loudest. I found an exhausted physician. He hastily examined our wounded and told me he would tend them when he could. We repeated our prayers and left.

At the garrison the constable greeted us. "Good to see you, Saulo, but where is your captain?" I told him the news. "Sad," he said, "one of many."

I described our battles in restrained terms. He appeared weary, though obviously satisfied with the outcome. One of my men began to elaborate. "Enough," I told him, "it will keep for another day."

"The Angolar war is over," announced the constable. "You are dismissed, but be cautious of raiders. About half of the rebels escaped, most of them toward Porto Alegre. Some of our slaves went with them. I sent a company of soldiers, but I fear it may be too late. Alegre may suffer the same fate as we." He pointed to the rear of the building. "We have many women and children in the armory. You may want to look there for your families."

I found my children, Joseph and Mazal, the center of attention. For a change, Suryiah greeted me and the children did not, the latter barely concerned with the ruin around them. Kiman's wife was there too. As she ministered to his arm, I wished I had a woman so inclined. My tenant families were also in the armory, the men absent, pressed into settlement work. "Nawar and his brood stopped here," said Kiman's wife. "They went to his farm. We hear it's destroyed, everything but the house. Somehow the rebels missed it."

I remembered my journals hidden there—hopefully safe—and felt a sudden relief. "Keep the children here," I told Jubiabá's sister. "We'll send for you in a day or two." I offered a prayer of gratitude to Yahweh for my children, my first Jewish prayer in some time, thanking also the Christian saint of children whose name I did not know. Then, in dread of what we might find, Kiman and I hurried to my farm through the fire-gutted settlement. Clustered at the edge of town, groups of people sat huddled near their fires, everyone living out-of-doors, grateful for the dry season.

Chapter 14

Except for the goats, pigs, and horses that foraged in my garden plots, little remained of the farm. Our houses were burned and the canefields black. Kiman found a supply of salt fish in the rubble of his house, and we took the charred mess down to the Vascão, washed it and ate our fill. With little to do for the moment, our families safe and the two of us exhausted, we lay down in the shade and slept.

In a short while Kiman woke me. "Hear noise, master."

I listened and heard something. "Goat," I mumbled, adjusting my repose and closing my eyes.

"No Saulo, a man noise. From Horté farm."

I struggled to my feet and picked up my poleax, the damned weapon part of my life now. "Let's take a look." As we neared Horté's we saw buzzards circling.

We found him hanging by his arms from a tree in his yard. He'd been flailed. The buzzards made their ill-tempered croaking sound and lumbered away. We cut Horté down and laid him on the ground. Frantic eyes stared from his bloody face. He gasped violently and began to talk. "My niggers did this. Where'd they go?"

"Most of your slaves fled with the Angolars," I told him. "We heard you'd been killed."

"I am not dead yet. Where's my family?"

Horté was dried blood from head to foot—amazing he'd survived this long. "I don't know where your family is, but we better get you to town."

For the second time that day Kiman and I carted a man on a litter to the hospital. Horté was immensely heavy and, as we struggled along, he asked a stream of questions. His fanatic eyes flashed when we told him of the executions at the slave port. "I will see more of them hang!" he shouted.

Some soldiers straggling back from Alegre caught up with us. Most of the rebels, they told us, had escaped into the jungle after sacking the town. "...headed toward the old fugitive camp on the mountain," one man said.

When they saw our burden and offered to carry Horté, he began to buck and thrash. "Take me where they're hanging those bastards," he raged. "Take me!"

"He's going to the hospital," I told the soldiers.

"No!" screamed Horté. He pitched himself from the bloody litter and squirmed in the dirt. "You men take me, not the Marrano. I got gold sovereigns. I'll pay."

The soldiers appeared confused. I'd grown sick of Horté's insanity. "Where is this gold, Nuño?"

"It's hidden, Jew. I'll not tell."

I had never seen anyone so crazy. I dashed my palms together dismissively. "Take the lunatic," I told the soldiers, "but see you get his gold before he dies."

• • •

Horté did not die. He stayed a day at the slave port, unable to rise from his litter, urging the hangman on. When he fell into a stupor, the soldiers carted him to the hospital. By then he had gangrene in an arm and a leg. The surgeon took both. The nuns looked after Horté and a priest administered the last unction. By hate alone, Nuño Horté survived. Sometime that week, his starving wife Isabel and the children wandered into my farm. We were living in thatched lean-tos, which reminded me of my first days in the Jew yard. As for the Horté farm, the place was abandoned except for the soldiers and degradados digging for gold.

"What happened?" I asked Isabel.

She eyed me suspiciously while she and the children gobbled the lentil soup we gave them. "The rebels took us to the mountain back of Alegre. After a few days they turned all the whites loose. Seems our slaves talked them out of killing us." Isabel finished her soup and looked for more, then put an infant under her filthy shift to nurse. "My husband dead?"

"No, he's at the hospital." At the time I knew little else, and nothing of the amputations.

She gave an indifferent shrug and glared at her offspring. "Go to the river and bathe. Wash your clothes too."

"You can stay with us, Senhora Horté, until—"

"Why are those men digging at my farm?"

"Your husband promised them gold if they took him to the slave port to see the hangings."

She choked, laughing. "We got no gold, but those thieves can spade my yam patch if they want."

My workers built a lean-to for her. Then we put everyone to work on farm repair. Since less than two months remained before the rainy season, we focused on housebuilding. Jubiabá arrived from town and moved in with the Kiman family, keeping her distance from me. She and her sister conducted school for the children under the trees. I wanted to talk with her, ask if she was pregnant, but found myself so occupied, I never took the time.

I intended to put in a sugar crop and needed cuttings. North along the river I had a small cane field not yet ripe and too green for the rebels to have burned, but someone had gone through it one night and cut all the tops. We made cuttings from the shortened ends and packed them in wet earth and cane sops, hoping they would root. I sent Kiman to find better ones and discover who raided my field. He returned a day later with Nawar and two carts of cuttings. Kiman gathered the workers who quickly began to unload and set the starts in our root plot.

I hugged Nawar. "What do I owe you?"

"Nothing. The plantation's got two green fields with enough cuttings for everyone."

"Do you know who raided my cane?"

"I suspect, but it's not important." He shoved a letter my way. "In town, this came for you. From Majorca." I held it like a poisonous snake. "You never wrote them, did you?" I shook my head. "You disappoint me, Saulo. I will say no more."

"I promise I will write. My parents too if I ever hear from them."

Nawar moved to other subjects. "You better send Isabel to see Nuño. He's bad. Lost an arm and a leg."

"Ouch! Which side?"

"Right arm, left leg. Might be able to get around if he lives."

He went on to tell me about his farm and the plantations, their situation much the same as mine. Two sawmills on Tomé's north end still operated, and planking would soon be available. The governor's home and chapel had been burned and Doria, just as we commoners, was living in a lean-to. I assumed his first priority would be to rebuild the church and rectory, and I would soon hear from him. Nawar stayed the evening. Next morning we drove his carts back to town. Isabel Horté rode with me. I had not opened the letter from Majorca.

A short distance down the road, Isabel spoke up. "You know that insolent ninny's telling everyone she carries your child?"

"Jubiabá?" This knowledge did not surprise me, but now I had to decide what to do.

"All those blackies want to be free. They'll do—"

"She *is free*, never a slave."

Isabel jounced along, her feet dangling over the back of the cart. Finally she said, "How can I run my farm? Nuño's probably dead."

"I will run it for share. Fifty percent." She stayed silent and chewed on the idea the rest of the way to town.

We found Horté in the hospital yard where he rested with the other wounded, fanned by slaves to keep off the flies. He looked more dead than alive. He stared at the two of us in confusion. After an impossible silence he asked, "Why do you keep company with that Marrano?"

I smiled. "You visit with your husband, Sra. Horté. I'll be back." I left with Nawar to return his wagon. We rode together, the second cart tied behind.

"What will you do about that pregnant African?" Nawar asked. "As I said, she will make a fine wife."

"For the sake of God, does everybody on the island know?"

"I do know that Doria considers you and the constable heroes of the Angolar war. You're in his good graces, but not mine." We came upon a smooth stretch of road where he clucked the horse into a trot, then he sliced a hand through the air in frustration. "How is it you're able to make decisions in battle, yet cannot write letters you must? Or show responsibility for a girl who carries your child?"

"I don't know why, but there remain certain things I cannot do. I know I am overwhelmed with the commonness of violence and death, and I've never killed a man before. Now I have led men in battle and— Ah! I'm also a farmer and have demands there. I've offered to run the Horté farm for half share and need more cuttings. Will you sell me—?"

"I will *give them* to you, Saulo." He made an exasperated shake of his head. "Have you heard anything I've said?"

At the Nawar farm I visited with Yasemina and her daughters. The sight of the two older girls reminded me of Miriam's last days. I expected Yasemina to ask about Jubiabá, but she did not. When the slaves finished loading a cart with cuttings for Horté's, I drove back to town. What remained of our ruined little city was pitiful to see. Buildings no longer stood in view, and I could stand on my wagonseat and see all the way to the harbor.

Off the main thoroughfare I heard screaming and spotted the commotion a short distance away. A young woman writhed with her back exposed, tied by her hands to a post, guarded by soldiers, and lashed by my old vereador, Felix da Tavora. A crowd of citizens looked on.

Feeling suddenly at war again, I jumped from the cart, seized a pike from the nearest soldier and battered da Tavora with the shaft. I turned and threatened the soldiers as they advanced. They recognized me, and stopped. Da Tavora struggled to rise from the ground. I put the point in his face. "Our city is leveled, Felix, and you have time to beat a woman?" He tried to wriggle away, but I held the spike to his throat. "Remove your shirt and give it to her. I will not have a women shamed in public."

"But—"

I brought the point across his cheek. "Do it!" Felix sat up and struggled out of his garment. Blood streamed from his face. My madness surged. I again menaced the soldiers. "Untie that woman and give her one of your shirts. Felix's is too soiled for my taste." They did my bidding. "Lift her into the wagon." They helped the sobbing woman onto the seat. I took my place beside her and drove off.

I held my tongue until calmness returned and my breathing slowed. "What is your name?" I asked.

"My name is not important. I am a degradada and most grateful for your kindness." She spoke with a heavy Castilian accent.

"What did you do to—?"

"*Washing!* I do people's washing."

She appeared a sturdy woman, with something familiar about her. I nodded to the pile of cuttings behind me, and said, "I'm a planter and can always use another pair of hands. Do you want to work at my farm?"

"Oh, yes. I have been here only a month and lost what little I had in the fire." She dried her tears on her sleeve. "I do not have a husband, and people have no washing now, only the clothes they wear." At the hospital I told her to sit in the back of the cart so I could talk with Isabel Horté. I found her waiting for me in the courtyard. Nuño was propped against a tree, looking worse than ever.

"My wife says you'll run the farm for share. Fifty percent's a Jew's bargain, but what choice do I have?"

"I have starts in my wagon for half your farm. I will find enough for—"

"I'll not have you using my wife!"

"I expect her to run your place until you can take over. I will supply most of the labor." His glare moved to Isabel when he realized I had not understood him.

"She won't tell me if those mountain niggers *used* her."

"Your slaves protected your wife, Nuño. I doubt if anyone touched her." Isabel stared blankly. "I'll prepare a contract and—"

"I got a better idea," he growled. With these words, Sra. Horté became distressed and cast her eyes to the heavens. Nuño continued. "That oldest daughter of mine is as pretty as any. She's fourteen. I keep two-thirds and you can have the girl."

"Your daughter's not a day over ten, Horté, and obviously your mind has cracked. Half or nothing. For all I care, the Crown can take your land back." As much as I disliked the man, seeing him in this disgrace was pitiful. And his injuries were frightful! For the first time in ages, my feet ached. Torture. Torture at the hands of fanatics just like him.

Isabel headed for the gate. "It's fifty percent," she said. I followed her.

At the cart I made introductions. The woman still did not give her name. I helped Sra. Horté—my new partner—into the seat next to me and we started for the farm. I explained the young woman's situation and asked Isabel to take her in. "You will need a helper. I'll have Kiman finish your house first."

She took a green stalk from the cuttings and chewed it. "That will be fine," she said, then after a few moments, "Nuño was never like this before we moved here. This place has made him crazy. That's how he got hurt the first time, in a fight with a slave. We were serfs back home, and this island was supposed to be a chance for us. Here we had a farm of our own. But no one told us about the fever sickness."

At my farm we'd planned a feast that afternoon to celebrate our good fortune at having cane starts. As we neared, the smell of food cooking filled our nostrils. My arrival with another wagon of cuttings and a new worker caught everyone's attention. When Kiman's wife heard of the woman's plight, she took her home and applied an unguent to her back. They returned a short while later and pitched in at the rooting beds to help pack the cane starts. I found it hard to believe that our new arrival could look so fresh after her ordeal in town.

I asked, "What gave Felix his excuse to beat you?"

She gave me a troubled look. "Nearly the same offense that got me labeled a degradada in Lisbon."

"Oh?" About then school let out. The children came shouting down the hill, Mazal with them. They crowded around, asking favors, curious about our new arrival. Jubiabá stood a distance away, arms crossed, wary. I presented my brood to the new woman. "This is Joseph and Lael, Michal and—"

Her eyes grew large. "Those are Old-Testament names. You're a Jew?"

I shrugged. "Supposedly a Novo Christão, but— Well, even the monkey is called—"

"I am called Ariella."

My turn to be surprised. "You are in good company."

She smiled. "My Hebrew's not very good."

I looked at her, confused.

"You spoke in Hebrew. I should tell you..."

I began to babble in my father's tongue—comprehending. What had happened? Everyone looked. I ran to my lean-to and found the letter from Miriam's father, broke the seal and eagerly read it. Sadly it contained not one word of Hebrew. I had not one thing to write with or upon, but burned wood was everywhere. On the back of the letter, with a crumbling slip of charcoal, I wrote the first words of the Torah, mouthing them as I wrote. The words sprang together in my mind—clear, the phrases deliciously familiar. I shouted them aloud. I looked down the hill to see people toiling as if nothing had happened. Everyone, I guessed, had grown accustomed to my odd manners. I clearly saw someone working next to Ariella, a man who wore a black coat and broad hat, Great-Grandfather Marcel. He spoke to her and they looked up at me. I waved in excitement. Marcel disappeared and Ariella stooped to her task.

I returned to the rooting beds. It had been so good to see Marcel and I knew, like always, that I and no one else had seen him, so I did not ask Ariella, but said, "You were going to tell me about da Tavora."

She again protested my use of Hebrew. "I am so poor with the language, Portuguese is difficult enough." Joseph chimed in to remind me he knew Hebrew. I was pleased he remembered. He'd not heard any since Miriam's death. Then it struck me, why had I not tried to speak the language with him, or Lael who knew a little, or any of the Novos? What brought it back? This involved Ariella somehow. And Marcel? I could not understand any of this. Miriam's words broke into my thoughts. Not Miriam, not Miriam—Ariella. What was happening? Here was the feeling I had lost so long ago when Miriam died, the transformation of my soul.

"... he used it as an excuse to beat me." Ariella had gone on for some time, and I had no idea what she'd said.

"I take it you're from Castile. How did you end up Lisbon?" Close to the subject it appeared, because she answered directly.

"My family and I fled Castile and crossed into Portugal at Vilar Formoso. There we found a immense camp of outcast Jews. The Portuguese stole everything from us before they let anyone go further."

I gestured to the girls. "Before they were shipped here, Michal and Louisa's family went through the same travail at Formoso. My departed wife and I adopted them after their parents died from the fever."

Ariella continued. "At the camp my parents and brother became ill, and since we had paid the entry tax, they insisted I go to Lisbon where they would join me. I, well all of us in the group who traveled there, expected to find a Jewish community. But the Jews of Lisbon had fled, leaving only old people. There was inquisition, not as harsh as Castile's, but I knew the Portuguese expected us to convert." Her face took on the sadness I'd seen earlier. I felt myself drawn to this woman and, though rendered speechless, I wanted to comfort her. "We were starving," she continued. "The authorities gave us menial jobs, cleaning privies, sweeping the streets. They took our men away, no one knew where. They forced some of the girls to whore for the soldiers. As for my parents and brother, I still know nothing of their whereabouts."

"I am sorry," I said. "But how did you end up a degradada?"

"I refused to whore, so I began doing laundry for the soldiers. What irony. My father made a comfortable living as a tailor, and our shop was well known for its elegant military uniforms. Then to end up in Lisbon washing filthy undergarments for soldiers. Well, after a while, an official in Lisbon came and told me I needed a license."

"Uh! They tax everyone that way."

"I had no money, so they assigned me a vereador. He was supposed to keep my fees until I had enough for the license. The vereador insisted I lie with him, then demanded a surcharge on the license when I would not. When that didn't work, he denounced me in public and had me shipped here."

When we finished packing the cane tops, everyone filthy from the work, we left for the Vascão to wash our clothes and bathe, the men in a nearby sidewater, the women downstream beyond a bend of trees. I wondered if they spied on us. I found pleasure that Ariella might be watching me. Then I thought of Jubiabá in the group of bathing women. What would she say to Ariella? With her shift off, Jubiabá's condition would surely be obvious.

Before going to the celebration at the tenant camp, I stopped at my lean-to. I hung my damp clothes in a tree and changed into the other set. I felt fortunate to have obtained a change of clothing at the garrison. Almost everyone else had only the clothes on their backs. I reread the letter from Miriam's father, full of hope and good cheer, about their life in Majorca, a peaceful life. There was scarcely a word about my parents, only that they left my mother and father in Porto Málaga six months ago, my parents alone with no word of my sister and waiting for a merchant to take them east. Miriam's father puzzled why he had not heard from her and assumed the letters had been lost in transit. He asked about his grandchild and wished us good health. I vowed to answer him the next day.

I struggled through the celebration, torn by my attraction to Ariella, thinking of the letter I'd write tomorrow, and wanting to talk with Jubiabá. I watched as some children ran up to Jubiabá and pulled at her shift. She straightened the fabric, for a moment the swell of her belly evident. With my insides full of knots, I walked over to Jubiabá. "Is it my child you carry?"

"Of course, Marcel. No other's."

"And what must I do? It is not my nature to ignore such things."

"You've done well so far."

"I apologize. I will ignore you no longer."

She gestured to Ariella. "Of course you will. You have a new interest. A Jewess who captures your attention."

"I don't know that. I just met her today."

"In half an evening you bedded me," she hissed.

I thought of the welcome she'd prepared three months ago, the delicious dinner, her eagerness to be with me, her caring for my children while I'd wandered the settlement. These women had a spell on me I found all too confusing, "What would you have me do?"

"You will do what you want, Saulo, that is the way of men. I expect your dusky child and I will tend house for you and your new wife."

"I don't know how you can—"

"It is written all over you, Saulo!" With a violent wave of her hand and stares from everyone, Jubiabá walked off.

Two events at the celebration that night did lighten my spirits. The first, eating spitted pork with Ariella and thoughts of Great-Grandfather Marcel comically aghast at the two of us. Why I thought this funny, I do not know. The second was to see Isabel Horté and her children enjoy the celebration. I guessed they had known little happiness in their lives.

In the morning I took Nawar's wagon back to him. On the return I stopped at the garrison to find materials to write my letter. The constable appeared glad to see me. Thoughts of attempting Hebrew with him crossed my mind, but I spoke only Portuguese, for I knew where I would speak my father's tongue that afternoon. The armory had been converted into a school and it overflowed with children, so I fled to a quiet spot under a tree to compose my letter—a painful task. When finished, I returned the quill and ink to the constable, and thanked him.

"Keep it," he said, and handed me a sheaf of papers. "Have more."

"This I will use. What can I do in return?"

"Nothing." He looked away and appeared thoughtful. "I misjudge you, Saulo. You fought bravely, better than any others. But now I have a complaint from Felix da Tavora. Yesterday you assaulted him. My soldiers bear witness."

"Da Tavora abuses his station. He insists on money and favors, especially from women. To see the violence he inflicted on that woman— Well, it appeared unjust." I wondered how far this might go. I had stopped paying da Tavora's extortion a month ago and assumed he'd found something better to do. I took a silver reis from my pouch. "Will this settle the matter?"

The constable fully understood the transaction. "He owes the surgeon fifty coppers for sewing his check, and then there are my soldiers—" He extended a thumb and forefinger. "Perhaps two."

I handed him two silvers and gestured with the paper. "Shall I write an apology?"

"No, Saulo. This will be quite enough."

My next stop was the cemetery and Miriam's grave. I walked by freshly mounded earth, the final resting place for citizens killed by the Angolars. For a while I sat quietly by Miriam's gravemarker and watched the priests and mourners go through their rituals. With great sadness I recited the husband's kaddish, then read Miriam her father's letter. Next I read aloud my letter to her parents.

"This is the most sorrowful letter I will ever write. Almost a year ago dear Miriam died of the bad-air fever, our first child dying within her, her love for you and for me on her lips. I sit by her grave and read her this letter, begging her forgiveness and yours for waiting so long to write you. My only excuse is that her passing left me desolate and unable to write. Miriam was the best wife any man could wish for, and I now grieve with you at her loss.

"I, we, are not without family. Miriam and I adopted four Tomé children of deceased Jewish parents, Joseph, now age 5, Lael 3, Louisa 5, and Michal nearly 8. ..."

My letter went on—hopeful for their prosperity in Majorca, asking questions about my parents, and telling of my life and farm. I wrote nothing of São Tomé's affinity with sorrow. Their daughter's death was sorrow enough. My sadness lightened by Ariella, though she and Miriam were not alike, yet Ariella had drawn Marcel back to me. All this Catholic talk about souls. Did Miriam and Ariella share a spirit?

"I have much news," I told Miriam in Hebrew. "And my ability to speak thus is part of it. When you and our son left us, I found myself no longer able to read or understand Hebrew. I prayed for Great-Grandfather Marcel, but he did not come. I cursed God and became a Catholic." I continued, telling her of the children, the Angolar war, disasters at the farm, and our recovery. "The Catholic saints have helped me through these times, yet I feel I'm still a Jew. Maybe I am both." I told her of Kiman, Nawar, and Horté, though did not tell her about burning my Torah and the house.

"I have made a free-African girl pregnant and don't know what to do." Could Miriam hear me? I suddenly hoped not. "And last, I've met this Jewish girl, Ariella, a degradada from Castile. She seems the reason I am able to speak my father's tongue again. I might someday care for her as much as I care for you, Miriam. So you see, leaving me here alone was a dangerous business."

A voice came from behind me, Bartolis and his girl-like squire. "I suspect that language is Hebrew. And what is it you say?"

I gestured to my wife's marker. "Hebrew indeed, Job 40"—the first answer that came to my mind. A terrible choice.

"A strange passage to pray at a grave. Have you rebuked God?" The squire crossed himself and knelt to pray.

"To assure the saints, Father, I have not rebuked God."

"And Hebrew?"

"In deference to the Church, I know the Latin Bible is the clergy's province. I thought it might be permitted in Hebrew."

He gave me a brittle smile. "I suspect you said something else, Saulo." He paused to survey the graveyard. "There are many souls here to tend, and we owe you a debt for your bravery against the Angolars. Say a confession on Sunday. I will let this pass."

I felt angry that he suspected my lie, but I responded cautiously. "Thank you Father Bartolis. That I will."

He blessed me and walked off, then stopped when he noticed his squire still knelt. The priest, without a word to the kneeling figure, strode back, grabbed the boy's vestment collar and jerked him to his feet. The child looked at me, his face shadowed in fear, hands clasped together tightly, knuckles white. This scene left me puzzled and upset. I wanted to say more to Miriam, but decided to wait, and whispered a quiet good-bye to her and our dead son. At a distance I followed Bartolis and the squire from the cemetery. The priest's arm encircled the child's shoulders, almost dragging the boy.

Before going home I stopped at the hospital, the current place for mail dispatch, and left my letter for Miriam's family. Though only a day had passed, I decided to visit Horté. I found him in the courtyard where two nuns were helping him use a crutch. The doctor sought me out and told me Horté could return home in a week. As usual, my neighbor remained wholly disagreeable. I left, determined that I would work only with Isabel to run his farm.

Arriving home in the early evening I found my lean-to swept and ordered, my clothes folded on my pallet. As I walked across the hilltop I met Jubiabá coming from the tenant camp. She carried a basket of food. "You were absent all day," she said, "so I brought you dinner." A pleasant change. Usually I took meals in common with the workers. "Is your home fittingly clean?" she asked.

"It is, thank you. Are the children fed?" They had been staying with Kiman's family until I could rebuild my house.

"Yes, I saw to it."

We sat on the hillside, saying little, the Vascão in the distance. We ate pork and yams from the day before, bananas, sugared onions, and drank black syrup beer. Jubiabá wore an intoxicating perfume. As darkness settled, she went inside the lean-to, removed her clothing, and bade me lay with her. I could not refuse.

In the morning Kiman and I went to the Horté farm. Despite my night with Jubiabá, my mind was a jumble of conflicting thoughts, including a crass eagerness to see Ariella. As loving as Jubiabá had been, how could I be so easily distracted?

Ariella was not at Horté's, having left early with the workers to prepare the fields. Isabel greeted me as she led her children around to do their chores. I noticed her ten-year-old daughter—how Nuño could have offered to sell me this child was beyond my understanding. I told Isabel of my visit to the hospital, that her husband could return home.

She gestured at their meager housing. "What am I to put him? He will be of no use to us."

"There are many maimed men who do a good day's work," I said. "He will in time."

"I will do the work, he can watch the children."

I explained that Kiman would start her house as soon as we got wood for the floor. "An African style," I told her, "easier to build and better than Portuguese houses in this climate." I nodded at her cart which stood in the yard. A lone horse grazed nearby. "I will arrange for your floor planks if you'll pick them up. You might as well pick up your husband too."

"How am I to pay for this house?" Her direct manner surprised me. I had intended to talk business, but not so quickly. The oldest girl brought cups of yerba buena. Isabel and I sat on a bench under a tree while Kiman looked over the ruins of her burned house. "I don't want the new one there," she called out and directed him across the clearing. "Use the high ground. Not so muddy when it rains."

"You probably won't need money for house-building or repairs," I said. "Governor Doria told me the Crown will pay for almost everything. He dispatched a caravel to Lisbon and expects a fleet of supplies and builders in return. Even what we do now will be repaid."

She seemed surprised. "I have never heard of such a thing."

"Our little sugar island is an asset to Portugal. The Crown is quite generous when they want to restore commerce." I discussed the need for slaves to work her farm, and we agreed on six families. "I will buy them and they'll be my tenants, paid with my fifty percent. I will furnish the labor, you provide everything else."

"Nuño won't like the tenant idea."

"I don't care what Nuño likes. The workers will live here and be in your employ. Yours, not his."

Across the clearing Kiman drove stakes to mark the house piers. Isabel considered my proposal as we watched him work. "It is more than fair, Saulo, the worker plan too, particularly if these new slaves turn out like yours."

We finished the details of our agreement as the sun neared midday. I kept looking across the fields in hopes I might see Ariella. "I'll write a contract," I said.

"Your word's good. Neither Nuño or I can read."

Her children were leaving for school at my farm. They carried fruit and yamcakes to eat while under the trees with Jubiabá. "Does your oldest girl read?"

204

"She does, thanks to that pregnant ninny of yours." Isabel gave me an indulgent smile.

I ignored her remark. "I'll write a contract anyway. Your daughter can read it to you." I helped Kiman finish and we took our leave.

Following our noon meal, we drove two carts through town to the slave port. In the chaos that followed the Angolar war, we had acquired three stray horses. Kiman and I drove two of these in hopes someone would spot and claim them.

One of the toughs that ran the slave port met us as we approached. The captaincy of the place had fallen to a gang of five degradados, all scum. Bones and sculls were scattered along the beach—the only vestige of the Angolar rebels. Bodies of more recent dead were stacked in open pits. Without regard to the ruin of our colony, the commerce of slavery went on. The place overflowed, slaves arriving, others prepared for shipment, a ship unloading, two waiting in the bay, all the enclosures full. Hundreds of slaves sat chained under the trees awaiting their fate. Except for the carcass of a dog which some men fought over, there appeared to be no food. Men worked the branding irons, the outcries and the smell. Never had the world witnessed such a loathsome scene.

I addressed the degradado. "We want ten families with—"

"Families? Most are split." He looked at me as if I had asked for the moon.

"I want ten families from those new ones. They're not split up yet. Healthy men and women, at least two children each, big enough to work."

He called several of his black workers over, explaining. They left to inspect the new arrivals. Kiman and I followed at a distance. "What do you think of this?" I asked him, recalling when I had first seen slaves chained on a caravel in the sea off Porto Novo.

Oh, Saulo, there been slavery always, but ..." He searched for the words.

205

"The size of this place?"

He nodded gravely. "The *big* size of this place."

The sorting took an hour. Finally we had nine families and a possible tenth, the last headed by a large, imperious man whom Kiman had chosen. "Why do you want him?" I asked, "he looks like an assassin." The man's back was scarred with recent whip marks, and the port workers used a prod to make him face us. He had a wild animal stare to his eyes. His wife and three children clung around him as we looked at each other.

"I know of his tribe," Kiman said. "Proud people. Work hard."

This man spoke Guinea, so I addressed him directly. "Kiman says he knows your tribe, and that you are hard workers."

"He knows nothing! No tribe. The people are fugitives in the jungle, starved and hiding from the slavers."

Since Kiman had already explained my tenant operation, I said, "All the more reason to work for me. Yes or no?"

"Why should I? A month ago I was a free man."

"A month from now you'll be skin and bones like the others. If you survive they will ship you north. There's ice in the winter and your family will be gone. Work for me and you'll be free again, your family with you." I pointed to the new people clustered around our carts, eating the food we had brought for them. "They no longer have chains; at my farm they will eat their fill."

His wife began to wail. "Shut up," he muttered. He looked me in the eye. "At Pinda the sailors took many girls, including our daughter, a pretty child, but feeble of mind. She knows only her family and cannot care for herself."

"If I find your daughter, will you take her back?"

His wife looked at him, pleading. "Yes," he said.

I took a blank slave invoice, wrote down the girl's name and description, then called a degradado over. "Someone took this man's daughter in Porto Pinda. He wants her back."

The degradado studied the paper; I doubted he could

read. "She's a whore now."

"You have a ship returning to Pinda?" He nodded. I took the invoice and penned a further note. "Give this to the captain. Tell him I am Nasic's agent."

The man's eyes widened. "Yes sir. You still wish to buy the Negro families?"

"I do, and I'll pay twice what that girl is worth when you find her."

"We'll have to use Portuguese coin in Pinda, sir, no cowries, bracelets or neck—"

"You will *get* coin. I've never paid slave specie. But what's the problem there?"

"Portuguese money is all they want these days. There is some kind of inflation. We've got mountains of coris beads, copper bracelets and cowries piled on the beach at Pinda. A month ago that's all the slavers wanted. Now we can't give the stuff away. They're melting down the bracelets for ship's plate."

Throughout the conversation Kiman had been translating my Portuguese for the African. At words about the daughter's possible recovery, his wife began to caterwaul. Again the husband silenced her. I asked his name. "Pongué," he told me.

"Work for me Pongué, yes or no?"

He held out his manacled arms. "Yes."

We settled, took the families home, the little children in our carts, the rest walking, their eyes wide when we passed through the burned-out town. With the promise of more food at my farm, I had no fear of runaways. I left them at my worker camp to bathe and eat. The six families for Horté's could move there when we had shelter for them. Before I left to tell Isabel about my purchase, Kiman drew me aside. "That man not name Pongué, that tribe name. His family last Pongué alive."

"The last? How is that?"

"His tribe believe if man taken slave, then no longer live. You offer give life back."

"All his tribe are slaves?"

"Many slaves, some dead. Slave hunters burn, steal crops. People starve. Go to slave place. Sell self, children for food. This man Pongué must now live for whole tribe."

I drove my cart to Isabel's where I found Ariella returned from her work, telling the children a story. She looked fresh and beautiful, and took note of my arrival, then continued with the children. When finished, she came over to greet me. I said, "It appears you're getting along well."

"Oh, yes. Isabel and I have become fast friends. If you don't mind eating with the children, would you stay? We have plenty." I could not help smiling at the sound of Ariella's Castilian lilt as it softened her Portuguese.

At dinner I wished to talk of personal matters with her, but with so much company, I spoke only of the farm, our new workers, the story of Pongué's family, and the scene at the slave port. I was surprised that neither woman showed much concern for Pongué or the plight of the slaves.

With our meal over, Ariella and I prepared to take a walk. Isabel, sounding like an old benot-levayah, directed us to a seat by the fire. "You two sit where I can keep an eye out for mischief." She waited until we settled, then left to tend the children.

At first I remained tongue-tied as I searched for something trivial to say. Then my mind became a jumble of thoughts, none likely to woo her. Did Ariella know about Jubiabá's pregnancy? I settled on telling her about Miriam, our four children, and the visit to my wife's grave.

"You still love her," she said.

"Yes, but life is fleeting. I miss a woman's company and want a son of my own." Jubiabá barged into my thoughts, my discomfort grew. I touched Ariella's hand. "I must go. My day will be long tomorrow." She gave a sulky smile which reminded me of Miriam.

Though it was pitch dark, the horse easily found his way to the tenant camp. I sought out Pongué and left him to care for the animal. This new man appeared already settled, eager to work. I took a pitch torch and walked up the hill to my lean-to. I found my clean clothes laying in the dirt while inside two pigs quarreled on my sleeping pallet over scraps of food. Jubiabá, I thought, and chased them out.

I confronted Jubiabá in the morning. Defiant, she did not offer an apology. "I made dinner for you last evening, but you prefer the company of that blue-eyed Portuguese." My new workers looked on with great interest. Though they did not understand the language, here they saw the amazing sight of a black girl berating the plantation master. I walked away. I wanted no more confrontation.

Kiman and his wife watched with amusement. The wife finally took Jubiabá's arm. "Come, dear niece, morning chores await us." Jubiabá, with an insinuating smile, pulled the fabric of her shift tight across her belly. The two women strode off.

At any moment I expected Ariella and the others to show up for work. Not wishing further conflict, I sent Kiman with some men to the Horté farm. "Start the houses," I told him, "and have Horté's workers stay there to help. I'll run the crew here." He gave me a knowing nod.

The arrangement worked. We built planter houses at Horté's and on my farm, worker houses, and we flooded some fields from the Vascão. Within a week we had the wet fields cleared and planted, house piers up, floors laid, walls staked, and roof thatch started. A letter came from Governor Doria with a list of settlement projects he wanted me to supervise. Although the relief fleet from Portugal was probably six weeks out, our mills produced enough lumber and mud bricks to keep our rebuilding going.

With each day's passing Jubiabá seemed less sullen. I began to hope I might spend another night with her, a thought I could not contain. One morning, as I bound thatch to the roof of Kiman's house while Jubiabá handed the bundles up to me, we spotted Ariella hurrying our way. Jubiabá gave me a sour look, then turned with a smile to Ariella.

"Saulo," said Ariella, "there's trouble. Nuño's back and

Isabel needs you." I climbed down, wondering what the women might be thinking. I glanced back at Jubiabá as we hastened away. She gave me a look that would have driven Satan from hell.

Ariella ran ahead and urged me to follow. My grim mood told me not to hurry, not for Sr. Horté or anyone. A quite unexpected scene greeted me at the farm. Nuño—master of his plantation—lay in the yard like a discarded carcass, screaming in rage, his one arm shielding the sun from his eyes, his crutch out of reach. Ariella and Isabel stood looking down at him. The moment I appeared he directed his anger at me. "You have profaned my farm, my family, my life!"

"I saved your life."

"For what? For this? A nigger house, tenants instead of slaves?" He groped for his crutch, then flapped his hand at Ariella. "A Jew-degradada in my home?"

I picked up the crutch and poked him. "We will help you walk." When he said nothing, I grabbed his foot and gestured to the women. "Let's pull him into the shade." The women took his arm.

Nuño began to struggle. "Does your Jew-woman know you got that black Jezebel pregnant?"

Ariella dropped her hold. She looked at me and Isabel as it we'd hit her. Isabel stared down at her husband. "He heard it elsewhere. I've told him nothing."

"You have both deceived me," cried Ariella. Her shoulders slumped, and she backed away.

Isabel and I dragged Nuño under a tree while we watched Ariella. She went to one of the other houses and began to work there. "I am guilty of the worst perfidy," I said, "and I've broken her heart."

Isabel looked glum. "What did you expect? Go on home. I'll do what I can."

I found Kiman and told him the story. He shrugged and smiled. "Ah, Saulo," he said.

"Finish the houses and keep working the fields," I told him. He nodded. "You want to make Pongué the foreman at

Horté's?" The man had shown himself to be an able worker. "Move him over there?"

He nodded again. "Where you go?"

"I've Doria's projects to look after. I need to get started."

"Ah, Saulo."

"None of this is funny," I said, but Kiman's smile remained. "Tell Pongué to take directions only from Isabel, and caution him not to kill Nuño." He bowed in mock ceremony, then helped me hitch a wagon with one of our stray horses. Leading the horse, I trudged up the hill to my new house.

As I put the things I needed for town into the cart, my children showed up, the four eager to show me their new pet—another gray monkey, a female that scampered behind them with Mazal. "My Mazal has a darling," said Joseph proudly.

"Jubiabá told us they will soon have babies," added Louisa.

Good for her, I thought. "Then you will all have monkey pets." The children jumped and giggled. "Now go and eat. You have school soon."

Chapter 15

I bade the children good-bye and drove the cart into
town where I saw much construction progress. The church
stood ready for roof timbers, with the rectory not far
behind. I was amused to see priests living in the Jew-yard
while nuns occupied the nearly completed rectory. The
church bell hung in the town square from a makeshift
tripod. The bricks in use were of my style—pleasing, yet
sadly remindful of Leah. Father Bartolis and the sugar-mill
mason stood at the rear of the church directing construction on the back wall. I spread my hands. "All we need are
benches and we can have Mass."

Bartolis mirrored my tone. "If you wish, Saulo, we'll
celebrate a Mass just for you." Disturbed by our jest, the
mason crossed himself.

"Thank you, Father. Governor Doria asked me to oversee
the construction here, but I see the mason is ably in charge.
It appears I can move on." The mason remained solemn
until I said to Bartolis, "I've learned much from this skilled
gentlemen. You may trust him with any project."

The priest gave me a curious look. "I expect your farm,
and that of our brother Horté's, is prospering?" Perhaps an
idle question, but the man's manner made me uncomfort-
able.

"Yes," I answered, "though half of our fields are still rock
hard." I left quickly, happy to be away from these puffed-up
Catholics, yet feeling that something remained unresolved.
Next I stopped at the public bath and walked through the
ruins, gratified to see the pool and water channels had not

been damaged. One of the women who ran the bath approached. She wore scant clothing, her generous figure visible beneath her garment. I found myself enticed by her flirting.

"Greetings, Master Saulo. I hope we'll be open soon so you'll visit. Or if you care to stay now…"

Tempting—an easy solution compared to the difficult women at home. For some reason I thought of Pongué's daughter and my desire left me. "The church and rectory will be finished in a week," I told the woman. "The bath is next."

I drove the cart to Nawar's farm, thinking it a welcome place to spend the evening. I'd not been there in a few weeks and was astounded when I entered his gate. Sprawled between his home and the nearest field stood a city of slave huts, mostly lean-tos and a few roughboard hovels. I quit my count at fifty, about half of what I saw. Yasemina hailed me as I drove up, and explained that Nawar would be home soon from the fields. A group of white and mixed-blood children sat in the shade and recited lessons with one of her daughters.

I gestured to the huts. "What is this, Yasemina? Looks like you have quarters for two hundred slaves?"

"Yes, and they'll be back this evening, cooking, complaining, their ninnies running everywhere."

"A boon for planting. How did you get so many?"

"A Crown loan." She cast her eyes downward. "I thought you knew?"

"Knew what?"

"Bad story, Saulo. Go care for your horse. I must wait for husband to tell you."

I watered and staked my horse, wondering at all the slaves, then brought my things into the house and chatted about trifles with Yasemina. Seeing Nawar in the distance, I walked out to greet him. He urged his horse forward, dismounted, and embraced me. "Good to see you, Saulo."

"And you too, friend Nawar. Yasemina won't tell me the story behind your city here."

"You've not heard that Doria's made good his reparations promise?"

"I thought that was in the future, with the relief fleet."

"Yes, but in the meantime he's allowed us unlimited use of workers from the slave port, and at no cost. The Crown plantation has over five-hundred. We've got most of the burned fields irrigated and ready to plant. Now we're clearing as much new ground as we can."

"Isabel and I could certainly use a few hundred. We've less than thirty between us."

"Ah, Saulo."

"That's the third time I've heard that today. I'm sick of it. What's going on?"

"I heard Doria warned you, Marcel. Your worker scheme is crosswise with island policy. No reparations for you and your—"

"But *you* have tenants."

"Only three plantation foremen, and then with Crown permission. Not all my workers as you've done."

I threw up my hands in frustration. "Doria did warn me. But with the war chaos I thought no one would notice."

He put an arm round my shoulder and led me toward the house. "You misjudge the governor and his spies. And now you've extended your affront to Horté's."

"What must I do?"

"Yasemina has made a delicious beer of yams, black syrup, and ginger. Let us drink before dinner and contemplate the fate of rebels like you. Perhaps you owe our esteemed governor a visit."

Except for the many ants that floated in the beer, it was excellent. We relaxed on his steps, spit ants, and watched slaves, driven by armed overseers, troop back from the fields. I recognized a few of the guards, some the vilest degradados. "How can you sleep at night?"

"I sleep fine. The guards are also supplied by the governor."

"I'm referring to the guards." He appeared unimpressed. "Do not think lightly of this," I said. "There is a criminal faction who kept their weapons after the war. Sooner or later they will threaten us." One of Nawar's foremen came to report. I stood to greet the man, an acquaintance from town, a displaced sugar merchant whose warehouse had burned in the war. When the man left, I turned to Nawar who obviously did not share my concerns, his current interests only with his farm and the plantations. "What happens to all the slaves when planting is finished?"

"I hope to keep the best of them. About half. The rest will go back, shipped north, I suspect. Doria has promised a free slave for every three acres we open up."

I found this prospect depressing, and wondered how my farm could compete. Across the flat fires began to smoke. "At least they have food," I said. "Not like a month ago."

Nawar plucked an ant off his tongue and examined it, asking, "If God gave us Dominion, why are there ants in my beer? And why can't we keep them from our sugar?"

"I believe God instructs us through imperfections, some small, some immense." I spit an ant into my hand and poked it around my palm. "If you set this alongside the death of Miriam last year, or those in your family, or the sea of enslaved humanity out there, the ants have no significance. Yet we have as little control over them as we do over plague or the cruelties that men do."

Nawar looked thoughtful and flicked the ant away. "So tell me, Saulo, how are these imperfections supposed to instruct us?"

"I'm not sure," I answered. "Perhaps they encourage wisdom." Then added, *"Slowly* encourage wisdom."

At dinner we drank great quantities of beer and my tongue loosened, opening a subject I'd wished to avoid. Nawar said, "Here's a chance to use some of your accumulated wisdom. Even the most devout Moslems and Christians acknowledge their bastard children. You cannot ignore Jubiabá's."

"That doesn't mean I have to marry her. Maybe I'll take up with one of the bath women."

Yasemina gave me a level stare. "You show concern for

slaves, but won't marry Jubiabá who carries your child—a free black, the most beautiful girl on São Tomé." Nawar looked smug, and Yasemina's swelling pregnancy reminded me that Jubiabá was nearly as far along.

"You know what's wrong with this island?" I fumed. "It corrupts civilized conduct. In my homeland, no Christian, Moslem, Jew or *heathen woman* would talk like that. As for the insolence of the women on my farm—"

"My wife speaks the truth," said Nawar, and turned to Yasemina. "But our friend Saulo deserves understanding. This Ariella is someone to replace Miriam."

"No, you people *do not* understand! Besides being born into it, one may *elect* to become a Moslem or Catholic, or forced into conversion, but no one *chooses* to be a Jew. We are *born* as Jews—no other way."

"If Jubiabá's child is a son," asked Yasemina, "is he a Jew?"

Speechless, I staggered off to bed, thankful for the tolerance of these friends. Surely I had insulted them, yet they did not chastise me.

Next morning, just as I left the Nawar home—my head still spinning with Yasemina's question and aching from drink—I came across the degradado from the slave port driving a cart with Pongué and a girl in the back. The man stopped in front of me and said, "They told me I'd find you here. I got that girl."

Pongué climbed down. "My daughter from Pinda. She's hurt. This man won't let me have her until you pay."

"What's the problem?" I asked the degradado. "You know I'm good for the money."

"The girl's got a broke arm and she's sick. If she dies— I don't get money for a dead ninny."

I looked at the girl. She sat there drooling, confused, her arm hugely swollen and covered with sores. I glared at the slaver. "Did you break her arm?"

"No, she come that way. She's an imbecile; no one told us."

"You read my note to the captain."

The degradado looked at me blankly. "I forgot."

I touched my purse and asked, "How much?" It was fortunate that Pongué did not understand Portuguese. At this moment he might have killed the man.

"The captain told me she cost nothing. Them whores was happy to —"

"How much for finding her, her passage, your trouble?"

He hesitated and eyed the purse on my belt, then produced a slave invoice. He knew he'd hang if he cheated me. He shoved the paper my way. I told Pongué to put the girl in my wagon. The invoice showed fifty reis for shipment and no other costs. "Fifty is fair," I said, knowing that bribes and so-forth had cost him more than that. "Is your boss going to stand the other costs?" The man nodded and looked disappointed. I gave him a silver and fifty coppers. "You lived up to your part, here's a hundred more. I better not find out you hurt her." He flicked the reins at his horse and left quickly.

I climbed onto my seat and looked back at Pongué. He stroked the girl's face as she lay there, talking softly to her numb eyes. I started for town. "We'll see what they can do at the hospital," I said, but felt sick at heart and fearful of what awaited us.

Once there I sought out a doctor I knew. He looked at Pongué and the girl, then shook his head. "We don't treat slaves."

"They're not slaves. They're my tenants."

"This is a Crown hospital. The governor and the Growers' Association have their rules." He looked more closely at the girl. "You know the policy, Saulo. Officially there are no tenants on Tomé, only free whites and blacks, degradados, freed blacks and slaves. The hospital is not for slaves anymore than it's for pigs or goats."

Pongué looked on murderously, not understanding everything, but likely enough. I pleaded with the doctor. "She looks terrible. You can't ignore her; these are my workers. This man is her father and foreman at Horté's. What am I to do?"

"Take her home. The slave women will care for her." He crossed himself. "An idiot girl— No use anyway, she's going to die. Likely a blessing."

I drove Pongué and his daughter to the Horté farm where his wife—raving loudly as always—and the other women took the girl. Pongué gave me a veiled look. "Thank you Master Saulo."

I shook my head. "I wish there was more I could do."

When I got back to my farm, Joseph ran up. "Papa, Papa, Mazal gone. Gone to forest with darling. Have baby."

"He'll come back like he did before." Joseph, remembering, nodded agreeably. He did not whine as I would have expected with such news. His conduct gave me an idea. "Do you want to go with Papa for a few days?"

"Oh yes, yes!"

"I'll get your things from the house. Go find Jubiabá or someone and tell them."

So we set off for Doria's. Joseph sat next to me, proud as a rooster, chattering without stop. I answered him in Hebrew, and soon we were both speaking it. He demanded a Hebrew name for everything we saw, then repeated the words to himself, smiling to me when he thought he had it right. Here we were, my son and I. As a child, had I chattered like this when I rode with my father and Diaz into the Christian sector to deliver bricks? I did remember how pleased I'd been to go along, though feeling a little fear from the strange surroundings. Did my father or his father ever ride like this with Great-Grandfather Marcel? I pictured the old man sitting next to us amused and approving.

On the road to Doria's we saw several farms that swarmed with slaves. I stopped at each, finding only one mill construction in need of help. "I'll return after Doria's," I told the owner, and continued on.

Doria's retinue was camped in makeshift dwellings and tents, the governor living in what remained of de Caminha's chapel. I found him at work among the slaves as they set piers for his new house. There were many white women and children about, and I wondered which belonged to him. A cluster of children in school sat under the shade trees. "Go sit with them," I told Joseph. "I'll come for you when I finish."

With Joseph gone, I looked around, seething with anger at all the slaves I saw and my experience at the hospital with Pongué's daughter. Before I could rehearse my complaints, Doria hailed me. "Saulo, how are my settlement projects coming along?"

Though furious, I calmly told him of my visit to the church and rectory. "I plan to tour farms in the next days," I added, and gestured to his house. "Everyone's building the African style now."

"They're most handy, and the slaves know how to build them. I've not been here in the rainy season, but I understand that rats are a real problem then. Raised structures really keep them out?"

"The infestation hit the isle a few years ago." So did we, I thought. My vexation suddenly boiled over and I hopped from one foot to the other, trampling imaginary rats underfoot. "Rats, rats, Portuguese vermin! Just like home! Rats!"

Doria backed away. He thought me possessed, which at the moment I was. "What's wrong with you? I'll call the priests."

I began to shout. "Call whom you like! Call someone to explain why the hospital won't treat my workers. Why everyone has reparation slaves but me. I too have a crop to plant!"

The slaves stopped to stare; so did the women and children. Squires ran up and put themselves between me and the governor. "He's mad," Doria said.

"I may be mad. Who wouldn't after the way I've been treated?"

He looked at me closely. "Tell me the devil hasn't taken you?"

"Only anger takes me, governor. Anger at being so mistreated. After I've served you as Crown Mason and in war, I—"

"It is *only* because of that service I have not jailed you. Maintain a civil tongue, Saulo, or you will know my wrath." He bade all his men leave except one. "You defied my policy against making slaves tenants, my direct request to you. At the very minimum I will withhold the Crown's generosity."

"But sir, I feel it is wrong to enslave people."

"This is outrage! You are the only person in the world who thus believes. Now you encroach on your neighbor Horté and install tenants there. Your choice is to reverse your inflammatory tenant program or do without Crown help."

"For my construction overseeing, will I be paid for that?" With an ever-diminishing purse, I needed money. I still owed the lumber mill, and soon would have to borrow from Nawar.

He tapped his foot. "I don't know."

"Reparations for my lost crops?"

"Now we have something to bargain over, don't we?" From the corner of my eye I saw Joseph. He'd scrambled onto the wagonseat and sat there watching. My anger lessened and Doria took note of Joseph. "Who is this young fellow?"

"My son Joseph Saulo," I said, seeing Miriam in his eyes.

"He looks a fine lad." He called to Joseph, "Come down boy, we'll have a closer look at you." Joseph hesitated; I motioned it was all right. He got down and walked over, bowing with great dignity. "And manners, too," commented Doria, "quite unlike his father." Joseph beamed. "What does your father do when you disobey?" Joseph stuck out his lower lip and slapped his behind. Doria laughed. "And what should *I* do when your father disobeys *me?*" Joseph trotted over and made a motion as if to hit me.

I picked up my son, setting him back in the wagon. "He'll make a good governor someday." I put my foot on the hub and started to climb in.

"Where are you going?" asked Doria.

"To Gustavo Barreto's. His new mill is about to fall

down."

He shielded his eyes and looked at the sun. "Go tomorrow. Stay here this evening. Perhaps we can settle our differences." He pointed toward the cooking area near the chapel. "See that big pot? It's full of lobsters, caught just today. Tonight we'll have a feast."

That evening we held our feast of lobsters, yams, honey, roasted bananas, and gallons of beer—so much beer that I felt I could reason with Doria. Drunk as he was, the governor refused to discuss anything of substance. I drank little, remembering my aching head from the morning. Studying his retinue and the women and children, I reckoned the families belonged to his squires and none to him. A black woman served us, and Doria remained gracious to her— perhaps his mistress, but she was obviously a slave.

Joseph enjoyed his food and the jollity and, after two cups of beer, soon ran around with the rest of the drunk children. Later Doria directed us to sleep in a vacant hut, but we soon found ourselves kept awake by babies crying and ants in our bedding. After an hour's struggle, we shook out our sleeping covers and moved to the back of my wagon where we lit camphor wicks to keep the flying pests away. My son smiled at the sky as if he understood its mystery. There we slept, a blanket of stars overhead while smoke from the wicks curled into the blackness.

Next morning I woke early and roused Joseph. The two of us ate a first meal of bananas and yam cakes bought from a slave family. With no one awake except the slaves, and no construction that needed my attention at Doria's, we hitched the horse and headed to Gustavo Barreto's. With the horse's first step, the issue of Crown payments continued to rankle me. I reined the animal, found my quill and ink, and wrote two invoices, one for the month I planned to spend on settlement projects, and the other for my farm losses. I pinned them to the chapel entrance and Joseph and I continued on.

Gustavo emerged from his doorway just as the sun peeked through the trees, illuminating his new home. He and his slaves obviously knew how to build a house, but understood little about laying a mill foundation. "Greetings, Saulo and son Joseph, come join us for morning repast."

We drank yerba buena and nibbled on sweet maize bread while his wife busied herself with cooking. His children were curious about Joseph. I gestured to his oldest child, a girl about nine. "We'll have to work most of the day on your mill. Can your daughter look after Joseph?"

"Certainly," Barreto replied. "They school at Doria's. He can go with her."

Joseph, who'd already made friends there yesterday, said it would be fine. After breakfast we went to the mill. According to my instructions from yesterday, his men had dug up most of the foundation and removed the bricks. The workers finished while Barreto and I walked the Riberio Negro looking for gravel to line his foundation. We found a bed of black pebbles just below the watercourse where his mill sat.

"This will do fine," I told him. We had his slaves scrape mounds of pebbles from the stream and wheelbarrow them to the mill site. Using a notched stick I called a slope level, I showed Barreto and his foreman how to dig the trench so it would project a respectable wall. His wife brought a cart with midday supper and, after eating, we dumped gravel into the trenches, leveling the fill with a grooved-plank water level. Next I showed them how to place the first bricks, drive tie stakes, and set plumb lines to ensure a straight wall.

Barreto produced a large flagon of beer from his wife's cart. We drank, watching his foreman and slaves build the next section of foundation. "What do you think of this weather?" he asked, casting his eyes to the trees above us. A breeze from the east ruffled the leaves. Our weather had been cool, unusually mild.

I tracked his gaze. "One needs a west wind before we get rain. It'll be late this year, perhaps a month."

He nodded in agreement and made a cross. "God makes

the weather. Perhaps he's forgotten our little island."

I finally broached the question which I'd been wanting to ask all day. "What reparations did you get?"

"A note signed by the governor, a surety paid when the fleet arrives, quite generous, more than my crop and house were worth." He took a swig of beer and handed me the flagon. "I hear the governor's withheld your payments. How's that set with old Horté?"

"Nuño's furious at my worker policy. He doesn't yet know about the reparations or extra slaves." I took a drink. "Isabel is in charge of the place, and Nuño's finished. I don't care what he thinks." I passed back the flagon. "Do you believe my policies undermine the island's slavery?"

He grew thoughtful. "You've done me a great service today and I do not wish to insult you."

"Well you're an odd bird, Barreto. No one else minds. Speak what you will, I'll not be insulted."

He squinted at the sun. "In a word, Saulo, 'yes.'" He stood and yelled to his men. "Finish up, that's all for today."

We drove his cart back to the farm house. On the way he said, "Stay for dinner, rest this evening. We have sea turtle and mangos, surely more maize bread, honey and beer."

Well, I thought, lobster last evening, now sea turtle, an abomination trip in many ways. But it certainly wasn't when I saw Joseph, who talked so much about his day that I told him to wait until later. Afterwards, as he and I rested in the back of the wagon, we revisited the sky. "Those stars guided our ship here almost four years ago, Joseph. Somewhere behind us is the North Star." I tried to point it out, but could not find it. "And south, right over my foot"—I traced its outline with my toe—"is God's Cross."

"What are stars, Papa?"

"Perhaps little windows into heaven, the light of God to challenge our musings."

"I've seen falling stars, what are they?"

"Maybe the wingbeats of Gabriel. Nawar's a Moslem; they believe Mohammed flew to heaven with Gabriel and met the angels. There he knelt in the presence of God."

Joseph stared a long time. "Do we believe that, Papa?"

"No, but I do not deny its possibility."

He turned to look at me, his face a dark outline. "Did Mama follow the stars here too?"

"Yes, in a different ship. Before I got here."

"Is Mama in the stars now?"

"Yes, Joseph, oh yes. She is the brightest star we see each night. The one right there."

"I wish I could talk to her."

"But you can, dear son. She will answer you in your dreams."

I listened as he talked, held his foot aloft, and touched the bright star with his toe. "... and we miss you, Mama. Papa told me to look behind the brightest star for you. Can you see me? That's my foot. I'm a good boy, and we're having a fine time. Today I went to school at the governor's. Yesterday Papa did a funny dance and showed Senhor Doria how to kill rats. When we're in the wagon and no one can hear us we speak Hebrew." As he continued, I understood fully for the first time that Joseph believed that I was his father. I fell asleep, the promise in my heart that he would never know otherwise.

Over the next weeks we worked our way across Tomé's north end, each day nearly the same, improving sugar and sawmill construction, home building and irrigation works. We usually supped with the farmer and slept the night in our wagon. The Crown plantation east of the slave port required five days of my time, as they had many projects needing attention. We settled in, bedding with the foreman's family in his African house.

The house brought back angry memories. Here the previous foreman had raped Miriam, this current structure built over the ruins of the last. That foreman had died from the bad-air fever a month or so after returning Lael. At the time I felt pleasure at his death, and vowed, as it is now for Joseph, that I would be the only father Lael would ever know. But what *did* Lael know? So young when the foreman took him, and for such a short time—hopefully he would never remember. I recalled I still owed Nawar for ransoming Lael.

Nawar was overseer at this plantation as well as others. He showed up one day to review the construction work, and carried with him news brought by slavers from Elmina, news that now swept the colony. "King João is dead," he told us that morning. "Our new regent is Manuel I, a cousin of João's. His officials will arrive with the relief fleet." I couldn't understand all the fuss—one tyrant replacing another. Nawar and I took our construction tour. "I understand Joseph is with you," he said.

"He's having a grand time and likes the school here so much he wants to stay."

"If he only knew what happened in this place, or remembered." Nawar smiled, reflecting back. "You've come a long way, Saulo. I am proud of you."

"I could not have done it without you and Kiman. And by the way, I still owe you for Lael's ransom."

"In that matter there is no debt. It is my gift."

"That's not—"

"Saulo, do you know why I'm really here?"

"Since you ask that way, obviously not."

"The governor says you left a bill for a month's work. He wanted me to look in on you."

"And?"

"As you do with most everybody, Marcel, you've bound him up. He doesn't know what to do. You're working even though he may not pay you."

"The governor has his job, I have mine. If a mill falls down, they blame me, paid or not. You can tell him that." I lifted my hands in frustration. "If he doesn't pay, may I borrow from you on next year's harvest?"

"Yes, Saulo. My purse is yours for the asking."

That evening Joseph said, "Can we sleep in the wagon, Papa? I like the stars." With no threat of rain, I agreed. He picked the brightest star and began his talk to Miriam. "Today I went to school at Senhor Nawar's plantation,

Mama. I like my teacher, but not nearly as much as Senhorita Jubiabá who I really like. She is very pretty and all the boys are in love with her. But I think she has a husband because she's going to have a baby." While my son continued his scandalous story, I whispered a prayer and begged Miriam for understanding. When Joseph grew quiet, I began to tell him about Joseph from Genesis. He stopped me. "Papa, *I know* about Joseph. Jubiabá told us in school."

"All right, young man, you tell me." And so he did, in an excited mixture of Portuguese, Hebrew, and Guinea, carried away by the adventure, adding scenes known only to him. When he finished I said, "Some story, Joseph. Is that the same one Jubiabá told?"

He rolled in his blanket and looked at me. "I couldn't remember, so I made things up."

"Genesis is sacred text, Joseph. You choose to embellish the Word of God?"

He thought for some time. "I don't know, Papa. But why did his brothers throw him into a pit and sell him to the Pharaoh?"

"Because they were jealous. What did Jubiabá tell you?"

"She scolded me. I'm not supposed to ask questions about the Bible." Again he turned thoughtful. "Do you think Lael will sell me?"

"No, Joseph, you are not for sale."

He giggled. "So Papa, why did the Pharaoha want Joseph for her husband when she already had one?"

"Pfsss! How did Jubiabá answer that one?"

"She got angry when I asked it."

"Maybe she didn't know the answer. God understands everything, Joseph, but He gives us much to puzzle over. It is His way of teaching us."

And so went our nights, Joseph's wild Scripture stories and my tales of Miriam and his grandparents—those in Majorca, and mine God-knows-where, of Aunt Leah, of Lisbon and the sea and my journey here, and of Golem, Germo, and Fr. Norte. It became evident that Jubiabá and her sister had often told Bible stories about my family names, Lael, Michal, Louisa and, "Even King Saul," said Joseph. "I think Jubiabá loves you, Papa."

Chapter 16

When we left the plantation, I drove the horse along the route of my Angolar battles. At locations where my comrades fell I got down from the wagon and prayed. What a terrible place for men to die. I looked up at my son on the wagonseat. Would he someday pray for me? He seemed indifferent to my prayers, wanting only to see the slave port. But as we approached, it appeared busier than ever, so I decided to go around. Anchored offshore—tended by lighters, its draft too great for the harbor—was a three-masted caravel, the first I'd ever seen. I turned the horse toward the beach. From the distance we watched the back-and-forth activity, slaves and supplies ferried to the vessel. Joseph and I imagined the ship running sails full in a vast sea.

In the next days we continued south along the island's west shore, new territory for me, having always gone to Alegre on the island's east side. The green mountain loomed above us; thin plumes of smoke rose from its flanks. Angolar camps no doubt.

Near Rio da Névoa we came to the farm of a Novo planter, a Lisbon Jew who had been on my ship. He and I talked of old times. I found him to be a competent builder with no need of my help, but the day had grown late, so Joseph and I decided to stay with his interesting family in the comfort of his restored home. His wife, also a Jew—his third, the first two having died of fever—grew up in Setúbal, and had arrived a year ago. At dinner she described her journey from Lisbon. "They told us we were the last Portuguese Jews for São Tomé. Everyone else has fled the Inquisition or been expelled."

"Where is your family?"

Her look told me I should not have asked. Nevertheless she continued. "I have received only one letter. My father is in Burgundy where the Black Death kills nearly everyone, including my mother. My sister and two brothers died on their way through Castile. My father says the Inquisition is closing in on him. I'm the only one safe."

"I often ask myself if we're better off on this island." I noticed all the children had left to play except Joseph and an older boy who sat listening.

"We're better off left alone," the husband answered, "but that will never happen." He looked at his son. "Go outside with your new friend, we have private matters to discuss." The wife began to clear the table. "Marcel, have you heard the complaints against you from the Growers' Association? You're in hostile territory here. The Association has strong supporters on this side of the island."

"What now?" I said, weary of Association gossip.

"They'll deny you privileges if you don't abandon your worker policy."

"Let them, I don't care."

"You will care. They—well, all of us—have the governor's ear. Things are about to change." He continued, reciting agreements between the Association and Doria, "Free warehousing, collective harvest labor, Crown-guaranteed sugar payments, first rights to new land ..." The list went on.

"I've heard none of this."

"I heard it just two days ago from the manager at the d'Ouro plantation south of here. You said you're going there. You'll meet him. He and Doria are close friends."

His wife brought the yerba pot and sat with us. From a skin pouch she slipped a handful of silver and copper coins onto the table. "Have you seen the new money?" the man asked, separating some coins. The coins were Portuguese, but quite unlike any I'd seen before, with a cross on one side and a head relief on the other. "These are silver cruzados," said the farmer, "four times the value of a silver reis. Same proportion for the coppers."

In the candlelight I studied a coin with its stern faces. "Is this King Manuel and...?"

"Yes. Manuel and Queen Isabel."

"Isabel?"

"Yes, the daughter of Isabella of Castile."

"Quite a catch for even a Portuguese king."

"Laced together in a devil's bargain," said the wife. "Manuel secured Isabel's hand with his pledge to expel or convert all Jews and Moors. Thus the Inquisition."

"One man's king is another's oppressor," I said. "I've come to expect only the worst from these damned Christians." I spun a coin on the table. "Where did you get these?"

"From a slaver. Money back for a Negro girl who died. He told me this is the only specie they will accept in Pinda. Everywhere Crown pursers are exchanging cruzados for reis. I expect they will arrive here with the relief fleet." His wife dropped the coins back into the pouch. "How would you like to get an advantage of twenty percent when you exchange your reis?"

"What advantage? If Doria doesn't pay me, I'll have naught to exchange."

"As a member of the Association, you'll get an extra twenty percent from the pursers. Doria has agreed to it."

More bad news—they would squeeze me from all sides. We walked to the porch and called into the dark for the children. South of us dim fires glowed on the mountainside. "Angolars?" I asked.

"Yes. They're raiding in Alegre. I expect they'll strike here one of these days. Everyone calls it 'The Forest War.'"

"Are you worried?"

"Not yet. They'll trouble the farms below here first. So far they've stolen only ninny women and children. Everyone speculates the Angolars believe we won't bother them if they steal only blacks."

Joseph and the other children emerged from the night. They helped move the wagon closer to the house. As we prepared our bed, Joseph asked, "Papa, the kids told me we ate gray monkey for dinner. You don't think it was Mazal?"

"No, my son. Your pet is safe on the other side of the island with his new wife." With this assurance, Joseph went right to sleep. A slim moon hung in the night sky, and I gazed at the heavens, whispering a prayer to Miriam as many thoughts crowded into my mind: Ariella, Jubiabá, Association threats, my financial travail, the Forest War. Since I did not share my friend's lack of concern about the Angolars, I resolved to borrow a weapon from him in the morning. On this trip I would not venture beyond the big plantation at Rio d'Ouro, but take Joseph back to my farm and go to Alegre from there. At last I fell asleep, Angolar battles raging in my dreams.

After our breakfast, Joseph and I prepared to leave, a basket of food from our hosts setting behind us. The farmer also provided me a crossbow, a half-dozen bolts, and a light pike. I set the crossbow on the seat between us. "Thank you," I said, feeling comfort from the weapons.

"Safe journey," he offered. "I hope you don't have to use them."

We drove the horse south, passing two farms which I planned to visit on my return. Joseph wanted to hold the crossbow, so I and finally let him, warning, "You must hold it carefully; it is wound up and ready to shoot."

He hefted the heavy weapon. He breathed, "Wupp, wupp," taking aim at this tree and that.

I looked toward the green mountain where wisps of clouds tore across the highest spire and spilled toward Africa. I pointed. "That's a sign, son. The weather is about to change. Our rainy season might arrive after all."

Atop a grassy headland, the broad Atlantic before us, we paused for noon supper. I wondered about the navigator Columbus and the new lands to the west. Everyone these days talked of his discoveries, great isles of gold and treasure, strange fruits and animals, mermaids, outlandish

231

natives who go without clothes, of women warriors—the Caribs—who husband and eat human flesh and fight savagely alongside their men.

"Look, Papa," cried Joseph, "there's the three-master." Rounding the point from the north ran the magnificent caravel hard-heeled on a southern tack, her red-crossed canvas full out, sides glistening light as the port wave broke across her bow. We watched her crew stretch and haul as she came about, the sails ripple and slacken, then fill once more. The ship rolled starboard and drove north-west, copper flanks exposed, her prow crosscutting the ocean into a froth that glinted in the sunlight like diamonds.

"There is no more beautiful sight in the world," I said to Joseph, then thought of the ship's human cargo in the dark hell of her hold, the slaves bound like the cluster of crossbow bolts at my feet. This idea of slavery burdened me, but I would not trouble my son with it. *You are the only person in the world who thus believes.* Perhaps Doria was right.

We staked the horse and let him graze as we ate our lunch in the wagon. Joseph again asking about the monkey meat, the two of us watching the great ship work her way into the west sea. Occasionally she'd disappear behind the point, then emerge further out, finally falling below the horizon.

"Where's it going, Papa?"

"I would think to Portugal, but she seems headed more west than north. Maybe it's the wind."

We neared Rio d'Ouro in late afternoon. About a half-league out we came upon a sign nailed to a tree with the decayed body of a black man hung next to it. DEATH TO ANGOLARS, it read. Joseph raised the crossbow and aimed. "Wupp, wupp." When we approached the plantation, the manager, a recently arrived Portuguese named Pedro de Abreu, rode out to meet us on a fine-looking horse. "Saulo, I heard you were coming." He spied my crossbow and pike. "Good, I see you're armed. I hear you are quite the soldier."

"Only when life requires it." I looked around. "I see no

war damage. Did you escape the rebellion?"

"Yes, but they sacked the farms above here first and drove our comrades to my gate. We had enough fighters then to hold them off. Two days later a force came from the slave port and we trapped them between us. Killed the lot."

"You know they are stragglers raiding at Alegre?"

"Oh yes. We're ready if they come." He led us around his construction. This was the Crown's newest and largest plantation, four-hundred acres. I estimated it required at least five-hundred slaves. On the mountainside where the d'Ouro ran its steep course, we staked out a site for his sugar and lumber mills. I showed him where to place his waterwheel in the exposed riverbed so he could work one bank for grinding and the other for lumber.

The forest rose lush around us. "You have fine trees for lumber," I said. He seemed impressed with my plan. "I expect to use the same two-mill arrangement at my farm if I ever get around to building it."

We followed the rough path back along the river to its mouth where de Abreu laid out his ideas for a slave port. "This harbor's better protected than the one north, and deeper; we can get the large ships almost to shore." Joseph excitedly told him about the three-master. "Yes sir, young man," the planter said. "Ships that size can bring three-hundred slaves at a time from Pinda." He swept an arm across the flat. "We've got room for ten-thousand Negroes right here. Figure we'll build barracoons from one edge of the trees to the other." His voice lowered as if he spoke in confidence. "Whoever named this the River of Gold got it right. I've made application to the Crown for Tomé's sec-ond, *and last,* slave transport license. I'll put those damned degradados out of business."

"What does Governor Doria think of your plan?"

De Abreu looked surprised. "I haven't asked him yet. He's got his hands full getting our island back on its feet. Though I did petition him to make me overseer at this plantation."

This man was so full of himself, I decided to egg him on.

"A reasonable petition, Pedro. With your farm so far south, the Crown could use an overseer down here. Anyway, Nawar's burdened with too many plantations as it is."

For a moment he looked guarded. Perhaps he suspected my mockery.

Our tour completed, Joseph and I followed him to his house, one of conventional style, several rooms, wood-sided with a roof of shingles and thatch. The house sat on piers, its one compromise with Tomé's jungle. His wife, a mannerly Catholic Portuguese was dressed in a brocade gown preposterously out of place, one suitable only for the royal court. She welcomed us inside and served a snack of pickled fish, sweet cakes, and cardamom tea. We ate in the sitting room on a table set with matched porcelain and attended by a liveried slave girl. I'd not seen such pomp since my visit to de Caminha's residence three years before. The mistress of the house presented her many children, then shooed Joseph and her brood outside.

I wondered if this woman was like Miriam's mother struggling with travail and the Inquisition, or in this lady's case, contesting the disorder of São Tomé. What had she abandoned in Portugal to be a rich farmer's wife on a miserable African island? Given her appearance, it had to be a step down. And why did I think of Miriam's mother more often than my own? Elcia, my mother so strong and able to withstand—

Saulo," said de Abreu as he broke into my thoughts, "I hear that besides a warrior, you're a man of reason."

"Depends on the subject."

"The subject is your tenant program." His wife excused herself and sent in the servant girl to clear the dishes. I motioned him to continue. "I am head of the new Planters Association. We feel your policies endanger the commerce of our island."

"I've been over this all before, but I'll listen to your version." He explained in the same terms I'd heard a dozen times earlier, sounding like Doria's footservant. I wagged my head disdainfully. "I own the last farm on the east road and run another next door. Though not as far from town as you, we're quite remote. I can't imagine my policies tempt slaves elsewhere."

"I assure you they do. This is a small island." He rose and beckoned me outside, leaving our disagreement for later. We ambled along the edge of his fields, many of them irrigated and already planted. Our conversation ranged from weather, to planting and harvesting, the sugar and pepper trade, and Doria's governance. This man, though certainly good company—as cultured as Nawar and de Caminha—now and then let a hint of malice creep into his manner. It was only a matter of time.

At dinner his wife set a sumptuous table with yet another set of matched porcelain. Her uniformed slaves served venison, roasted bananas, and cooked greens with a flavor much like the beet leaves we ate in Lisbon. We drank ample wine, a fine vintage from Madeira, and got quite drunk, the wife so much so that she fell on the floor and had to be carried to bed.

The drink emboldened the man and he began to lecture me on the Association and slave commerce, possibly saying more than he intended. "Your friend Nawar doesn't understand the slave and sugar trade as I do. I imported sugar in Lisbon, but here—" He struggled to his feet, returning in a minute with a handful of coins. "Do you know what these are?"

I picked up a gold one, half the size of the others, though with the same markings as the cruzados I'd seen the day before. "What's this?"

"A *gold* cruzado. A *cruz*. Seventy-five silvers."

I turned it over. "Why not a hundred? Same proportion as the coppers and silvers?"

De Abreu remained standing, though he needed to steady himself on the table. "Slavery, Saulo, slavery. A healthy buck slave is worth seventy-five silvers which converts to one gold cruz." His face became strangely comical. "Slaves have become coin of the realm."

Interesting, I thought, realizing there was much I

needed to understand. I bade him continue.

"The Crown will replace reis and accept no slave specie except cruzados." He pointed to a carved elephant tusk on the floor. "And ivory of course, always ivory." He drained his goblet, refilled it and offered me the flagon.

"Thank you, no. I need a clear head to understand all this." I'd had quite enough already.

"You should drink more, Saulo. I do not trust a man who refuses drink." He gulped his wine and continued. "By restricting payments to cruzados, the Crown will break the back of the unlawful slave runners. You should see what's happening in Pinda. The unlawfuls have thousands of slaves. The Crown won't buy them because the sellers don't have proper licenses. They're letting the niggers starve." He made a slashing motion with his hand. "Or they kill them."

"How can they enforce such a thing?"

He looked amused. "The local constable hangs any trader who buys unregistered slaves." He sat down, his eyes wild from drink. "In Lisbon, before those imbeciles drove you Jews out, I had much commerce with your people. So once I explain the slave-trade business, I'm sure you will understand the foolishness of your tenant scheme." De Abreu began moving coins on the table. "A healthy male Negro is worth one of these." He set aside a gold cruz. "Let's say he weighs one-hundred-fifty pounds. How much is one-hundred-fifty pounds of sugar worth?" He separated some silver cruzados. "About seven silvers and change, right?" I nodded. "Saulo, you haven't been a Catholic so long that you can't recognize a ten-to-one advantage."

"Ten-to-one," I said, my jest wasted. "Now I see."

"No, you don't." He emptied his flagon and shouted for more. A slave girl hurried in with a replacement. "That three-master you and your boy saw? That was São Tomé's first slave shipment to Brazil, the place Pinzón discovered, the Portuguese lands across the sea."

I'd first heard talk of Brazil a month before. Portuguese settlers were clearing land there for sugar plantations, and the demand for slaves would be enormous.

"That caravel, Saulo, probably carried three hundred slaves. How much do you think that's worth?"

"Three hundred gold cruz," I answered, weary of the conversation.

"*Yes,* I think equal to nine million copper reis. *Nine million!* The same boatload of sugar would be worth a tenth that. Now do you understand why we cannot allow you to hazard our slave commerce? Why we must force you to desist?"

"No, but you've been too fine a host for me to disagree. And your excellent Madeira has overwhelmed me. I must sleep." I wobbled off to find Joseph and bed.

In the morning, while our Portuguese hosts still slept, we hurried our leave. My head throbbed and Joseph complained of hunger. I handed him the remainder of yesterday's lunch as our wagon bounced out the gate and up the road. He devoured two bananas and, after knocking ants off a piece of meat, ate it carefully, mumbling, "Not monkey, not monkey."

I considered making an excuse when he asked why we'd left so early, but instead told him the truth. "The planter wants me to turn my workers back into slaves. I won't do that and I'm tired of arguing about it."

Joseph gave me a curious look. "I don't understand, Papa."

"You know the Bible story, Joseph, how Pharaoh made slaves of the Jews? Should we treat Africans that way?"

He nodded gravely as we passed the warning sign and rotted Angolar body, then put a hand over his mouth and looked at me, his eyes wide. "I don't know, Papa."

"Well I know," I said, and continued on, describing my money distress, wondering aloud what to do.

These words put Joseph to sleep, his head resting on my arm. At the next farm north we found the planter in great distress. Behind him his slave camp was in disarray. "I wish you'd been here last night, Saulo. You could have helped fight the Angolars. They stole five of my black women and killed three men." The bodies were on the ground in front of a smoldering ruin that had been a slave hovel. A group of women keened over them while men and children looked on.

"I am sorry, Paiva." Here was a man that I held in high esteem. Trapped in town the day of the rebellion and unable to return to his farm, he had fought the Angolars with me. "What happened?"

"They came in the night. Went around the de Abreu plantation. Too well defended."

"Maybe they did. We didn't see anything."

"You know," he went on, "this could become a slave revolt if we let it." He gave me a blaming look, and I could sense more lectures coming. Indeed so. Over the next days I heard endless complaints and threats about my policies as I worked at his farm and the neighbor's north of him. I helped with construction, said little in response to their comments, and kept an eye on the mountain and the rain clouds that gathered there.

Late on the third afternoon the rain started, ushered in with a deafening thunder clap. Joseph and I made plans for home—time for planting. I spent a sleepless night as I listened to the deluge and worried about an Angolar attack at my farm, mine located much closer to Alegre than this.

In the morning Paiva's wife fed us. She claimed she did not know her husband's whereabouts, but we found him soon enough. He and a group of planters confronted us on the muddy road outside his farm. The men sat their horses and blocked our way. "What's this about?" I asked, knowing full well.

My earlier host, Pedro de Abreu, spoke first. "We have a petition which requires you desist from your tenant practices." We faced off, everyone wearing broad-brimmed straw hats and large jungle leaves to keep the rain off. Regardless, we were all soaked to the skin. "If you do not," he went on, "you will be refused all Association privileges."

The situation should have frightened me, instead I felt only anger. "You dare threaten me? I have just helped at your farms. Some of us have risked our lives together fighting Angolars. My farms operate under *my policies*. It is not your concern." I glanced at Joseph. He sat there glaring at the men, hat tipped up as rainwater dripped from his chin, black curls pasted to his forehead, the picture of childish courage.

Paiva spoke next. "You will be jailed, Saulo. The governor will declare you in violation of Crown law."

"We battled a common enemy, Paiva. You saw how bravely Kiman fought. We had many loyal blacks with us. Should they be punished for their valor?"

"He's got two nigger foremen!" someone shouted.

"Your words only increase my resolve!" I shouted back. "More than once Kiman has saved my life."

"Read him the petition," de Abreu ordered. Two men rode next to the wagon, one withdrew a parchment from a watertight skin, the other held a leaf to shelter it.

I took the crossbow from Joseph's lap with one hand and seized the petition with the other. Leveling the weapon at the nearest planter, I jammed the bolt point through the parchment. "Reclaim the petition at your peril." I prodded Joseph with my elbow. "Give me the pike, son." He did so, and I laid it across my lap.

"Now you threaten us, Saulo? You see we are unarmed." They backed away.

"By your numbers you threaten me." I crumpled the parchment and threw it beneath the wagon. "Your petition will not stand." I eased my horse forward, then stopped to confront Paiva. "Tell them how Kiman led us to safety off the island, of his courage in battle."

Joseph and I bounced up the road. I looked back to see a rider dismount and retrieve the petition from the muddy track. "I'm scared, Papa," said Joseph. "How could you do that?"

I patted him on his leafy hat. "You didn't look scared, and I did it with your help." I handed him the crossbow and slid the pike behind me. "Do you remember my tales of Great-Grandfather Marcel?"

"Yes, Papa, the Saddiq."

"He once told me to know my conscience. With that in mind, I owe Kiman a debt beyond any I can ever repay."

"What you did back there, is that what a Saddiq does?"

"I'm not sure, Joseph. Perhaps, but I know that courage is part of it." I wished to tell him how our loyal friend, Kiman, helped rescue his mother three years ago from rape and bondage, but that was a story so painful I could never tell. I moved to a new subject and I said, "The winter rain in Lisbon is chilly, so cold it makes you shiver."

Joseph put out his hand. "This isn't cold."

"Sometimes there's snow, frozen water from the sky, and ice so slippery that Aunt Leah and I could not stand up on it."

He examined his wet hands. "No, Papa."

"You question your all-knowing father?"

"Yes, Papa," he said meekly. A look of uncertainty shadowed his face.

"Joseph my son, I am honored to be doubted by someone as brave and wise as you; but whether you believe me or not, the trees of Portugal shed their leaves in the fall, except for evergreens which have prickly needles and smell like camphor." He looked more doubtful than ever. "All right, I will show you. I'll take you and Lael to climb the green mountain. I've seen evergreens up there."

The road entered a thick jungle. Wet foliage nodded in our path. Joseph began to giggle. I looked to see a frog the size of my hand sitting in his lap. "You have a new pet." He reached for it, but the frog jumped onto the horse's back and then to the ground. Thunder burst overhead and suddenly the trees rained frogs. Dozens of the green creatures fell about us. Joseph overflowed with laughter as he reached for the animals, then tumbling behind me to chase the ones in back. Quickly his laughter turned to screams. A black mamba choking on a frog twice the size of its head writhed in the wagonbed.

"Snake!" Joseph screamed and scrambled back beside me. He hid his face in my shirt. I laughed at the twisting apparition. "Bad snake, Papa. Not funny."

"Here's a chance to show what a brave boy you are. You can tell Jubiabá and your friends how you saved us." He peeked at the snake. "He's choking on that frog, Joseph; he can't bite you." The boy looked more closely. "Take the pike, slide it under its belly, and flip it out of the wagon." He picked up the pike and began poking. The mamba struck at the weapon, smacking its head, frog and all, into the point. "Throw it out, son, I don't want blood over everything." Joseph hefted the snake over the side and it vanished in the bushes.

"That was The Serpent from The Garden, Papa" he said proudly. "I'll tell Jubiabá."

Yes, I thought, and I will tell Jubiabá that I will acknowledge the child growing in her womb. Our child.

Chapter 17

The horse trudged on. Around midday we came to the Rio da Névoa farm of the Lisbon Jew. Though not with the group this morning, I knew he shared their views. Joseph wanted to stop for supper, to dry off and see his friends. I needed to return the weapons, but I decided to wait. Perhaps I might need them. "We'll pick some fruit on the way," I told him. "It will have to do until dinner." But along the way we could not find any fruit within reach, even when I stood on the wagonseat and swung the pike.

In the rainy dusk we neared the slave port. Uncertain of my ability to find the nearby plantation in the dark, I decided we'd stay the night at the hellhole that loomed ahead of us. The degradado who had delivered Pongué's daughter peered out of a stick hovel. He looked as if he'd rolled in the mud. "If you're looking for a dry place here, Sr. Saulo, we cannot help you."

I gestured to his hovel. "Why don't you have thatch on that?"

Another man—equally dirty—appeared next to him. "We was going to have the niggers do it, but they all got sick."

"What's wrong with them?"

"Don't know. About half are dead. A lot of em have purple spots. We got it too."

Foreboding invaded my heart—the malady that had infected our ship and killed so many. And now it had a name: slave typhus. "They know about it in town?"

The man shook his head. "No, we was afraid to tell them."

A third degradado with fever-madness appeared and struggled toward us. I stared at him through the fading light. His face, the spots—he had it for sure. I turned the horse, retreated, then stopped. "Go back inside," I shouted. "I'll send a doctor from town." The sick man stepped back. I addressed the other two. "How many slaves here?"

"Alive? Maybe five-hundred."

"No one leaves this port! Any ship that shows up, send them off, no one lands. Run up the yellow flag." Then a panic came over me. "How many slaves have you sent to the settlement?"

"About a thousand this week. Before the rain hit."

"I'll get the doctor," I said and headed the horse into the gloom.

Of course there would be no doctor to send; they would be too busy with the rest of the colony. I gave the horse his head and hoped he would find his way in the dark. Joseph began to cry and complain. Neither of us had eaten since morning. I put my arm around his shoulders. "I'm hungry too, son, but the slave port has plague. We must keep going." I knew we would not stop anywhere.

"When will we eat?"

"When we get home tomorrow afternoon. I guess we should have kept those frogs and that snake."

"No, Papa," Joseph whimpered, his head on my arm. I relaxed the reins; the horse stopped and put his head down to graze, his chomping mixed with the night sounds around us. We sat in the pitch black and I used the time to think. Joseph shifted against me. As if Jubiabá and his sisters and brother sat in attendance, he began an elaborate story. "Papa and I were passing through this scary forest where it rained frogs. Big frogs. The horse got very tired of wading through the big frogs, so we took off his harness and let him walk. We hitched up the biggest frogs and made them pull the wagon. Papa doesn't know how to drive frogs, so I had to do it."

"Hitch up!" I called to the horse. We moved on. "Good story, Joseph. Tell me more."

"Well, pretty soon it began to rain black mambas. Mambas with two heads, one a snake head, one a frog head. Papa tried to cut them in half with his sword, but it broke. But *I* had a *magic sword* and killed the evil snakes. We roasted them for dinner. I ate snake heads and Papa ate frog heads." Joseph grew quiet, frightened by his own story. He began to shiver. Oh, he couldn't be getting sick, not this darling child. I reached behind me, pulled forward some of our clothes, and draped the driest ones around him.

I considered the plague. Half the people on the island might die, maybe more. How could we protect ourselves? I thought of the ruthless measures de Caminha took when we first landed. His actions were what kings and princes often did to protect themselves during times of plague, retreating to their rural estates to keep great distance between them and the infected public. With God's help, I would save my family. Let others infected with slavery suffer its curse.

"All right, Papa, you tell a story."

"My story is Psalm 107." And so I recited, *"Oh, give thanks to the Lord..."* God delivering us from our enemy, out of the wilderness, from darkness and hunger. God's mercy for those who did not believe—and then did—breaking their chains, smiting the enslavers, shielding the wretched from the gates of death and raging seas. Joseph's shivers ceased. He slept.

Through the murk of darkness I saw a torch at the farm just west of the governor's, the horse had found his way. We continued on to the governor's where I saw more torches and turned into the yard. In an open window of the chapel I could see Doria and two other men. I got down, knocked on the door, and returned to the wagonseat. When the door opened, I saw several people lying on the floor. Bartolis and a physician stood with the governor.

"It is I, Saulo, who calls from the dark. Do you have the sickness here, Governor?"

"Yes, everyone has it. It's the typhus."

"I saw it at the slave port."

Bartolis peered out at me. "Why do you travel at night, Saulo?"

Joseph came awake and asked if we were home. "I must return to my farm," I said to the men. "We are afraid to stop. South of the slave port there is no sickness." A plan began to form in my mind.

"Stay the night here, Saulo."

"Thank you, Governor, but I must go." I turned my horse. Doria shrugged and pushed the door shut.

Joseph pulled at my arm. "Can we get food here, Papa?"

"No, we can't stop. If the plague has not infected our farm, Joseph, I have a way to protect us." As we moved up the road, I wished we had a pitch torch. A good one would burn even in the rain. I could have begged one from Doria, but feared getting close to him. I urged the horse forward. If he wandered off the track, we would wait until daybreak. The darkness folded around us. Joseph began to shiver and cry. "No, no my son," I said, "no tears. Tell us about the brave boy in your story. How you saved Papa." He began, but fell asleep before the mambas rained down. At some point I also slept, then woke when the horse snorted and veered to one side. I reined him back and continued on. Behind in the dark someone moaned—everywhere the typhus stalked us. We rode into a gray dawn, finally stopping in a grassy place to let the horse drink from a rainwater pool and graze. With nothing else to fill our bellies, we drank also.

In the sodden tent camps of the town, many citizens lay ill, tended by the weary. In desperation I repeated my psalm. "*...And they drew near to the gates of death. Then they cried out to the Lord in their trouble. And He saved them out of their distresses.*" Joseph and I passed nightmare scenes of dead and dying, afraid to stop even when someone we knew called our name, family and farm my only concern. We continued through town and onto the road which led to my loved ones. Hunger gnawed my gut, my head light from lack of food. Endless rain.

245

Ahead, a child clothed in brown struggled along the road, a hood covering his face. He held a jungle leaf folded atop his head and peered up as we came near. The shock of what I saw took me back to Lisbon when the soldiers had returned Germo from the mob. Here stood Bartolis's child squire, his face bloody and bruised. I could not help but stop. "What happened young man? Who did this?" Though recognition flickered through the pain of his eyes, he said nothing. He grasped the muddy wheel rim and held it. I lifted the reins, intending to urge the horse on. If we took the boy with us, we risked bringing plague to my farm.

I asked, "Are you sick?" He shook his head. "Take off your hood." He hesitated. "If you want to go with us, take off your hood!"

He did so, dropping his leaf in the process. Though he had whip marks and cuts, I saw no sign of the typhus. As if he'd lost his world's only possession, he kicked forlornly at the leaf. At my insistence he exposed his arms, also cut and bruised, but showing no evidence of the sickness.

I felt his forehead, then helped him into the wagon. I prayed again, "God grant me safe passage with this child through the gates of death." The rain stopped at last, though low clouds remained; the world steamed around us. Our noble horse labored on. To my relief, Joseph began his stories, telling the boy our frog adventures. The newcomer remained silent. He rested behind us among our things in the wagonbed, his face averted.

"He does not hear me, Papa."

"He does, Joseph, but he is hurt and can't talk." Or, I thought, sick with plague.

My gratitude became twofold when we entered my farm. All around I saw fields of planted cane. A patch of scrub cane grew near the road. I stopped and cut several pieces for us to chew. I saw two groups of workers in the muddy fields, one nearby and a second with Kiman some distance away. At the first group I asked about the sickness—none here, and no one had heard about it. I handed the boy and Joseph to a woman and hurried on to speak with Kiman.

"When was the last time anyone went to town?" I asked him. "Or someone from town came here?"

"Week maybe. Why?"

I told him of the typhus. "No one from here is allowed to leave. Keep all outsiders away." I motioned toward Horté's. "Have someone go over there and tell them."

He looked to the fields. "How long, Saulo?"

"A month at least. This is much more urgent than planting."

Fortunately we had a single lane that served both my farm and Horté's. One guard station should do. "Build a hut at the road entrance. Three guards there at all times." I gave him the pike, the crossbow and bolts. "Show your men how to use these."

He nodded and said, "Master been gone long time. Much to tell."

"Not now. Come see me after you've put the guards in place." I saw two women taking the boys up the hill to my house. I followed, hungry, tired, eager to see my children, and grateful to God we had no typhus. The women prepared food and looked after the boys. I left the horse with a tenant and changed into dry clothes. "Where are the other children?" I asked, expecting to hear they were in school.

"Planting, Master Saulo. Everyone plant cane." That pleased me. In Kiman and Pongué I had chosen able foremen.

Joseph and I stuffed ourselves with lentil soup and maize bread. The new boy ate little. He slumped in the corner on the spare pallet, looking slightly better with a clean face and dry clothes. I had watched closely when the women undressed him. He showed more bruises and whip marks, but displayed no plague. Joseph soon fell asleep on his straw bed and I on mine.

In the late afternoon I awoke to bright sunlight and a brisk wind, a delight after so much steamy rain. The two boys still slept. I walked to the edge of the hill where every field below me appeared planted. To the west and at Horté's the work continued. With the sickness everywhere,

I wondered what planting progress could be made in the settlement. Then I agonized over the possible fate of Nawar and his family. In the distance I could see Kiman and his helpers finishing the guard shelter and covering the roof with thatch. Though not yet in their view, I spied an oxcart coming up the road from Alegre. A woman lead the animal and someone rode in the wagon behind her. A figure or two were prostrate in the wagonbed. I hurried down the hill, and arrived at the farm entrance as they pulled near. "Stop," I shouted, and indicated a spot about twenty feet away. "What do you want?" The woman looked exhausted.

A man and an almost-grown boy were stretched out in the back of the cart. They had typhus. The other rider, a girl about eight, got down and stood beside the woman. "We come from Alegre," said the woman. "There is sickness there. Our doctor is ill with it. I am taking my son and husband to the settlement hospital."

"The sickness is there also." I pointed. "Please go. We are not infected here, and we wish it to remain so."

"We come from a good planter's family, kind sir, but we have no food or money. The Angolars robbed us on the way. Can you help us?"

I felt for my purse and found I'd left it at the house. I looked to my men. None had money, but one had a skin of beer. I took the skin and laid it in the road near the woman.

She picked it up and motioned her daughter back to the cart. "Bless you, sir."

"Bless you, madam." I gestured toward town. "The hospital is two hours away."

None but us had escaped the plague. The Angolars were sure to have it too; perhaps it would kill them off. I pointed to the spot where the woman had been. "That's it, Kiman. Twenty feet. No one gets closer."

"Yes, master." He instructed his men in Guinea. I bade him walk with me so we might catch up. "Pongué daughter dead right after you leave," he said right away. "He and family in your debt."

248

"Pongué owes me nothing. How's the planting going at Horté's?"

"Half," answered Kiman. "Like here."

"Good. You've both done well in my absence. How is Horté?"

"Master Horté sit yard all day. Curse everybody." The hint of smile crossed his face.

"Yes?"

He broke into a wide grin. "Ah, Saulo. Four women live close now. Jubiabá and sister move to Pongué family. Your children live with them. Next door live Ariella and Sra. Horté. All friends." He dissolved in laughter. "Call selves 'Saulo's forbid—'" He struggled with the word.

"Forbidden?"

"That it, 'forbidden harem.'"

"So I'll have to face the harem to see my children?" Kiman's annoying smile continued. Since his wife was Jubiabá's aunt, he was the requisite male for this discussion. "I plan to recognize Jubiabá's pregnancy."

"That good, master. Make Kiman wife very happy. Give baby Saulo name?"

"Yes. Will you present my offer to Jubiabá?"

"Yes, but not marry her?"

"No, not marry her."

"Saulo want marry Ariella?" I nodded. "This right thing. Isabel Horté not bless Saulo until he claim Jubiabá baby."

"How do you know all this?"

"Women tell Kiman wife everything."

The next day I screwed up my courage and went to Horté's. There sat Nuño who glared from his lean-to and cursed when I approached. I ignored him, went to look for my children, and found them in a nearby field planting cane starts. They squealed with delight when they saw me. "Papa," shouted Lael, "Joseph told me you take us to climb big mountain."

"That's true, my son." I opened my arms in a generous manner. "I'm proud to see how well your planting's going. You are good children." Michal and Louisa, muddied up to their knees and elbows and full of mirth, curtseyed. A ways off I saw Ariella, Jubiabá, her sister, and the young squire all working together. I sought out Pongué and his wife, and located them in a distant field. I paid my respects.

I decided next to test the waters with Isabel before approaching the women. I found her preparing noon supper in a hut at the edge of her largest canefield. She looked up when I shouted my greeting. "Welcome back, Saulo. I hear you're protecting us from the plague."

"We will see. This is a terrible time. I fear for everyone."

"Only this colony affords such an advantage. On these two farms we get to do what royalty has done for centuries. It may save us." From her pot she ladled turnips and a portion of meat onto a wooden plate. "Try this."

I sat on the only stool in the place and ate. The meat looked familiar. "Is this turtle?" She muttered something. I put a piece into my mouth. "Look, Isabel. I'm eating it."

"Thought you Hebrews don't eat turtle and such."

"On Tomé we eat everything. Which reminds me, where's Mazal?"

"Still on his honeymoon."

"Joseph doesn't seem to mind. I'm surprised."

"The boy's grown up since your trip. Never seen such a change in a little one." She wiped sweat from her forehead. "Now he's like everyone else—indifferent."

"You'll be happy to know I also grew up on the trip." She folded her arms. "I plan to acknowledge Jubiabá's baby."

"So I've heard." She tapped her foot, though her demeanor did not change. "It's about time, Marcel. I suppose now you'll ask for Senhorita Ariella's hand?" Her stare remained coy and unyielding.

"You know, Isabel, this turtle is really good. Still alive when you dropped it in the pot?" I stood and handed her the plate. "Since you're Ariella's benot-levayah, I am asking your permission."

"You must first get Jubiabá to accept your acknowledgment." As if staring down a snake, I backed toward the door. Isabel shook her head at my antics. "You know, she may not accept."

A short distance away I encountered the women and the squire as they headed to the hut for supper. I was surprised by the size of Jubiabá's belly. "May I walk with you ladies." Jubiabá and Suryiah put their noses in the air, Ariella smiled modestly, and the young squire gave me a faint nod. He looked much better than he had yesterday. Since the women clustered together, I walked alongside the squire. "It appears you fare better," I said.

"Thank you Master Saulo for bringing me here. I owe you much."

"Work like everyone else and you owe me nothing. I'm pleased you're here. What is your name?"

"Fernão."

"A surname?" I asked. He put his head down and ran to Jubiabá's side. She turned and put a finger to her lips. I followed the crowd until they got their food, then asked Jubiabá if she'd walk with me. She handed me her plate and walked beside me to a log bench. I helped her sit. She did so with obvious discomfort.

"I'm so big, Marcel, and six weeks still to go. Maybe it's twins."

"One or two, Jubiabá, I will petition the Church to bless them and bestow my name." Her cheeks reddened, but she remained silent. We sat without talking while Jubiabá ate quietly. Occasionally she brushed tears from her eyes. Finally I said, "Thank you for taking care of the children and Fernão. What happened when I asked him his name?"

Though she would not look at me, she said, "His last name is Bartolis. He is Fr. Bartolis's nephew, the son of his brother in Porto."

"Was it Bartolis who beat him like that?"

"Yes, the boy confirmed it. I am a sincere Catholic, and this knowledge troubles me."

"We'll keep him here. No one should—"

Jubiabá turned, tears and anger mixed. "You have shamed me, Marcel. What am I to do in this condition? I cannot return to my Congo family with a white-man's child in me, they will think me a whore. And I will not give up this baby." She smoothed the fabric over her middle. "Yet I gave myself freely to you. I am the fool."

"I, too," I said.

Jubiabá put my hand on her belly. "Feel him move, Marcel. He likes turnips."

"He?"

"Only a figure of speech. I'll not have my face witched, but I know you want a son. I will do my best." She straightened up. "I accept your acknowledgment even though it means you will marry Ariella."

I inclined my head. "Explain how you are now friends with her."

"Ariella is most generous, without a shred of contention. She has offered me friendship and understanding." Jubiabá sighed and looked away, her lovely face still damp with tears. "But mostly it is because of you, Marcel. I wish to be part of this family."

I took her hand. "I do not deserve this."

She put her fingers on my lips. "What you did for Pongué's daughter, what you did for Fernão, what you would do for any of us, Marcel. You treat us all like family. We know you are kinder than any man." With dignity she struggled to stand. I helped her. "When will you marry Ariella?"

"Not until the plague is gone."

As we walked back to the others, she said, "You must grant me one request."

"I will try."

"If our baby is a boy, we will name him Marçal."

"I agree of course; and if a girl, her name is Leah."

Really, I thought, Marçal the African Jew, the Portuguese Catholic Novo-Marrano- mulatto-bastard. Your son— Son of the failed Saddiq.

• • •

Word of my farm's reclusion spread quickly. A few days into it, Kiman in great distress came to see me. "Someone leave plague bodies in night near guard hut. Not know what do."

I left my breakfast and followed him down the hill to the tenant houses. We took a horse and a rope, and walked around the hill to the farm entrance. A week of rain had turned the roads into a sea of mud. "No one heard them?"

"No master."

"I better not hear your men were sleeping." He remained silent. Two bodies were stretched in the road near the guard hut, those of a naked black woman and a child. Though mud covered the bodies, I could clearly see their plague spots. A rope must have been looped around their feet, and they had been dragged a great distance. I began to yell at the men. "This is what you'll look like if you sleep on the job!" They hung their heads. "If you spot intruders, kill them." I turned to Kiman. "On dry nights light a fire; when it's raining, burn torches." Though the men thought me brave for dealing with the bodies, but I knew better, assuming I had immunity to the typhus from my voyage here. I took charge. Not wishing to touch anything attached to the dead, I used a pike to fit my rope around the corpses, then pulled their heads together in a grisly twosome. The horse dragged them into the jungle on the far side of the road. I undid the rope and left everything. I returned to the guard hut and said, "If the weather dries out, burn the corpses." I looked up at the hut's entrance. "What is *that?*"

"Igbo zindika," answered Kiman. "Drive off sickness."

Above the entrance hung a hideous mask of black straw, white eyebrows and giant eyes, a flared nose and jagged-tooth mouth. Heads of dead parrots drooped from the hollow of each eye. I struggled to hide my amusement, then burst out laughing at the absurdity. Kiman poked it with his pike. "Leave it," I told him. "That thing would scare off the devil."

The farm's infamy grew each time travelers passed my gate. Tales of witchcraft sprouted as quickly as my new canefields. One afternoon during a dry period, about a week after the incident with the bodies, I was told the constable waited at the gate to see me. With the typhus raging, he could only bring me the worst of news. He and two soldiers stood by their horses and kept a distance—his way of acknowledging my efforts. "It is good to see that the plague has not taken you, Constable, but I fear for our colony."

"Your fear is justified beyond all measure, Saulo. You remain free of the sickness?"

"Indeed so."

He looked up at the igbo mask and crossed himself. His soldiers made the sign also. "Your success breeds many enemies, but I am not one. With this magic of yours, you will outlive us all." He paused, his head down. "Oh what calamity I have to tell. I do not know where to start."

"We need to hear. We've had no news."

"Nawar is dead, Saulo. So are Doria and Bartolis. Many others."

The shock of his words! My head reeled. The worst news I could ever imagine. How could my best friend and comrade be dead? "I am beyond sorrow, Constable." I looked to Kiman. Grief shone in his eyes, and he nodded in disbelief. "Yasemina? Her family?" I asked.

"Yasemina is well, but she lost both sons and a daughter."

Unbearable tragedy, I thought. "Are you again in charge of our colony?"

"Yes, and with no end of impossible tasks. Last week two slave ships flying the yellow flag of plague returned with many dead. Even though Elmina also has plague, they were refused port there. We refused them as well. There may have been a third caravel, but it was lost at sea. We allowed only those not infected to come on shore from the two ships. Then we towed the vessels to open water and burned them. I can still hear the screams and see people jumping. The hakifi fed well that day." He kept glancing at the igbo mask. "What is that? Do you know from a distance the face looks like a cross?"

I studied the mask. "I don't see a cross. It's just a joke."

"The thing is a sacrilege. I heard about it in town. Many

accuse you of witchcraft. I suggest you take it down."

Suddenly I appreciated the seditious nature of the thing, and had no intention of removing it. To change the subject, I asked, "What of the Angolars? It would be just due if the typhus killed them."

"I understand they have it, but less than others. We hear it started with them in Pinda." He moved his straw hat to better shade his eyes. "And now I come to the Crown relief fleet. After all our waiting, they fled yesterday without landing. Short of water and food, their seven vessels now wander the ocean like lost souls. They sailed here from Elmina hoping we had no typhus. They may return to the Canaries or even Lisbon. I told them to try again in a month."

"Will our plague be over in a month?"

"Oh, I hope so. It's slowly lessening." He stared at my men who loitered behind me. "Saulo, you've armed your slaves. Uh, tenants. That's causing great concern."

"Slaves fought alongside us in the war."

He raised a hand in frustration. "I know, but you must understand there are people who—"

"To hell with them!"

He touched his hat and mounted his horse. As they moved off, I shouted, "Constable! Tell Yasemina I will come see her when the plague abates. Let me know when there has been no typhus for two weeks." He again touched his hat. As I watched them leave, I considered the frayed remnants of Colony Tomé. How could I live with the knowledge of Nawar's death? *"With your magic, you will outlive us all."* Where was the magic to bring back my friend?

Kiman and I walked up the road, adjusting our hats in the blazing sun. "Before Master Saulo," Kiman said, "Master Nawar best friend I have."

"Mine too," I replied, recalling how I'd first seen the two of them in my cell the day they freed me from de Caminha's torture. "Nawar was my patron, he helped me succeed and took Miriam and me into his home." I put my hand on Kiman's shoulder. "He is the reason we work

255

together on this farm." The two of us continued our mournful walk, finally turning around when we reached the corner of my last field. As we grew closer to the hut, I studied the mask. Indeed its features looked like a cross. I imagined hearing Nawar laugh at the ridiculous thing.

Kiman noticed also. "I take zindika down, master. Priests not like."

"Leave it up," I said. "Its magic seems to work."

Chapter 18

In a month or so the typhus ran its course. As traffic on the road increased, more news reached us. I hoped that the sickness had done what I could not. With Doria's death and that of many planters, perhaps the Association's complaints against me might fade to the single voice of Pedro de Abreu, the Rio d'Ouro plantation manager. I heard he'd replaced Nawar as Crown Overseer.

With Nawar's passing, my money problems grew more perilous. Because I was the only farmer on the island with a crop fully planted, perhaps the fleet pursers would advance me a loan. With Doria dead, I also planned to ask them for my Crown Mason's pay—enough to carry me until harvest five months hence. Given Tomé's current situation, I doubted they would support the Association's twenty-percent cruzado exchange scheme.

Often I took my evening meals at Isabel Horté's mid a host of family and friends, Isabel and her brood, my children, Jubiabá, her sister, Fernão, sometimes Pongué and family, and of course Ariella. Occasionally I brought cursing Nuño his dinner, feeding him in his hovel as one might a dog. Ariella and I took walks. She knew my intentions, but we did not discuss marriage, my telling her I first wanted to pay respects to Yasemina and get Nawar's death behind me. And, though I did not say so, I needed to talk to Miriam.

With no reports of plague for ten days, I hastened into town. Fully a third of the settlement had perished. I found Yasemina and her daughter in low spirits, lost in grief. "I grateful you come, Saulo. My sons are dead, and daughter,

257

and beloved husband." She patted her swollen belly. "Soon
I will have this child and no father to provide for him." The
three of us grieved together, crying, recalling stories of her
family and the many contributions they had made to mine.
We had shared great joy, and endured so much.

"Kiman is sorrowful too," I told them. "I will send him to
see you. When I visit Miriam's grave this afternoon, I will
pay respects to your loved ones also."

Yasemina sent her daughter to the kitchen to prepare
food and drink, then looked at me with deeper sadness.
"Saulo," she said, "my prosperous life is ended."

"My workers will plant your farm. And I'll send someone
to manage if you wish."

"With only one daughter now and no sons, I wish to
plant nothing. But I must plant for husband's heir. It is
law. When Nasic hears, he send Nawar's oldest son to
claim farm, son of other wife."

"We have a month, I'll think of something."

"What can you do? Already Doria's lackeys nose
around—they have nothing else for their time. Widows
without male heirs cannot keep farms."

I wondered about these lackeys. "I expect to petition the
pursers when they get here for my wages and a loan, but I
suspect Doria's people might block that too. Did Nawar tell
you I'm short of funds?"

She nodded and fetched a purse. "He left bag of silvers
for you." She handed it to me. "Not much. I kept some for
self." She gave me a grim look. "I must turn over my
husband's property to his heir." The daughter brought our
repast and we ate quietly.

I asked, "Who is this heir? Will he let you stay?"

"He is sixteen-year-old son of Nawar's Congo wife. He
has own family and will not let me stay. His tribe is jealous
of Nawar's love for me. This will be their revenge."

The irony grew clear. "We're about to have mulatto
plantation owners, not just our little plot farmers. I wonder
how that will sit with slavers like Pedro de Abreu?"

"Typhus killed his wife."

"What a shame. I met her, and she was a gracious Senhora."

"De Abreu moved to the plantation near slave port, right into my husband's shoes."

I took the hands of Yasemina and her daughter. "I'll go see the constable. There must be a solution. If not, when the new governor arrives, I'll appeal to him. If all fails, you may live at my farm." Finally I thought of something uplifting to say. "You may be happy to know that I will give my name to Jubiabá's baby." They sang out their approval, and I went to look for the constable.

I found him within the hour. He heard my complaint but brushed it aside. "Yasemina's correct, Saulo. Property passes only to males. Even if she remarries, her new husband has no right to the farm. Plain and simple, what's Nawar's is not hers. She must stay there until the heir shows up. I'll find some slaves to work the place for her. If the heir doesn't appear within a year, the Crown is the new owner."

"Her new child could be a boy."

He shook his head. "You know as well as I the baby must be baptized before the pervious heir dies."

"Then I'll buy her farm and—"

"Saulo, you have bigger problems than saving Nawar's farm. There is a frenzy of accusations against you. Overseer de Abreu is in league with the two priests left alive."

"Of course! I avoided the plague and my crop is in. They're envious. And it all goes back to how I treat my workers. I'd hoped they'd be too busy for mischief."

The constable shrugged. "These types always find time for mischief. Regardless, they intend to prosecute you for spreading the typhus and African witchery. De Abreu blames you for his wife's death, claims you used devilcraft to avoid the plague."

"Can't you stop them?"

"I can refuse them, but only until the fleet gets here. With King Manuel's representatives, pursers, new priests, perhaps— Before they sailed off I told them Doria had died, so I expect they'll bring a new governor with the fleet, or soon after. I am a Novo like you, a temporary constable. Remember how Doria punished me when he arrived? I'm not going through that again. I may leave Tomé, get on a slave ship and go to Brazil."

This possibility was not news. Novos were now free to leave for other colonies. The constable had no wife or family. In Brazil he could become a wealthy planter or merchant. "One way or another," I said, "I'm losing my friends."

He looked exasperated, much the way Nawar did when we disagreed. "Why can't you be a good slave-owner like the rest of us? I have never seen anyone stir up trouble the way you do."

"It's in my blood," I told him, and left to visit Miriam.

I found the graveyard crowded with mourners and burial parties. The two priests hurried from one group to another, made quick blessings among the forest of wooden markers and moved on. I knelt at the markers for Nawar, his sons and daughter, whispered a Hebrew prayer for each, and added, "I will miss your wisdom, my friend."

At Miriam's grave I sat quietly, wondering where to begin. Finally I said, "How simple life would be if you and our son were alive here with me." I told her of Nawar's death and the plague, of our escaping it, Yasemina's plight, of Joseph, Lael, Michal and Louisa, about Fernão, told Miriam of my hope to someday receive letters from our parents, and recounted my farm's success. "In a few weeks Jubiabá will have her baby. Boy or girl, I will give the child my name. Then I will marry Ariella." I laughed at the thought of my life's confusion. "To top it all, we have an igbo mask at the farm entrance. Everyone thinks I'm a warlock now." Though it's considered bad luck, I told Miriam, "Marçal or Leah are the names for Jubiabá's baby"

• • •

The relief fleet arrived earlier than expected, having found safe anchorage at Elmina where the plague had spent itself. Seven glorious ships stood in our harbor—fine looking caravels, two of them three-masters. The fleet admiral, captain of the largest vessel and a prince in the House of King Manuel, was full of good cheer and eager for his army of masons, carpenters, and millwrights to begin work. King Manuel's wisdom in sending this man soon became evident—he exercised commanding authority over the ship captains, pursers, and other Crown minions.

Because of my position as Crown mason, the constable included me among the welcoming officials. I sensed bad blood from most of the delegates around me, Overseer de Abreu, the two priests who demanded I return Fernão Bartolis, my old vereador Felix da Tavora—now captain of the slave port—and others whose tongues wagged about witchcraft. When I learned the admiral was also a master shipwright, I pressed my possible advantage, engaging him in discussions about construction and shipbuilding. "Saulo," he said, "are you not the inventor of those clever bricks everyone uses?" He shook my hand vigorously and ignored the others who vied for his attention. "I also understand you're a man of great controversy."

"More often controversy chooses me; but I'm surprised anyone from the mainland has heard my name."

"Captains returning home have mentioned you. Your slotted bricks now serve as ballast in the most modern ships. I will show you. My two largest caravels have them." His face brightened with a thought. "I hear Saulo delves in African witchcraft." A stir went through the delegates who listened intently.

"The gossip of malefactors," I replied, gaze fixed on my detractors.

Our group adjourned from the town square to the beach where slaves had prepared a noon supper under colorful canopies brought from the ships. The admiral invited me, along with the mayor of Alegre, the constable, and de Abreu, to sit with his party of master craftsmen, ship captains, and other officials. In a curious breach of custom—not including the fleet clergy at his table—he ordered the priests to an adjacent seating with our local churchmen. As we approached the head table, someone called attention to this and the admiral replied, "I charge myself with rebuilding your settlement. I charge my priests with rebuilding Church Tomé." He carefully considered his next words. "My arrival brings great tidings from His Holiness in Rome. But that most joyous announcement must await Sunday Mass."

To me this meant the new pope, Clement VII, had proclaimed the São Tomé Diocese, a dangerous event for Novos. Local Church power would doubtless increase. I thought of Governor Doria—arrived less than a year ago— and remembered how hard he worked to establish the diocese here. Now he, King João, and Pope Alexander who first received the diocese petition, were all dead.

The admiral directed me to sit at his right hand, the constable at his left. My fellow Toméans fumed to see the chief fleet officer flanked by two Novos. I took the occasion to further my advantage and asked, "With your permission, sir, before I occupy the honored seat, may I inspect your marvelous stores?" He acknowledged me with a subtle cant of his head, and appeared amused by the turmoil he'd set in motion. With a gasp from those who watched, I pulled my knife from its sheath, placed it across my plate, and ambled away to inspect the goods from the ships.

All morning sailors and slaves were unloading a myriad of supplies—lumber, bricks, polished masonry, iron staves, barrels of cement, decorative latticework, copper latten, assembled mill wheels, sawmill blades and grinding stones, hardware of every kind, and roll after blessed roll of cloth mesh. I walked quickly through the stacks of goods, searching for the bricks, finding them, excited to see that they were of Leah's design.

After lunch the admiral and his party finished their survey of the town and moved on. Taking horses, we toured north-end farms, the slave port, and the nearby Crown plantation where Pedro de Abreu had built his new home— surprisingly one of the African style. He made apologies for not inviting us inside, explaining that he was still mourning his wife. I suspected a different motive, as I knew he kept company with a beautiful slave woman who fancied his wife's clothes. He and da Tavora had obtained the admiral's agreement to double the size of the slave port, committing a third of the relief supplies to the task. De Abreu, had also abandoned the idea of a port at his d'Ouro plantation.

At day's end we assembled on the beach, fleet squires and craft chiefs busy with their construction lists, the admiral and captains conferring and barking orders. Fires from the noon supper had been put to good use. Sixteen large hogs, split, spitted and roasted, now awaited our appetites. Most of the crews expected to camp on shore, many of them planning to seek the public bath and recreation with the whores. The admiral, however, along with the ship captains and some officers prepared for their return to quarters. He came over to me with a twinkle in his eye. Behind him sailors loaded his boat with half a pig, bananas, and other food. "Tell me Saulo, do you care for pork?"

Perhaps this admiral was a Portuguese less burdened with prejudice. "I've made the adjustment, sir."

"I hear Tomé pig is the world's sweetest. Would you care to dine aboard my ship?"

"You honor me, sir, but I must tell you that there has been little cane to feed these hogs."

"I appreciate a truthful man, particularly when it involves food." He directed de Abreu, the constable, and the Alegre mayor to the boat of his second-in-command, the captain of the other large caravel. Then he addressed the crowd. "We have made a fine start today. Tomorrow morning we will assemble in this place to begin reconstruction of His Majesty's colony." As the throng dispersed, he turned to me. "There is someone I want you to meet, my master carpenter. He is the shipwright responsible for four of my fleet's vessels; and a delightful dinner companion. The admiral led me to his boat where he introduced a short, typically thick-shouldered Portuguese with a heavy, black beard. In another circumstance I could have easily mistaken the man for a peasant.

His rowers set our boat into the twilight, the last rays of sun illuminating the fleet's magnificent masts. I stared in awe as we neared the admiral's ship, thirty feet longer than any I'd ever seen. "Gentlemen, I have never been aboard a vessel this size. I hope we have time for a tour."

"If it pleases you," said the carpenter, "we will tour in the morning. This one I built from her keel up."

We boarded, attended by two white-liveried boys who looked Indian, their tinto complexion much like Nasic's and Nawar's. "Your stewards are from India?"

"Yes," answered the admiral.

"Slaves?"

"No, their parents lend them on contract, usually seven-year indentures. Many such boys serve our fleet these days. They are hardy and intelligent young men, able to withstand much travail at sea." We climbed to the high deck for a better view. "Do you know we voyage as far as Cathay these days, around Cabo de África, across the Ocean of India to the edge of the world?" He described the explorations in detail, and described the ever expanding Portuguese Empire. I knew some of what he told me, but found his descriptions of strange and unfamiliar lands fascinating. Afterwards he said, "When we finish work here, Saulo, I plan a slave voyage to Brazil with two or three ships, depending on how many blacks we can round up."

The carpenter spoke. "I will be chief of construction at our new Brazil settlement. You should join us. The sugar lands there dwarf what we've seen here. Land, sugar, slaves. The riches of the New World will be ours."

The admiral repeated the offer and added, "By the size of our fleet you can see the Crown's dedication to sugar commerce."

I told him I'd consider, hoping they would let it drop. I thought of my family, and knew Tomé was as far in this sea as I ever wanted to go.

The stewards served dinner on the high deck, our conversation emboldened by a cloved Spanish wine unlike any I'd ever tasted. A breeze sounded in the rigging, reminding me of my days with Norte in this harbor. "It's a fine thing to get away from the island flies and mosquitoes," said the carpenter.

"They're so much part of life here," I said, "we rarely notice. It's particularly bad in the rainy season. Whoever sent those rounds of meshcloth deserves sainthood."

"If it's true," observed the admiral, "that all the farms now have their houses rebuilt, we can devote our time to the towns and mills." He tilted back in his chair. "But that's for tomorrow. Since you, Saulo, appreciate fine ships, we'll tell you about our works at Lagos..." The two men droned on—ship design, engineering, construction—as I struggled against sleep. Eventually the carpenter excused himself and went to bed.

"I am gratified to see that your supply of bricks are of my design," I told the admiral. "Though I must tell you—"

"In the morning you will see hundreds in my ship's hold set in ballast stacks, filthy with bilge however. We secure them with iron rods. Your design has replaced our need for rocks and wooden cribs." He laughed and slapped the table. "You know the natives of Cathay have a style of brick like yours? Claim they've used them for centuries."

"A few years ago my sister Leah invented them in my father's brickyard."

He looked astonished. "Unusual for a girl. Where is she now?" I told him what I knew, and of my parents, and suggested he might support a letter to the Crown inquiring to Leah's whereabouts. My request troubled him. "Marcel, if not for the Inquisition I would gladly pen such a letter and send it with a returning captain. In the current situation, however, it might call attention to your sister and put her in danger."

The stewards served mugs of hot spirits, and the admiral rose and bade me join him at the rail. The dark sea spread below us all the way to Africa. "As a Prince of Portugal," he began, "I tell you in confidence that cousin

265

Manuel is sometimes the fool, a lackey to his wife and that damned Isabella. The mistreatment of Jews is the shame of our country." A steward refilled our mugs from a steaming kettle. "I worked with many Jewish shipwrights and engineers, intelligent associates, faithful to their craft—all fled or perished in the dungeons. *Now,* when it comes to famous mariners, that most-high admiral, Columbus, is rumored a secret Jew." He grew thoughtful. "No doubt some Church auditor might locate your dear sister. Those petty thieves keep thorough records in such matters." He shook his head and lifted his cup to the darkness. "To sister Leah. May she remain safe."

The admiral turned to me. "I sense you have no interest in Brazil, so perhaps you will consider another possibility. Amsterdam is the safest place on the continent for your people these days, and Jews there are among the wealthiest slave traders. We need a Crown agent there—I'll be your patron. It's cold in winter, but you'll be among your own and unhindered in religion."

"Thank you, sir, I will consider it. Though I must say that Tomé feels very much like home these days." I finished my mug of spirits and tipped the bottoms over the rail. Its slurry of spices drained silently into the water below. I turned to the admiral. "From you and others I've heard many voices who oppose the Inquisition. So who supports it?"

He waved a hand. "Greed, kings and Church. It's like plague, a force of nature."

I slept that night in the booth of an absent officer, in a real bed with sheets and straw fill. An hour before dawn a powerful wind woke me. Moments later lightening flashed outside the porthole, thunder boomed, sheets of rain fell and the ship pitched violently. I immediately became seasick, went to the rail, and vomited over the side. The carpenter came over and slapped me on my rain-soaked back. "If you are this poorly seasoned in a trifling blow, Saulo, I wonder how you'd handle a deck-washer?" I forced a smile, then turned to vomit again.

After a while the storm lessened, though rain continued. The admiral had his boat lowered, signaled the other captains our intention to go ashore, and promised my ship's tour for another day. The moment I stepped onto the beach the sickness left me. Around me, gangs of sailors and slaves worked feverishly to shelter stacks of goods beneath the canopies. We gathered under a separate canopy and laid out our plans for the settlement.

The admiral assigned fleet craftsmen to each project, making Overseer de Abreu and Felix da Tavora responsible for the Tomé work force. This meant mixing my tenants with slaves. I decided to tell my workers I'd deal harshly with anyone who mistreated them, and so informed the overseer and Felix. The two sullenly accepted my words.

Having spoken earlier with the admiral about my money problems, he directed the chief purser to pay me for both mason's labor and reparations. Midst rankled looks from de Abreu and other hostile planters, I stood quietly as the purser counted out my cruz.

The rain quit around midday. I set off with a fleet millwright, three wagons of supplies, and twenty slaves. We drove to two farms on the south edge of town to repair their sawmill and make improvements in a shared cane grinder. I divided the crew between the projects, and journeyed to my farm, promising to return the next day with my workers in tow. From the supply stock on the beach, I had taken several bricks of polished masonry, intending to someday carve proper grave markers—in place of the wooden ones—for Miriam and the Nawar family.

When I arrived home, I found a group of workers replacing failed cane starts in the big field below my house. This task needed another week's work, so I decided to send the men to the construction tomorrow and keep the women and children here to finish. I changed my clothes and went to Horté's. Nuño and his oldest daughter were the only ones there. The two sat together on a bench where the girl was teaching him to read. "This is a smart one," he grunted, and struggled to stand, showing me his wooden leg carved

267

from a tree branch. "She made this, and a crutch too." With his old crutch and the new one, he performed a short hobble. The new crutch fit into his armpit and could be moved along by the arm stump lashed to it. For the first time since I could remember, Nuño had no angry words for me.

"Papa's a good student," said the girl. She helped him back to the bench.

"That I see. Soon we'll have him planting cane. Where is everyone?"

"Planting," the girl said, and pointed me in the direction. I walked through the wet fields until I spotted the women and children working together. My children, clamorous and muddy, crowded around. Jubiabá, looking immense, smiled at me. I found Pongué and told him my plan for tomorrow, then went back to work with the women and children until sundown. Soon I was as muddy as the rest.

Our meal that evening included the familiar crowd and a newly chastened Nuño. I was the center of attention; everyone wanted to hear my tales of the relief fleet. Ariella, though thoughtful and attentive, encouraged me toward Jubiabá. "Walk with her," she told me. "The babies are probably only—"

"Bab*ies?*"

"Oh yes," said Jubiabá who'd overheard. She stood and stuck out her belly. "I don't need a witchwoman to tell me I'm carrying twins, anyone can feel them." Jubiabá and I took our walk. "In a week or so," she said, "you will have your two dusky sons, Marçal Primerio and Marçal Segundo. Then you can marry Ariella."

"Does the marriage trouble you?"

"Not as much as it will trouble you, Saulo. Ariella will not sample your bed unless we share your house."

"The Church will forbid it." The idea seemed insane, yet forbidden and enticing.

"The priests will see me as the humble servant, Marcel." She gave me a challenging look. "Suspect Novos need a Catholic in their household."

. . .

At a packed Mass on Sunday we received the announcement. Indeed Clement VII had proclaimed the São Tomé
Diocese. The admiral provided details. "The Church will
honor your island with a resident bishop." I wondered how
long this bishop would last. With the rainy season barely a
month old, the fever had already extracted its toll. In under
a week, half the fleet's persons were sick, and three had
died.

"This hellish place deserves its reputation," the admiral
told me after church. "We must finish before the fever kills
us all." I expressed my regrets. "I'm going to assign you a
special task, Saulo. You and my chief carpenter will be in
charge of restoring the old de Caminha estate. With the
chapel there, the place is an ideal residence for your new
bishop. When you finish, you will start on the new governor's residence in town." By now the chief carpenter, the
constable, and a sullen de Abreu had gathered around. I
wondered if the admiral still expected to persuade me
about Brazil and had assigned the carpenter to that end.
The way the carpenter's eyes fell upon me, I knew he was
someone I could trust. In the next few days I intended to
explore the subject of Amsterdam with him, a preferable
place where I could be among my own. But even given a
safer life there, I would not broker slaves. Perhaps they
needed a Crown builder in the land of the Dutch.

The admiral summoned the entire company, including
da Tavora, the two priests, Doria's remaining squires, and
several planters. He stood on a bench and addressed us.
"Before I departed Elmina, I sent word to Lisbon of Governor Doria's death." The priests, then all of us, made the
sign of the cross. "So I believe your new governor will
arrive in a month or two. Hopefully you may expect the
bishop soon after." He nodded to the constable. "Your fine
garrison commander has informed me of the Angolar
threat. I will personally write a letter to King Manuel and
request troops. It will go out on the first ship." He glanced
at the threatening sky. "We have a stock of new weapons

on my ship, and I wish to show them to you. Most are destined for Brazil, but I will demonstrate their use and leave several here. They're called muskets." We all listened with interest, as we'd heard rumors of these shoulder cannons, and were eager to see them. As the admiral implied, we had also heard they did not work well in the rain.

The next day I took Kiman, Pongué, and a dozen of my workers to de Caminha's estate. It seemed Alvaro's ghost had reclaimed the place, with Doria's brief presence almost forgotten. I owed the admiral a great debt. Working on this residence and that of the new governor's set me apart, placing me favorably in the eyes of Church Tomé and the civil governance—an advantage I sorely needed. What a fine governor this admiral would make. But I knew he had bigger plans.

Chapter 19

In early afternoon, the second day at de Caminha's, Ariella and Fernão arrived in a state of great distress. She sat terrified in the wagon while the boy, his head down, held the reins. "Oh Saulo!" cried Ariella, "terrible news. The Angolars came while we were in the fields! With no men to protect us they took many black women, boys and girls too."

My first thought went to Jubiabá and the babies. "Did they take Jubiabá?" I asked.

"Yes, and—" She looked fearfully at the workers. They crowded forward to listen. "The wives of Pongué and Kiman, Suryiah and many children." She recited a long list.

Impossible! How could they take Jubiabá, so obviously near her time? The carpenter pushed though the crowd. "Go tend your to troubles," he told me, "and see the admiral. He will give you some men." It wasn't sailors I needed, but weapons and my old troop who knew warfare.

I sent my workers home with Ariella. "I will be there shortly. Prepare yourselves. We're going after them."

Kiman and I took my wagon to the garrison, hoping to find the constable. From there I went to a nearby construction where his men told me he was working. He listened without emotion to my plight. "Forgive me, Saulo, but I don't believe there is a white man on this island who will fight alongside you. You have curried too much favor with—"

"Then just give me the weapons! Don't you understand?

271

Some of those taken were free Negroes. You have an obligation. At the very least will *you* fight with me?"

He shook his head. "You may have your weapons, but I will not go into the jungle after blacks, citizens or otherwise. Another two months and I will be sailing the ocean sea to Brazil."

Returning with me to the garrison, the constable gave me what I needed—crossbows and bolts, pikes and poleaxes. Silently, we loaded the weapons into the wagon and left. I thought of finding the admiral to ask for muskets, but it was raining again. I glanced at Kiman. He looked terrible.

On the way home I prayed for Jubiabá and the other captives, thankful the rebels had not taken Ariella as well. As in the past, Angolars believed nobody would come after them if they stole only blacks. One of the women taken spoke the Angolar language; perhaps my people had a chance. "The raiders hurt no one," Ariella had said. "Ten came from the jungle and surrounded us with spears. They forced me, Sra. Horté, and the white children to one side. I threw myself at the feet of the leader and pleaded for him not to take Jubiabá. He just stepped over me and took them all."

We drove toward my farm. For a while Kiman remained silent, then he began rocking, wailing his lament in a tongue I did not understand. My thoughts went to Pongué's wife—her oft-crazed manner placed her in great peril.

Though the hard rain continued, everyone at the farm made ready, the children included, younger ones fearful and crying for their lost friends. By nightfall we had assembled a week's supplies and loaded three carts. I decided to take fourteen fighters, eight men and six of the largest boys, selecting men who had lost wives or children—they would fight the hardest. That still left enough men to guard my field workers.

Rising before dawn, we ate a hurried breakfast and headed south. Kiman, Pongué, and I drove the carts. As we cleared my gate, Kiman stood on his wagonseat, took down the igbo mask and set it behind him. In all our times together I had never seen Kiman so grim. And I felt absolute torment at not having left guards to protect our women. In Alegre I found the mayor and several fleet workers busy with construction. I asked for their help. They eyed my armed Negroes. "If anyone can find the Angolars," said the mayor, "maybe your crowd can. The niggers have been stealing our slaves ever since the uprising and we can't find them. Maybe they know how to find each other." He refused to provide me men, claiming he needed everyone for construction. "But you can re-supply here, Saulo. You'll be a hero if you recover our slaves."

We turned back to the Rio de Sul, and took the rough track up the mountain, the same road Miriam, pregnant with our child, and Joseph and Lael and I once walked with Kiman to the fugitive camp. I never dreamed I would again enter this jungle. As we paused to let the horses drink, two wretched-looking Negroes appeared from the jungle. Though each carried a spear and shield, they made no threat. "What do you want?" I asked in Guinea.

"We know you look for Angolar," one replied. "They took our wives and ninnies. We help you find them, get families back."

They looked like starved rebels to me, perhaps a trap. Pongué spoke to them in Angolar; they appeared to not understand. I called him and Kiman to my side. "Guinea runaways," said Kiman. "No Angolar. Maybe help. Maybe not."

I told the two to follow us. "Give them each a yam cake," I said. The starving Guineas thanked me profusely. Further on, the track became quite steep. We got down from the wagons and led our horses. The jungle closed in, the rain started anew, the mountain disappeared into the clouds, and these new arrivals filled me with apprehension.

We came upon the fugitive camp. Though abandoned, it appeared someone had been living there. The common hut had been partly rebuilt with a makeshift roof and a store of dry wood. We made camp. Pongué put the men to work while Kiman and I questioned the two Guineas. "The planter refused to search for our families," one said, "so we ran off." He pointed to the mountain. "We lost Angolars a ways from here, but know where to look. Saw their smoke. They have two camps league apart on east side." That made sense, they would have moved once the season changed. "Man named Mbundu leads them," his companion added. "He is the cruelest Angolar." Knowing what lay up-mountain from my time here before, I wondered how Jubiabá and my two tenant women with kanga babies could have managed this steep and dangerous mountain-side.

In the morning we unpacked the carts and moved our goods to the backs of the horses and men. Above our camp, the Rio de Sul came together from three streams, each with its own canyon. We decided to take the eastern canyon, hoping we might pick up the trail the Angolars used when they crossed from the Alegre Road to the mountain. The day before we had searched from the road, but found nothing. Pongué suggested they'd scattered into to the jungle to leave no trace.

We marched from the fugitive camp. The rain fell and the tree leeches covered us as if we were in water. Every now and then we stopped to pull them from ourselves and the horses. My men swallowed the leeches whole, eager for more. I would not stomach the things and waited for dinner.

That afternoon, more than a league from where we started, cutting through jungle so thick we could see only ten feet ahead, we stumbled onto the trail from the east. Kiman in the lead stopped, put his finger to his lips and motioned me forward. He pointed to muddy footprints that headed down the trail, fresh enough that water still ran into them. "Two," he whispered as he spanned the tracks with his hand. "Maybe escape people." The prints appeared small enough, perhaps a woman, and definitely a child. Uncertain what they might find, I sent Kiman and three of my strongest fighters down the trail after them, positioning the rest of my men in defense in case the Angolars came from the mountain above.

I sent Pongué with other men up the trail. "Wait a few hundred yards above us," I said. "If you see anyone, retreat here. We'll trap them." We waited on guard in the bush. The clouds cleared, the jungle steamed. Stinging pests drove us mad.

Kiman and the men returned in an hour with one of the stolen wives and her son. Kiman carried the body of her baby wrapped in a kanga. Fortunately this woman's husband had traveled up the trail with Pongué. She and her family had been with me several months, hard workers all, and I did not want to lose her or the husband. Usually these Negroes cast off or killed a wife suspected of being raped, a practice similar to honor slayings among Moslems. While killings of this kind were common on the African mainland, more often a Tomé wife found herself beaten and banished to another farm, her children taken away.

The woman looked around fearfully for her husband, took the dead baby from Kiman and threw herself at my feet. "They did not touch me," she pleaded, holding up the child's body. "They killed this little one because I would not submit. Ask my son." The boy looked away. Had the Angolars killed the infant? I suspected they'd raped her and she'd killed the baby to cover it up. When we rescued my people, I would face this problem again and again—the men talked of little else.

I took Kiman with me up the trail. "What will you do if your wife has been used by the Angolars?" With his wife five months pregnant, and their only child, a year-old-daughter also stolen, he said nothing. I stopped and grabbed him by the shoulders. He stood more than a head taller than me. "We both know Miriam was raped more than once. Though it gave me much pain, I put it aside. Her sons are now *my* sons. We—"

"You not Guinea!"

"And neither are you. You're a free Christian, and so is

your wife. We will set an example." He jerked from my grasp and continued up the hill. In a minute we came upon Pongué and the others. I told them what had happened. "If any man beats, banishes, or kills a wife or daughter because they were violated," I went on, "I will sell him to the slave port and keep his family." The men turned silent and sulked ahead, occasionally glancing back. Kiman told them about Miriam and me. Upon entering the camp, I gathered everyone around me. Kiman repeated my story and threat. That settled it for now. The family buried their baby.

We continued our march up the mountainside, spending a miserable night in the rainy jungle. In the morning, with information from the two Guinea runaways and my tenant woman, we approached the first Angolar camp and found it deserted. In the afternoon we found the second camp, also deserted. Both appeared emptied just the day before. I again asked my tenant woman about Jubiabá. "We were in the first camp," she told us, "but I heard Mbundu took her to this one. Her sister too. He's going to make them his queens."

"What about the babies? She's so close." One of the runaways had listened to our conversation and understood that Jubiabá was my mistress.

"Master Saulo," he said, genuine concern in his eyes, "if African, Mbundu keep babies. If mixed blood, maybe kill them."

We set guards around the second camp and stayed the night, my sleep interrupted by hellish forebodings. At dawn I took Pongué and two others to scout the mountainside. I included the husband of the rescued woman—I did not trust him. He'd been sullen to her, and had barely acknowledged the death of their infant. I sent Kiman and a few others ahead to search the Angolar trail beyond our camp.

My group scaled directly toward the mountain spire, a likely place to spot the Angolar fires. By midday, battered and sore, we found ourselves climbing hand-over-hand up a cliff of sharp, wet rocks where low jungle plants grew thickly—one slip and the fall would be fatal. We reached a collar of black rock a few hundred feet below the mountain-top with a view along the entire east slope of the island. Ten leagues north the smoke of the Tomé settlement rose into the sky. On the mountain's near flank I saw no sign of the enemy. I looked back and could see smoke from our camp. Had the Angolars seen it too? Had they extinguished their fires, knowing we hunted them? We took handfuls of evergreen needles, twisted them, and rubbed the sweet-smelling sap on our sore hands. This was a sad day—here stood the trees I'd promised to show Joseph and Lael.

Back at camp, Kiman had three captured Angolars. One lay dead, the igbo mask covering him. The other two hung nearby, strung by their hands from a thorn tree, faces covered with stinging pests. Brutal, but I understood Kiman's intent—we were short on time. He gestured to a small deer that roasted over the fire. "On hunt."

"What have they told you?" I felt no sympathy for them.

"Told place of main camp. Mbundu, Jubiabá and sister not there."

"Then where are they?"

"Say not know. Mbundu know we seek him."

I considered the captives. "Take them down and keep them alive; they'll be useful tomorrow." Kiman nodded gravely.

While the camp readied itself for the next day's battle, I considered my possibilities. Likely the enemy greatly exceeded us in number. Though I could not defeat them, we had advantages—my men possessed superior arms and were accomplished fighters. Further, we would have no women, children, or captives to guard. Assuming the Angolars had crossbows, I told everyone to cut vines and weave them into shields. "Cut grass too," I said. "Cover the tops of your shields with igbo hair. Use charcoal to give them eyes and a mouth." That evening I dined on venison with my war council, Kiman, Pongué, and the Alegre runaways, these last two uncommonly strong despite their gaunt appearance. In the end I accepted the advice of the

277

Africans: "We must be more savage than our enemy."

We set out at first light leading a single horse loaded with supplies. The rescued woman and boy remained in camp to gather food, cook, and look after our other horses. Our march took two hours. On the way we remained braced for a surprise attack, but it did not come. As we neared the Angolar camp, runners spotted us and rushed ahead in warning. With one of our captives in the lead and bearing a white flag, my crossbow point to his back, our little army marched in. We stood together in Old Testament formation, a flat line, shield-to-shield. Hidden by several fighters in front of us, Kiman, Pongué and I held our crossbows. At my signal, the men in front of us stepped aside to reveal our weapons. The man next to me raised his poleax with the impaled head of the dead Angolar from our camp. I pushed the second captive forward, a lanyard around his neck, his hands tied, the igbo mask covering his face and upper body. He screamed for his comrades not to kill him.

We faced forty fighters, several with crossbows. When we entered the clearing, they had stamped their feet and pounded the ground with spears. At the sight of the igbo mask and severed head, the Angolar mob grew quiet and listened to the pleadings of their man with the white flag. He presented our offer to the headman: We would take only our people and leave them in peace. One of the Alegre Guineas next to me hissed, "That man is not Mbundu." Behind the enemy cowered many settlement captives. My eyes searched for Jubiabá and could not find her. The parley with the headman had gone on too long. At my signal our line gave a war shout and moved a pace forward. The man with the poleax flung the severed head at the enemy's feet. They brandished their shields, but stepped back. Our hostage dropped his flag and fled behind them while the headman began screaming.

"What does he say?" I asked Pongué.

"We can have our people."

I walked toward the enemy, the second hostage in front

278

of me still tethered by his leash, crossbow in his back. When only a few feet from the Angolars, I stepped out and aimed the crossbow directly at the headman. "What about the pregnant woman and her sister?" I shouted. Pongué moved next to me and translated. Now the headman faced two crossbows. Behind him a captive's shrill voice rose above the noise. It was Pongué's wife, and I believe I saw my comrade smile. The headman shouted back and threw his hands in the air.

"He claims Mbundu took the women," Pongué said. "He doesn't know where."

"Tell him we'll take our people and the two Guinea families."

Not recovering Jubiabá felt horrible, and I had no idea what to do. Maybe our rescued people might know something. I dragged the captive back to our ranks and had Pongué ask him, "Is that headman related to Mbundu?"

"His brother," came the reply. Could I seize this man? Trade him for the two women? I'd return later and take them by surprise. My captured people began to straggle over, everyone there except the two I most wanted. A small clubfooted boy and some others came our way. One of the fugitive Guineas ran forward and lifted the lad over his head. These were good men; I'd keep them both.

The remaining settlement slaves began to shout and cry for release. They attacked the rear of the Angolars, hurling stones and chanting. The captives in neck leashes struggled to free themselves. Here and there people fled. Half the enemy had their backs to us, loosing arrows at the disorder behind them. We had them off guard. With a war shout I compelled my men forward. "Take the leader and his people."

Quickly my courageous fighters surrounded the headman and a few others. We killed any who resisted. Two of my soldiers went down, one man lifeless, the other struggling. We herded the new hostages to our lines, while the three of us with crossbows guarded the retreat. I looked down to see my shirt covered with blood, a broad gash

279

across my chest—a trivial price for taking these hostages.

I split my force in two. The smaller group I sent with Kiman down the trail with our rescued people, the escaped slaves and the hostages. Pongué and I with my larger force attacked the Angolars as they came after us. The jungle was thick and forced the enemy onto the narrow trail. We drove them back in retreat, then hurried to join the others. Catching up, I realized we'd won a worthy victory, rescuing two-dozen people, but we had more wounded than I first thought. These we carried or dragged along.

I stopped a moment so I could send a message to the Angolars. As I did, Kiman's wife ran up to me. "Bless you for this rescue, Saulo. My husband told me of your threat to the men—it will save us much sorrow."

"What about Jubiabá?"

"Mbundu knew she was more than a slave. He disappeared with both women the day after we were stolen." With great sadness she looked around. "They are my nieces. What am I to tell my brother?"

"The babies?" I asked. She didn't know and shook her head. I pointed to the hostages. "We still have a chance." For my messenger I picked the Angolar who'd worn the igbo mask. He had an arrow sticking from his back—let his fellows care for him. Our captive headman wore a fancy copper bracelet with a blue stone. I put it on the messenger's arm. With Pongué as translator I told him, "Tell Mbundu we want our two sisters and the babies returned. We give him three days." One of the Alegre Guineas said he had a boy missing. I told the Angolar we wanted him too. "We will wait at the old fugitive camp. If you do not deliver our people, Mbundu will never see his brother again." I put my knife to the messenger's throat. "Go!" He scuttled painfully away, the arrow twitching from his back like a devil's tail.

My orders at the first camp were to care for the wounded and feed everyone. The rescued men wore coarse vine yokes braided tightly around their necks. We carefully removed these. The skin underneath was putrefied. I took stock of our situation. With the enemy close by, staying in this camp was perilous. My reclaimed workers appeared in fair shape, having been captive less than a week. The husbands continued to regard their wives and daughters with suspicion. With everyone angry and fearful, no one celebrated the rescue.

The other rescued Africans were a sorry lot, filthy and starving, the little ones' bellies swollen from hunger. Except for a brother and sister among the children, none seemed related. Though all had family still held by the Angolars, no one wanted to return. Since we could make the more distant abandoned camp by evening, I directed an immediate retreat. We loaded the wounded onto the horses, carried our supplies, and headed back along the canyon. Just then an Angolar woman rushed into our midst, begging to stay. "She's likely a spy," I told Pongué. "Put her with the hostages."

Near nightfall we arrived at the new location. I set an ample guard. It had rained and misted all day, now a heavy rain drenched us. Fire was impossible. We sat huddled under leaves, ate salt fish from our supplies, and waited out the night. Three of our wounded died in the early hours; and in the morning we buried them and began our march, this time along the steep mountain traverse of the Angolar trail. The horses skidded down the muddy path, slowed only by men hanging on to their tails. Bless these animals, without them we might have failed. In the middle de Sul canyon we discovered a concealed trail that headed straight toward Alegre. If so, the fugitive camp was just a league-and-a-half away, an easier route than the trail we'd cut five days earlier. I sent runners ahead, and they returned in a short while with good news. The rain let up, and by late afternoon we struggled into the fugitive camp. Seeing my wagons sitting undisturbed in the clearing, I prayed our good fortune might hold.

The following day I became an unwilling slave trader. I intended to keep the two Guinea families, and so informed them. They agreed to take the orphans, all big enough to work. That left three rescued Alegre men and a woman, and the Angolar woman. I'd offer them to the Alegre planter to partly compensate for the Guinea families. I took several men, two carts, and the five slaves into Alegre.

There I found the mayor and explained my situation. He accepted the slaves for the planter and offered to sort out the ownership. He congratulated me. "You are the first to recover anyone from the Angolars." He remained grateful, but stopped there and did not ask details. He left the impression he had no stomach for fighting. When I told him about the hostages, he said, "I hope you get your other people back, Saulo. If not, we need workers. We'll pay full price for those men." A sad outcome. If I sold him the hostages, it meant I'd not recovered Jubiabá and the babies. From the Crown warehouse the mayor gave me the supplies I needed. We returned to the mountain.

Next morning I sent almost everyone home with Kiman and Pongué. I kept eight of my best fighters and a few women to cook. My foremen returned with the wagons the next afternoon.

The three days passed and we heard nothing. We scouted our original trail to where it crossed the Angolars' and found it well trod—they had again gone raiding. My hopes of recovering our lost souls fled with the tracks going east down the mountainside. I worried they might attack my farm; but since they knew and feared me, hopefully they would stay away. I sent a few more people home, but kept a half-dozen fighters including Kiman and Pongué. The hostages remained chained with irons I'd brought from Alegre.

I held council. Kiman and Pongué were both as anxious as I to find Jubiabá, her sister, and the babies. "What next?" I asked.

Kiman shook his head. "Not know, Saulo. Wife say must find."

"Stake a dead hostage in their trail," suggested Pongué.

"No. If they wanted these people, we'd have heard something by now." We had questioned the captives and learned nothing. I refused my men's suggestion for torture. Being chained to trees in the rain and deprived of food was torture enough.

We waited two more days and went searching, this time to the west, crossing on foot to the island's miserable, rainy side. There we found Angolar dry-season camps, but no sign of anyone living or traveling there. Through broken clouds I gazed down at the Rio d'Ouro plantation and its fine harbor. We stayed out several days, muddy and exhausted, and found little except the odd bomajiti trees with their gigantic, wide-flung roots and an occasional sign that someone had once lived beneath them. Heading back the last morning we approached the camp where we'd battled the Angolars. We peered through the jungle and saw they had new captives, but none from my farm.

The next day at the fugitive camp I unchained the headman, cut a gold cruz in half and handed it to him. Perhaps Mbundu might honor a gesture of mercy. The headman kept turning the coin over in his hand. He knew gold of course, but did not understand a coin. "Bring our people back to my settlement farm," I told him, "and I'll give you twenty-five of these. That's enough to buy freedom for twenty-five Angolars." I gave him food and sent him up the trail. We loaded the other hostages into a wagon and went to Alegre where I sold them, chains and all, for six gold cruz. With Brazil's demand for slaves, the price for Africans had doubled. I would have given six-thousand to get Jubiabá back.

In solemn procession, the rain falling as ever, we headed home on the east road. I sent my prayers through the rain and clouds to the mountain and its secrets.

• • •

At home, the farm seemed to be running itself. My cane grew thick and lush. The admiral had heard tales of my difficulties and sent millwrights to complete my grinding and lumber mills. I ate dinners at Horté's and spent time with Ariella. She cried over the missing women, and my heart broke at my failure to find them. How many months must pass before we could marry? And marriage with such overhanging sorrow? I did not know what to say. Was Jubiabá alive or dead? The babies? Her sister? In a week I'd go back and search again.

The rainy season had about eight weeks more to go. With my crops flourishing, I could finally look forward to a good harvest. Yet I remained heartsick, reminded by the farm children who pined for their favorite teachers. Clear skies or rain, I stared at the mountain, beset by my neglect at having left the women unprotected. I had deceived myself with arrogance, shown off to the admiral by taking all my men to work his projects. Yet why had Kiman, Pongué, *or someone* not raised a caution? I despised being considered a lord by my workers—these people who never questioned my judgment. I sought counsel with Isabel and Yasemina, the latter cradling her healthy new son. Both women encouraged me to keep searching.

In the following weeks we thrice scoured the mountain, captured Angolars, learned only that the Guinea family's son had died, sold the captives, got one of my men killed, spied on their camps, and discovered little else. The women and Mbundu had disappeared, yet people claimed they'd seen the Angolar chief during settlement raids.

When I went to petition the constable and admiral, I discovered the construction progress in town was amazing. Despite the rainy season, the settlement appeared nearly rebuilt. "There's still much to do," said the admiral, "but we've got the colony back on her feet, and the Crown will have its sugar."

I showed them a map I had drawn, and explained of my search. "They've got two, maybe three camps," I pointed out, "and perhaps a hundred slaves—stolen or fugitive. When the rain stops, they'll move to the west side. I believe that's where we can capture them."

The constable and admiral smiled at one another. "By then," said the latter, "we'll be on our way to Brazil." He handed the map back. "Give this to the new governor. I'm sure he'll seek your advice once our soldiers arrive. Hopefully both he and the new bishop will arrive before I leave."

"In the meantime the Angolars—"

He bade me quiet. "In the *meantime,* Saulo, you will have crops to harvest. I did not repair your mills to leave them idle. Let our soldiers fight the battles."

Over the next days I tried to organize an army, figuring to attack early in the dry season at the first sign of Angolar activity on the west side. Since the cane needed a month without rain to cure, no one could harvest yet. I needed fifty good fighters, and sought them from planters who had lost the most slaves. Presenting my case to these men, I explained my map and kept repeating, "Besides getting your people back, there's money to be made. A healthy Angolar is worth two gold cruz." I'd improved on Pedro de Abreu's reasoning. "That's a ton-and-a-half of sugar." After two weeks' frustration—the dry season closer at hand—I quit. For all my efforts, the planters had pledged me few men. I would have to take on the Angolars myself.

One afternoon, while fine breezes cleared the sky and the admiral, constable, and half the relief fleet made ready for Brazil, our new governor sailed into port. What a surprise, none other than Pedro de Caminha, nephew of our respected first governor. After his introduction by the admiral at church the following Sunday, and a celebration in the afternoon, Pedro moved into the restored de Caminha residence, the very one prepared for our new bishop. At the celebration I heard talk of this, and asked them about it. The two traded tight smiles. "I assure you," said Pedro, "our esteemed bishop will be most happy with the residence in town you so ably built for me."

How strange. I looked to the admiral, but he remained indifferent. "Besides," the governor continued—he made the sign of the cross—"I wish to honor the new bishop by praying in Uncle Alvaro's chapel." Both men gave simpering laughs at the comment, and the governor put his hand on my shoulder. "I honor you too, Saulo. For was it not you who built that fine chapel?"

"Thank you, Governor," I replied, and strolled away,

immensely puzzled at what I'd just heard, yet smiling about my Hebrew symbols scattered throughout the chapel.

Chapter 20

A few days later the colony bade farewell to the admiral, the constable, and the relief fleet. Four vessels full of slaves sailed for Brazil, and five, including the governor's two, left with slaves for Elmina and Portugal. Because of threats from the Barbarossa pirates, all ships now sailed in convoy.

We had acquired a new constable, an able captain from the admiral's fleet who had fallen in love with a mulatto girl and elected to remain on Tomé. The admiral realized the island needed a qualified soldier to head our garrison, so he had granted him a quarter-percent share of Crown export taxes as an incentive to stay. I befriended our new constable soon after his appointment.

When I heard reports of camp smokes on the dry side of the green mountain, I made plans for another foray. The governor's ships had brought a large store of muskets. With the dry season at hand, I decided to try them. I told the constable my plans. "...lost a man on my last expedition," I said, "and we need to be better armed." He gave me four muskets and demonstrated their use. I did not ask him to accompany me, knowing he'd received orders to wait for the Crown force to arrive.

As word of my preparations got around, Governor de Caminha called me to his residence. "You stir much passion among the islanders, Saulo. And from what I see, you look as determined as everyone says."

"I consider that a compliment, sir. The Angolars still have two women from my farm. Educated, free blacks, both teachers, Crown citizens. The Lisbon force may arrive too late to save them."

"I understand one carries your child."

"Almost to term when stolen, perhaps with twins. Two more Portuguese subjects." Our discussion ranged over many subjects and, as I expected, the governor spent excessive time on my tenant policy.

When finished, he accompanied me to the door. "You will find our new bishop extraordinary, Saulo. And while I strongly object to his appointment, also to his politics *and* his person, you may see him as a confederate." When I asked for an explanation, he said, "You'll find out soon enough." We waited while a squire brought my horse. "Godspeed in finding your people," he called as I mounted up.

• • •

A week later my men and I marched from the fugitive camp on a westerly track, all of us on foot, leading pack horses. I thought the Angolars might be spying on the west-side road, so we came along the east road, hoping to remain undetected. My force included the Guineas whose families I'd rescued. The two men had proved themselves tough, loyal fighters. With these two, along with Kiman, Pongué, and I, we formed a musket corps, four of us with weapons, and the fifth Guinea our loader and kindler.

My east-side approach paid off. We found the first Angolar camp in the location where I suspected, unguarded, with the men away on a raid. Of the twenty or so women and children, I spotted no mulatto infants. We trussed up the Angolar women and runaways and freed the Tomé captives, untying wrists and cutting through neck yokes. I questioned everyone, including the Angolars with Pongué translating. "Mbundu might be with the raiders," he reported, "but they have not seen our women since they were first taken." Discouraging news, no different from what I'd heard weeks before.

Considering the island slave owners would not share the risk of this expedition with me, I told the recovered slaves I'd not force them back into bondage. They could stay in the jungle. After more questioning, we left the camp guarded with some of my fighters and the freed slaves.

Based on what I'd been told at the camp, I set an ambush on the trail, selecting a vantage point above a steep decline where we could look down on a grassy flat a thousand feet below. The next morning we saw the raiders as they moved across the clearing in our direction—seven or eight Angolars and perhaps a dozen captives. They faced a difficult climb, and we would catch them tired and unawares. For the ambush I had chosen a length of trail free of heavy foliage. They would all be within sight when we attacked.

Once the Angolars were among us, we rushed from hiding. Believing musket fire would force a quick surrender, I killed the first man who raised his crossbow. I hoped it might be Mbundu. The enemy froze in their tracks and surrendered. We rounded them up and freed their captives. The latter group fled down the mountain. This seemed too easy—the musketshot had made the difference.

My Guineas examined the dead man and the others. Mbundu was not among them. Even with smoke curling from our tinder cups and muskets stuck in their faces, the Angolars refused our questions. Finally Pongué said, "They don't understand muskets. They think we have a cannon somewhere." As the kindler handed me my reprimed weapon, Pongué strode forward with his weapon and blew the head off the dead man. The Angolars threw themselves facefirst into the dirt and jabbered for mercy. I bellowed, "Where is Mbundu? Where are my two women and babies?" Pongué again translated.

I received immediate answers. "Mbundu and queens in secret place," one man said. Another, "None of us know where they are. Mbundu finds us. He will hide until you no longer seek him."

"What about my people?" I demanded.

"Pregnant queen have babies," the first man told us, but he did not know their fate. He stuck a finger in his neck. "Mbundu warriors protect him. A killer guards each queen and holds a knife to her throat. If you attack Mbundu, the women die."

I conferred with Kiman and Pongué. "Do you believe them?" I asked. Both thought the captives truthful. I sat on a log and pondered this impossible turn of events. Should I wait until Mbundu drops his guard? Even if Jubiabá's babies lived, there seemed nothing else I could do. Finally I said, "Yoke the Angolars and get the people from the camp."

In an hour they returned, herding the bound Angolars and runaways while the freed slaves walked ahead. Stray children ran here and there. A head count revealed that all the slaves had decided to go back to their farms rather than starve in the jungle.

After a steep, three-hour march down the mountainside, we arrived on the Alegre road above Rio d'Ouro. While everyone drank from a nearby stream and the local slaves gathered for their walk to Alegre, I considered what to do. The law was clear for runaways: I'd hand them over to the constable; he would return them to their farms and whatever punishment awaited. Despite the malice I felt for our captured Angolars, their children did not deserve their parents' fate. Through Pongué I told them, "By tomorrow afternoon we will be at the slave port. It is the place from where you escaped almost a year ago. There I will sell you. Because you are enemies of this island, you will be branded, shipped elsewhere, and separated from your children." What an odd turn of events. Last year we would have hanged these rebels. Now they were too valuable to kill. I pointed to the Alegre slaves who would soon start for their farms. "Give your children to them," I urged. "Your offspring will suffer less."

The Angolars had endured slave ports and shipment, and knew what sorrows loomed ahead. As in a scene wrought straight from Isaiah, they impelled their children to the Alegres, the older ones weeping, dragging the little ones. Two kanga infants were handed along as well. For a second time I examined these two closely, ensuring they were not mine. Then I cast my eyes to the mountain that still held Jubiabá, her babies, and Suryiah.

In a mood of intense failure, I turned my group up the west road. We faced a long, two-day walk. As we journeyed, I returned most of the recovered Africans to their farms, affirming to the owners they were not runaways. Many farms had great numbers of Africans in worker camps the size of small towns, and most of the planters were the same who'd threatened me with their petition before the typhus plague.

We arrived at the slave port the following afternoon. I was astounded to see how much the place had grown, though conditions remained as wretched as ever—row after row of barracoons, bodies dumped into open pits, animals feeding on them, more dead in the water, and all the harbor busy with black cargo. If the ghosts borne of Tomé rose from the underworld and lusted for space, our island would stand shoulder-to-shoulder with their sorrowful multitudes. The port's stink of death and burned flesh assailed me. Throughout our march I'd looked forward to being rid of these Angolars. Now, as I thought of the outrages they would suffer, my soul recoiled. If not for slavery, my travail—and theirs—would not be.

I separated the Angolars from the runaways, and readied them for sale. Felix da Tavora, master of our island's uncommon hell, ambled our way. He'd acquired a shabby captain's uniform and looked the fool. "What are these skinny niggers you bring me, Saulo?" He puffed himself up. "Thought you don't deal slaves?"

"Angolars, Felix, hardened by the jungle. Twenty cruz for the bunch."

He rubbed the scar on his cheek I'd inflicted a year ago, then hooked his walking stick under a woman's chin and tilted her face to his. With dignity, my captives endured his inspection. Finally he asked, "You selling all thirteen?" He knew my intentions and also knew me eager to be away from this place. He intended to draw things out.

"My next stop is the constable's. He'll hang them." I

291

nodded toward the harbor. I knew everyone considered Angolars the hardiest of slaves, many of them immune to bad-air fever. "Those Brazil captains will pay two cruz apiece, Felix."

He sullenly counted out the money, handed it to me, and again fingered the scar on his cheek. "Don't rush off, Saulo. Stay for supper."

Putting a hand to my dagger, I acknowledged his insult but went no further. I secured the coins and gestured to my little army, their disdain for this slaver written on every face. "I sup with my Negroes, Felix."

Two hours later, weary and sore, we reached the town garrison. A soldier I knew—and distrusted—met us in the yard. He, like most others, regarded my armed men with suspicion. "Where's your commander?" I asked.

He crossed himself. "I am commander. Our constable died two days ago. The fever." This was terrible news, to lose my new friend and no longer have an ally in this office.

I gave the soldier the runaways, but kept the few rescued slaves that remained. I believed the soldier would exploit these blacks and demand money from the planters, claiming he'd recovered them, or punish the Africans for his own pleasure. I'd planned on returning the muskets, but now kept them, knowing I might never again be able to borrow weapons from the armory. We took our leave before the new constable thought to ask for them.

After dropping off the remaining slaves, we arrived midday next at my farm with naught to show for our round-island walk but exhaustion and a few extra cruz. I sat on my house steps and soaked my aching feet in the basin I'd fashioned for Nawar. "My friend," I pleaded aloud, "how I need your counsel."

A day later I invited Ariella and Isabel to dinner at my home. I told of the journey and my failure to find our missing family. Yes family, for that is how I felt about Jubiabá and the babies, and Suryiah.

"No one could have done more, Marcel," said Isabel. Ariella agreed. Isabel continued, "If it is His will, God will deliver them to us. In the meantime you and Ariella should marry. Jubiabá expects it." How tragically these words fell on my ears—words I'd longed to hear now drowned in remorse.

Ariella told me the details of the constable's death and of his widow. "She now expects his child, Marcel. We should marry while God gives us time. Even thought it's the dry season, the fever still takes many."

"Legions are gone," I observed, "yet the cane ripens with indifference." I looked to Isabel. "God makes us wealthy with sorrows, Sra. Isabel, and soon with cruz." I pressed Ariella's hand to my lips. "In a month our first sugar will be milled and drying, a time for rejoicing. Let us marry then."

My Ariella smiled. "I accept your proposal. It will be a fine time."

Isabel gave a mischievous look. "If he's arrived by then," she said, "maybe our new bishop will marry you." She brushed a silencing hand through the air and smiled at Ariella. "Someone has told me tales of secret marriages, and I have grown curious. At some time might you and your betrothed have a private ceremony?"

Ariella's eyes were full of light. "Think what you will, Marcel, this idea was not mine."

• • •

Rumors swept our colony like wildfire and became more scandalous with each telling. First, slave captains who arrived from Elmina claimed the new bishop was black. They added a name and an appointment by Pope Clement, "Bishop Henrique Cão, son of King Henrique of the Congo," they said. Plausible—people had spoken of Cão, a priest who studied in Rome and Portugal, perhaps the Church's first black prince. A bishop to serve our island so riven with strife.

As Tomé bent to its harvest, the rumors grew. A planter who came to visit Nuño claimed they had organized a protest, that their lot included priests preaching warfare from the pulpit. I valued this disorder and encouraged the protestors at every chance. Let these Catholics fight among themselves.

I centered my energies on the harvest, supervising the cane crush at my mill, feeling much pride as my first syrup flowed into the boiling vats. The sweet vapors delighted my senses. Ariella worked with me daily, and we talked of our wedding two weeks hence, fueling our anticipation. A single thought seemed to arrive in both of us at the same moment, though Ariella voiced it first, "Can you wait until the new bishop arrives, Marcel? Only a matter of weeks perhaps, and if indeed he's black—"

"He can marry us. We'll thumb our noses at the colony."

"Her smile brightened further. "Isabel's mischief comes home."

We both laughed and thought of Nuño. He'd grown fond of Ariella. This would put him in an ill-tempered pickle.

• • •

With news of Cão's arrival, the Catholic rebellion turned sinister. We had just put our first sugar to dry when we heard he'd come ashore with a force of armed brothers. He would receive his investment at church the following Sunday. Rumor had it rebel planters planned to murder Cão at the festivities afterwards. Deciding to stay safe at home, we worked the farm that Sunday, but Nuño insisted on going to church. He took a cart and horse, and insisted that a daughter to drive him. Isabel refused to let either girl go, and sent a worker instead.

Nuño returned late in the afternoon, drunk on wine and disbelief. He sat propped up in the wagon bed, cursing. "He's a nigger all right; and he's got de Caminha and that constable wrapped around his little finger." He struggled to stand, leaned on the back of the wagonseat and pissed over the edge. The women turned away in disgust, but I found it pure comedy.

"So the rebels failed to murder him?"

"Of course," said Nuño, grappling with his pants. "The constable disarmed everyone before church. Cão's got those soldier-priests, half of them niggers too. And the man's ugly! *Never* seen a man so damn ugly." Sad to regard Nuño reverting to his old ways.

Ariella, Isabel, and I went to services the next Sunday. Nuño refused. He, along with many others, spurned Cão and, encouraged by a rebel priest from Alegre, threatened to assemble their own congregation. I carried a petition for the new bishop, asking him to marry Ariella and me. As expected, the constable and soldiers met everyone at the entrance and collected weapons.

Cão, despite his regal bearing, was indeed ugly—a large, squat man of perhaps thirty years, with drooping mouth fixed into a fleshy, round face that possessed large, bulged eyes low-set like a demon's. He sat unmoving on the pulpit, and spoke only after Mass. "Please excuse the brevity of my comments," he said in an eloquent voice. "As I do at times, I suffer from the fever and must rest. Nevertheless, two subjects compel me to issue the following decrees: The first is to inform those who oppose my office that you have one week to renounce your opposition and pledge fealty to me and The Mother Church. Otherwise you will be excommunicated. The second is a fine of twenty silver cruzados on any planter who kills or maims a slave without just cause."

The latter edict threw the assembly into chaos. Most everyone considered slaves property, to be treated like oxen. The congregation stood in protest. "Just cause?" someone shouted. Angry words rose from the crowd. An acolyte assisted Bishop Cão—who walked with the awkward movement of age—from the pulpit while a priest tried to calm the mob and explain. We left the service, the protest still raging. I reclaimed my dagger and passed my petition to the bishop's scribe.

Near the end of the next week, on an afternoon while I labored at my mill, Lael and Louisa excited and out of breath ran up to me. "Papa! Papa!" they shouted. "The bishop and his soldiers are coming to see you." And here they came. Cão rode a beautiful chestnut stallion, escorted by four mounted brothers. The escorts wore red hats and the white sash and red cross of the Knights Templar. They carried lances and wore breastplates.

I knelt in the shadow of the bishop's horse. "Your Excellence, your presence honors me."

He dismounted and extended a hand. "Stand, Saulo. No one is more honored than I."

"Sir?"

"I have read your petition, but that is not why I have come." He directed me to walk with him toward the Vascão. A knight on horseback followed a step behind. "When I inquired about you from Governor de Caminha, he told me Saulo is the only planter on the island who holds his workers as tenants. He implies you are quite the rebel."

"In some eyes."

"The governor suggested we are confederates. Is that so?"

"Based on your edict, sir, the twenty-cruz fine, I believe we may be." I wondered how a man of such unlikely countenance could appear so kind and courtly.

"I would like you to convince me of this. Please take me on a tour of your farm so I may see for myself."

I brushed at my clothes. "I am filthy, sir. Permit me to change first."

"Nonsense, Saulo. I admire a man who toils with his men."

While a worker went to get my horse, I showed the Bishop my sugar and lumber mills, surprised when he took a lance and waded the river with me, balancing himself with the shaft. "I hear you're an accomplished soldier, Saulo. What do you think of my men?"

"They would do any army proud." I knew about these knights and their campaigns against defenseless Jews and Moslems. "Templars?" I asked.

"Modern Templars. A gift from Clement VII, Order of St. John, trained with the Knights of Rhodes." Though I made no show of it, he sensed my feelings. "They bear you no malice, Saulo."

My horse arrived and we mounted up, riding toward Horté's with the knights behind us. "Thank you for the assurances, Bishop Cão" I said, "but what can one expect from a suspicious Novo?"

"Your bishop is as much Novo as you, my friend. Before I embraced The One True Faith, my Bakongo religion was certainly further from The Mother Church than Judaism."

He grew curious when we neared a cluster of workers returning to my tenant camp. After their ablutions to the bishop, he addressed them in Guinea, Angolar, and a Congo tongue I did not recognize. He soon had a lively conversation going. My children showed up, along with young Bartolis, the Horté daughters, and our many black orphans. I attempted introductions over the voices that rose around us. After a while Cão turned his mount back the way we came and summoned me to go with him.

"I trust nothing displeased you, Your Excellence?"

"Quite the opposite, Saulo. From what I see you are more a Christian than most."

As we headed for the farm gate, I felt relief at the absence of the igbo mask there. "Sir," I said, "have you considered my petition?"

He turned his palms to the heavens. "Indeed I will honor your petition, but first I must ask a favor." We rode through my gate where he stopped to face me. "I understand you constructed the beautiful home where I now reside."

"Yes, Your Excellence, but what is the favor?"

"Tuesday, join me at my residence for noon supper. We will eat, drink, and set a date for your marriage." All at once Cão appeared to bear the world's weight on his shoulders. He made the sign of the cross. "This favor I seek, it is one by which you could be most helpful to me."

Bidding him good-bye, I turned my horse and headed at a gallop for Horté's. I quickly found Ariella. "A favor?" she asked, "what could it be?"

"Don't know," I whispered, "but he suggested he'd marry us." We glanced at Nuño who dozed in the shade a few yards away.

To my astonishment, Governor de Caminha presented

himself at my mill the next morning just as Bishop Cão had done the day before. Accompanied by an outrider and a horsecart which carried two female slaves and quantity of goods, he heartily called, "Greetings, Saulo."

"Governor," I answered, "it is an honor to see you."

"I have brought us a flagon of Malaga and an excellent basket of red bass caught early this morning. Might we lunch together?" He pointed to the cart and the slaves. "They will prepare a delicious repast." De Caminha pondered my look. "No surprises, Saulo. I feel we must get to know one another. And it is a beautiful day for such activity."

While his slaves built a fire and prepared the meal, I took the governor on a tour of my sugar works. His outrider-turned-steward followed with a wine jug and dutifully replenished our goblets with the strong Malaga. After several fillings the governor said, "I understand you had a distinguished caller yesterday?" I confirmed the bishop's visit. "And what do you think of—" He took draught of wine and used a sleeve to wipe his mouth— "of what everyone's calling 'the Crown's mistake?' You know King Manuel pressed this bishop upon us?"

"From what I see he's a reasonable priest, concerned with the sins of his flock."

"I knew you might say that, Saulo, given that Cão proposes ruinous changes to our slave commerce." The steward called us to lunch, and we seated ourselves at a table set under the trees. De Caminha, unsteady from drink, looked at me dazedly. "What did he tell you?"

"About slavery? Nothing. I believe he might have intended to, but the subject did not come up."

The fish, vegetables, and fruit were quite delicious, and I thanked the governor. He ignored my words, guzzled wine, ate great mouthfuls of food, and stared at me with malice. When I attempted light conversation, he began to shout slanders against the bishop, the drink slurring his words. I felt much of his anger was directed at me. He looked over his shoulder at the steward who stood nearby and lowered his voice, "I can't oppose Cão openly, you know. The Crown would recall me, but that black devil's up to something." I had remained silent only a moment when he jumped to his feet and began to shout. "I bring you fine food and drink, wishing to discover what you know, and you mock me with silence!"

"Sir?"

"You're in league with this so-called bishop! I know you've asked him to perform your wedding." With these words de Caminha grabbed the table and overturned it, covering me with food. The effort made him stumble backward and he fell to the ground. "Goddamn you, Saulo! I should have never—" He struggled with the steward who rushed to help. Once on his feet, he slumped against the wagon, then crawled into the back. "Get me out of this place," the governor shouted. "I have no business with traitors." His servants stacked the supper goods around him and left.

I stood and contemplated this insane event, eating a bass while a gaggle of pea fowl fed on the spoils around me.

De Caminha's curses nagged at me all afternoon. Traitor? Had the bishop told him about my petition? Did the governor have spies in the Cão household? And to what end? It was he who suggested the bishop and I were confederates. Though I could make no sense of any of this, my apprehension grew. At dinner I lied to everyone, telling Ariella and the rest that de Caminha had merely drank too much, turned sick and gone home.

That evening, alone in my bed, another visitor arrived. "Marcel?" I asked, "why in a dream? Never before have I dreamt of you."

"Never before have you neglected me so."

"The world overwhelms me, Grandfather, yet I call for you only when I fear. There is little I fear these days and I am addicted to vainglory, no longer the Saddiq."

"Many think you are, Marcel, though the Saddiq is rarely judged in his own time on earth."

Great-grandfather vanished as always, and I awoke with

a chill on my heart.

· · ·

On Tuesday, expecting after de Caminha's visit to be waylaid on my way to town, I took Pongué and another man with me to visit Bishop Cão. We arrived there without incident, and I soon found myself walking with the bishop in his new courtyard as he proudly showed me his garden. "Tomé is blessed with a multitude of God's wonders," he said. "Planting them in my garden brings His Works closer to me." As we seated ourselves for lunch, he offered a prayer of thanks, then said, "Regarding your tenant policy, Saulo, you must be a man of great valor to take such a stand in a colony like this." His attendants brought lavish plates of food.

"It is a stand which logically occurs to me, sir, and my workers are more productive."

"Not a labor of conscience?"

"It could be. When I was taken from my family and shipped here, beaten, tortured, treated like an animal, I knew the misery of slavery. For those around me, and myself, I wanted away from it."

"Perhaps you're my only confederate on this island." That word again, one that I was learning to dread. Was this connected to the favor he wanted to ask?

The bishop continued. "I have seen the plight of Jews in Iberia, and the better life they have in Rome. We have a large community of your people in my city of Ambasse. They certainly aren't the malicious demons the Church makes them out to be."

"I'm surprised to hear the phrase, 'your people.' As I said, I am a Novo Christão."

Cão rubbed the skin of his arms. "As your heritage binds you to Jerusalem, my flesh tethers me to Africa." His large eyes grew moist. "This skin, this black gold enriches the kings of Europe and Africa, and sadly, my Church." As tears ran down the man's face, his countenance appeared more gloomy than ever. He seemed to sensed my thoughts with his next words. "By any earthly standard I am not a handsome man. This sad face you see— Well, as a child I was tormented by the other children because of my appearance. But then as a young man I discovered the teachings of our Lord. In God's eyes all men are beautiful."

An attendant brought a handkerchief. The bishop wiped his eyes and blew his nose. "Understand that I am a first-generation Christian, Sr. Saulo." He crossed himself. "So I have taken Christ's teachings to heart. Perhaps more-so than many of my colleagues in the Church. My sentiments put me at odds with both Church and governance."

"I am not sure you've told me your sentiments, sir."

"I consider black slaves fellow Africans. This puts me in opposition even to my father who, as the first Christian king of the Congo, sells his own people like cattle. Starvation and decimation stalk the land of my birth, pits brother against brother, mother against child." He settled his sad eyes on me. "I am preparing a tract which I shall send to King Manuel requiring better treatment for our slaves. Nothing to upset their precious commerce, mind you, but I believe Catholic Law extends to all men. Slaves must be baptized and given sustenance, their families kept whole."

"Whether Jewish conscripts, slaves, or defeated Moors, nowhere in Christendom are men treated so. What you suggest is without precedent."

He made a gesture of frustration. "Manuel claims he supports me; yet even my father opposes my position, and the powers in Lisbon may only be humoring me, hoping I will lose interest now that I'm isolated here." He offered his profile. "Nevertheless I am devoted to Catholic Law. *With my hand*, the instrument of God in Christ's Church, I will enforce it." He asked my permission for tea. The attendants cleared the plates and brought cool buena and sugared figs. Cão drummed his fingers on the table. "How strongly do you favor my sentiments, Saulo?"

"I believe it is evident in the way I treat my Africans."

The bishop stood and bade me follow, examining his plants as we walked. His attendants trailed behind with the figs and tea. "On my journey here from Lisbon we made

301

port at Elmina. Injustice to slaves in that frightful place confirms my fears. But my tract must describe the wretched conditions of several slave ports. Though I have not visited them, I hear the slave stations farther south are just as terrible. The court flatterers who surround King Manuel tell him these places are nearly Edens, and he seems to believe it. Only first-hand accounts will convince him otherwise, and—"he paused to strip wilted flowers from a bush, then straightened up slowly—"I need a second party to observe these abuses. It will add credence to my tract." He put his hands together in prayer. "Which brings me to ask my favor: I request you journey to Pinda for me to detail the suffering of slaves there."

I could not believe my ears. A knot formed in my stomach, my face turned flushed and hot. "Sir, when? I hope to get married soon. Such a journey would—"

"Are you ill?" he asked.

I wiped sweat from my forehead with my sleeve. "Perhaps a touch of fever, Your Excellence."

He turned to an attendant. "Bring our guest a damp cloth of camphor."

I rested on a nearby bench and, with the cloth on my forehead, I felt a little better. Cão looked at me earnestly. "My friend, I have much to discuss with you. Do you feel well enough to continue? You look improved."

Despite my ill-ease and shock, his request intrigued me. And if I did not hear him out, I would dishonor this man. "I am better, sir. Please go on."

"The ship I seek for your passage could be here any day; and Pinda is a mere seventy-five leagues away. You'll be gone only a week or so." As I listened, my confusion grew. For some reason the idea of this journey frightened me. "You have my word, Saulo, I will honor your petition of marriage and unite you and your bride on the eve of your return. So will you accommodate me? I wish to discuss the details of your travel."

On the way home I drove the horse while Pongué and the other man ate food sent with us from the bishop. "I told

Bishop Cão I'd decide in a day or two," I said to Pongué. "He suggested I wear a priest's disguise. Since you're my only worker who speaks Angolar, if I decide to go, will you accompany me? I'm supposed to have a manservant." I knew he relished adventure.

"With pleasure, master. I will sail with you to Pinda on a deck without chains." He grinned broadly.

Pongué's glee did nothing to dispel my gloom. These days three-masters made up nearly the entire fleet, so in a way the prospect of a short trip to Pinda excited me, but there seemed something wrong with its purpose. Could my report truly benefit Cão's tract? Who would care what I thought?

Concern about the trip tortured me over the following day as I considered my decision. What would Great-Grandfather Marcel choose in this circumstance? I thought I knew. Then there was the question of marriage. If I refused the bishop's request, could I still expect him to marry us?

I waited until evening before I told Ariella. She stood listening, arms folded, the angriest I'd ever seen her. "Oh," she protested, "what a terrible idea. What about our wedding? You belong here on the farm with me and our beautiful sugar crop, not on some dangerous errand for God knows—"

"It is not dangerous, Ariella, and Pongué will accompany me. I'll be gone a week, perhaps two at most. As for harvest and milling, Kiman runs things quite well."

She stepped back as I reached for her. "You cast your lot with the most hated man on the island!"

I felt my own anger rising. "I have sought your counsel, and you respond like this? You told me you liked the idea of Cão's marrying us. If I don't help him, he might not—"

"Well I've changed my mind," she said harshly. "Anybody can marry us. What if someone finds out what you're doing?"

"Finds out that I travel for the Bishop of São Tomé? Why are you acting like this?" She refused to meet my gaze, began crying bitterly, turned and ran up the steps to

Isabel's.

Confused as usual, I set out for home. Once there, sitting by the candle and recording the day's events in my journal, I struggled to quell my apprehension. What on earth was I afraid of? My own behavior puzzled me as much as Ariella's. A shaggy moth the size of a small bird whirred onto my page. I caught it gently and closed my hand around its struggling body. Its strange eyes glowed fiercely in the candlelight. I walked to the door, pulled the net aside, and threw the moth into the night. "Seek your fate elsewhere," I called after, then studied the golden dust left in my hand.

Bishop Cão's request blessed me with opportunity, a noble cause for a Saddiq. Here was a priest with the compassion of Fr. Norte—a bishop no less—who shared my distaste for slavery, did not hate Jews, and who sought my help. I must ignore Ariella's anger and overcome my own fears. "Be true to your namesake," my father had whispered that night in Lisbon. "There you will find courage." Of course I would undertake the journey for Cão. This is what a Just Man must do; and perhaps my report would make a difference. I resolved to send word to the bishop in the morning.

· · ·

Several days passed before Cão's livery and a priest showed up with instructions and clerical attire for Pongué and me. He thanked me profusely for my decision, then got down to business. "You must cut your hair thusly," he explained, showing me his bowl-shaped trim, "and you must crop your beard short and neat, not the unruly thicket I see on your face. As for the manservant, he must be clean and tend to your every need." The liveryman brought in two sets of clothing, sandals, and rosary beads, a brown cassock for Pongué with a black waistband, and a gray, hooded cassock with a gold waistband for me. Lastly he handed me a heavy cross on a brass chain. The Saddiq as Catholic priest. Then it struck me, might Cão be a Just Man? This bishop seemed to qualify, and legend has it the Saddiq is more often a non-Jew. Only time would tell.

My cassock hung entirely too long and full. The priest gave a hearty laugh when he saw it on me. "Have one of your women fix it," he told me. Pongué, who stood a head taller than I, would find his garment adequate. As the priest prepared to leave, he said, "His Excellence has arranged your passage with a captain known for his Christian charity. We expect the ship from Pinda within the week."

"A slave ship?" I asked, Christian charity I wondered.

"It is a trading ship that sometimes carries slaves. He plies the trade between here and Pinda." Not a satisfactory answer, but I let it go.

Late morning of the next day, as I drove a cart overflowing with cane stalks to my mill, the tolling of the village Angel bell reached my ear. I thought of the priest's garb that hung in my house. My decision to do Cão's bidding warmed me, but Ariella had not relinquished her anger. As I considered how to win her over, I spotted two riders hurrying down my farm lane—the priest from the day before and a Templar.

"His Excellence begs you come see him," the priest said. "It is of utmost importance."

"Certainly," I answered, and left the cart with a nearby worker. I sent a runner to my stable and mounted behind the Templar. We rode to my house where I changed clothes. Before I had fully changed, a tenant arrived with my horse.

As we spurred our horses for town, the priest explained. "Yesterday, after Wednesday Mass, a group of men gathered in the square to celebrate. No one paid much attention to them, and Bishop Cão returned to his rectory office. Perhaps an hour later they turned into a mob and stormed the rectory, threatening to kill the bishop. They tried to start a fire, but the Templars put it out and drove the men away. In all of this His Excellence strictly forbade the Templars to injure anyone." I recalled Ariella's words, 'The most hated man on the island.'

"Much damage to the rectory?"

"Only a little. When the mob heard Bishop Cão had fled

305

to his residence, they headed there. The knights were horseback, so they arrived ahead and chased the rioters away."

"What does this have to do with me?" I asked.

"Bishop Cão has prayed daily over your journey. He must talk to you in person."

We arrived at the church where three formidable Templars guarded the entrance. Inside I found the bishop kneeling before the altar, praying aloud in Latin. I knelt at the first bench and appeared to pray. When the bishop finished his devotion, a priest informed him I'd arrived. "Saulo," said Cão as he took my arm, "I thank you greatly for your decision. Heaven will reward you. Let us go to my embattled rectory; there is much I must tell you." Inside he settled behind his desk and called for refreshments. An acolyte brought honeyed tea. When the door shut, Cão began his story. "This attack yesterday is another sign that God instructs me to relieve the suffering of my African brothers. As I journeyed here from Lisbon, I prayed day and night over this. When I heard there lived a white man on this island who might share my views and I sought him out. That of course was you."

"Yes sir."

"What you do not know is"—he crossed himself and made a silent prayer—"I believe God has given me other signs. Your name for instance, Saulo descended from King Saul of the Hebrews, is also the name of the Apostle Paul— *Saul* of Tarsus, Christ's messenger on earth."

"This is a heavy burden, Your Excellence. I wish you had told me sooner."

Cão rose to his feet and strode around his small office. "But I *could not* tell you sooner. Don't you see, you agreed to the journey without my urging. You have innate valor."

"Yesterday's attack, how was that a sign?"

"I forgive your lack of Christian knowledge, Saulo, but you should know that mobs and temple priests, along with the Romans, assailed the Apostles and Christ's early followers. The mob yesterday cast me in company with The

306

Host."

None of this cheered me—I recalled that most of these people were eventually murdered. We talked a while longer, then Cão sent me home in the company of two Templars. The Saddiq, Church lackey, guarded by sworn enemies of the Jew.

Back home I busied myself with the harvest and milling, awaiting word that the Pinda ship had made port. Attempted conversations with Ariella proved futile, although occasionally I caught her looking my way.

Yasemina, her daughter and new son, and a cartfull of goods arrived a few days after my visit with Cão. "Nawar's heir is here," she told me. "We are dispossessed."

"My farm welcomes you. I will have Kiman build a house for your family at Horté's. There is more open land there." Remembering that her daughter had helped the nuns in the town school, I said, "After harvest, Isabel's oldest girl and yours can teach school here. It's too far to send the children into town, and dangerous with the Angolar threat and all the settlement angry at me." Yasemina offered her thanks and left for Horté's, promising to intercede with Ariella on my behalf.

Almost a week went by before Bishop Cão's agent appeared and announced the ship from Pinda had arrived. "We will come for you tomorrow afternoon," the man declared, and handed me a letter of transit with the bishop's seal.

"Is the caravel a three-master?" I asked, excited at the prospect.

He shrugged. "I do not concern myself with such things. Just make yourself ready."

I sent word to Pongué, planning to tell everyone else at dinner. That evening at Horté's it was obvious that Yasemina's intercession had not worked. Ariella scowled at me, turned quickly and left. I made light of her behavior and we sat down to dinner.

Afterwards, all the children gathered round laughing while Yasemina cut my hair and trimmed my beard, while

Nuño glared and muttered curses from his corner. Even Pongué allowed his wife to trim his fuzzy hair and clip the few whiskers from his chin.

The next noon Yasemina brought a delicious supper and waited with me for the bishop's coach. "Ariella still loves you," she confided. "She says she will perish if anything happens to you."

"Nothing will happen. I'll return and Cão will marry us." We sat on the brow of the hill overlooking my farm, the Vascão, and the distant road. I opened my journal. "See," I pointed, "every day I will keep an account. In a week or so I will read it to Ariella and win her back. This is a favorable time of year for the trade winds. I wager my time away will be short."

I withdrew Leah's gold chain from my pocket and said, "You and your beloved husband were there when I recited my marriage declaration to dear Miriam. So now—" I wrote out my declaration, carefully tore the page from my journal, folded the necklace within the paper, and gave it to Yasemina. "Please tell Ariella that her gift is not yet complete. In Pinda I will select a jewel of brilliant turquoise that will rival the blue of her eyes."

Chapter 21

In a short while we saw the Bishop's carriage as it came along the road. Yasemina's dark eyes welled with tears. "This is a good thing you do, Marcel." I sent a runner for Pongué and collected my travel things. Yasemina laughed as I donned my priestly garb, settled the heavy cross and chain over my head and adjusted it around my neck. She straightened my hood. "Better take a vow of silence. No one will believe you're a priest." I made the sign of the cross and blessed her, then Pongué as he trudged our way in his acolyte's attire. We must have looked quite the pair, the tall sturdy black man and the short Jewish priest. In the blistering heat of this afternoon and our heavy garments, we both began to sweat profusely. We loaded our things into the carriage and bade our good-byes. Yasemina took Pongué's hand and gestured to me. "Take good care of him."

My manservant bowed. "For master and friend, Ma'am Yasemina, with my life."

Our journey began as Yasemina watched from the hill. The horse pulled us along my lane and up the road to the settlement. I felt relief at finally being on our way.

In town we stopped at the church where Bishop Cão gave us his blessing. He handed baskets of food to his liveryman and a purse of coins to me. "Give Captain Suárez fifty silvers for your passage."

"Suárez, sir? A Spaniard?"

"Oh yes, a most gracious one; owner of his own ship as well. I came down with him from Lisbon.

So this was the captain of local trade and Christian charity, one sailing under the Spanish Alliance, the devil's bargain between Manuel and Ferdinand written with the blood of Portuguese Jews. Regardless of Cão's like for the man, I suspected Suárez could not to be trusted.

"You make a worthy looking priest," observed Cão.

"I'm not sure, Your Excellence; but I believe myself worthy of your charge, and will return with a full report"

At the harbor, the sun setting over the jut of land west of the city, we greeted Captain Suárez. My heart quickened as I spotted the three masts of his glorious ship. Though the captain carried himself in the arrogant Spanish manner, he spoke passable Portuguese and seemed reasonably gracious. He accepted the food and payment, then penned a note to Bishop Cão, handed it to the liveryman, and sent him on his way. He addressed me as "Father Marcel." Just how much Cão had told him I did not know, but none of it was his business. I introduced Pongué and thanked him for the passage. "We expect to spend a few days in Pinda," I told Suárez, "and return when you sail next back to here."

"Will you stay with the friars, Father Marcel?"

From the corner of my eye I saw Pongué's face light with humor. "Yes, Captain Suárez, I carry letters of introduction from the bishop." As the sailors rowed us to the waiting ship, a full moon rose from the African waters and chased the sun from the sky. I noticed the ship rode high in the water. "Are you returning empty to Pinda?" I asked.

Though my question seemed mild enough, it distracted him. "No, father,"—he paused and squinted at his vessel— "we will load cargo at Porto Alegre, sugar, yams, and lumber." Once alongside the caravel, the sailors held the ship's boat while we climbed the rope web to the deck. "Show the priest to his quarters," the captain told an officer, and ambled away—not the reception I'd expected. Regardless, the tiny booth proved sufficient. It appeared to be that of an absent mate's, with a raised pallet for me and a straw pad on the floor for Pongué.

After stowing our things, Pongué and I sat on the deck

and ate dinner from one of Cão's food baskets as we watched the moon illuminate the settlement and mountain beyond. Pongué carved beads from a length of snake vine while I whispered a prayer for all that lay before us. Dare I consider that God has dealt less harshly with me than with Job? Two missing children and their mother, one dead wife, my sister Leah's fate unknown? Only this? Yet plague and fever spared most of my family while others on São Tomé died. Why does this not make me grateful? And to what end does God tempt me over happiness with Ariella?

Before us moonlight glinted across the water and the dark mountain rose in its mystery, the twin crests fretted with silver clouds. Yasemina's plight came to mind, reminding me I must prepare a testament when I return, willing the farm to Joseph and Lael. Did this thought mean I'd abandoned my search for Jubiabá, her sister and the children? The idea sent a chill along my spine. Behind us the captain and officers, who continued to ignore us, began a lewd drinking song on the highdeck. Since they excluded me from their revelry, perhaps they really thought I was a priest. As we prepared our beds, Captain Suárez rapped on the entry and peered inside. "Father Marcel, no alarm if you hear us take sail by moonlight. The trace of clouds tells me we may get a favorable wind before morning."

We'd slept maybe three hours when the ship began to pitch on the swell. The wind sang in her rigging. I expected seasickness, but found it not upon me. The ship sat at anchor so that it pointed prow-first into the wind, giving the deck's movement a pleasant rhythm. We dressed and went outside. The moon sat high above the west horizon, with dawn three or four hours away. All night we'd heard the crew at work to ready the ship. Suárez knew his weather.

The breeze swept in from the north and required a difficult harbor exit, though once on open sea it promised a straight run to Pinda. I excitedly explained these things to Pongué, adding, "We'll see if this captain is up to getting us out of the harbor. It won't be easy."

Suárez met the challenge with ease. His crew mounted the small foresail and held it sharp to windward while others kept the helm to port. The ship bucked crossways through the waves and moved deftly out of the harbor. The sight and feel of this was intoxicating. Soon I would be sailing the broad sea on a three-master. "We'll run down the east side of Tomé," I told Pongué. "If the moon's high, we might see our farm." He seemed unimpressed and complained of seasickness. I wondered about Ariella.

Once on the open water, the sailors mounted only half the sails and held our course on a hard northeast tack. This made no sense since they could have mounted sails full and gone windward to Porto Alegre. But this captain knew his ship; perhaps he didn't need a full rig for the short trip there. Before we knew it, the ship came about and began a tack northwest past the low headland of the settlement. "Well," I said to Pongué, "I guess we'll approach Alegre from the west. It seems out of the way."

"We can look for Angolar fires on the mountain," he suggested, appearing a little less ill. When Ilhoa de Cabras came into view, the crew dropped one sail, and left only the foresail and half-a-rig on the midmast. I found this so puzzling, I left Pongué to speak with the captain on the highdeck. I had not gone ten feet when I heard my companion curse. Turning, I saw four men knock Pongué to the deck. As I rushed to his aid, a gang of sailors surrounded me. I held them at bay with my dagger.

"You can't kill everyone, Saulo," growled Suárez who appeared from behind his men. "Give up."

"I can kill *you!*" I shouted, and set after him. A blow from behind put me on the deck, my dagger clattering out of reach. They trussed my hands and tied me to the midmast. Though Pongué fought violently, they threw him into the hold, his curses raging from beneath the deck until something silenced him.

"What are you doing?" I demanded. "This is criminal!" By now we had rounded Cabras with the slave port in view, the first color of dawn lighting the waters.

312

The captain looked at me with insolence. "Da Tavora will explain it."

To no avail I struggled against the ropes, struggling also to understand this betrayal. There seemed many possibilities. As the ship made its way into the slave harbor I saw a boat on the water rowing to meet us. In the bow stood Felix da Tavora. Once on board, my old vereador strode up to me and spit in my face. "I see you've got the Jew," he snarled to Suárez. "Where is his man?"

"In the hold," answered the captain. "Another slave to sell."

"Watch that black," said da Tavora. "He's a crafty bastard." He turned his attention back to me, his eyes small and forbidding. "So, Saulo, thought you were off on some errand for the nigger bishop, did you? If you survive, we'll sell you with the rest." He took a whip from one of the sailors and lashed me across the face. Even in torture or at the stake I'd never known such shock and pain. If I could only touch my face—it felt like he'd put out my eye. I turned my head to avoid the next blow, but it fell on my shoulder. "I don't want him to miss the excitement," da Tavora said, and tossed the whip to a sailor. He put his fingers to his cheek. "That's repayment for this, Jew. And there's more."

Longboats full of slaves began to arrive from the port. Driven to climb the rope web, they were forced into the hold and chained. Blood kept running from my eye into my mouth and it caked on my lips. The sun bore down terribly upon me. I pleaded for water, but all day received only a meager sip from da Tavora when he stopped to brag. "We're taking these black devils to Brazil," he said. "We'll make a fortune when we sell them."

"Then sell me too, but let me live. I need someone to tend my face. Pongué will do it."

"Not a chance. That one's chained with the rest."

"Free me and I'll see that you get only exile, not the gallows. By the time you provision the ship, the bishop will hear of this."

"Guess again, Saulo. We sail before dusk. We'll sell slaves in Elmina for provisions there."

I hoped against hope this might be true. In Elmina, Nasic would discover this iniquity and free me, but surely da Tavora remembered my friendship with Nasic. I could only pray he'd forgotten. Oh how I wished I could touch my face, and Elmina was a week's sail away—two weeks if this unfavorable wind kept up. Would they leave me to die, lashed to this mast? This fate I could not allow. I began to shout for Suárez, pleading for water. Finally the captain appeared. I said, "If I am to survive for the slave market, I must have water." He summoned a cup and a sailor held it to my lips.

By now the ship's hold stood full, and more blacks were being chained on deck. With the sun low over the water, this hellish ship would soon set sail. I weighed my chances, trying to decide among perilous choices, then continued my plea to Suárez. "I am known in Elmina. Keep me alive and you can ransom me and Pongué. Enough cruz to provision the ship." I doubted the captain would fall for this, but perhaps it provided an opening. Though I wanted to ask him if Pedro de Abreu had a hand in this treachery, I knew the question would work against me.

He gave me a hard smile. "Do you really think us fools? We know you're friends with Nasic the slave broker. If you live, we'll simply hide you below."

"How can you dishonor Bishop Cão in this manner?" I thought about the spies in his household, the tea and fig-bearers that day in his garden.

"A man of his color cannot be a priest, much less a bishop. It is a privilege to dishonor him."

"Your scheme is folly. You'll lose your ship. One cannot sell stolen slaves in Elmina *or* Brazil." I felt the edge of madness—the thirst, and the pain from my ruined eye.

He jerked his thumb to the blacks crowding the fore deck. "I hold title to those buggers. I'll sell *them* for provisions. If da Tavora told you Brazil, he does not understand. We travel to the Spanish lands north of there. In those

314

Americas I can sell whatever I wish."

The caravel left harbor as the sun slipped into the sea. I prayed for Pongué and my family, beseeching Marcel to appear. If my beloved great-grandfather heard my prayer, it took the form of a fresh south trade that caught us as we left São Tomé, a wind which might hurry me to Elmina before my death. The irony of this hideous journey, to sail as a captive from my home into a rising moon. On the receding island, canefield fires lit the landscape and smoke obscured the flank of the green mountain just as they had when I arrived on this sea almost five years ago.

By morning a fever possessed me, my head in delirium, the sun reflecting off the waters, blinding. They could not have tethered me in a worse place, the aft side of the mast as the ship sailed north where sun broiled my body all day and shade from the sail fell just out of reach. Not a wisp of cloud appeared to soften the sunblaze. I no longer prayed for Marcel, I prayed for death. Good-bye dear Ariella, you must never see me like this. Near evening da Tavora and two slave-port degradados appeared. I pleaded again for water. "Drink our spit," they shouted, and let fly in my face. They brought their dinners and ate in front of me. Too sick for hunger, I did not care.

On the second day slaves began to die and were thrown overboard. I prayed to join them, to embrace the hakifi in the bloody jaws of the sea. I do not remember when or how long I lost my senses, but found myself one night free of the mast, chained with a slave iron to a column next to the highdeck, a bowl of water and hard biscuit within reach. I had no hunger for the biscuit, but drank the entire bowl of water, then vomited into my lap. I felt carefully for my ruined eye. I had no eye, only the empty socket of bone. The delirium took me.

In the morning I saw the African coast. This meant I'd been insensate for days; and though it seemed the fever had lifted, I could not take a full breath. The air rattled in my chest. I ate the biscuit and called for more. An officer brought hardbread and filled the bowl with water. "How long to Elmina?" I asked.

He studied the mizzen pennon which stood straight in the breeze. "A day, maybe two."

I gestured to my eye. "Please bring me a poultice for this."

He stepped into the light and looked up to the highdeck. "I'll do what I can." He came back after a time with some bananas and a cloth to clean my face. "I have no poultice," he said, "but I'll see you are tended to."

I raised my body. "Like the slaves below, I lie in my own waste." Then I noticed the man was mulatto. "Why do you care for me?"

He crossed himself. "I hear you and your slave were emissaries for Bishop Cão. The bishop held Mass on this very ship on our way from Lisbon, and in Tomé he blessed me. What the captain and da Tavora do is wrong." He called two sailors. The men stripped me and doused my body with seawater, then rinsed my clothes and put them back on me.

"Do you risk punishment for this?" I asked.

The officer smiled. "No, Captain Suárez is in all manners avaricious. He owes the crew wages, and knows I want to leave the ship at Elmina. I've no wish for Brazil or any unknown place. I persuaded him to give me your custody in lieu of pay. He and the degradado reluctantly agreed." He pursed his lips. "I imagine Bishop Cão will reward me for your rescue."

"He will indeed, and so will I." I guessed a one-eyed farmer would not fetch much on the slave market. I ate a biscuit and some fruit. "You must save my man Pongué." I coughed, taken by a fit of it.

He nodded. "I will do so before Elmina."

I gripped the cross around my neck. "Is my eye really gone?"

He put his face near mine. "It appears so." Again my senses abandoned me.

I awoke in the late afternoon. They'd moved me to a different spot with a pad under my body and a sackpillow for my head. Though still shackled, but with a chain long enough to let me stand, I found food and water nearby, and a chamber pot. I stood for the first time in days, leaning on a wooden column that supported the deck above. I immediately felt dizzy and dropped to my knees. They had tied a cloth around my head and over my bad eye. Surely I looked as rough as any sailor. Da Tavora came near as I knelt there. "Too bad you might live," He said and placed a finger aside his eye, running it over the lid. "But you will always have something to remember me by."

In the night the terrible fever and cough seized me again. This was not the bad-air fever, but something worse, much worse. My body racked with cramps and my bowels flowed without control. In the morning the officer brought water and a towel. He watched me with pity as I struggled to clean myself. "Our good wind continues," he said, "almost a gale. I expect we'll make port in an hour or two. You will have to go below deck and stay there until just before the ship sails. Then I'll take you ashore and find a physician." I looked to see the mainmast topsail furled and lashed, the lanyards standing in the breeze. Perhaps Marcel still answered my prayers, but could I live for two days or more in the hold of this ship? "I need Pongué," I cried. "Get him. I'm quite sick."

He acknowledged my request and headed for the hold, but had gone hardly a pace or two when a commotion erupted on the highdeck. Suárez began shouting orders to the crew. Sailors hurried from every direction and gathered at the stairway a few feet from where I was shackled. A lookout climbed the mainmast and stood in the nest. He pointed aft towards the coast, shouting, "There he is! Corsair! Corsair!"

"What's happening?" I asked one of the men.

"Barbarossi!" he said in a terrified stammer.

I stood, straining to see their ship. In the distance a black menace appeared against the coastline, its oar banks catching a glint of sun. It was a low-slung, square-rigged galley, an unusual ship in this sea. Perhaps it was Barbarossi, but they could never catch us running downwind in this gale. The mulatto officer came down the stairway and I called to him. "Is there just one of them?" Dizzy again, I sat down.

"Yes, and we can outrun him." He pointed forward. "That's the Elmina headland. I reckon the fool will break off before we make port." He left to help the sailors prepare the cannon.

"That pirate's no fool," I called after him, "they're up to something." I rattled the chain on my leg. "Turn me loose. My health is ruined, I'm no danger to anyone."

"I cannot," he shouted back. "Suárez has the key. You'll be free in Elmina."

"Then get me Pongué." He ignored my words and hurried off.

My chest hurt terribly. Even my shallow breaths proved painful. I began another fit of coughing. My bowels turned liquid, and I soiled myself before I could get to the pot. Weary beyond belief, I reclined back in my mess and tried to sleep. The sky swam above me as the rough sea slammed against the ship's hull.

I fell into a stupor for about an hour until a howl of protest broke out among the crew. I struggled to my feet, again supporting myself with the column. The highdeck behind me blocked my view of the corsair, but I had no doubt it still trailed us. What I saw ahead in Elmina harbor froze my blood. The hulks of three Portuguese ships sat smoldering in the water as the wind whipped their smoke landward. Unfamiliar colors flew from the ramparts of the fort. Two sleek galleys rowed at us from the bay, the pirate soldiers standing ready as the wind relentlessly swept us toward them.

"Cut the halyards," commanded Suárez, desperate to slow our drift. The sailors complied and chopped frantically at the ropes. Sails, rigging and all plummeted to the deck. The foremast spar broke. Its canvas and lumber tumbled down on the screaming slaves. Vastly outnumbered, the captain and his men crowded the rail, keening in prayer, supplicating to their Christ. The wind and pirate oarsmen sealed our fate as the coxswains' drumbeats reached our ears, nearer and nearer. Suárez struck the flag and prepared to plead mercy. Panic seized the crew.

The mulatto officer came by. "Farewell, Saulo. This is from your cabin." He threw my purse at me.

"My leg iron!" I hissed. "And Pongué!"

"The key's in the purse," he said. "See if you can buy your freedom from the heathens."

Rumors had it these Turks behaved more charitably than Christians and, as I found the key and stuffed the purse inside my undergarments, I prayed I might experience this charity.

The Barbarossi crews boarded the ship at once, coming alongside with demoniac huzzahs. Hove to and grapples cast, the white-turbaned pirates swarmed aboard the caravel like sugar ants. I reached to unlock my shackle, then changed my mind. Perhaps if they saw me captive they would treat me better. I removed the cross from my neck and put it with the leg-iron key under my sleeping pad.

Ignoring the pleas from the caravel's officers and crew, the Barbarossi trussed the men as if they were market pigs, passed them to the galleys, and stacked them in rows like bundles of thatch. The slaves on deck remained chained in place, as did the multitude of Negroes in the hold. I prayed for Pongué and myself. From my limited knowledge of the Turk language, I understood that all captives, white or black, would become booty for the Sultan Barbarossa. No matter my fate, I felt pleased that Suárez and da Tavora were destined for the slave market or the oar bench.

By now we had drifted further into the harbor. The pirates attached one of their ships to the bow and began towing us toward the seawall. Despite my distress, I pondered the brash nature of these waterborne devils and admired their galleys. Here and there pots of blooming flowers hung from their spars.

I rested on my pad, mostly ignored, exchanging a smile or brief word in my poor Arabic with the occasional Turk who looked at me. As we neared the seawall, I saw corpses draped along its entire length, many of them disemboweled, two hanged by white lengths of turban cloth. I struggled to my feet for a better look, afraid one might be Nasic. Neither were. The majority of the dead appeared to be from the Portuguese garrison. Slave port or otherwise, this would be a tragic end to Elmina. I could only wonder if the pirates would soon invade Tomé.

In spite of the heat, I felt a sudden chill and fell back on the pad. An officer came by, a man of swarthy complexion who wore a white caftan and gold braid around his turban. "Who are you?" he asked.

"A Portuguese citizen and a Jew," I told him, having decided this was the best answer.

"Why are you dressed so?"

"The Christians did this to shame me. I am deathly ill and need a doctor. They beat me. I've lost an eye."

He fetched a man with a chisel and hammer, and struck my leg iron. As they helped me to my feet, the pad stuck to my back and revealed the cross and key. "Explain this!" he demanded. I stayed silent, my head spinning with the sickness. He fit the key to the broken leg iron and glared. "You're one of their priests," he said, and threw the cross into the sea. "We have a place for you."

I must have again lost my senses, for I next found myself ashore, being dragged along the fortress outwork. Behind me slaves from the ship's hold marched toward the Elmina fortress. I struggled to see Pongué, but could not. Many bodies floated in the water around the ship. At any moment I expected to join these dead, or those who hung from the seawall. Instead they cast me into a cistern that occupied a large space in the rock floor of the outwork. I pitched head-first into a mass of rotted bodies in the water. The cold saltwater-shock revived me. I discovered they had tied my hands. My death would come from drowning.

"I will live a little longer," I said, feeling rocks beneath my feet. The water, apparently leaked in from the sea, stood only waist deep. Perhaps I was dead, enveloped in a scene wrought from the Christian hell. Attached to the reeking bodies, large-clawed crabs fed in mindless clicking. Here and there floated rats, eyes white and bulging, mouths gaped open in death. Though my arms were trussed behind me, I found a sharp point of rock and worked the rough cord against it. After some struggle, I freed myself. The effort left me breathless and coughing. The fifteen-foot cistern walls were covered with slime. No possibility of escape. The light above told me night was fast approaching. I took a cruz from my purse and tossed it up to the surface. It clinked on the stone plaza above. As twilight deepened with the echoing calls to prayer, an Arab chanced by and picked up my coin. I feebly shouted to him, but he went on without looking. I noticed the water had dropped slightly, likely caused by a receding tide. In desperation I threw up another coin and a dead rat after it. Now darkness covered me—no hope till morning. How long could I last? I struggled to keep from fainting, against hunger and thirst. To succumb meant death. Hour after hour I kept myself from madness, imploring Yahweh, Christ, and Great-Grandfather Marcel to help me.

Sometime in the night the water drained from the cistern. The crabs were replaced by rats, their eyes gleaming in the dark. From a distance, torch or lantern light flickered around the rock circle above me. I dragged bodies into a pile and sat upon them, sleeping for a time. The rats did not bother me. They seemed content to feed on the putrid corpses.

At first light, seawater began to flow in from a jagged crack in the rock floor. Rats scurried away into channels that in years-past must have supplied fresh water. Stuffing bodies into these channels, I trapped a dozen rats in the cistern, then went among the rot, kicking the brutes to death, their corpses my only connection to the outside world. The Saddiq, insane tyrant of the death hole.

I tossed another coin and rat up to the plaza. In time the

321

water—only the neap tide—rose just to my knees. I had fallen into a stupor when a splash awoke me; someone had kicked a rat back into the pool. I tried to call out, but had no voice. Desperately I threw another rat to the surface. Like a shadow, a Negro Arab in a blue turban peered down at me. The man reminded me of Nasic's slave. He held my cruz, his face a question.

I showed him more coins. "Get me out of here," I wheezed in Guinea, "and all these are yours."

"No," he answered, his eyes without pity, "you are condemned. In time I will get the coins from your corpse." With his foot he pushed one of my rats over the edge. It grazed my shoulder. "Vermin to vermin," said the Arab.

Could there be a chance? I choked out the words. "I am brother to Nasic." I threw him another coin. "He will reward you." With veiled eyes he picked up my cruz. After a moment he held the coins over the pit, then dropped them into the water and disappeared.

I sat in the fetid heat for hours, alternately sweating and freezing, my body shaking. The seawater drained out of the cistern, then filled to the previous day's level. Thoughts of my death seemed to rise with the water. Why had I not told the man my name? In hunger and thirsting madness I began to kill crabs, cracking their large claws against the rocks and greedily sucking out the sweet juice and meat. No abomination ever tasted so good. As the water receded, I blocked the crack with bodies, trapping crabs as I had the rats, smashing more of them against the rocks. "You first shall be my supper," I raged, "before I am yours." Though it was vile beyond words, I had food and liquid, yet felt myself grow weaker. "I am alive and eating," I told myself. "You shall not die in this pit."

Night had nearly fallen again when I heard a familiar voice. "Saulo, friend of my brother, is that really you?"

"I am dying. Get me out of here."

Two men put a ladder into the cistern and climbed down as Nasic made his apology. "When the ropemaker told me of the lunatic priest in the pit, I ignored him. What use do I have for a priest who claims my father as his? Then that thief Suárez told me it was you."

One man hoisted me on his shoulders while the other supported us on the ladder from below. In this manner they carried me to the surface and placed me on a litter. As he examined my eye, Nasic wafted a hand in front of his nose. "You stink worse than the holds of my slave ships, Saulo. You're a mess. We must have you bathed and in the hospital."

"Anything, Nasic, thank you. Please get me water."

I remember my final rasping plea, for him to find Pongué.

• • •

A day or so later I awoke in the hospital, Pongué sitting cross-legged at my side. Both my arms were bandaged below my elbow. They had bled me. A worm of blood seeped from under one dressing. Pongué held a bowl of fermented milk to my lips. "Master, drink this."

I gulped down the milk and tried to sit up, but found myself so weak that I fell back. "I am alive," I said to Pongué, "though feeling no better." His chest and arms showed crusted lash marks. "How do you fare?" I asked.

"I fare well, master. Grateful to be free of the barracoon." Tears came to his eyes. "And grateful to find you alive."

Early next morning Nasic arrived with a doctor. I watched with vague interest as the latter cast an astrology and prepared to bleed me. "I can bleed my own self to death," I told him as I struggled to breathe. He left in a fit of ill-temper.

"Ah, Saulo," said Nasic, "profane as ever."

I gestured to a Turkish warrior prostrate on the next pallet, his spear and shield propped against the wall. "And you are as durable as the moon, Nasic. How did you manage to survive this?"

"Manage? I am *rescued* by my Moslem brothers and have accommodated quite well. They do not fault me for my Portuguese business. What choice did I have?" His eyes rose to the heavens. "But I am uncertain what to do about

Suárez and his degradados; one must admire their enterprise, yet they stole my property. Though now I have my goods back, and a caravel and more slaves to boot." His voice lowered. "I think I should only lash them, Saulo, lest the Portuguese return to examine my record. So far I've persuaded my fellow Moslems to spare many of Elmina's Crown citizens."

"I suspect Overseer de Abreu is involved in this Brazil scheme. Da Tavora is too stupid to manage this."

"I shall ask around," said Nasic. His tall slave appeared with a basket of food and pot of broth. The slave propped me up and spooned the delicious liquid into my mouth, but soon my cramps and shaking cut this pleasure short. I reclined back on my pallet. Nasic looked truly distressed, then his mouth sealed into a grin. "You may not die on me, Saulo. Suárez told me of your mischief with Cão. I will hang you myself for soiling my commerce." I struggled to speak, but Nasic raised a hand. "I know your little errand was destined for Pinda, but there too I hold the franchise."

As he continued his pointless chatter, I fell into a troubled sleep, dreaming of Bishop Cão and Great-Grandfather Marcel. The two sat in the bishop's sunny garden and played draughts, attended by a white slave without a tongue. An occasional moan lifted from the slave's mouth. "What God does this?" I asked. Great-Grandfather advanced a piece, Cão countered. "Do I have a soul, and what is its destiny?" The moaning slave moved between me and the players. "Father Cão! I have been rescued by slavery, the wholesale evil we both oppose, delivered from one hell to another." A woman with lifeless babies in her arms replaced the slave. The garden players dissolved behind her.

For days I hung in a stupor, Pongué always at my side. One morning I awoke to thunder, yet through the window the skies were clear. Everywhere men ran and shouted. Pongué came from outside, lifted me in his arms and walked to the hospital rampart. "Sea battle," he said. At the harbor entrance a magnificent four-masted caravel stood in, guns booming along its flank. Beyond range of the pirate guns, the Portuguese ship skipped cannon shot across the water into the helpless Barbarossi galleys, one already in flames. I watched as the two others were smashed to kindling, sinking, taking their chained oarsmen into the sea. Except for the few pirates who struck for the seawall, the majority of them struggled and drowned, their swimming abilities no better than mine. Longboats put out from the four-master, our sailors fired muskets and their lances flashed, slaughtering those pirates found clinging to debris. Seaward of the harbor, a group of three caravels held station. All flew Portuguese colors. My spirits rose—I might again see my children and beloved Ariella.

The battle's outcome was never in doubt. With the sinking of the ships and most pirates drowned, the remaining Barbarossi watched helplessly from the seawall. As our marines moved to take the port, the enemy fled to the countryside. Soon Portuguese troops surged across the plaza and into the buildings. They caught the Turkish soldier from the bed next to me as he tried to flee. They ran the man through and pitched him over the wall. In clear Portuguese, I announced myself and Pongué. "Your armada is a beautiful sight," I said. "Where did you come from?"

"Lisbon," answered a marine. "We were on our way to São Tomé to fight the Angolar rebels."

"How did you know the pirates had taken Elmina?"

"After we captured a galley full of Portuguese prisoners and looted cannons. The *arrogance* of those Turks, running without an escort." He gestured to the plaza below where pirates being put to death screamed in agony. "Today we won a victory for Christ and king."

In my strongest voice I said, "Tell your captain the local Portuguese slavemaster dresses like an Arab. His name is Nasic and he is an ally. He is not to be harmed." How silly, I thought. Nasic will outlive us all.

Indeed the fat chameleon came to visit me at sundown, and he assured me that all was well. They had placed me on a raised pallet, and Nasic settled himself in a chair next to the bed while his tall slave prepared an opium pipe. "Take a draft of this," he suggested. "It's more help than any physician can provide." Immediately taken by a coughing fit, I could not breathe in the sweet-smelling vapor. "Too bad," said Nasic, and returned the pipe to his lips.

The Vespers bell, silent these many days, rang across the fortress. A priest appeared accompanied by a Portuguese physician. The former carried a sick child of about ten. They placed him on the Turk's pallet. "A Jewish boy?" asked Nasic.

"A Novo Christão," countered the priest.

"I am a Novo." I said and strained to get a better look at the boy. "I thought the shipment of Jews ceased a year ago?"

"It seems our blessed Inquisition has burdened the kingdom with fresh hoards of these mongrels. What better place to send them than Tomé?"

"Ah yes," said Nasic, "the Crown will rid the island of the Angolars and import new citizens to die of the fever." The priest cast a stern eye at us, then left with the doctor. I called out to the child in Portuguese, then in Hebrew. The boy stirred, but did not answer.

Later I awoke as the doctor examined the boy, then drew a cover over the child's face. After a while a priest and a nun came in, the latter praying while the priest applied the unction. The oil had a musk smell, and I began to cough. I caught my breath for a moment and said, "My regret, but you must move the poor boy out—"

The nun whirled to face me. "Marcel?" She bent nearer. "Oh Blessed Virgin!" she gasped. "Marcel!" She fervently crossed herself and clutched the crucifix around her neck. Who was this Bride of Christ who knew my name? "Marcel, it's me, your sister." She took my hand and kissed it. "I am Leah."

I tried to look, but my eye clouded with tears. This nun's face so close to mine glowed with health like no other. The playful eye crinkles and crescent dimples as she smiled. "Oh, it is you! It is you!" I cried. Leah knelt at my bedside and prayed. The priest, briefly annoyed at the interruption, sensed the moment's import and left to find other help.

Pongué threw himself at my sister's feet. "Ma'am Leah," he wailed, "Ma'am Leah," then looked at me. "Surely master we will get home now." He gazed up at Leah. "Master Saulo talks of you often." She smiled at him, obviously not understanding Guinea.

Leah reached for my eye cover, then drew back. I touched her hand. "The degradados put it out. I will tell you later, but even with one eye, my sister, you are the most lovely sight in the world. Are you here with the Jewish children?"

Through tears she began to talk. The words spilled out, then stopped when the priest and another returned. They wrapped the dead boy in a winding cloth made from the bed sheet and carried him from the room. Leah continued in quieter tones. "We had many Jewish children at Convent Silves." I did not tell her of our parents, once only four leagues away from Silves in Porto Lagos. "As the Inquisition swept through Portugal, more orphans arrived, Jews *and* Christians. Their parents—at the whim of Church and king—had been tortured and killed. Yet strangely King Manuel keeps many of Jews in his court, astronomers, mapmakers, and physicians, though rumor has it they have been forced to convert..."

I examined my sister's exquisite face, touched her fringe of hair cut short in the fashion of nuns. "How can you be part of a Church that so abuses—?"

She put a finger to my lips. "They gave me no choice, my brother; and as you know, I am a practical girl. With children to look after— Well, My Lord knows how I love children. I labored and studied, took my vows, and pledged to help every child I could." I made an effort to speak. "Shush!" This time she placed her hand over my mouth—a divine touch—and raised an eyebrow. "Dearest brother, I had no hope of regaining our parents once the persecution started. And I believed by doing God's work, caring for children, might allow me someday to find you." She made the sign of the cross. "So now the miracle I most prayed for has come to pass."

"Did you *choose* to travel here?"

"Forced to choose. The Inquisition holds children accountable for their parents' supposed sins, and inquisitors began to take our most innocent. But *I* stopped the practice at Silves." Leah leaned closer. "The convent was always short of funds, and taking care of new orphans threatened our meager reserves. When I heard that children might be turned away with no refuge, I volunteered to take our little ones to São Tomé. I petitioned the mother abbess, she informed Lisbon, and they agreed." She looked down the hall, cautious that someone might overhear. "Because of the fever, no one wants to travel here. They thought I'd lost my senses. I knew the alternatives at Silves were much worse."

"The priests I've seen don't appear to share your charity."

"Quite so. Most are here by penance, eager to deliver our wards and return to Portugal."

I drifted with her words and must have fallen asleep, my dreams full of terror. When I awoke, Leah and Pongué stood talking on the rampart outside my room. I listened with amusement as Pongué struggled with his faulty Portuguese. Then my dream returned and I began to rant, "I have feasted on the surrogates of the dead! Foul carrion-eaters of human flesh." Pongué and Leah hurried inside. She took my hand. I told her of Nasic, my rescue from the pit, the eating of crabs. "I will be damned for consuming such things, the vilest of the vile!"

"No, no," my sister said and sent Pongué for the doctor. She knelt to pray.

The Portuguese physician arrived and looked me over. "What happened to your Moslem colleague?" I asked. With rolled eyes and tilted head, he lolled out his tongue, pulled a hand over his head and made a strangling sound. What a waste, I thought. After examining me, the man stood and walked into the hall, conferring with Leah in tones I could not hear. Finally he brought forth a vial of camphor tonic which I sipped. It helped my breathing.

Over the next days Leah rarely left my side, while loyal Pongué saw to our every need. Through spells of weakness and sleep that held me like death, I told her of Miriam, the children, the tragedy of Jubiabá, my love for Ariella, the success of my farm and tenant scheme, and all my adventures. "There's so much on the island I want to show you, and many friends you must meet."

"We will get you well so you can—" My sister suddenly burst into tears and left the room. I lay there confused, but she soon returned and soothed my cheek. "Everyone says Tomé is a miserable place, yet it seems you have grown fond of it."

"Worse than miserable, yet my loved ones are there."

I told her of my unusual friendship with Nasic, of Yasemina and dear Nawar, the plight of our parents and Miriam's, their search for her, and our parents' letters that awaited her in São Tomé. She cried anew when I told her of Porto Lagos. "Why did you not write?" I asked.

"Oh I did, and often. I suspect the censor never let my letters pass the convent gate."

"When I heard you might be at Silves, I wrote you there."

She shook her head. "I never received any letters."

Leah became most fascinated with my mission for Bishop Cão, asking questions, eager to be in service to the diocese, and sympathetic to my loathing of slavery. "If you visit the slave dungeons here," I told her, "then you can gauge the savagery of this commerce." And, after considerable hesitation—I feared she would not believe me—I told her about Great-Grandfather Marcel, citing the many times he kept me counsel. To my surprise, Leah showed interest and did not take alarm.

• • •

One morning Pongué carried me to the rampart where we watched the ships ready themselves for São Tomé. "We must make ready too," I whispered, wondering when I had grown so weightless that he could easily carry me. The words struggled in my throat. "What will my Ariella think of me with only one eye?"

Pongué looked down with great alarm, rushed back to the room and placed me on the bed. He ran into the hall shouting, "Ma'am Leah! Ma'am Leah!" A priest heard the commotion and came into my room. He bent over, gesturing around my face. He began to chant in Latin and fumbled with his cross. Leah and Pongué came in, the two of them weeping.

I sat up, amazed to feel no pain, and saw from both my eyes. And what I saw! A host gathered on the rampart, the sun shining brightly upon them! There stood Great-Grandfather Marcel, Miriam with a little boy at her side, Golem, Germo, Fr. Norte, Nawar, all those I so dearly love. Marcel took me in his arms. "Come my beloved grandson, your family and friends await you."

"I have died too soon, Great-Grandfather. The life of the Saddiq eludes me."

"As it does every man."

I bade farewell to Leah and Pongué, but I do not believe they saw me.

Leah

Chapter 22

More than a half-year has passed since my brother's death. As I first set ink to paper and chronicle his final days in Elmina (while they remain fresh in my memory), I arrange his journals and prepare to write Marcel's story.

So no one will think me daft, I shall tell you now of his last moments at the hospital. With the aid of dear Pongué, Ariella, Kiman, Yasemina, and others who helped give names to the apparitions we saw, and having perused my brother's journals, I assure you Pongué and I truly witnessed the miracle of Great-Grandfather Marcel and the host that surrounded him, and also my brother as he rose to leave his pitiful remains, although—perhaps just as well—the attending priest seemed not to notice. I further attest that before he and the host faded from our view, Marcel appeared of good health, speaking with our great-grandfather in Hebrew, a language that I fully understood—a miracle, since I had not heard the tongue or spoken it aloud the past four years.

I felt sure Marcel wished to be buried in São Tomé, but the fleet captain refused to accept his diseased body for transport. As is custom, the surgeon removed my brother's heart and gave it to me in a lacquered box for safe passage. The strange Sr. Nasic, who appeared to grieve over our loss as much as Pongué and I, graciously buried my brother's remains in the lavish garden of his manor. "He has joined my brother in Paradise," Sr. Nasic told me, placing a polished rock on the grave in the thoughtful manner of Jewish mourners.

The criminals Suárez, his officers, the degradados and

331

Felix da Tavora were returned in chains to Lisbon for trial. The Crown magistrate sentenced each Suárez sailor to fifteen lashes at the slave pillory, and they, along with the caravel (declared forfeit) were pressed into Crown service.

When I arrived in São Tomé, I met with His Excellence, Bishop Cão to arrange for Marcel's funeral. It was then I began to understand my brother's influence. Meeting soon after with Marcel's family and friends, his stature grew further. I found myself overwhelmed by the affection everyone expressed for my brother.

Bishop Cão, distressed as any of us, took personal charge of the funeral arrangements. On a suffocating hot afternoon, in the cemetery next to Miriam's grave, the bishop's eulogy went on for over an hour as people began to faint. His testimonial would have gone longer had not His Excellence also fainted.

Considering what my brother had told me, and the accounts in his journals, Bishop Cão fares no better than before in his efforts to reform slavery. I find him a priest of most sincere piety, though he retains only a few followers. He is widely detested, particularly among the planters. As Marcel suggested, Cão's house has many spies and plotters. At every turn they frustrate his efforts to remedy the plight of Africans. The bishop seems weary from his lonely battle, and I believe he avoids assassination only by his dint of office. I did visit the slave barracoons in Elmina and here, and find myself in sympathy with Cão and my brother. Slavery is a blot on Christendom, second only to my adopted Church's hideous Inquisition.

Some time after hearing Bishop Cão's eulogy, I decided to tell His Excellence about Marcel's journals. "Dear Sister da Doçura," he said, "may I see these journals?" I could not refuse. When I advised him that most were in Hebrew, he raised no objection—appearing even more intrigued—and insisted I read some of it to him. As I read and translated, and regardless of the bishop's interest, I discreetly censored some passages. To my surprise, he made me chronicler and assigned me the joyous and heartbreaking task of writing my brother's history. I sincerely believe this assignment provides me license to write truthfully of Marcel's unusual leanings and blasphemous opinions. How curious that in exile I have more freedom than at home.

Oh the continuing irony of my journey to this island! A few days after my arrival, a fleet officer gave me two letters addressed to Marcel. It seems both letters had sailed here with our ships, held in the captain's safe of the very vessel on which I traveled. The first came from me, over a year old from Silves, renewing my pledge to find my dear Marcel. And the second letter! I cried tears of joy and remorse, and my hands shook as I broke the seal—before my eyes, there was our mother Elcia's handwriting.

My Dearest Son Marcel,

I send you our most thankful greetings from Antalya in the Ottoman. I write in place of your father because dear Benoni is away on business at a nearby fortress. We sailed successfully in lengthy voyage from Málaga to this Turkish port where we found a local khalif who made us welcome and, much to our relief, a small Jewish community. The khalif readily employs craftsmen of any religion if they have the necessary skills; in your father's case, as a mason to build fortifications. How pleasant to find acceptance in this strange land, a place that reminds me of Castile under the Moors.

Most regrettably, Miriam's family chose the less arduous journey to Majorca, expecting to join the Catalan community of mapmakers and scientists there. I pray the Inquisition will not soon invade that tranquil island and drive them elsewhere. I am sure they were devastated at hearing of their sweet daughter's passing. What a difficult time that must have been for you.

I will tell you something that your father (in deference to dear Miriam's memory) would never put in a letter: Miriam's mother complained incessantly about the names of your children. It seems, for her, the given names were too Jewish, Biblical if you will, and she wanted them more secular. Regardless, we wish Miriam's parents well and

333

miss their company. Which leads me to ask, have you heard from them, or any news of our dear Leah?

And here is a big surprise: You have a new brother and two new sisters, Yakub, age 5, and Rebecca and Sarah, ages 4 and 7. You, my son, are not the only one in our family who adopts orphans. The parents of these children, Spanish Jews from Porto Málaga, died during our voyage, and we took in their children.

Your father and I wonder if you and Ariella are yet married. I know how you miss Miriam, though in time your heart will heal...

My goodness the thought struck me, *Yakub?* I must write my parents who will be heartened to learn of my well-being, but shattered by the tragic news of Marcel. With their knowledge of my brother's death, and my father's insistence on having an heir with my great-grandfather's name, will little Yakub soon be Marcel?

I will tell them my brother led an exemplary life—the evidence surrounds me everywhere—and in my mind he wears the mantle of the Saddiq. Having read my parents' earlier letters to Marcel, I know they may be prepared for the news I am a Catholic nun. More difficult will be trying to explain the many hues of children who inhabit the Saulo farm and claim my brother's paternity. I pray for guidance.

• • •

In the months since I arrived on Tomé, much has happened. Our courageous soldiers hunted down the Angolars, ridding the island of those dreadful raiders. Their leader, Mbundu, was hanged in the town square, and more than a hundred of his followers were captured and sold into slavery. Unfortunately Mbundu took what he knew of Jubiabá and Suryiah to his grave—their fate remains unknown. The soldiers did, however, discover twin mulatto infants of the right age in the Mbundu camp, a boy and a girl, Marçal and—proudly for me—Leah, who now live with Yasemina and her children in my brother's house on the table land. With money from the successful harvest, Isabel Horté and Kiman purchased fifty acres of Crown land south of the Saulo farm. Marcel's children, Joseph, Lael, Michal, Louisa, and the ward Fernão Bartolis, live in the house originally built for Yasemina by Kiman on the Horté farm. The children are tended by Ariella and Isabel.

Nuño, Isabel's husband, moved to the slave port where he is now its captain. Though Pedro de Abreu, the Crown Overseer, was vaguely implicated in the scheme which led to my brother's death, no charges have been brought against him.

Since my brother left no testament, the farm ownership remains in dispute, though currently Joseph (with Lael subsequent) is the leading heir. Ariella, who continues to live with Isabel, is only two months from term with Marcel's child. Her claim of paternity (if the child is a male) would further complicate the inheritance. Then there is the mulatto boy Marçal, and one wonders if Yasemina will assert his claim. As the local diocese has final say in such matters, I feel assured Bishop Cão will settle it fairly.

There is another item of contention, but only if I let it. It is a personal disquiet I must reject along with all profane emotions, my gold chain thrown to Marcel that fateful night in Lisbon. Ariella wears it reverently. She knows its history, that it was once mine, and once Miriam's. Next to the child she carries, the necklace is her most beloved possession.

Within my brother's journals I found an item attributed to me that, lest God judges me deceitful, I must clarify. I did not invent the masonry with the support stays, but discovered the design while salvaging bricks in the ruin of an old synagogue near our home in Lisbon. It is by God's Grace that these bricks so bettered my brother's lot on São Tomé.

Would one think me vain at feeling slighted for seeing Great-Grandfather Marcel only once, while my brother claims many instances? Yet my great-grandfather visits me each time I transcribe my brother's writings, the Hebrew script clear as the dawn. My brother's voice resounds in me as if he were here reading his journals aloud and instructing the narrative. I am forever grateful, even for the briefest time we had together. Once this manuscript is completed, I will safekeep the journals for his children.

The indifference of time shall not dim Marcel Saulo's memory, for all who knew my brother consider him a man of true conscience. I, and those who loved Marcel, shall never forget him.

Your most faithful servant,
Sister Mãe da Doçura —Leah Anna Saulo

Acknowledgments

The author expresses his great appreciation to the following: Jill Cohn for her superb reference volumes; Hebrew linguist Dr. David Ezra; editors extraordinaire Charity Hogge and Barbara Lee Magin; singer Julie Larson whose lovely ballad, *Havem Kan Seile,* seems to capture every mood of this novel; Professor Armin Mühsam of Northwest Missouri State University for his literary critique; Sue and Jesse Oppenheimer for their encouragement and historical perspectives; the PBS series, *Into the Rising Sun,* which chronicled the Portuguese voyages of exploration; and to mystery writer Mark T. Sullivan who shared his secrets for voice, setting, and structure.

I am particularly indebted to anthropologist W. Thomas Ballard for his tireless research; to Professor Robert Garfield of De Paul University for his splendid book, *A History of São Tomé Island;* and to friend and novelist Dr. Sid Gustafson for his many creative literary and editorial contributions.

I also wish to acknowledge the several authors whose publications provided material for this book, and commend the reader to their fine works on history, anthropology, culture, the sea, Europe, Africa, and The Americas for this period of history: Ernle Bradford, Luc Cuyvers, Basil Davidson, Jared Diamond, Max I. Dimont, Robert Garfield, Johan Huizinga, Amin Maalouf, William Manchester, Teofilo F. Ruiz, Andre Schwarz-Bart, Dava Sobel, and Barbara W. Tuchman.

To read about the author, please visit our website at
www.saotomethenovel.com

Referral/Rewards™ – Burns-Cole Publishers